Maarten Maartens

Joost Avelingh

A Dutch story

Maarten Maartens

Joost Avelingh
A Dutch story

ISBN/EAN: 9783337301163

Printed in Europe, USA, Canada, Australia, Japan

Cover: Foto ©Andreas Hilbeck / pixelio.de

More available books at **www.hansebooks.com**

A Dutch Story

BY

MAARTEN MAARTENS

AUTHOR OF GOD'S FOOL

NEW YORK
D. APPLETON AND COMPANY
1894.

CONTENTS.

A

JOOST AVELINGH.

INTRODUCTION.

It had stopped raining.

Had it not stopped raining? The grumpy old fellow
who keeps the small grocery store on the Hoester road crept
to his door and looked out. You know the little shop, if
you know the neighborhood at all, the low house with the
lollipop jars in its square-paned window. The old grocer
stood shading his eyes with his hand to see better, as men
will do in excess of darkness—strangely enough—as well as
in excess of light. He was asking himself for the twentieth
time that evening whether it was worth his while to cross
the shining, slippery road and have his customary chat with
his friend, the innkeeper opposite.

It was not so dark but that he could see the long,
straight highway vaguely stretching away on both sides in a
shimmer of steaming wet beneath the glittering drip, drip
of its lines of trees. In fact, the light was coming through
more and more every minute. High up among the clouds
the wind was busy at his lace-weaving, lifting and spreading
and intertangling puffs of black and white and gray in an
ever thinner veil, for the moon to look through. And she,
as if to bid him continue, was sending forth feeble rays that
crept slowly down upon the little cluster of some half-a-
dozen cottages which lie huddled—like a knot in a rope—

halfway down the long, lonely road between Heist and
Hoest. Decidedly, the clouds must have stopped raining,
even if the trees had not.

The Baas came to the conclusion that crossing might be
worth his while. Whether it was a craving for the innkeeper's company, or for his customary steaming "nightcap," that influenced his decision, it were needless, and perhaps invidious, to inquire. He toddled through the mud
toward the dim light over the way.

"Innkeeper" is, in fact, although it has been used
already, too imposing a word to apply to old Wurmers.
The cottage opposite, with one narrow window beside the
door, and one square window over it, is the smallest even of
small Dutch public-houses. A broad hoop, painted a bright
green, with "Tappery, Slytery" on it in golden letters,
stands out above the entrance, and in the window a solitary
card, the advertisement of a Bavarian Brewery, hangs before
a blue wire-work screen. Within, all is stale smoke and
bitters. A low box of a room, with a bar, a number of
shelves full of bottles, a square deal table and two or three
wicker chairs. The grocer pushed open the door; the
master of the house came shambling forward. He was old,
like the other man, with faded red hair, and he walked
lame.

"A bad night," he said, "no customers."

"So much the better for the Temperance people,"
chuckled the grocer. "There's a meeting down at Heist
to-night. Ha! Ha! I know what they say: 'God made
water and fire, and the devil brewed fire-water out of
them.'"

"God made all things," said the other piously; he was
a pious publican, a Publican and a Pharisee, a type not unknown in Holland—nor elsewhere, for the matter of that.

"Even gin?" asked the grocer, with a queer grin, as he
took the glass Baas Wurmers held out to him.

"Gin more than most things," replied the republican sententiously. "At the marriage-feast of Cana, a village where it appears there were not enough wineshops—"

But the devil's reasoning on the devil's behalf was suddenly cut short. The noise of advancing wheels, to which both old cronies had been lending a vague attention during the last few seconds, stopped abruptly outside. A rough voice was heard calling and swearing. Both men hurried to the door as fast as their shaky legs could carry them.

A one-horse chaise was drawn up in the middle of the road, its lamps flashing in broad sweeps over the mud and dimly revealing under the hood the figures of two men, a younger one driving, and an older one at his side.

It was the older man who had cried out, and he now repeated his demand, in the same loud, blustering voice.

"A borrel," (dram), he shouted, "a borrel, you damned old stupid! What else should a man stop for at your hole of a house on such a damned cold night as this?"

The younger man sat silent. Behind, in the open dickey, was a servant, half-asleep.

The gin was brought without a word of greeting. Free Dutch burghers do not like being sworn at. It was gulped down amid a multiplicity of oaths, the last at the driver for tarrying; and then the carriage dashed off again into the darkness, its lights playing "catch me and kiss me" with the few moonbeams that lingered among the trees.

The two men stood watching it out of sight. "*Those* are not going to the Temperance meeting," said the tavern-keeper.

"Poor young fellow," muttered the grumpy old grocer. And they went in.

. . . .

The chaise passed swiftly down the road, hoof and wheels plashing straight through big and little puddles. Conversation there was none between the two occupants, unless an occasional muttered oath from the one, or an angry whip-cut from the other, can claim the dignity of that name. A good deal of intercourse, doubtless, may be kept up by such intermittent signs as these.

The younger man sat silent, with a white face and tightly compressed lips, holding the reins firmly, and driving fast, fast.

The older one, whose wrathful ejaculations had been gradually dying away in longer intervals, suddenly shook himself together and burst into a torrent of meaningless invective. His companion shrank slightly away, against the farther side of the hood, but answered never a word.

And then, a few minutes later, the angry man foamed over, as it were, bubbling and spluttering and choking, till he fell back in a heap, limp, clumsy, huddled up, his voice lost in a sudden whisper, a gasp—then a prolonged gurgle, broken once or twice by a stronger effort, like a groan.

The younger man sat silent, holding the reins firmly, and driving fast, fast.

And so they passed on swiftly between the dripping trees. The lights of Heist were standing out and growing larger every moment. The figure in the corner stopped its gurgling, gave a faint gasp, then another—and was still.

The chaise rolled along the road for some minutes longer, then jolted over rough pavingstones, between straggling oil-lamps. Suddenly the still, motionless figure fell forward; the young man sat silent, and drove on.

At last, with a clash that dragged the horse down on its hindlegs and sent flakes of mud flying up over both men and right back into the hood, the chaise stopped. Without heeding his reins, the driver jumped out and ran round to a house-door. He rang a furious peal that seemed to wake the servant in the dickey, who pulled himself together and tumbled out.

The door was thrown open; there was light in the hall,

streaming out to meet the carriage-lamps. A maid-servant had come forward, and, immediately after her, a little old gentleman in black.

"Is the Notary in?" said the young man in a dead voice; and the little old gentleman in black immediately cried back from the hall:

"Why, you see that he is!"

"There's something wrong, I believe," the other went on hurriedly, "we were coming to see you. He—" he pointed with his thumb over his shoulder—"he is ill, I fea —fancy. He—I don't quite know."

The Notary hurried to the chaise. He touched the man lying in it, lying half off the seat, with his body falling forward over his knees. He shook him gently at first and called to him in a voice growing shriller and more shaky every moment, then turned and impatiently summoned the young driver, motionless under the hall-lamp,—turned again and addressed the groom, awake now and curious at the horse's head.

Together lawyer and man-servant dragged the heavy, insensible body down out of the chaise, and laid it, all bespattered with mud as it was, on the marble floor of the bare little hall. They laid it down against the wall; where the maid no sooner saw it, motionless, with purple face and staring eyes, than she pressed her hand against her bosom and went off into a series of smart little screams, a tribute she considered she owed to her feelings. The young man stood as if struck to stone, with his fists clenched at his side. He did not offer to help the Notary who, rapidly taking the matter into his own hands, undid a red silk comforter tied tightly round the sick man's throat and, opening his underclothes, laid a more or less steady hand on the heart. While doing so, he cast one or two quick, cross glances at the young man under the lamp. "How white he looks!" he thought, "and how strangely he presses his teeth together! I should not have thought him such a coward. For it can't be his love for the old man that makes him look like that."

The subject of these considerations watched every movement eagerly. The maid sat down in a heap on the stairs, and moaned, and rocked herself. The Notary, running for some brandy, stumbled over her, and abused her in passing. The groom stood staring sheepishly; no one offered any assistance. It was the Notary who chafed the numb hands and forehead and poured a few drops down the throat and did a number of useless, and even of unwise things, from which he at last stood up, panting, despairing.

The young man broke the painful silence.

"He is ill," he said with the same toneless voice he had spoken in before.

"Ill!" cried the Notary impatiently. "Ill! He is dead."

The young man fell down on his knees and burst into a passion of weeping. "God forgive me," he cried, "I would give the world it were not so!"

PART I.

BEFORE.

CHAPTER I.

"A STRAP UNDER HIS HEART."

"AND this," said Agatha, as she tied a bow over one of many parcels, "is for Joost."*

"Poor Joost!" cried a chorus of voices. And then they all laughed.

The ladies of the family were assembled round a table in the big living-room—the home-room, as we say in Holland—portly, self-satisfied Mevrouw van Hessel and her three unmarried daughters, Agatha, Anna, and Elisabeth, or rather, to designate them in the euphonious accents of their native tongue, Agapict, Annemie and Bettekoo.

It was the eve of Santa Claus—the 5th of December, the most important social event of the year. In an hour or so Mevrouw van Hessel's married daughter would arrive with her husband the secretary and their three young children, and then the gentlemen would come in from the smoking-room, and there would be great goings-on round that big table laden with presents.

Joost was coming too. "Oh yes, of course; ask Joost,"

---

* Pronounce "Yoost" with a "y" as in yoke, not joke.

had said good-natured Mynheer van Hessel, as he stood with his hand on the door-knob a day or two ago.

"But Santa Claus is a family festival," expostulated Mevrouw, "and Joost is not one of the family."

"*Conceptus*," began Mynheer, very slowly and impressively, "*pro nato habetur quotiescunque de eius commodo agitur*, so you see, my dear, Joost has a right to come. Send him an invitation, Agapiet," and he opened the door and closed it behind him with wonderful rapidity.

Mynheer von Hessel knew that he seldom got his own way at home; he did not mind that as a rule, but he had also learned long ago by experience that his only chance of gaining respect occasionally lay in puzzling his far cleverer and more imperious wife. He remembered very little Latin out of his college days, but that little not infrequently came in useful.

"After all," said Madame, "men have far more opportunities than we." She admired what she considered her husband's learning, while she somewhat despised his want of sense. But in reality Burgomaster van Hessel was a sensible man, of very slender intellectual acquirements, with a turn for what he considered wit, and his friends tomfoolery. His intellectual acquirements, by-the-by, were the only slender thing about him.

So his daughter wrote her note, and received a favorable answer. "And this," she said, with her hand on a little brown paper bundle, "is for Joost."

"What is it?" cried mother and sisters, in a breath.

Agatha smiled, blushed, looked at her parcel, looked at them, twirled it in her fingers, and laid it down again.

"It is something new," she said, hesitatingly. "At least, you never hear of it here. But I thought—"

"What is it?" cried Bettekoo, who was always impatient.

"You know, I read about them in That Charming

Curate. It appears that in England they are quite a customary present to gentlemen, and so useful."

"But *what* are they?" almost screamed Bettekoo.

"A pair of embroidered braces."

"Embroidered braces," said Annemie, the beauty, slowly and sneeringly. "Who ever heard of such a thing?"

Agatha was not a beauty; she was only beautiful. At least, so all the good people thought.

A fair-haired, fair-cheeked maiden of nineteen summers, with graceful, gentle features and full blue eyes that seemed to say: "Love me, for I love others and deserve to be loved."

"Poor Joost," she said, "I thought it would be quite a new kind of thing to give him, and he wants, as I shall tell him, a strap under his heart."*

"But braces," cried Bettekoo, "Oh, Agapiet, to a gentleman!"

"We ought not to know they wear them," remarked the beauty, languidly. "Fancy, supposing they were to begin giving us stays!"

"It is not the same thing at all," cried Agatha, hotly. "In England everybody gives everybody else embroidered braces. I mean all the gentlemen; no, all the ladies, I mean. And the English are a very proper nation."

"I consider it an extremely improper and indelicate selection," said Mevrouw van Hessel. "No Dutch maiden who respects her feelings would allude to any such article in the presence of strangers. Nor can I allow any daughter of mine to give anything of the kind to a—a man."

By this time Agatha's cheeks were crimson. She ruefully fingered her little parcel; and the red rosebuds over which she had spent so many an hour, seemed to burn their way up through the paper and smart in her very eyes. She

* Dutch idiom.

knew that it was no use trying to reason with her mother, who habitually found all opinions unreasonable but her own. "So few people can argue," said Mevrouw van Hessel, meaning that, as a rule, so few people agreed with her.

"But I shall have nothing to give Joost!" cried poor Agatha.

Her father, entering at the moment, caught the words. "Nothing for Joost?" he asked, "How is that?"

"Agatha should have prepared a more appropriate gift," answered Mevrouw. "Some articles are not fit to be mentioned, and some subjects not fit to be discussed."

Agatha held out her parcel with a glance of mingled mirth and misery, and Mynheer van Hessel extracted the objectionable braces. He looked comically grave.

"They are very pretty," he said, "and— No; give them to him in a year or two."

"And why in a year or two?" queried Madame.

"It's a pity," continued Monsieur, "that you did not rather choose slippers, Agapiet. That would have been harmless, and an appropriate emblem!"

"I do not understand you," cut in his spouse,—which was true; she rarely understood his smallest jokes. "There is no reason why Agatha should give slippers, or anything else, to Joost. I have got something for him, and so have the other girls, and Kees. Agatha is growing too old for that sort of thing. And besides, it is her own fault, surely, but girls are so unreasonable."

"In England—" began Agatha.

"In England! We are not in England, thank Heaven," snapped Mevrouw, who was a good woman, but did not like being bothered.

"In England," said Mynheer, "girls talk of 'inexpressibles' and yet embroider braces. In England the highest honors are a garter and a bath. Never mind; tell him that, next year, you will give him the best present he can get, Agapiet."

"But then I have got nothing for this evening," said Agapiet.

CHAPTER II.

"SANTA CLAUS."

An hour or two later the big room was lighted up, and full of movement and conversation. A buzz of excitement round a table laden with parcels, large and small, some unwieldy, some fantastic: flower-pots, cigar-boxes, pails of water, piles of plates. It is the custom in Holland to send these Santa Claus presents, done up in so-called "surprises," no gift being in reality what it seems at the first moment. A book is a box. A cigar-case contains six real cigars and one imitation one with a breast-pin inside it. A plate full of food has a false bottom; an oyster hides pearl ear-drops; a dead mouse in a trap is caught with its neck in a diamond ring. Elaborate imitations of the most various articles are spread out in the shops, costing as much in themselves as many a handsome present; but most families prefer to spend their ingenuity—and not their half-pence—in the fashioning of their own surprises, often from odds and ends, and often from household articles "which please return," all little incidents of the current year, individual peculiarities and family traditions, being taken into due account. Nor are ill-natured jokes altogether unknown; many a learned professor or pompous official has been unpleasantly reminded of his idiosyncrasies on the Eve of Santa Claus.

Years have robbed the feast of much of its simplicity. There is no limit nowadays to the present-sending from

house to house, and the things themselves have grown costlier and costlier, till the whole custom threatens to become
a nuisance. The thrifty Dutchman, who rarely spends a
penny on ornament of any kind all the year round, over-
leaps all bounds at "Sinterklaas"-tide. And feasting—
gorging, guzzling—plays, alas, the most important *rôle* of
all; sugar—enough to nauseate a Polyphemus—being unfortunately the chief ingredient. Great blocks and rounds
of sugar (with a little fruit flavoring); chocolate letters, half-
a-yard long and a couple of inches thick; almond-paste
letters, still larger; ginger-bread dolls, weighing many
pounds of unwholesome sweetness — mountains of every
kind of rich foreign confectionery are spread out and piled
up in lines of shops, a very Paradise Row for the children.
All Holland turns out into the streets, and comes home
laden with parcels. All Holland is apt to eat itself sick,
and the doctors hold *their* feast-day on the morrow. If it
may be truly said that to the intelligent foreigner (with the
pictorials as his guide-books) Christmas in England is all
beef and plum-pudding, plus an occasional carol for the
sake of old associations, it is no less certain that Santa
Claus in Holland is all sugar-cake and gingerbread, but
then, it must be added, in common fairness, that the latter
is not, and does not pretend to be, a religious festival from
the first.

.   .   .   .

The van Hessels were simple, old-fashioned people, but
they had a large circle of friends. So their door-bell kept
ringing ceaslessly on that important evening, and after each
ring a maid-servant would come running in with a parcel, a
stiff cap and a beaming face. Then there were shouts and
cries and questions. For whom is it? From whom is it?
the latter question often remaining unanswered, for it is an
essential rule of the proceedings that all presents are from
"Santa Claus." The festival is originally a children's one,

and the good bishop, the great lover of children, rides round with his African servants at night, passing down all the chimneys, as you can see for yourself, if you look into the little boots at daybreak. There is a dreadful tradition that he asks the parents if he must leave presents or a rod? It is often mentioned during the year, but it would appear that no Dutch father has ever considered his own children so very, very naughty—whatever he might have advised if consulted about *neighbor's* " Jacky "—or else, judging by the exemption of some little wretches, St. Nicholas can not draw the line much under parricide.

But Mevrouw van Hessel's grand-children — the little Verrooy's—though they too had been threatened with the rod at intervals lately, had never really deserved it. The two youngest still firmly believed in Santa Claus, the eldest —six, and " no longer a child "—was beginning to waver and confuse him with her father. Her uncle Kees's reiterated assertion that the bishop was coming presently, that she would really—now really, you know—see him herself, was nevertheless beginning to tell upon her. In the meantime all three children, with sparkling eyes and burning cheeks, were skipping from one aunt to the other round the ever-increasing confusion on the table. There was a great gingerbread sweetheart for every one, of course, and an indigestible almond letter, and parcels innumerable, boxes and papers, taking up twice as much room again in the delicious medley of unpacking. Mevrouw van Hessel sat with a great sack of genuine potatoes before her among which she had long hunted for the hollow one; Kees*—twenty, and at college—had wanted to uncork all the bottles in his wine-basket (prevented in time) before he perceived that papa had stuck a banknote in an envelope behind one of the labels. And Annemie, the beauty, had, amid much laugh-

---

* Short for " Cornelius."

ter, unpacked a hat on which her younger brother Klaas *
had lavished cheap green and yellow ribbons, fastened together by a tiny Greenaway brooch. That was a pardonable
hit at Annemie's appreciation of her own good looks.

Joost was there also. He had not so many presents, because he had not so many friends. He did not sit staring
vacantly at half-a-dozen articles, wondering whoever could
have sent them, and what he was to do with them now they
had come. He was not troubled by the pre-occupation of
the girls van Hessel, lest they should reach a lower number
than their acquaintances, and Bettekoo's repeated : " Oh I
hope we shall pass the hundred this year ! " struck him as
foolish, if it struck him at all. He had unfastened his parcels one by one as they were brought to him, and guessed
at the donors. It was not so difficult under these circumstances because he scarcely had to look beyond the circle
around him. His first paper had revealed a card-case with
a little embroidered vignette. He had held it in his hand
for a long time, wanting to say : " Agatha," but something
that made his heart go pit-a-pat had forced out " Bettekoo."
He was quite sorry to find he had guessed aright, and then
ashamed of himself for feeling sorry. And so he had suc-
cessively found out Mevrouw van Hessel, Mevrouw Verrooy,
and Annemie; and now only one parcel remained. This,
then, surely, must be Agatha's. He took off a number of
papers and disclosed a small black leather case. His hands
trembled a little as he opened it and gazed down on a Meer-
schaum cigar-holder. He felt now instinctively that he must
keep back the one word that was pushing to the front, and
yet, looking round, he stammered out : " Agatha." There
was a general laugh, and Kees, the giver of the pipe, slapped
him on the back and cried " Bravo," and so Joost was miserable for the rest of the evening.

---

* Short for " Nicholas."

"Agatha's present is not yet quite ready," said Mynheer van Hessel. " I tell her she must wait to give it you until—"

" And here is something new," cried Mevrouw, as the folding-doors were thrown open.

A personage entered, of reverend aspect, with flowing beard of cotton-wool, robed in a crimson mantle and wearing a bishop's mitre. In his hand he carried a well-stuffed bag, and as he slowly advanced, he told his name and mission: St. Nicholas, the good bishop, friend and patron of all good children. The two smaller Verrooy's stood staring curiously; but when the Saint asked gravely, if there were any such good children there? the youngest promptly answered: " Yes," and they held out their hands for their presents and scrambled gleefully for the sweetmeats which were soon being scattered all over the floor from the Bishop's inexhaustible bag. But the eldest, " who was no more a child," shrank back nervously, being old enough to question, and would not take courage, till Kees, the very person who had done most to convince her, took pity and whispered: " It was only Uncle Klaas," thereby dispelling all belief in Saint Nicholas, in good fairies, ghosts, and good fortune— forever.

The disappearance of Saint Nicholas heralded the departure of the children who went off, laden with more goodies than they could eat in a month, and more toys than they could comfortably break in a week. Then, all the parcels having been opened, a lull fell on the party, till Bettekoo, who was the sprightliest of the family, proposed a new game she had recently seen played, a French game, you know,— they call it " Combles,"—in which every player has to give his definition of some " Comble " selected before hand. Le Comble de l'ennui, le Comble de la bétise, le Comble de l'avarice, and so forth; you agree on a special subject, and then give your idea of its non plus ultra; the best definition to gain the prize.

B

Le Comble du pléonasme was chosen, and Mevrouw van Hessel led off " with a reasonable argument," at which her husband shook his head. Then came Kees with " unnecessary superfluity," Annemie with " attractive beauty " (" very bad," said Kees) and Mynheer van Hessel with " unreasonable woman," accompanied by a triumphant look at his wife.

And now it was Joost's turn. He had got his pleonasm ready beforehand and was burning to say " Fair Agatha "; but at the last he feared it would be considered immodest, and so he said " good Agatha " instead.

" Right," said Kees.

" Why?" asked Bettekoo, who was not aware that Agatha means " good."

" You should have said, 'fair Agatha," remarked Mynheer van Hessel. " In my youth, when men were still gallant, every cavalier would have said ' fair Agatha'; but you youngsters can not turn a neat compliment nowadays."

It did not comfort Joost much after this that " good Agatha" gained the prize.

.　　.　　.　　.　　.　　.　　.

" Good-by," said Agatha, at the hall-door, " I—I had got something for you, Joost; only mamma did not like what I had chosen, and— "

" Ask Agatha for her present, Joost !" called out Mynheer van Hessel.

" I don't think mamma would like the present I *should* ask," said Joost to himself, as he walked out briskly into the frosty night.

———

CHAPTER III.

DRAMATIS PERSONÆ.

"You are a fool, Joost," said the Baron van Trotsem, next morning at breakfast.

Joost did not answer.

"You are a fool," repeated his uncle. Do you, perhaps, a student of medicine, a wise man, scientific and all the rest of it, mean to tell me you believe in Santa Claus or any saint, good or bad? Nonsense; you scientists nowadays believe only in the devil, whom you worship as the origin of evil by his new name of the great Microbe."

Still Joost was silent. He smiled to himself, for he thought that he recognized a saying of Mynheer van Hessel's.

"And did you enjoy yourself?" queried the old gentleman, as he poured himself out a cup of tea.

"No," said Joost.

"And I suppose you told Mevrouw van Hessel so!" sneered his uncle.

"She did not ask me," said Joost.

"And if she had done so?" the old gentleman paused, with uplifted sugar tongs, and regarded his nephew from under his beetling eyebrows.

"I should have told her the truth."

"You are a fool, Joost."

It was now sixteen years ago, that Joost Avelingh, a pale little orphan of five, had first crossed his uncle's threshold, and he had never since then spent more than half-a-dozen consecutive nights under any other man's roof. People often wondered how he came to be there at all. The Baron van Trotsem himself could scarcely have told. If any one had been able to give a fairly accurate explanation, it would have been the Baron's old nurse—ninety-three, and pensioned off, in a cottage on the estate, for many long years now—but the Baron's old nurse was childish, and past talking accurately about anything whatsoever. It was a pity; for she might have told of days in the early years of the century, when Dirk van Trotsem was a bright and loving, if somewhat wayward and imperious child, an only child, always playing alone, learning as it were to live alone, roaming far and wide through the woods of the ancestral home he dearly loved, and—later on—shooting through them day after day, with no companion but his dogs. She might have told of his passionate resentment when his father married again, after twenty years of widowhood, and of his equally passionate afterlove for his little half-sister Adelheid. She had once remembered all the circumstances of their affectionate intercourse; she had seen the girl grow up and twine her charms round her brother's impetuous, impressionable heart. She had seen them live together when the old father died, in the time when the sister was twenty, bright, gay and handsome, and the brother forty, a strong man, but affectionate, a country gentleman to the backbone, still fond of being left alone, knowing each inch of his own estate and loving it, and proud with an all-corroding, all-consuming pride of his great historic name and ancient lineage.

She could have remembered the great quarrel later on: the Freule's match with the village doctor in open defiance of her brother, the cruel separation—forever, as it proved—when he drove her from his door; the whole sad story; the old nurse could have told it once upon a time, and told it well. But so far she would have recounted nothing that all the village had not heard from its grandmother half-a-dozen times before. However, she could have gone much further and spoken of long lonely nights when the Baron stalked up and down his dark room till daybreak, and of gray hairs among the black, and deep furrows on the ruddy complexion.

"There was no doubt," as she said, at the time, "that the separation tried the Baron cruelly, for if there was one thing he loved more on earth than Trotsem Towers, it was surely his sister. And she, poor thing! Dear, dear, people complained of his not having a good heart, but it was all bluster—bluster and a heart of gold."

Therein, however, her judgment failed her. It was not all bluster. There was a burning wound, a depth of positive, continuous pain, such as few men can understand and still fewer sympathize with. To acknowledge, and fairly appreciate, the wrongs of injured family pride a man must have ancestors and an ancestral name of his own. They are a possession, as much so as houses and lands, or an honorable reputation; too often they form the owner's only property; to take them from him is theft, to strike at them assault. And the multitude, unjust in their ignorance, talk of "vanity receiving its due reward," as if it were the deserved fate of the proud possessor of a beautiful garden that roughs should climb in and knock off all his roses.

The Baron Dirk van Trotsem was not an intellectual, nor a well-educated, man. He had grown up, as has been said, pretty much alone and at haphazard, with an old nurse to look after his wants, and without seeing much of his father, who was a State-minister and occupied with public affairs. Even as the boy grew older, he avoided the society of his equals; but he turned instinctively to the men about the estate, and made friends with grooms, gardeners and gamekeepers. From his earliest days he developed a very passion for a country life, for country pursuits in all their forms. Before he could conjugate "amo, amas, amat," he knew the note of all the birds of his province. He never learned to write Dutch correctly, but as years went on, he acquired what may be called a personal acquaintance with half the trees on his large estate, an individual acquaintance which separated, and kept apart, the peculiarities of half-a-dozen trees of the same species, standing side by side. But, none the less, a bird was a bird, and a tree was a tree, to the Baron van Trotsem. Trees remained material for agricultural occupation, and birds—chiefly remarkable as game-birds, useful and harmful birds—were made either to be killed or let alone. He knew the varieties of primroses, and could even give you one or two Latin names (with a false quantity), but for all that they were yellow primroses to him—and nothing more.

His father had, after a fierce struggle, given up all attempts to send the boy to the University: he died, bitterly disappointed, soon after the loss of his second wife, whom he had been chiefly prompted to marry by the desire for a more promising son, and who only presented him with one little daughter. Dirk found himself his own master at the age of twenty-three, alone in a large old-fashioned castle with a middle-aged housekeeper, who had been his nurse, an infant, and a host of servants. He laughed at all ambitious advice, answered that to be the last van Trotsem was in itself a vocation, shot and fished over his property and explored every nook of it, putting to rights the many things his father had neglected, until each slate lay on the cottages and each twig fell from the trees according to the strictest rules of economical accuracy. There was not a better managed estate in the country than Dirk van Trotsem's; there was no budget in commercial Amsterdam more beautifully worked out than his. The Baron could not reason logically, but he could cipher with the best. His father's bookcases stood untouched and dusty, but he had his private library, consisting of three volumes: his mother's Bible, Rietstap's "Noble Families of the Netherlands" and the account-book of the estate. The first he honored from a distance; the second he admired and often looked into of a Sunday; the third he studied all the week.

In short, Dirk van Trotsem was a hard-headed, not too

soft-hearted, old-fashioned country gentleman, with an immense idea of the greatness of his race, and of himself as its
representative, but not otherwise of noticeable vanity; a
good landlord because a so conscientiously painstaking one;
and a good citizen, because, although he usually voted for
nothing at all, he never voted for anything wrong. Sentiment first came into his life when his little half-sister began
to attach herself to him, and within a short time he had
given his whole heart, such as it was, to the child. She was
beautiful, and he worshiped her beauty; she was affectionate, and he went a-begging for her kisses; she was imperious, and he bowed his neck to the family spirit. The control of the estate was his daily bread; the coming home to
Adelheid a jam-puff at the close.

There was nothing romantic in his love, for all that. It
was good, solid, every-day, wear and tear affection. He
liked Adelheid, not for any far-sought reason, but for what
she really was to him: a van Trotsem, his sister, a sunbeam
in the gloomy house; and, as years went on, a quick, if careless housekeeper. He liked her to play the piano to him in
the evening, although he never recognized the tune; he
liked her to listen to his interminable stories about the cows
and the crops, and that in spite of the ignorance she revealed when he asked her opinion. And, under his rough
exterior, his heart, ever quicker than his head, swift to flame
though slow to melt—was unsuspectingly susceptible of the
caresses his little sister bestowed on him. It lay dozing
like a cat, but it purred when stroked.

Then came the dispute, when Adelheid's spirit asserted
itself in quite an unexpected manner. She was barely
twenty; she had fallen in love with Dr. Avelingh and declared herself resolved to marry him. The village doctor!
a poor man!—that did not matter—but a bourgeois! An
honest man, and a clever!—Faugh! All gentlemen are
honest; and cleverness is not a gentlemanly quality at all.

There was a regular tussle. According to Dutch law, a woman can not marry without her guardian's consent till she is twenty-three, so Dirk had several years before him. He shut up his sister in the castle and used all his influence to drive her lover from the village. But the doctor set his back to the wall and stood firm. And Adelheid took to feminine arguments, and began to look pale and wan and fading away. So Dirk sent for a great man from Utrecht, and cast murderous glances into the doctor's dispensary as he drove his visitor up from the station. The doctor returned them defiantly, and took off his hat to his distinguished colleague.

Was the Utrecht Professor in the lovers' secret? Or did he guess it, and are there still romantic medical men? He took the Baron into a side-room and told him that the invalid was dying of heart-disease which indulgence of her fancies alone could cure.

"You must let her do as she likes," he said.

"Thank you," answered the Baron, "and to begin with I'll see you d— driven back to the station."

After that Baron Dirk locked himself up in his study and had a bad time of it for an hour or two. He swore at the doctor, the professor, his sister, himself, his ancestors, the medical profession, the world in general, Heaven, Hell, and then at the doctor again, and the devil—he mixed these two up rather toward the end.

Then he unlocked his door, and went up to his sister. He remained standing in the middle of the room, at some distance from her couch.

"Freule Adelheid van Trotsem," he said, "I have come here to ask you to choose, once for all, between your name, your rank, your kindred, your home, me, my—my—love on the one hand, and on the other hand—the village doctor."

He paused. A slight flush crept over Adelheid's pale face. She hesitated a moment—not from indecision.

"I choose the doctor," she said softly.

"Thank you," he replied. "I shall be at the Stadhuis * on Monday, the 17th, at twelve o'clock, to give my consent. To-day is the 7th, the banns will take you till Monday. No, I forgot. Excuse me. I must go to the Horse Fair on Monday. On Tuesday, the 18th at twelve o'clock, I shall be at the Stadhuis."

He turned to go.

"Dirk," she cried starting up, "I must, I must—Dirk, let me—"

The door closed upon him. Those were the last words he spoke to her. He saw her once more, at the Townhall, as he had promised, then never again.

She left the neighborhood with her husband. The latter was for braving out his noble brother-in-law's wrath, but she loved that brother too much for such a measure. They crept away, "like criminals," said the doctor, as he helped his wife into the cab.

How the Baron got back into his room, after the interview described above, he never knew. Before he realized what he was doing he had broken every chair within reach, what with swearing and raving and stamping about. He was ashamed of his behavior during many ensuing weeks, and persistently deprived himself of smoking—yes, actually, smoking—till he had paid for every penny of the damage in that manner.

These fits of passion grew upon him, as time went on. He was past forty when his sister left him, when he suddenly awoke to the consciousness of the fact that he was a very lonely, dull and, as he considered, ill-used man. He buried himself anew in the administration of his property, and from being strictly just, grew stern. He would break out into rages about nothing, pouring down over the heads

---

* Townhall.

of his servants abuse which was really aimed at his sister, and still more at himself. Not that he thought himself to be blamed in any way; if anything, he was angry for having acted right. He had had no occasion, while his sister occupied his house and his affections, to trouble about love-making, and now it seemed too late for anything of that kind. Besides, there were stories abroad of an earlier love affair— but we need not dwell upon these stories here. In fact, circumstances were broadening all the shadows in his character and stunting the naturally feeble sunbeams; he was growing into an unreasonable, unamiable man, with a heart prematurely seared.

Two years after their parting on the Townhall stairs the brothers-in-law met again, this time on the steps of Castle Trotsem.

Adelheid Avelingh was dying and she had sent her husband to her brother with a message of peace. The doctor went—he would have done anything for his wife at that moment; who would not?—and Dirk, called out by a servant, received his enemy on the threshold. The message was delivered coldly and formally: a prayer for one more meeting before the end; the answer was given more briefly still: an outstretched hand, a finger pointing down the avenue; that was all. The doctor turned to go, with rage and contempt unspeakable battling in his heart, and did not dream that the other stood there completely unable to utter a word, fighting with a tempest of sorrow and fury at himself, at his sister, at the man before him, in efforts that sent the blood beating thunder against his brain and swam a red ocean before his eyes.

Dirk van Trotsem watched his rival pass out of sight in that crimson mist: then he stumbled forward, stretching out one hand vaguely and feeling with the other in his tail pocket, while the first and last tears he ever shed since his childhood trickled heavily down his cheeks.

A couple of years again passed on, and then little Joost
Avelingh was brought to his uncle's house. And this was
how that came about. The widower, a strong, healthy man,
fully occupied by his profession and the care of his only
child, was suddenly struck down by an internal inflammation which carried him off in less than a week. During
the first days he was full of the knowledge that the disease
could be stopped; then came the fatal change, and he knew
that he had but a few hours to live. He sent for the
minister of his village, a good man, with whom he had had
some intercourse. But when the minister came, he was
nearly speechless. He pointed to the child playing with
his cart and horse but a few feet from the bed.

"To the orphanage," he gasped. The minister stood
amazed.

"Surely," he began, "your relations, or your wife's—"

The dying man signed impatiently for writing materials.
They were brought him. He scribbled down hurriedly:
"To the orphanage—only—*not* his uncle." The minister
bent over him. He had large, dark, penetrating eyes—
fortunately, or who knows where little Joost might have
ended his days? He looked right into the dying man's
soul. "On whose behalf do you make that arrangement?"
he asked "Your own, or the child's?"

Avelingh winced: he seized the scrap of paper and wrote
eagerly: "The child's."

The minister bent down closer, till his face almost
touched the other's. "On whose behalf," he said, slowly
and solemnly, "do you make that arrangement? Your
own, or the child's?"

The doctor started up so suddenly, that his interlocutor
recoiled. Supporting himself as best he could, Avelingh
sought the child, silent, struck still amidst his toys, staring
open-mouthed. With a swift wrench the father tore the
scrap of paper right across, and fell back. It was the one

great self-renunciation of Avelingh's life, made in the hour
of death. He lay unconscious till the evening, when he
died.

After all debts were settled, the minister found himself in the possession of five-year-old Joost, an insurance
policy of three thousand florins* and three hundred and
twenty-nine florins, fifty-five-and-a-half cents of ready-
money. He sat down and composed a lengthy epistle to
the Baron van Trotsem, in which he, with much elaborate
care, gave a description of what had taken place and asked
for instructions with regard to the future of the little
orphan. Ought he to have told so much? He discussed
the question at length with his wife, and came to the conclusion that the father's memory was ruined, in every case,
beyond retrieval, and that the knowledge of the facts might
rouse the pride, if not the magnanimity, of the child's noble
relations. The answer to the letter came unexpectedly, by
telegram: "Send child." The minister's wife began pack-
ing up Joost's little belongings, with a heart full of mingled
feelings, when a second telegram arrived: "Keep child.
Will pay expenses." But before the change was fully discussed, a third telegram appeared, which proved to be a
repetition of the first. Still later, during the course of that
ever memorable day, two other contradictory missives came
rushing in; all the village street was in a ferment—the
minister's quiet neighbors pressing their cheeks against the
panes for another sight of the wearied telegraph-boy. At
last came a fresh telegram with definite instructions: "Send
child unconditionally. Never mind further telegrams.
Van Trotsem." The minister obeyed with alacrity, and his
wife and her charge were already some way on their journey, ere he opened the last telegram and read: "Keep child.
Will pay expenses."

---

* Two hundred and fifty pounds.

Joost Avelingh was received by servants on his arrival at the castle; rooms were assigned to him in a side wing, and a Swiss nursery-governess procured. The choice unfortunately proved an unwise one; the nurse was an ignorant and unscrupulous, though a smooth-faced and smooth-mannered, woman, and Joost found himself suddenly transported from the free, intellectual intercourse with a father resolved to make a clever man of his son to a nursery full of ghost stories, small lies and small persecutions. During the first year or two he saw but little of his uncle, who dreaded the pain of the whole connection. Those years gave their definite impulse to his impressions of both past and present. The image of his dead father deepened upon his childish mind with all the glory of a lost happiness; the grim uncle, seen at rare intervals and never caressed, became the embodiment of terror. Joost had an old picture book, his favorite, with the story of "Beauty and the Beast." With a child's contempt of incongruities, he clothed his uncle with the name and attributes of the Monster and his father with those of the unfortunate Bride. It was a dangerous game that van Trotsem was playing; and he lost it in the end.

Joost had been two days in the castle before uncle and nephew met. "What is your name, child?" said the uncle abruptly. "Joost," replied the nephew, and added, "Avelingh."

It was the first time that the Baron heard the boy's name, and he was angry at himself for being so angry that his sister had called her baby after her husband, and not after him. He turned abruptly and left his little nephew standing on the grass-plot, all in a tremble at the fear of having done something wrong.

As Joost grew older and his character developed, his uncle began to take a greater interest in him. They were very different, and yet in one or two things they were strangely alike. Joost also early displayed a taste for wan-

dering away into the woods alone, to his uncle's disappointment, who now, irrationally enough, was in want of a companion. But Joost did not get intimate with nature, at
least not in his uncle's manner. He would lie out in some
sun-checkered copse or by some murmuring stream, en-
joying himself with an intense enjoyment, but when he
came home, he could not tell what he had seen. One day
he stood listening to a singing bird, lost in a rapture of delight. His uncle came suddenly upon him, and, momenta-
rily pleased at the boy's evident pleasure, asked him what
kind of a bird it was. "A—a lark," said Joost, confusedly.
"The boy is an utter, hopeless fool," thought the uncle, for
it was a nightingale. Van Trotsem came to the conclusion
that a boy who wandered out into the woods without caring
for them, must be after some secret kind of mischief, and
he forbade the lonely excursions, though he would never
have stooped to asking his nephew to accompany him.
Joost, whose one great pleasure those moonings had been,
acquiesced sullenly. It was like the Beast to shut the fair-
est chamber up.

Other subjects with regard to which they came near
enough to clash would not be difficult to find. The Baron
was by nature straightforward, but the quality had been
warped by years and misfortunes, till he had learned to ac-
quire a certain amount of astuteness. Joost was also strictly
truthful, but, with him, the habit was more a carefully in-
culcated one, his natural tendency lying in the direction—
not of untruthfulness, but of the avoidance of all unpleasantness whatsoever. His father had never told him a lie or
even joked him untruthfully; he soon got to see that his
nurse had a whole list of deceptions ready and measured
them out, as required, by the yard. His uncle too, strictly
honorable in all transactions, did not consider a "fancy"
answer to a child in the light of a really responsible full-
blown lie. And so Joost soon found himself at sea, though

he stuck hard to his ideas of truth, imbedded as they were, in his dead father's—Beauty's—memory.

He had been a year or two at the Castle when Mevrouw van Hessel—not by any means always distinguishable for tact—asked him in the Baron's presence, whether he did not love the dear good uncle—who was so kind to him—immensely. Joost lifted up his great dark eyes to hers and said softly but resolutely, "No." An awkward silence fell upon the company, and the child stole a timid look at his uncle with oh such a fear bumping at his heart. It was this incident which revealed to the Baron what a turn things were taking. He drove back, his little nephew sitting opposite, without a word, simply because he did not know what to say. "He will murder me when we get home," thought little Joost. "Never mind, I shall go to Beauty." But the next morning the Baron called him out, not to stab him on the terrace, as he expected, but to show him a little pony he was to have for his own. It was partly the Baron's tribute to the boy's intrepidity and partly a shamefaced attempt to gain his affection. Joost's eyes grew even larger and rounder with pleasure, yet in the first moment he shrunk back with a half-nervous awe from the living, prancing, palpitating wonder before him. His uncle saw the movement and, crying out that the child was a coward, stung to the quick, he ordered the groom to take the animal back to the dealer's. Joost never saw that marvelous vision again except in his dreams; it often came to him then, and he kissed it and fondled it. He thought his uncle had arranged the whole scene to punish him, to insult him; and he clenched his small fist beneath the coverlet.

There came a time when Baron Dirk would have been ashamed to confess to himself how anxious he was that the child should take to him. He was full of false shame, was the Baron—like all egotists—of false shame and true pride. And in spite of his desire he did nothing—or the wrong thing—to gain Joost's love. He would sit opposite to him sometimes in silence for a-quarter-of-an-hour, with his hands on his knees, his great red face bent forward and his fierce, prominent eyes staring, staring at the child, seeking to stare into his features—as it were—some resemblance to the dead Adelheid. It was a futile undertaking, for Joost was like his father, and like his father alone. It was a terrible ordeal to the self-willed old man to see thus ever before him this living monument of the whole cruel, painful story.

Several years had passed before he spoke to the boy of his mother. He did so one evening, in the twilight, suddenly, with an impetuous effort. But he struck no answering chord; Joost could remember nothing of her. The child sat silent for half-a-dozen moments, and then called to the dog. A burning desire had often come over him—almost insupportable at first—to speak to some one of his father, but an instinctive tenderness held him back. He had grown to be twelve before the subject was broached at all. And then it came up quite suddenly. Joost had recently acquired a habit of throwing back his black locks with an impatient movement of the head. It was a daily bitterness to his uncle's heart, for it had been the high-spirited doctor's favorite gesture, the scornful shake with which he had flung from him the Baron's brutal attacks. " Don't do that! " said van Trotsem one morning, exasperated beyond endurance. " Don't do that; it's ungentlemanly! "

The word stung Joost out of his life-long reticence. " Papa used to do it," he said. Suddenly, in that moment, the memory flashed upon him across the years.

" Your father," shouted the Baron recklessly, " was not a gentleman ! "

The child started back. " You lie," he cried. His uncle struck him, for the first time, a blow across the cheek.

The blow was never repeated, but it marked a fresh turning-point where the paths of uncle and nephew went still farther apart. Joost never forgot its disgrace, and, as he went up to his room, he vowed that he would nevermore give his uncle cause to strike him again. He was by nature uncommunicative; he now grew taciturn. See what came of resenting wrong—fresh, insupportable insult! He would render it impossible. Before all his uncle's gibes and reproaches he henceforth sat silent, sullen, often apparently sleepy, thereby maddening the old man more and more, and ignoring the one means by which he might have fronted and routed him. The habit, thus assumed in youth as a preventive against violence, grew upon him. It was easy, after all; and you soon get indifferent. It never left him afterward.

CHAPTER IV.

JOOST STUDIES MEDICINE.

WHEN Joost attained his thirteenth birthday, it became evident that he must go to the Public School at the county town. Till then he had been educated in a happy-go-lucky manner, the village schoolmaster coming up in vacant hours and setting him long tasks to fill up the intervals. French he had learned from his early governess, and he spent too much of his free time in the disused library, reading and re-reading the French classic poets, and even the great masters of French prose. His selections were often not those a careful mother would have made. He knew La Rochefoucauld and Le Sage well before he was twelve, and was not unacquainted even with Rabelais. Then he dived into French translations of the Greek and Latin authors—a chance volume of Herodotus led him thither—reading on "fast and loose" as they say in Dutch, and forgetting what he could not understand. His uncle disapproved of the whole taste without being able to control it. What rational boy would prefer a book to a boat, a pen to a pony? Joost would willingly have accepted the pony and the boat too, had his uncle offered them. He was now driven to the library by sheer ennui, and it was a blessing he enjoyed himself there. He did not care for the society of the children of those grooms and laborers his uncle was so familiar with in his own haughty manner. He idled out into the gardens and composed verses. They were not very good verses, and he was by no means a nineteenth-century Milton, but they kept him innocently employed—for he could not publish them.

Even Dirk Trotsem would have comprehended that such a boy must be properly educated, had he been left to find it out by himself. But the village schoolmaster spared him that trouble by telling him plainly, that Joost now knew all he could learn at home. And the old man, who looked upon his nephew as a continual worry, an annoyance and a reproach, who had no common interests with the lad and no agreeable intercourse, and who even felt at times that he positively disliked him—the old man now suddenly realized that he could not let the child leave the house. He hated the idea of being left alone in it; there would be nobody to talk to, nobody to talk at, if you will, nobody upon whom to pour out his grievances. The next worst thing to keeping Joost was letting Joost go. Both were evils; his life was made up of evils; he was an ill-used, undeservedly persecuted, miserable, righteous old man.

So the boy remained at the Castle and drove over to school daily, a drive of some nine miles. He got on better with his companions than might have been expected. His heart warmed and thawed amid all that bright young life. He was quicker than most boys, certainly, and more reflective, born with what the poets call an "inward eye," but once out in the open air with schoolfellows, he became a different creature. He could run with the swiftest and laugh with the loudest, and he showed quite an unexpected courage in hitting out when attacked. In athletic sports and games he did not excel; "I can only run away," he used to say in later years. But he had a frank, ingenuous manner, which goes home straight to boys' hearts—no one but a bully would have struck Joost Avelingh.

His uncle—guided therein by the Public School masters—had destined him for the bar. It seemed the natural thing, and Joost was well satisfied it should be so. By the time he was eighteen, and in the highest class, he looked upon the matter as definitely settled and made all his plans accordingly with Kees van Hessel, his class-fellow and chum. They were to go up together.

But in the long vacation—at the last moment almost—a sudden change came. The old Baron—he was just about sixty by this time—called Joost into his room. He sat in the armchair by his desk, looking straight in front of him out of the window, with his back turned to the youth.

"I have been obliged to alter my arrangements," he said, abruptly; "you will study medicine."

Joost stood as if a thunderbolt had fallen on his heart. Perhaps—who knows?—if he had burst into hot reproach and refusal, he might have shaken his uncle's purpose. But that was not Joost's manner with regard to "the transaction of unavoidable business," as he had come to call his intercourse with his uncle. He hesitated for some time; then he asked quietly and, worst of all, sneeringly: Might I know your reasons for so sudden a change?" Now that he was no longer a child, he had got into this dreadful sneering accent with his uncle, unconsciously, as a man of superior intellect is apt to do under oppression. It was the worst tone of all with van Trotsem, who could not have told why it stung.

"I have my reasons," said the Baron, shifting his account books.

"It is, therefore, I should like to hear them," said Joost. There was a long silence. The big dog at the Baron's feet rose up, stretched himself, lifted his head, gave a long look at Joost, a deep sigh, and lay down again. The Baron kicked out one foot, unintentionally, and struck against him.

"I may say on my side," continued Joost, "that, although I am a doctor's son, or perhaps, on that account, I have a particular, a peculiar dislike to the study of medicine. I loathe it. The idea of always puddling in putrid matter is especially obnoxious to me. You may wish to know this."

The Baron nodded his head once or twice. "That comes true," he said aloud, more to himself than to Joost, "quite true." He took out, mechanically, a sheet of paper from the blotter before him, held it up for a few moments without reading the contents, and then put it back. Joost noticed the paper; is was of a peculiar pink tint, covered with writing in a large, florid hand.

"Quite true. Quite, true" said the Baron softly.

"And therefore," repeated Joost, "I should feel obliged if you could communicate your reasons to me."

The old man now for the first time turned round and looked at his nephew. The dog came up and put his nose against Joost's hand. "Joost," said the Baron, quite kindly, "believe me, I have my reasons. I consider them imperative. I am sure they are right. I can't tell you; at least, I don't wish to. I want you to begin studying medicine to please me. You'll like it afterward. I know you will. They say so; do it to please me."

The tone of the voice—almost imploring—was lost upon Joost. "Thank you, sir," he said, coldly. "I do not believe I need trouble you for any reasons. I am confident I know them. In fact, I should say I had stated them my-self—just now."

He turned to go. "What!" screamed the old man, starting up and shaking his fist. "Damn you, you thank-less scoundrel. Damn you and the bread you eat. Medi-cine! You *shall* study medicine! I'll make you study it! I'll—damn you, what do you mean by your insolence? What was good enough for your rogue of a father is good enough for his blackguard of a son! Damn you!"

Joost stood looking at him for a moment, then smiled—the faintest ripple of a smile—and left the room.

He really thought that he knew the reason. He believed that the whole comedy of preparation had been played by the old man for the sake of this final coup. He had been led to make all his plans for the future, that the disappoint-ment, the humiliation, might be the greater in the end.

"He may well do it for love of me," muttered the Baron to himself, as he fumed up and down his sanctum. "Why should that not be the best reason of all? As good any day as the other. Why should he not care for my wishes, the ungrateful vagabond? Talk of filial affection! If such a thing exists, he ought to feel it for me! And his father, whom he has never seen since he was a child! Whom he owes nothing but beggary! Doubtless he would gladly do it for his father. He sha'n't do it for his father. He shall do it for me."

"And he enjoys it," said Joost to himself, alone with his cigar, by the pond. "I tell him it means life-long misery to me. And he enjoys that. That's what he wants. I hate him. Great Heaven, how I hate him! Can it be wrong to hate as I do? With such a cause."

He was debating with himself, smoothly and leisurely, whether he should turn his back upon his uncle and his uncle's house forever. He could enlist as a soldier for Acheen.

That meant a horrible death in a year or two. Friends —the most intimate, to whom he had confided something of his troubles—had advised him to enlist. They were snugly settled in their own homes, and it sounded well. He might come back a general, with the Military Order of William on his breast. He might—Joost thought of the unspeakable horrors of Acheen, and shuddered as he looked down into the blackness of the pond.

He was well aware of his poverty. He had been too often taunted with it for the ghost of a doubt to be possible on that score. The exact amount of his possessions stood out before him, as he had heard it a hundred times from the lips of his uncle : three thousand three hundred and twenty-nine florins, fifty-five and a half cents, "the interest —you know, Joost, goes in keeping you. It really all goes; or would you desire me to give you a written account?" He was too much a child of the nineteenth century and he had been too accurately enlightened by his uncle not to know that a couple of thousand florins were at best but a loosening rope over the precipice of starvation. And besides, even what little he had was in his uncle's keeping. That uncle was rich enough; it had been Dirk van Trotsem's mother whose money had bought off the mortgages on the estate and restored the family to their pristine glory. The second wife, Joost's grandmother, had been as poor in her own right as the old Baron, her husband, was in his.

Joost could not escape from his guardian, even if he wished it. For the ensuing five years he was bound by the law to obey in all things. If he fled, he would be brought back with contumely. He could not, therefore, obtain a situation and "honestly earn an independent crust." He could only attempt to run away—run to sea, in fact. Not all young men have a natural aptitude or inclination that way (if they had, there would be more good admirals); Joost looked down again, this time at his own reflection in the pond and the red spot of the cigar. He was too old and too tall for a cabin boy. Decidedly the idea was unpractical, and Joost, being practical, walked up the terrace and rang for some coffee.

.   .   .   .

So Joost Avelingh studied medicine. He began his work with a rooted dislike, and the farther he went the wider that dislike spread out, until his life was overshadowed by its branches. The young men of his own rank, or rather of the rank his uncle's position had brought him, were law students, and naturally kept a good deal to themselves, though they made an exception, as far as possible, for Joost. His own fellow-students were rough lads of the lower middle class, who laughed at the airs he gave himself, and despised him for his dislike of his profession. He turned sick at the sight of blood, and even the professor burst out laughing. The smell of the laboratory, the touch of all that putrescent flesh were horrible to him. Often, after lecture, he could not eat a morsel. His daily occupations became a terror. He fled from them—whither? It is a wonder now, looking back, to think he did not fly to his own ruin; he sought a refuge in his old favorite, literature, and thereby escaped many a danger.

He lived in rooms of his own now. It was inevitable on his going up to the University, but it was also desired on both sides. The time had long gone by when the Baron was anxious to keep his nephew near him. He saw that the young man avoided him, and he also was quite content they should see but little of each other. He regretted sincerely that there should be so little sympathy between them, and he laid the blame on Joost.

If there was in Joost's character a strongly marked fault growing out of a virtue—what the French call: *Un-dé-faut de ses qualités*—it must have been the intense longing for approval and admiration which was part of his affectionate-ness. He was anxious to do all men a pleasure, but he was also anxious to be thought pleasing by them, and it was an extravagant enjoyment to him to know that they thought him pleasing. He wanted to be liked and honored and praised. Why not? He wanted affection. But in his present position he could not get what he desired. Besides, in any case, he was not a man to be popular at a Dutch University. He drank but little; he swore not at all, and he never played.

And so Joost Avelingh had spent three years at the University: he was therefore now, at the age of twenty-one, about half-way in the Dutch curriculum. He had even passed his first examination, although with but indifferent success.

He went over to his uncle from Saturday to Monday according to agreement. The rest of the week he worked as little, and read as much, as he possibly could. He dreamed of the great things he might have done, and thought himself a good deal cleverer than he really was. Most young men do, and that is why the very clever ones are so unbearably conceited. During the vacations he returned home, "by royal command" as he expressed it. He was at home at the time of that Santa Claus evening when Agatha van Hessel—"fair Agatha"—sent him away empty-handed.

CHAPTER V.

THE ICE-PARTY.

"I should ask her, Joost," said Kees.

They were skating leisurely up the crooked Rhine on their way past Utrecht to the quaint old town of Ysseltein.

Behind them skated the rest of the party. They intended making quite a day of it and were in high spirits accordingly. Mynheer and Mevrouw van Hessel had driven over with several other middle-aged people, and the young ones were now skating to join them. There was to be a simple luncheon when they reached their destination, and then all were to skate back again along the white canals.

"I can't think," Joost had been saying, "what I can have done to offend Agatha. I suppose I have no right to expect her to give me presents, but she always has done so till now on St. Nicholas eve. So I suppose she's offended about something."

"I should ask her, Joost," said Kees.

"You don't know anything about that thing she said she had got for me?" continued Joost, wishing his friend would be more communicative, "and which your mother—er—er—disapproved of."

"No," said Kees truthfully, "only that my father said she could give it you next year."

"Anyhow," Joost went on grumbling with a lover's inconstancy, "she didn't give me anything. So I'm sure that she's offended. I wonder what I have done."

"Ask her, Joost," said Kees imperturbably, pulling a long whiff from his short curved pipe.

"Ask her! Ask her!" cried the other, losing all patience, and sweeping round the corner with a flourish that almost made him lose his balance. "How can you be so provoking, Kees? I can't go up to your sister and say: 'Freule, why don't you give me presents?' I might as well stop a young lady in the street and say: 'Freule, why don't you give me yourself?'"

"You might," said Kees. "And the young lady might be my sister, or she might not. Look here, Joost"—he struck with a short stick he was carrying at a lump of snow that lay handy, "you have known Agatha ever since she was a child. You like her, and she likes you, and if you can't ask her by this time whatever you want to, you must be a duffer. That's my opinion, and I don't consider myself a fool."

Joost skated on in silence. A year ago he had come to the conclusion that he was in love with Agatha van Hessel, and he had found amusement and interest in developing the tender passion ever since. So by this time it was a very serious thing indeed. At least, so he told himself. She occupied his thoughts, and he liked to have them so occupied. Of course she had early taken possession of his verses, and her presence in them had materially improved these works of art. The idea of his having somehow displeased her worried him, chiefly because it hurt his comfortable self-esteem. He did not like people to be dissatisfied with him. He liked to please them.

"Van Asveld," he said presently, "is a cad."

"Of course," acquiesced Kees. "Nobody doubts that, I suppose."

"Then why did you ask him?"

"My dear fellow, man is a gregarious animal, and only a gentlemanly hermit could keep himself clear of cads. I am content, therefore, to draw the line at officially recogized, objective cads. I exclude all honest people in fustian, but the subjective broadcloth cad, the coronetted cad, I admit. I must talk to somebody. At least, that's my opinion, and I don't call myself a fool."

"No," interpolated Joost, "leave that to me, as your father says. No offense."

"The van Asvelds are an old family," continued Kees. "Title pretty old too. Besides Arthur's a relation of yours."

"He is no relation of mine!" shouted Joost with unnecessary vehemence. "He is only a cousin of my uncle's, as I have told you a hundred times." He cast furious glances behind him, where Agatha was skating, at some distance from them, hand in hand with the objectionable Arthur.

"Oh very well," said Kees coolly, "most people wouldn't think it mattered much. By-the-by, how is the old gentleman?"

"Wonderfully amiable. He presented me with a check for a hundred florins* this morning as a tardy Santa Claus gift. As far as I can remember—and I've been thinking it over all the morning—it's the greatest proof of his affection I ever received in my life."

"Let us hope he will continue to improve," said Kees. "The older he gets the more may he give you, till he cuts up and gives you all."

Joost flushed up.

"He must be very rich," Kees went on, "with all his hoarding and his capital administration of the estate. All's well that ends well, Joost. You'll be a great landed proprietor some day. My father says Dr. Kern told him the old man may last twenty years longer, but there's every chance he won't last two. He's got something the matter with his heart and he's apoplectic too. You knew that didn't you? Well, don't tell him I told you. *He* does. Kern told papa some weeks ago. My opinion is you won't have a chance of killing many patients, Dr. Joost.

Joost skated on. It has been said that he was a child of the nineteenth century, the age of gold, but it is due to him to add that, although he knew the importance of money, his was anything but a mercenary mind. He had fully understood that his uncle was rich, and that he was poor, and that, furthermore, he was dependent on the old man for support—the fact had been stated to him with sufficient plainness and frequency. But he had never real-

---

* About £8 5s.

ized that there could be any other connection between him and his uncle's money. Baron Dirk never spoke of the subject. And, for Joost's thoughts, it had lain too far outside the sphere of "practical politics." The Baron was not an old man—sixty-three, Joost thought; he might, as Kees Hessel had said, live twenty years longer, and by that time the best part of Joost's life would be over. The subject was too far away for immediate consideration. However it be, it is certain that Joost had never looked upon himself in the light of a possible possessor of his uncle's wealth till the morning of that 13th of December, when Kees Hessel, probably impressed by what his father had repeated of the doctor's indiscretions, first stated the desirable eventuality in such unmistakable terms.

"And a good thing too," continued Kees, breaking a long and awkward silence. "And I quite agree with my father, whatever mamma may say, that you are a very advantageous *parti*."

"Of course, a bird in the hand and all that's quite true," continued the ingenuous youth, "but as matches go nowadays you're a good one. And if I said what I thought—but I can't say what I think."

"I wish you would," said Joost. "You are like the celebrated foreign King—France, wasn't it?—who never thought a foolish thing and never said a wise one. At least, if one is to believe your own account."

"Well, I will say it," cried Kees. "My advice would be: Don't bother about Agatha's being offended with you, but ask her to marry you. She likes you; my father wants it. You like her, I am sure, for you're always jawing about her. *J'aime; tu aimes; il aime.* Make it: *nous aimons*, and have done with it."

"Thank you," said Joost stiffly, drawing himself up as well as he could while skating so fast—for he had spurted as if in a race during the last speech—"Thank you. You are very good, and your advice is undoubtedly attractive. But I shall never propose to any woman till I am in a position to maintain her."

"Oh very well. Don't be waxy. I don't consider myself a fool, and that's my opinion. Only mind Arthur Asveld doesn't forestall you. I don't think he will quite wait for love-making till he is able to support a wife." And good-natured, self-satisfied Kees buried his chin in the collar of his pea-jacket and tried hard to reanimate his perishing pipe.

They were nearing their destination. They had been skating on and on along the narrow river which lay as a gleaming band across the flat, frozen landscape. Barren it was and hushed, as if in death, beneath its white coverlet, but not bleak. The wintry sun shone out too cheerily for that from his pale, silver-blue sky, lighting up every sparkle in the wide expanse, and sweeping great shadows—you could not tell whence—across the ice-band down the middle. The rare trees along the banks—a cluster of poplars, a row of straggling willows—stood out, black and gaunt, against heaven. Here and there untidy bushes formed a sort of fringe. From these a bird would start up occasionally and shoot on ahead over the river. In the full, clear winter stillness they could hear his parting rustle; the notes of bells came ringing from peaked church-towers in the distance. Children called out to them, standing among the hens before red-roofed, snow-bedizened cottages along their road. And as they passed the full-bellied Dutch barges, motionless by the frozen river-bank, a head with a pipe would lift itself slowly from the companion and lazily follow them, and half-a-dozen chubby, red-comfortered children, pottering about on their own small skates, would come after them with a merry hue and cry, trying to keep up with the older riders.

The town, small enough, and huddled together, appeared against the horizon long before they were near it. It lay, flat amid the far-stretching flatness, with a steeple here and there, first gray, then, as they approached sufficiently to see the snow-patches, all red and glistening white. The others had been gaining on them while they talked, but after Joost's rejection of his friend's advice, they hurried on in unbroken silence, Joost skating ever faster, with a grim frown on his dark face, and Kees keeping up with him as a point of honor. As they neared the town, however, Kees slackened his speed, and Joost looked round at him.

"I think we'd better wait for the others," puffed Kees. "Politer, you know."

"No, sir," said Joost, "You're beat. But all right; I'll wait."

"Oh very well," laughed van Hessel. "It's quite true. We've been going too fast for any sensible man these last ten minutes, and that's my opinion."

So they made up what quarrel there may have been, and skated back very leisurely to pick up the others, talking of University affairs the while. Joost's face did not cloud over again, till he saw Agatha coming up, still hand in hand with van Asveld.

The Jonker Arthur van Asveld was a fellow-student of the other young men, and in their set. When they first went up to the University he had highly disapproved of the admission of a medical student into a club of "jurists," and had loudly expressed his disapproval. Of course some one had told Joost. He was not himself a very attractive personage, but in accordance with Kees's candid confession, he could scarcely be called an unpopular one. He was very stupid and boasted of his stupidity, he was very impecunious, and lived on his debts and his losses at play. He was very corpulent, and thereby proved a claim to good-nature. He was fairly good-looking and extremely licentious. He had a good many claims to popularity in the circle in which fortune had set him. The Jonker Arthur was a connection of the Baron's, being the son of that gentleman's cousin. He had come up to Utrecht from an out-of-the-way village where his widowed mother tried to keep up her rank on £500 a year. The Jonker now spent seven or eight hundred at the University.

. . . .

There was quite a merry company of them round the luncheon table of the hostelry of the "Golden Cow." A long table in a low, sanded parlor, a white earthenware service of coffee-things and a shining black slop basin, plenty of double rolls—"cadets," as they call them, mealy, pasty, nasty things—with thick slices of red beef or Dutch sweet cheese between them, and a dish of oranges to wind up with. Good spirits, glowing cheeks, and keen appetites; what would you have more? The Jonker Arthur asked for a pick-me-up.

Mevrouw van Hessel, portly and commanding, sat with the kettle in the little burnished peat-stove beside her, overlooking the company. She did not approve of Annemie —the beauty—'s tendency to flirt. It was an imported custom, she thought, and not an improvement on the silent, still Dutch manner of old. Still less, however, did Mevrouw approve of her spouse's inclination to follow his daughter's example. Bettekoo had brought a friend, a charming young thing of seventeen, in swansdown and curls. Mevrouw promised herself to speak to van Hessel at some more convenient time.

Verrooy, Mevrouw's son-in-law, had come over with them. There was not much to be said of Verrooy. He was " Secretary " to the Board of the Village of Hoest, because his father-in-law was Burgomaster of the village of Heist, and because the son of the Burgomaster of the former place wanted to be appointed to the Board of the latter. It was very simple. Some day he would become Burgomaster of some other village, when he had money, or influ-

ence enough, to get the place. Verrooy was not clever.
He could skate well, and he had a fine, light-blond mustache. "It had not been a very good match," thought
Madame van Hessel, as she looked across at her son-in-law
eating bread and cheese. "Agatha must do better, but
then Agatha was good-looking, not so fine a girl as Annemie
but far better than Clara, who had something that was almost a cast in her eye. Clara's had been a love-affair. She
had surrendered to Verrooy's mustache, and now the
mustache bored her. Oh, those love affairs, they always
turn out badly."

Joost sat between Agatha and Annemie, and, in a fit of
caprice and shyness, flirted with Annemie. It was a mistake
on his part, for Agatha naturally turned to her other neighbor and bestowed—not her sweetest smiles, for Agatha was
certainly not a flirt—but such second-best sweet smiles as
she had on the Jonker van Asveld. Arthur was delighted,
and grinned, and paid her such compliments as he found in
his repertoire, compliments which had already often delighted the ladies he usually spent his evenings with. They
did very well, he thought, brushed up and burnished, to set
once more before an honest girl.

"Well, Joost," cried out Mynheer van Hessel from his
end of the table, his volatile mind suddenly "butterflying"
away from the rosebud next to him. "Kees tells me you
beat him in skating this morning. So much the better; I
congratulate you." He lifted up his coffee-cup and flour-
ished it gracefully toward Joost—"I drink to you gentlemen of the medical profession. You remember the old
saying: *Medicina autem est ars tuendi*, etc. *La médecine
est l'art qui tue.*" He laughed heartily over his own joke.
It was an old friend that had gone through life with him,
and he loved it accordingly. He could not have remembered when first they met.

"Thank you, sir," said Joost. He was beginning to find

the fat Burgomaster rather a nuisance. He turned again to Annemie.

But Mynheer van Hessel was a born button-holer. He could not bear to let you go, till you tore your coat in escaping. "You must excuse me, you know," he went on, "I have always had a prominent ' *os humoris*,' a mouth for humor, as you doctors say, and I like my little joke. I was remarking only yesterday—"

"Did you say anything?" Joost asked abruptly of Agatha.

"I should like a little water," the latter answered meekly.

Mynheer van Hessel was left, open-mouthed, in the middle of his recital of yesterday's witticism. Two young men had swooped with a rush toward a bell-rope in a corner; four legs and four arms had got remarkably intermingled; there was a clutch at the rope, a violent peal, and then the whole concern came down, and the antagonists rolled up against the wainscoting together, with outstretched arms and exclamations. "Damned clumsy," hissed stout van Asveld in Joost's ear. "It was," Joost whispered back, "only: balls will roll, you know." A peal of laughter greeted this misadventure.

"What's the matter?" said the Burgomaster. "A ring for Agatha? There Joost has the first right."*

.   .   .   .

When they got up from table to go and see the quaint old town and the ruins of the castle, Bettekoo—Benjamin, as her father called her—ran up to him. She was full of excitement and animal spirits that day, what with the cold and the fun. "We can't all troop along like a flock of

---

* For the satisfaction of the captious reader who objects that the Burgomaster spoke Dutch his poor little pun is here given in the original: "Luiden voor Agaatje. Dat mag Joost bezorgen."

sheep, papa," she cried. "You must let me marshal you like a school-mistress. Mamma will take Verrooy, papa will go with Jennie (the young charmer in swansdown), Kees may have me, Joost will take Agatha—"

"But will Agatha take Joost?" interrupted the Burgomaster.

There was a moment's awkward pause. The wretched man availed himself of this to make matters worse by adding: "*Pour ceci et cela il faut bien être deux.*"

"Thank you, no, Bettekoo," said Joost, hastily flushing and stuttering. "You must really excuse my disobeying, but I have already arranged with Annemie."

And so Arthur van Asveld went with Agatha. She had now been tied to him for several hours and was getting very weary of his inane conversation. Mevrouw van Hessel looked on, concernedly. The excursion was not one of un-mixed pleasure to the good lady. She had some serious objections to Joost, but she disapproved utterly and unmiti-gatedly of van Asveld.

Agatha's difficulties, as it happened, were, however, by no means over. The party ultimately retraced their steps to the river, and, the girl having lingered to speak to her mother, it so chanced that, when she came down to the bank, she found both young men looking out for her, and casting terrible glances at each other. Both advanced simul-taneously; both—exactly at the same moment—bent down to fasten her skates.

"Excuse me, van Asveld," said Joost in a voice which he in vain sought to steady, "it is my—er—privilege to help the Freule with her skates."

"By what right but impertinence?" queried van Asveld. "If the Freule allows me to assist her, I shall do it."

"Mynheer van Asveld," cried Joost, suddenly dropping out of the familiar "thou," "you will leave this skate to me." He seized hold of it as he spoke.

"Mynheer Avelingh," replied Arthur, scornfully accentuating the "Mynheer," "you are probably crazy."

"It is like you," said Joost quietly, "to quarrel before ladies. Let the Freule decide for herself."

Agatha looked from one to the other. Their angry faces warned her to settle the dispute at once. She addressed Arthur. "Then, Mynheer van Asveld, if you will be so kind—"; she turned to Joost, "because you know, I know you longest, Joost."

It was rational and graceful enough, surely, but Joost walked off in high dudgeon. She eyed him in despair, for, she felt, that, were it only for appearances' sake, she could not again ride all the way home with van Asveld.

Practical Mevrouw van Hessel came to her rescue. She had come to the river-bank to see them off, and now she called Joost to her. "Will you start with Agatha, please," she said, "while van Asveld attends to Bettekoo." So Arthur, much to his disgust, had to remain behind with "that child."

Joost and Agatha skated off in silence, side by side. Joost offered no assistance, but glowered straight in front of him. His companion was not a very efficient skater, and after they had gone some distance, she stumbled, and would have fallen, had he not caught her. They righted themselves with some difficulty, Joost stamping himself straight on his skates again.

"Would you give me a hand?" asked Agatha, humbly.

He held out both, with no very good grace, and they skated on again.

They had turned a corner and passed under an old wooden drawbridge. The glow and sparkle had gone out of the landscape. The sun hung low, and half-way veiled, behind a line of pink clouds. The whole scene was gray and cold and hazy. There is nothing so ashen and death-like as the sunset of a fine winter's day.

They had skated on for nearly an hour in silence. They had distanced all the others, for Joost dragged Agatha forward, and were now apparently quite alone amid that misty waste of snow.

"And you flirt," burst out Joost, suddenly, "with one, and the other. A. for my fan; B. for my gloves! And, later on, I daresay, A. for my hand, B. for my heart! You are a bad girl, Agatha!"

It was very childish. And what did Agatha's flirtations matter to him? He had been ruminating the subject all day.

Provoked by Kees's advice, disgusted with Mynheer van Hessel's stupid banter, he had only just now made up his mind to be very circumspect. The Burgomaster's hints, especially, provoked him. They had led him firmly to resolve to make no advances to Agatha van Hessel. "No, he was not the man to be bullied in matters of that kind. He would show the Burgomaster that he, Joost Avelingh, was no fool. He would marry whom he chose, and as he chose, and, however much he loved her, he would not propose to Agatha at any man's bidding or prompting—not he."

The sudden attack on Agatha was childish under any circumstances. She was inclined to be very angry, and give him such answer as he had deserved. But, after all, Joost was Joost. They had known each other from childhood, almost as brother and sister; she could take a good deal from him that she would not have borne from another. And she stole a look at his dark face, looking so cross and handsome with the black eyebrows knit, and the mouth set square under the little black mustache. Poor fellow, how good and silly he was. She pitied him and his foolish anger.

"Joost!" she said gently, reproachfully, with a world of tender, laughing, half-vexed consolation in the word "Joost!"

She turned her kindly, clear blue eyes upon him. He

thought he had never seen her look so bewitching as now, in her tight-fitting sealskin. A little ear lay close to him, resting on the light fur collar, and her masses of yellow hair were coiled under a sealskin cap.

"Agatha," he burst out, "I love you. And that's why! And that's all."

They skated on. He held both her hands, and she could not well withdraw them without falling. He pressed them —that was unnecessary—and she could not well return the pressure without accepting him.

She returned it.

They skated on. He bent his tall form and kissed her. There were icicles in the little black mustache and in his wavy hair. Nineteen and twenty-one, and a winter's evening. A sinking sun and a violet haze; a pale heaven with a single star in it, and a gleaming stretch of ice across a boundless snow plain. She rested her head on his shoulder, against the shaggy peajacket.

And so they skated on.

CHAPTER VI.

WEIGHED IN THE BALANCE.

WHEN the van Hessels turned the corner from which they could see their house, the first object that met their view was Joost Avelingh standing on the "stoop."

"Dear, dear, how tiresome!" said Mevrouw to Mynheer. "I suppose he is waiting for an invitation to dinner. It really appears to me that we have been seeing too much of that young man lately."

Mynheer van Hessel lay dozing in his corner. He knew

he was in disgrace. Ever since they had set down their last
guest a few minutes ago, he had pretended to be asleep.
Madame had a way of ticking the middle finger of her right
hand against the back of her left when she was displeased.
She was ticking now.

"You will not ask him," said Madame.

"No, no!" answered the fat Burgomaster, cautiously
opening one eye. "Oh, no! Quite enough gayety for one
day."

"Quite enough tomfoolery," began Madame, severely.
The Burgomaster shut his eye hastily and buried his red
face in his furs.

The carriage drove up to the house. Joost came forward, astrakhan-cap in hand, with a beaming face.

"It was very good of you to wait," said Madame, as he
helped her to alight. "You should not have done that
merely to say good-by. Good-by"—she held out her hand
at the door.

The Burgomaster came tumbling out after his wife.
"Joost," he said, "Oh yes. Capital fun, wasn't it? Hope
you enjoyed yourself. Good-by!"

"Mynheer and Mevrouw," said Joost, "I have proposed
to Agatha, and she has accepted me."

Mevrouw van Hessel was a fine woman, a big woman, a
woman of the world, with a handsome face and bearing,
despite her increasing girth. She turned slowly half-way in
the hall-door and looked at Joost. She looked at him. His
eyes fell.

"Bravo," said Mynheer van Hassel. "So far so good."

"So far," said Mevrouw. "Perhaps. But no farther,
at least to-day. These subjects, as you know very well, are,
as a rule, first discussed with the young lady's parents."

"I thought that Mynheer had already sufficiently sig-
nified his consent," stammered Joost.

Mevrouw shifted her ground. "Quite enough has been

done for to-day," she replied, " if not too much. You can come up to-morrow and speak to Mynheer. Good-by !"

She walked into the hall. Mynheer followed after, but, as he passed through the doorway, he turned round and winked at Joost. And so that young gentleman went home, consoled for Mevrouw's " brutal behavior."

. . . .

" I will not talk on the subject to you to-day, Agatha," said Mevrouw, as she stood dressing for dinner. " No, I positively refuse to give any opinion. You have thought fit to act and judge for yourself, so, really, you can not be much concerned to know my impressions. I must speak to your father first, above all things. I suppose you remember that he is half-way in his studies, and not at all clever at them, and that he has not a penny. In my days girls consulted their mothers. I consider it very unmaidenly and immodest to act otherwise. There, there. It all comes of reading English novels. But I must speak to your father first."

That father was spoken to in the privacy of the connubial chamber. " It all comes," said Mevrouw, " of your fooling, van Hessel. I can not imagine what has possessed you during the last week or two. Since Santa Claus evening you have been in this stupid mood. It's not to your credit. What with Joost, and that little Jennie what's her name, you have made a fine exhibition of yourself to-day."

" My dear," the Burgomaster ventured to remark, " you are unreasonably jealous, like all lovely women. As for Joost, Agatha might do worse."

" It has always been a mystery to me," Mevrouw went on, to herself in the glass, " how the big world continues to be governed by Majesties, and the little world by Most Worshipfuls, whose wives know them, and appreciate them. My dear, could you be so obliging as to tell me how long

Joost and Agatha are to be engaged, and what they are ultimately to live on?"

Mynheer stepped up to Mevrouw, and twice or thrice solemnly shook his finger in her face. He looked so knowing
and so stupid, she laughed in spite of herself, and caught
his fat hand and kissed it.

"Madame," he said, "your husband is not so stupid as
you think. He should say, with all deference to your superior wisdom, that Joost and Agatha will live on old van
Trotsem's money."

"When old van Trotsem is dead, *and* has left it to
them," remarked Mevrouw, contemptuously.

"I am in a position to affirm," said the Burgomaster,
falling into the tone he assumed at Board Meetings, "that,
to begin with, the old gentleman's health is not nearly as
good as people usually think. That, however, is neither
here nor there. But I have also every reason to believe
that, dead or alive, van Trotsem looks upon Joost entirely
as a son."

"Indeed?" said Madame, doubtfully.

"If I confide a secret to you, I lose it," continued her
talkative spouse.

She smiled. She may have had one or two secrets from
him; he certainly had none from her.

"But it may not be going too far to tell you that about
a month ago I had some business to transact with van Trotsem. He made a good job of it."

"I have no doubt," interposed Mevrouw.

"Not to my disadvantage, my dear. There was a third
party. Well, when it was over I congratulated him, as we
walked away. 'What's the use of the money to me?' says
he; 'I must go and leave it.' 'Not just yet!' I said. With
that he mumbled: 'H'm, H'm. There's no one but Joost.
I've only got Joost, and a thousand florins more or less
won't matter much to him!' I have never known him so

talkative in these fifty years and more. It must have been the successful bargain; and perhaps the consciousness that 'all's not right inside,"—the Burgomaster tapped his manly breast.

"And that," said Madame, "that, and the doctor's chatter, accounts for your tone these last few weeks."

"It does, my dear, that, and my natural affection for Joost and Agatha. I love Joost as my own son. And I flatter myself that I have brought the two dear children together, and managed the whole business wisely and well."

"What you say about Joost's prospects proves nothing," said Mevrouw, "nothing definite at all."

"Definite! No, my dear, but it gives us ground to work on." The Burgomaster began leisurely settling a white cotton nightcap, with an imposing tassel, over the gray fringe round his bald head. "I shall tell Joost to-morrow that I will speak with his uncle. All will depend upon that. I must have the old gentleman's word of honor —word in writing, that is better—*littera scripta manet*, you know, with regard to his plans for Joost both now and afterward. All will depend upon that; it is the *sine qua non*."

"Certainly," said Madame.

"I don't myself think there will be much difficulty, or I should not have gone so far with Joost. The old gentleman told me at the time that he thought young men should marry early. 'Marry and settle down,' he said, 'it's too late afterward :' and he looked quite unhappy, poor old wretch."

"He is a very disagreeable creature, and very rude," said Mevrouw. "I suppose he wouldn't specially object to Agatha?"

"Why should he? You remember about my sister?"

"Of course."

"So he can't disapprove of the family; and why should

he? I should say we were quite half-way between him and Joost."

"Well," said Mevrouw, "we must wait and see. I can not say I approve of the whole thing. There is much to be said against it."

"There is, my dear," remarked Mynheer, lifting himself up on his pillow to look for the extinguisher. "And therefore, if you understood Latin, I should immediately say to you: '*Audiatur et altera pars!*' and you would admit that I was right. Van Trotsem must be a very rich man; I should value him at a hundred and fifty thousand a year * at the least."

And he put out the candle.

CHAPTER VII.

THE CLAIMS OF RANK.

JOOST AVELINGH drove back to the Castle, with his head in a whirl. He drove fast, recklessly fast, as was his habit when under strong excitement. His agitation will be forgiven him by all who have ever been in a similar position; and to few men has the great decision come so suddenly. But an hour or two ago, he had been firmly resolved to wait, and do nothing in a hurry. If anything could have kept him back, it would have been Mynheer van Hessel's manner, but how charming and innocent and thoroughly girlish she was when she looked up at him and said "Joost!" There was a little mockery in it, perhaps, never mind; there was plenty of affection and good-nature. Who

---

* About £12,000.

could resist her? Not he. And so he was actually engaged!

He did not make much of Mevrouw's objections. Perhaps it would have been better for him if he had. It is not always good, as has been often remarked before now, for the course of true love to run too smoothly at first. And Joost's was true love. Did he doubt it? No, no; if he ever doubted, it was not on that first evening, when he drove home all aglow, through the cold.

He went up straight to his room and dreamed all night of Agatha. What with the day's fatigue and excitement, he overslept himself. It was half past ten when he walked into the dining-room, and saw the remnants of his uncle's meal. The old man breakfasted punctually at eight, and could not bear his nephew not to be present. Joost strolled out on to the terrace, and the first thing he became aware of was a chaise coming up the avenue. It drew rapidly nearer, and he soon recognized Arthur van Asveld in the driver.

During the first half of his homeward journey yesterday, silent and angry at Agatha's side, he had been full of plans to shoot, smash, horsewhip or otherwise damage the fat body of the Jonker, but now, standing there, and watching his rival, he felt quite magnanimous toward him.

"Good-day, van Asveld," he called out. "Coming for some more shooting? Can't, while the snow lasts."

"I know that," the Jonker gave answer, in a far less cheery voice, "I should say, on the whole, that I might know as much about shooting as you do. Is Cousin Dirk in?"

"I suppose so," said Joost.

The Jonker jumped down. "I want to see him," he said. "Tell some beggar to announce me, please."

It was not by any means the first time the Jonker called at the Castle. He had made a point of looking up his distant relative as soon as he came to the University.

He had got on very well with the old Baron. In many points, in fact, he got on far better than Joost. His tastes were rough and uncultivated like van Trotsem's; he enjoyed a round oath, a coarse joke and a good glass of wine. He came to dinner once or twice in that lonely house, and kept the grim old man in a roar with his stories all the time. Joost sat silent and disgusted. The guest was not afraid to speak out, and give as good as he got. He abused the wine roundly once, and the old noble actually sent down for the best that he had in his cellar. Next time Arthur asked for "that Rothschild," and got it. He asked for an invitation to shoot over the place, and got that too. He was a capital shot and a thorough sportsman. His heart was in it. When the Baron discovered that, he was truly and unfeignedly delighted. They went out together for hours. (The doctor had told van Trotsem to give up shooting; but the old man obeyed neither this nor any other advice.) When they came home to dinner, the Baron ordered up a couple of bottles of champagne, and they discussed the day's adventures enthusiastically, until, what with the lateness of the hour and the excellence of the wine, Arthur had to spend the night at the Castle. The old man liked him, after a manner. It may be doubted whether, in his heart, he did not esteem Joost far higher, but he liked to have the other with him at times.

"And what brings you here this morning?" the Baron said, as his visitor entered the room. "No shooting, with this weather, at any rate."

Arthur was not at all pleased to see how every one connected his appearance at the Castle with shooting, and with shooting only. He sank down in an armchair, without waiting to be asked.

"I have not come about shooting, Cousin Dirk," he said, "I have come to see you."

The old man wheeled round in his chair. "See me!" he

said, fixing his protuberant eyes full on Arthur. "There's not much to see in me. Do you mean to say you have come all this way to look at me? I never was much to look at, and I don't improve, I fancy, as years go on."

"There's nothing more to see," said Arthur imperturbably, "than an old Dutchman who looks every inch, what he is, a gentleman, and the representative of one of the greatest families in the country. That's all. But I didn't mean that. I meant I'd come to call on you and talk with you about some matters chiefly interesting to myself."

"Humph!" said the Baron.

"They concern you too, however, Cousin Dirk, because, after all, I'm one of the few relations you've got. I've never asked you for money yet; have I?"

"No," said the Baron, "because you know you wouldn't get it. I can't go giving all you young men a dollar to-day and a gold-piece to-morrow."

"Quite true," remarked Arthur. "You don't mind my smoking, do you? Pretty well accustomed to smoke, this room is, isn't it? Quite true. And I haven't come to ask for a dollar now. Heaven knows I'm beastly poor, but I don't want any of your money, while things go on as they are."

"Do you mean to say," asked the Baron, "that you have come to ask me for it when I am dead?"

"No, sir," replied Arthur with a certain warmth, "I do not. Look here, Cousin Dirk. I've been wild enough these last years. I'm sick of it. I'm no good at the University. Any fellow would be wild in my damned circumstances. There's no use in behaving myself. I've got no money. If I settled down respectable, the regular thing, and all square, and married—I should have to marry: I couldn't do it without—Look here, Cousin Dirk, I may as well make a clean breast of it—Would you, for the sake of our relationship, and the name I bear, and all that, pay off my debts, and give me a fresh start in life."

"How much would do it?" asked the Baron, sitting bolt upright in his round desk-chair, and twinkling his eyes under their bushy eyebrows. There was a wicked gleam in them, but the guileless youth could not see that.

"The debts," said Arthur, "would tot up to about twenty thousand odd." *

"And then there would have to be something like the same sum to buy you an occupation of some kind."

"I suppose so," said Arthur.

"Damn you!" suddenly screamed the old man, opening his eyes wide enough now, till they almost seemed to start out of his head. He whisked his chair round again; his face was purple. "Damn you; have you anything more to ask? Damn your impudence! What do you mean?"

Arthur was very much taken aback by this outburst, and considerably disappointed, but he did not lose his presence of mind. "I meant what I said," he answered coolly. "Don't damn me, if you please, sir. There's never been another gentleman damned since the devil was. And I won't stand it."

"I shall say what I choose," shouted the old Baron, exasperated. "Leave the room and the house this moment; or I'll send for a servant to turn you out." A handbell stood on his desk. He stretched out his arm to it.

Van Asveld rose from his lazy attitude. "No, sir!" he said in a loud voice. "Gentlemen can settle their disputes without treating menials to cheap amusement." He dropped his voice and his dignified manner almost immediately. "Trust me," he continued, rolling a loosened leaf round his cigar. "Nothing helps the socialists more than our quarreling before the servants. If you consider my troubles, and

---

* £1,655.

the misfortune of my race, food for rage or amusement, so
be it. It is not my fault that I misjudged you. If Joost
Avelingh—" he hesitated.

"What about Joost Avelingh?" asked the old man. "No
lies!"

"I do not intend to tell them," replied the other haughtily. "Joost Avelingh is not a gentleman, you will admit
that. I am; and I had hoped that, speaking to one of the
first gentlemen in the kingdom, I should have been understood. I had surely a right to presume that, loving your
own name as you do, you might have some indulgence for
my love of mine."

The old man shifted his gaze uneasily. Arthur saw his
advantage, and followed it up.

"I am an unfortunate gentleman," he said hurriedly,
"doubly unfortunate in being so poor and so well-born.
I have never asked you for a penny. I did not come here
to-day to beg. I came to concert with a gentleman of equal,
of superior rank, my relation, what means could be employed
to save an honorable name—a name he bears among his own
quarterings—from disgrace. I wish you a good day, Cousin
Dirk."

"Hist," said the old man, "come back! sit down!
What do you want? I won't give you money. Whom do
you wish to marry? Have you got any one? Marry a rich
girl."

"Who will have me?" said Arthur. "I don't want to
marry a poor one, but I don't want to marry for money. I
was thinking of Agatha van Hessell. They're very well off,
are they not, Cousin Dirk?"

"I don't believe it," said van Trotsem, "I have my
doubts about van Hessel. He lives in good style and
spends, I should think, more than his income! We shall
see! We shall see!"

"Then I won't have her. And if you care for the hint,

cousin, mind Joost doesn't pick up my leavings. Start me
fairly in life, and I'll propose to Jennie Melasse. I met
her only yesterday; her father was a sugar-planter; but
you can't have everything, and I dare say he'll consider the
coronet worth paying well for."

"You'll have money enough if you get *her*," said the
Baron. "It's your business, not mine. I won't give you a
half-penny at this moment; so it's no use asking. But I
tell you what. I don't mind promising that, for the name's
sake—for the name's sake, mind, not for yours, you scoundrel—I'll remember you handsomely in my will. You can
trade upon that, if you like, with old Melasse, or the Jews.
I don't think I shall last long; and I've nobody in particular to leave my money to."

Arthur looked crestfallen. "Thank you, Cousin Dirk,"
he said, "and that is irrevocably all?"

"Irrevocably all," replied the Baron, turning to his
papers, "and I shall damn you, if I choose."

Arthur held out his hand with a bow. "Do so, Cousin
Dirk," he said. "Only mind you don't damn yourself."

CHAPTER VIII.

THE CLAIMS OF LOVE.

THE Baron, left alone, found plenty of food for his
thoughts. One idea, however, soon floated uppermost.
"Mind Joost doesn't pick up my leavings." The suggestion seemed to move him strangely. He rang his hand-bell.
"Is Mynheer Joost up now?" he asked the servant. Mynheer Joost was sent for. The man found him pacing up
and down his room with long strides. He had just given

orders for his horse to be saddled. He was going to ride over to his interview with Mynheer van Hessel.

"Sit down," said the old man, when Joost appeared before him. "Sit down. Did you enjoy yourself yesterday?" He talked on for some time quite kindly about the ice-party, so kindly that Joost thawed and gave an account of the proceedings. He might have enjoyed such a rare talk with his uncle, had it not been that his thoughts kept flying off to the coming ordeal, and had it not been, also, for the rooted dislike which made all intercourse with the old man so irksome to him. Since the great wrong the Baron had done him, three years ago, the cup of Joost's bitterness, daily fed with fresh aloe, overflowed. Their relations had not improved of late years. All Joost's thoughts of his uncle were influenced by his dislike of the profession to which that uncle's wish had condemned him, and the old man's feeling for Joost underwent the daily influence of the nephew's tacit avoidance and dislike. Their paths, once parted to right and left, now led them farther apart the longer they pursued them.

"And were there any pretty girls?" asked the Baron. He was trying to manœuvre, and he thought himself wonderfully skillful.

"There was Jenny Melasse," said Joost carelessly. "Some people think her very good-looking. Mynheer van Hessel seemed to be of that opinion."

"Well, the Hessel girls are not much to look at, excepting Annemie. Now, Agatha I should consider quite a plain girl." He said this, oh so slily, and stole a cunning look at his nephew out of his wicked old goggle-eyes.

Joost was silent.

"Should you not, Joost, call Agatha van Hessel quite a common-looking girl?"

"N—n—no," said Joost, "I should not consider her that."

E

The old man talked on about the van Hessels, with awkward questions and remarks. Joost sat on thorns. He was most anxious to put off any discussion of the subject with his uncle till after he had seen the Burgomaster. He tried to turn the conversation, but in vain. The Baron reverted to Agatha, her flirtations, her marriage prospects, till Joost felt it would be neither honest nor prudent to conceal the truth any longer. He walked up and down the room once or twice with rapid strides; then he came and stood with his hand on his uncle's chair. After all, this was his only relation; the house was the home of his life. His heart felt very tender at that moment.

"Uncle," he said quite softly. The old man pricked up his ears at the change of voice. "Uncle, I don't want to deceive or distrust you. I've a very important subject to speak to you about, a very dear subject to me. What would you say, my good uncle—would you be very angry with me if I were to tell you that I love Agatha van Hessel—be she pretty, be she plain—and want some day to have her for my wife?"

There was no response. The Baron's face was turned away, but Joost could hear him puffing and snorting. At last came the words: "I should say, Joost, it can't be."

They were practically as unexpected at that moment as they were foreseen in theory. Joost had dreaded but little opposition from the young lady's parents; he dreaded none from his Uncle Dirk. But he kept his temper, fortunately. "Not just yet, of course, uncle," he said, still softly, "I quite understand that I must be ready, and earning my livelihood somehow, as a doctor"—he gave a slight shudder—"before I can marry her. But I could be engaged to her, as is the case so often, and make her my wife as soon as I am able to do so."

"It can't be, Joost," said the old Baron, still sitting in the same attitude. "Nor now, nor ever. If it could be done at all, it might as well be done now. But it never can be."

"My dear uncle," said Joost, still gently, "I should like nothing better than to have your approval. And I still hope you will give it. What can we do otherwise than marry? Agatha and I both think this marriage was made in heaven."

"Agatha and you?" cried the old man. "How far are you, pray? Married already, perchance. Not valid in Holland."

"Sir" said Joost, "only yesterday evening—I can assure you, only yesterday evening—was the subject first hinted at between us. How it came, I do not know. Please do not ask me. All I can tell is, that now we both know we love each other, and as for the rest, God help us through." His voice faltered. The hand that rested on his uncle's chair shook slightly.

The Baron pulled himself together; also with a visible effort. "It can't be," he said huskily. "You can never marry Agatha van Hessel."

Joost's knees gave way beneath him. Almost unconsciously, he slid down by the chair and clasped his hands across its low, round back. "Uncle Dirk," he cried, and there was a thrill of entreaty in his voice, "tell me, what have I done to you that you persecute me thus? Great God, whatever my father's or my own sin may have been, is a life of suffering not atonement enough? I do not deny that I have often wronged you. Be merciful now. I have endured enough. You are an old man, near the grave. God be pitiful to you as you show compassion. Oh, if you only knew how I *want* somebody to be kind to me to-day."

He was altogether unstrung, moved in the very depths of his nature. It was not a moment to weigh his words or even to fully realize them. He had a vague idea they were not very dignified. What of that? Agatha's happiness was worth the sacrifice of a little dignity. His love was all so young, and sweet, and tender, he could have cried like a girl that morning and not been ashamed of his tears.

The old baron winked his eyes, and spoke very gruffly. "It is your happiness, after all, which I seek, Joost," he said. "In my own manner, after my own lights, perhaps. I deem them best. What you say is hard to hear; we have somehow got awry, my boy. I dare say some of it is my fault. I asked you to trust me about your studying medicine. You never did so from the first. I can not help that. And now I must once more ask you to trust me about this matter. It is for your own happiness. You never can marry Agatha van Hessel."

Joost sank his head on his hands. He did not speak.

"I swear to you it is for your own good," said the old Baron solemnly.

Joost made an impatient movement with his bent head.

"Damn you, can't you believe me?" cried the Baron, fretfully. "You would make a cart-horse lose patience. You give up Agatha from this moment, do you hear?"

Joost again shook his head without lifting it.

"Do you mean to say you ignore my wishes?"

Joost rose to his feet. His face was very calm and white with suffering. "Sir," he said, in a firm voice, "I shall ride over to Mynheer van Hessel to-day, as I was on the point of doing when you sent for me. I shall tell him what has passed between us, and I shall ask him to let me marry his daughter when I am twenty-three."

"Do," said the old man, trembling with passion, "and tell him from me that, if you marry Agatha van Hessel, you shall never, living or dead, have another penny of mine."

"I will, sir," said Joost calmly.

"Do," shrieked his uncle, "and come back for dinner, and give me van Hessel's answer."

CHAPTER IX.

"FOUND WANTING."

WHEN Joost Avelingh was ushered into the Burgo-master's room, he found Mynheer van Hessel seated at the writing-table and Mevrouw by the window.

Mevrouw looked stern and uncompromising, Mynheer well satisfied and comical. The latter motioned Joost to a chair.

"Well, my dear young friend," he began, "and so we have been love-making on the ice! 'The heart may glow in winter's snow,' as the poet says. And now we have got to discuss consequences."

Poor Joost had his battle to fight all alone. It was so true, as he had told his uncle, that he was thirsting for some one to show him kindness, some one to sympathize with him and talk the whole matter over. He was an impressionable, warm-hearted young fellow, soft-hearted at bottom; just the kind of still, undemonstrative man who has every need of a woman's affection. He had never known what the term meant. He had never—never—felt the touch of a woman's hand on his forehead; never—before yesterday—heard a tender word, other than purely conventional, from a woman's lips. He thought, with a shudder, of the Swiss nursery-governess of his early years. He was not by nature reticent or unemotional; his character had been forced from its natural groove by the negative influence of his surroundings. The sternness of his dark young face; the sad look in those great eyes told but a portion of the heart's story. At bottom there was a half-acknowledged yearning for warmth, brightness, softness, a "wanting to be loved." There was also, it can not be denied, a "wanting to be admired," but is there not that in every male yearning for affection? Only women love for love's sweet sake. And with Joost the de-

sire was strongly developed. He wanted people to be good
to him and love him for what he was and what he did. The
Dutch have a very graphical expression for the whole sentiment, borrowed from horticulture—" He wanted to be put
out in the sunshine," they say. Joost Avelingh's heart, a
fair plant enough, and intended by nature to bear sweet-
smelling, soft-colored flowers, had never been put out in the
sunshine.

An hour or two ago he had been happy and confident
enough, in spite of all natural nervousness and impatience.
For the first time he had felt a woman's affection. It had
wrapped itself round his poor numbed heart, and he felt like
an outcast in a blanket. What wonder he did not stop to
analyze the nature of his feelings, nor inquire too closely if
the gratitude, the gentle sympathy, he felt toward this
woman was exactly and accurately that particular feeling
men label " lover's love! " It was love, a strange, new feeling, love to a woman, reciprocated and revealed in the inter-
change. The man who, from his childhood upward, feels
the warmth upon his heart of his mother's unfathomable
tenderness, his sister's admiring affection, the friendliness of
more distant relations, the liking of his sister's friends, that
man can properly distinguish and select, and say: " Nay,
but, distinctly from all other sentiments, this woman I love
for my wife." Joost Avelingh, when he saw the first beam
break through a loophole, cried out : " It is light! " He had
liked Kees Hessel and one or two other boy friends ; he had
liked the van Hessel girls ; he had liked some of the servants
about the estate ; he had loved tenderly, truly, the dogs and
the horses, and some rabbits he had had years ago, and a
lame squirrel and a couple of birds ; he had revered the
memory of his dead father as something beyond, on the
border, somewhere where heaven and earth must meet. He
was twenty-one ; he had never loved human soul before.

And now he sat there facing Mynheer van Hessel, with

Mevrouw a little in the background to his right. And the weight of his uncle's rejection lay heavy upon him. Instinctively he felt that the fat Burgomaster's kindly manner must not be considered to count for much.

"And so," said the Burgomaster, "we have got to consider consequences."

"I imagined, sir," answered Joost, "that from what you let drop at intervals I had a right to assume you would not look with disfavor on a possible suit of mine for your daughter's hand." He had prepared this speech on his way to the house, and it came out with a rush and a hitch in the middle, as such sentences are apt to do.

The Burgomaster crossed his plump hands over his capacious waistcoat, and twirled his thumbs. From Mevrouw's corner came a quick, subdued little cough. The Burgomaster looked in the direction of the sound. This subject, broached at the very beginning, was the one on which he had been specially warned not to commit himself.

"My dear boy," he said, "we will not discuss that. Yes, undoubtedly, young people make love, and it is very pleasant. There is no reason why they should not. They do not always marry the person they first make love to. I myself—" another and a sharper cough from Mevrouw's corner —"Oh, well, sometimes they do. So much the better for them, when they can! When they can! And as the old Latin maxim says—"

"And if we were to give you our daughter, Mynheer, how would you expect to support her?" The words came from Mevrouw's corner. Joost turned quickly in that direction. Mevrouw sat looking out of the window with immovable face, tapping one finger on the back of her hand.

"Yes," said Mynheer hastily, "yes, I was coming to that. If we were to give you our daughter, Mynheer, how would you expect to support her?"

Joost turned back again. "Mevrouw," he said, Mynheer,—I beg your pardon,—Mevrouw, I should work for her."

"Yes," said Mynheer, "very true and very good. Most estimable. But you would have to work a good deal."

"I should do that," said Joost.

"And a long time. Look here, my boy, let us come to business, and be practical. Ask your uncle when he can find it convenient to receive me. Then, I will drive across and talk the whole matter over with him, and, when we have settled it all, as no doubt we shall, then Agatha and you may be as happy as the day is long. We old people, whose hearts have done flaring up and settled down into a steady glow, we old people must look after the bread and butter, while you young ones go gathering honey. Even St. John couldn't live on honey alone. It's very provoking and prosy, but it has to be seen to. So I'll learn what your uncle says first.'

Joost had been shifting about on his chair trying in vain to check the Burgomaster's eloquence. "I can spare you the trouble," he burst out at the first opportunity, "I have spoken to my uncle already."

"Already! Dear heaven, how impatient these young people are! With all the world before them! And what," said the Burgomaster smiling, "what does your uncle say?"

"That if I marry Agatha van Hessel, I shall never, living or dead, have another penny of his."

"What!" cried the Burgomaster, dropping his hands from his lap and starting forward. Mevrouw turned her head from the window.

Neither spoke for a moment; then both spoke at once.

"Why won't he have you marry?" said the father.

"How dare he not approve of my daughter!" said the mother.

Joost looked backward and forward. "He refuses his consent to my marriage," he said, "because he resists anything and everything that could bring me a spark of happiness. He refuses it, because it is the one interest and amusement of his life to make me wretched. He hated my father for the life-long wrong he fancied my father had done him, and the one object of his hate has been to wreak that wrong on me in a life-long misery. It is my right, and my duty, to tell you this."

He paused. His auditors sat silent. "But I will baffle him," he continued more brightly, "and you will help me, will you not? Mynheer and Mevrouw, we do not want his consent. I am twenty-one. Before I have finished my studies I shall be twenty-three. Before I am able to support Agatha I shall—" he smiled a pitiful little smile—"be a good deal more, I fear."

"The idea," said Mevrouw, "of his not thinking our daughter good enough for his nephew!"

"It is not that, I can assure you," cried Joost. "The better the match, the worse he would like it. Did he not force me to study medicine because he saw I was bent on a legal career? He would consent to my marrying a scullery-maid. He thinks Agatha too good for me; indeed it is that, Mevrouw! And he is right there," added poor Joost in a low voice.

"That does not matter much," said Mynheer with an impatient wave of the hand. "As matters now stand, it is evident—"

"I will work for her!" cried Joost. "What do we want the old man for? I don't ask you—Heaven knows—to let me marry Agatha before I can support her. I only ask you to let me work and wait. Hundreds do, surely! I've not got on as well as I might till now, it's true. But this is different. I shall work differently if I work for Agatha!"

The Burgomaster looked down at his embroidered slippers. Their intricate pattern interested him. The usually loquacious man was unpleasantly silent.

"Hundreds do it!" repeated Joost. "Only let us be engaged, and have this object in view. It will help me with my studies! It will show my uncle you do not want his support!"

Again there was a short silence. Mevrouw broke it. "Perhaps," she said kindly, "your uncle's opinion may change. Perhaps you have vexed him about something. The best thing will be for Mynheer van Hessel to see him about the matter before we decide upon anything."

Joost shook his head sadly. "When my uncle says a thing like that he means it," he replied. "You will not get him to change. He bade me give you his message."

"Then," said Mynheer briskly, suddenly finding his tongue, "there must be an end of this. Fooling is all very well and wholesome, but not too much of it. There are comedy-marriages and marriages in real life. In the latter kind the couples have something to live on. And if it is true, Joost Avelingh, that you are a penniless young man with no reasonable chance of ever being anything else—well, I'm very sorry for you, but you know the old proverb:

> ' Enough breeds more : but all confess
> That nothing's child is nothingness.' "

"Am I to understand," asked Joost when he could speak, "that you refuse me—incontinently and irremediably refuse me—your daughter's hand, unless my own holds my uncle's money-bags?" There was a slight touch of contempt in his tone.

"You put it very melodramatically," said the Burgomaster. "Yes."

"But I love her!" cried Joost, "I love her! We don't want more money than will do to keep us. We shall earn that in time."

"You are silly, Avelingh," said the Burgomaster, "positively silly. ' Perette sur sa tête portait un pot de lait.'

Make the best of it. We don't, as I remarked just now, all marry our first love."

"Mynheer! Mevrouw! I told you it was my uncle's one object in life to make me suffer. He has been successful enough till now, heaven knows. And are you going to help him to be successful to the end?"

"You are melodramatic, I tell you," began the Burgomaster angrily.

"Mevrouw, you have been kind to me for many years. You and yours have been pretty much the only people who ever showed me kindness. And are you going to turn against me now?"

Mevrouw did not answer.

"I tell you I love her and will work for her!" cried Joost, starting up. "And Agatha!"—he veered round suddenly and came toward her. "Agatha! She loves me too! She has told me so! What will you answer your daughter?"

The Burgomaster had seized upon the opportunity Joost gave him, and had risen also. "Come, come, Avelingh, be a man," he said. "This must end. *His autem rebus peractis domum profectus est.*"

Avelingh came toward him. "What will you answer your daughter?" he said.

"My daughter will ask no questions," replied the Burgomaster coolly, opening the door as he spoke, "nor will she make any arrangements for herself until she is thirty. Remember that. 'C. C.* article so much,' as we used to say at college."

"I will never give her up," said Joost, as he passed out.

Mynheer came back to Mevrouw. "Unpleasant," he said, "tiresome. Very absurd. And really rather insolent, *au fond.*"

---

* Civil Code.

Mevrouw did not answer.

Mynheer threw himself back in an armchair. "*Il y avait un p'tit amoureux*," he hummed, "*p'tit amoureux, p'tit amoureux.*"

"It is largely your fault," said Mevrouw suddenly and sharply.

"My dear!"

"Yes, your fault. It is quite true, as he said, that you egged him on. You have flung the girl at his head this many and many a time. We play a sorry part in the business, Henrik."

It was Mynheer's turn to sit silent.

"What wonder," she went, warming as she spoke, "that the poor thing thought she had a right to love him. Who knows in how far you first started the whole wretched idea in her brain? You have forced the subject upon them! You have taught them to love each other!"

"But, my dear creature!"

Mevrouw sailed toward him. "He loves her now," she cried. "It was pure, honest love that spoke from his heart and from his eyes. Is it little, perhaps, that he is giving up for her sake? All this money, to which we attach so much importance, and which you say is such a great inheritance. He never even mentioned it. He counts it as nothing before his love and her happiness."

She stood before her husband. There was that look in her eyes—the mother's look—which makes all women kin.

"And she loves him," she went on softly. "If the blame be yours, ours, so must the responsibility be."

"Nonsense! What do you mean?"

"If they love each other truly, sincerely, as deeply as this, they must marry, Henrik."

"Ridiculous!" cried the Burgomaster. "All you women are the same. Give the hearts a romance, and the best heads go."

"Who knows how much of the romance is of your making?"

"Pooh, I shall unmake it then. I at least love the child too much to sacrifice her life to a moment's folly. Whatever sentimental ideas you may have, I know too well what ruin means," the sentence ended in something like a groan. Such a sound from the jovial Burgomaster startled his wife.

"What?" she said. "How so? Ruin?"

"Nothing," he replied with a forced laugh. "Only, 'love may sleep on straw, marriage wants a downy pillow.' I won't have my daughter marry a beggar; simply because I can't afford it."

"He can wait, as he said. He can work. After all, we are well off and can help them."

"You do not expect *him*, I should hope, to earn much as a doctor?"

"Heaven knows I was sufficiently opposed to the whole thing. But if she loves him, Henrik?"

"Good gracious, Marian, are you a staid Dutch housewife? Are you fifty-two? Are you—"

"I am a woman," she interrupted with vehemence. "And I have a heart, even though I am Dutch! If they love each other they must marry, Henrik."

CHAPTER X.

MADAME DE MONTÉLIMART.

JOOST, riding home at a tearing pace, saw his uncle standing on the steps, watching him as he dashed up the avenue.

"Well?" said the Baron, with an ugly leer, "Well?"

He had bent forward, not without anxiety; one look at
the young man's face seemed to reassure him. Joost stood
still on the terrace. He flicked his riding-boot with his
whip.

"And what does Mynheer van Hessel say to your suit?"
queried his uncle. There was a mocking tone in the demand, as if he were triumphing over somebody or something, perhaps over his own anxiety of a few minutes ago.
Joost applied it to himself.

"Mynheer van Hessel," he said, "takes the worthy view,
the practical, common-sense, respectable view. He is quite
willing I should have his daughter; nay, he is most anxious. He offered her for sale himself. But you must buy
her for me!"

"And I'm damned if I do," said Baron Dirk.

"So I told him, sir. And so he refuses, unconditionally, to allow us to be happy in our own way. And so we
are not happy; we are miserable. So far, sir, I suppose you
are desirous of information. The rest must be indifferent
to you. Would you allow me to pass?"

"Listen," said the old man, striking his stick against
the moss-grown stones. "Don't sneer at me. I won't
stand it. I suppose you are very much cut up about this
matter?"

"I shall spare you the pain, sir, of further investigation
of my sorrow."

"Have you ever seen a madman, Joost?"

The young man was startled by the abrupt question. At
the first moment a doubt flashed across his mind whether
perhaps his uncle felt his own brain giving way. And actually, in the mood he was in that day, the conception
brought him relief. It would be better, happier—ay, even
calmer—to know the man was mad, than to think such
thoughts of him as were now surging through Joost's brain.
The flash of uncertainty lasted but a few seconds; then

came the revulsion of feeling as he thought he caught his uncle's meaning.

"You need not be afraid, sir," he said scornfully. "It is not madness. It is only just that existence of a heart which some men call disease."

The uncle winced. But he still evidently subdued himself by a mighty effort. Joost wondered in a sick, dreamy way, that there should be so little swearing to-day.

Van Trotsem pulled out his watch. He was a dirty, snuffy old man, and as he stood there, unshaven, without a collar—nothing but a black silk stock round his red neck—in much stained black waistcoat and trousers, brown coat and green Berlin wool slippers; as he stood there, his protuberant eyes staring at the great gold repeater which hung by a brown hair-chain from his neck, he certainly was anything but an attractive personage. Joost eyed him with unconcealed hatred and disgust. The soft feeling of that morning was fast fading away and making place for the old heart-hardening hate.

"It is still early," said the Baron, "your business with the van Hessels was settled more quickly than even I gave them credit for. Go and have some lunch, Joost, and at three be ready to drive out with me. At three exactly, if you please."

"Lunch!" the very idea filled Joost with rage and scorn. He lounged into the dining-room, for want of something better to do, and eyed the things on the table with very unmerited, individual contempt. The old butler crept in and placed a dish before him—his favorite dish, as he noticed—lady readers may care to be informed that Joost Avelingh's favorite dish was an omelette soufflée with rasped ham. He looked up, annoyed that the servants should pity him and yet grateful for all kindness, and said "Thank you." "His master had ordered it," said the man. Joost did not touch the omelette, but he cut himself a quantity of meat for all that, and drank several glasses of wine.

He went out on to the terrace again. The weather had completely changed since yesterday. In the night the wind had veered round to the southwest; it was thawing as fast as it could—and nowhere, perhaps, can it thaw as fast as in damp, changeable Holland—the air felt quite warm after the long cold; clouds were coming up, and there was a ceaseless drip of melting snow from the house, from the parapet, from the trees of the avenue.

The stable-clock struck three, and at the same moment an open chaise with a dickey turned the corner of the house and drew up at the steps.

The old Baron came out with a red comforter on. He stood a moment looking at the landscape. "It's a good deal to give up, Joost," he said, encompassing with a sweep of his arm all his broad acres and stately forests.

"Sir?" replied Joost—nothing else.

The old man chuckled. "Nonsense," he said, as he got into the chaise, "we are not going to give that up, nor anything else, except just a boy's fancy. Drive on, Joost. To the town."

They did not speak much on the way. The Baron talked agriculture, but without eliciting much response from his companion. They met the village doctor in his gig. He shook his head reproachfully, and he took off his hat.

"Damn him," said the Baron.

When they reached the town, the Baron Dirk began giving instructions, directing his wondering nephew till they drew up at the great entrance of a gloomy, many-windowed building. There were bars before all the windows. Joost glanced up nervously.

"You know where we are?" said the Baron.

"Yes," said Joost.

"Very well. Never mind. Follow me."

They got out. A porter, with a grim, stony face unbolted and opened one half of the massive door. He seemed to recognize the Baron and led them into a waiting-room. Joost looked round him in silent amazement. Had his uncle brought him here to leave him? Nonsense; the idea was too absurd. It was like the old scoundrel to think of such a thing, but, after all, he, Joost, was not a child, and the laws of the land were there to protect him. The old man took off his coat and comforter. Joost noticed with fresh surprise, that he had made himself spruce, with a clean shirt and collar and his old-fashioned best suit of black clothes. The adventurous instinct which sleeps in us all awoke in Joost's breast. He began to feel interested.

A bland gentleman came in and greeted the Baron. "It's a long time," he said, "since you have been to see us. You will find us quite well and happy. We are all comfortable here in spite of circumstances. Taking us all in all, I should say we are the happiest community of fourteen hundred souls in the kingdom." He chattered on till a smug-faced female in a dark cloth gown appeared at the door. Then he confided the Baron to this person's keeping, and bowed the two gentlemen out.

Joost found himself passing through long, dreary stone passages, with a number of doors on both sides. Strange noises came constantly from various quarters; dull thumps, grating laughs, and occasionally something like a muffled shriek. Vague as the noises were, there was an unnaturalness about them which made them strangely impressive. They caused Joost to shudder, while he laughed at himself for the feeling. On the stairs the little party met two men with utterly foolish, vacuous faces, dressed in a sort of gray prison garb. One of them gave a feeble laugh. The smug-faced female brushed past these and, unlocking what must have been the fourth or fifth door since they started, led her visitors into a little square entry. Then she threw back a green baize screen and announced in a loud, harsh voice: "Mevrouw the Countess receives!"

F

Following his uncle, Joost found himself in a good sized, bright-looking room, against the windows of which wide-spreading branches—gaunt and dripping at this moment—somewhat obscured the view. It was an uncomfortable item to notice that the windows were heavily barred. Otherwise the room was cheerful enough, not to say gaudy; furnished in many colored chintzes and bright ribbons, littered with all manner of knickknacks, and full of bird-cages of various shapes and sizes. In the middle of the apartment stood a little old lady with a stiff yellow curl on each side of her face, attired in a low-necked red satin dress. She was court-esying profoundly. Joost noticed that, while the two curls were golden, the hair under the head-dress of black lace and poppies shone forth a silvery white.

"I am glad to see you, Baron," she said smiling sweetly. "It is very long since you have done me the honor of a call. I was beginning to feel quite angry with you."

The Baron's eyes seemed to goggle more than ever. His face was once more purple; his heavy eyebrows twitched nervously.

"It is very good of Mevrouw de Montélimart to remember," he said.

The little lady waved her hand. "Excuse me," she said, "the Countess de Montélimart. I bear my title. I find it is necessary to do so here and to insist upon it.* Excuse me. Pray be seated, Baron."

There must have been two or three dozen birds in the room, large and small. A green parrot sat on a perch near his mistress. Two canaries settled down on her shoulder-knot. The twittering and whistling was deafening. "Hist," said the Countess, with another wave of her hand, as she sat down. Complete silence immediately fell on the whole company.

---

* Titles of nobility are never given in Dutch conversation, except by inferiors.

"They are not all my children," said the Countess apologetically. "Joko is"—with a wave at the parrot. "And so are Elvire and Elmire"—the same movement toward the canaries—"but the others are people of position in the neighborhood where I now live. You may have met some of them in society, before. They always come to my receptions. It is very fortunate, Baron, that you should just have come on my reception-day. Or did you know?"

"Oh—ah—oh—yes," said the Baron.

"Of course," said the little old lady, "I always send out my cards. My maid,"—another wave of the hand at the attendant, who sat sullenly looking out of the window—"my maid sees to that. Elvire show the Baron van Trotsem how you are progressing with your music. Elvire, sing!"

One of the canaries burst into a warble on his mistress's shoulder. She sat listening intently and nodding her head approvingly, but, half-way in the performance, the melody evidently got too irresistible for little Elmire's feelings, and he too lifted up his voice and sang. A flame of fury flashed into the Countess's eyes; in an instant she struck the little beast a blow which sent him rolling off his perch. "Obedience," she said, apologetically, bending over to the Baron, "is the mother of indiscretions."

The Baron nodded approval.

"You have forgotten," she said very severely, when she had stopped the canary's singing, "to introduce your son to me. I can not allow that."

"Good gracious, no," cried the Baron, "I beg your pardon, my dear countess. I most humbly beg your pardon. This is my nephew, Joost Avelingh."

"I knew he was your son at once by the likeness," said the Countess de Montélimart, smiling sweetly on Joost. "Besides, I had heard of your marrying again. I had a son of my own once, young gentleman," she continued turning to Joost, "such a fine, handsome creature. In the full bloom of health and beauty. And such a voice. His name was Dirk. Oh, how I loved him!" A tear trickled down the poor Countess's cheek.

"And he is dead, madame?" said Joost sympathetically.

"He is," sighed the Countess. "He died of the pip, but the doctor promised me he would have him buried in the garden. No wonder your father is proud of you," said the Countess. "It is a fine thing to have a son."

She began to cry so copiously and continuously that the attendant interfered. "There's Joko," she said in a rough, coarse voice. "Isn't Joko your son?"

The Countess broke into sudden smiles. "Joko," she said. "Show the gentlemen what you can do."

"Scratch my head," said the parrot.

"How dare you!" cried his mistress, once more in a violent passion. "Every parrot can say that, and no gentleman *would* say it. Something else. Quick!"

"Long live King William!" croaked Joko. "Long live King William! Long live King William, and the devil take the nurse!"

"Hush! hush!" said the Countess, with a frightened, cunning look toward the attendant. "I can't imagine who taught him to say that. It's very wrong, Joko, and very improper. Consider yourself in disgrace."

She turned to the window. Her bright little eyes never rested for one moment. "Refreshments!" she said, with that imperious wave of the hand. The woman got up, sullenly again, and went toward a cupboard. She extracted therefrom some empty glasses and decanters, and a biscuit-tray, and placed them on a little table by the Countess's sofa.

"Will you take Port or Madeira?" asked that lady with her hand on an empty decanter. "I am sorry I can not offer you bitters. They only allow them to the men. It is very unfair, I consider."

The Baron and Joost gravely chose Port wine and took their empty glasses. She seemed a little put out by Joost's not selecting a different wine from his uncle.

"I shall take Madeira myself," she said. "The rest of the company prefer biscuits." There were one or two on the tray, she broke off a bit and gave it to Joko, who plumed himself at this unexpected sign of returning favor and winked his wicked black eyes.

"The gentlemen and ladies are very well behaved," remarked the Baron.

"Are they not?" she said, with a pleased look. "Oh yes, I teach them good manners. And I have to clean all their cages myself. Is that not hard? Do you not think," another cunning look at the attendant, "that, with all the money I am paying here, they might give me some one to clean my cages for me?"

The old Baron stared in embarrassment.

"But I find time for other things," continued the Countess. "Look at this—" She took up a piece of fancy-work lying near. "Look at this, and tell me honestly, sincerely —now mind you tell me the truth—don't you think this is very well done for a madwoman?" She looked anxiously into her visitors' faces. The parrot took up the last word and yelled again and again: "A madwoman! A madwoman! A madwoman!"

The Baron rose with an ill-concealed shudder.

"It is very clever," he said, "very ingenious. Yes, quite so. I fear we must be going, my dear Countess."

"Going? Already?" There was a look of positive pain on her face. "I so seldom have anybody. Could you not stay a little longer?" She caught hold of his arm and clung to it. The attendant drew nearer.

"Don't go!" said the Countess, "don't go."

"I must to-day. I shall come and see you again!"

"Don't go, Dirk," entreated the poor creature, clinging

to him as they went toward the door; "don't go! don't go! I am not happy here." She dropped her voice to a whisper. "They are not good to me. Look!"—she pointed to several blue bruises on her naked arms; those bruises had fascinated Joost from the first—"she did that"—her voice dropped to a whisper—"She often does it. Never mind. Hush! She won't let me have Pears' soap in my tea. The doctor expressly told me I was to have Pears' soap and no other. It is matchless for the hands and complexion,"— "A madwoman!" yelled the parrot. "A madwoman! The devil take the nurse."

The attendant showed them out. "I presume she told you I ill-treated her, sir," she said, in an indifferent voice. "They all do. It is a symptom." Joost looked into her smug, villainous face and felt sure the charge was true.

They passed back through the same gloomy passages alive with half-smothered shrieks and laughs and blows. In the parlor the director joined them. "I hope you found the patient looking well," he said. "It is a sad case, an interesting case, very interesting. It must be about forty years now that she has been with us."

"Yes," said the Baron, "forty-two. I hope she is happy. I trust—I do trust—she is happy."

"Oh, she's happy enough!" said the doctor, coolly. "Never fear, my dear sir. I dare say she has been telling you she is ill-treated. They all do. It is a symptom. Perfectly absurd, you know. Impossible. Government institution. Government inspectors. Assistant doctor looks in daily. Now really, you know, perfectly absurd."

Joost gave a great sigh of relief when the open door fell to behind them and he heard the porter fixing the bolts. He took the reins and drove off.

"Well?" said his uncle, who had been watching him closely.

Joost gave a long shudder. "Why did you bring me

there?" he asked. "Have I not had enough to torment me already to-day? Great Heaven, what a place! It is the very portal of hell."

"Then you would not like to live in such surroundings? Not like to come much in contact with anything of the kind?"

Joost did not answer the question, which seemed to him to be devoid of meaning. He was extremely agitated. It seemed as much as he could do to hold the reins. His was, as has been said, an impressionable, tender heart, and the actual vision of that suffering with all its hidden possibilities had moved it to its foundations. What psychical agony, what physical torture did that long, gloomy building inclose? The inhabitants of the town, passing by, would look up with a smile and nod to each other: "The madhouse! Yes! Fortunately so admirably managed, you know!"

Joost shuddered again. On any other day he might have borne the sight better, but, unnerved as he was already by preceding events, he felt that this was more than he could bear. And his uncle watched him closely, silently. Not a word was spoken till they were half-way home.

CHAPTER XI.

THE CUP FLOWS OVER.

THERE was no more talk of agriculture; the old man sat muttering to himself and scowling. Presently he asked: "How old are you, Joost? Twenty-one, are you not?"

"Yes, sir," said Joost.

"*I* was twenty-one," said the Baron; and that was all.

The cloud had thickened and dropped while they were

paying their visit. It now began to drizzle. "No, no. No putting up the hood," said the Baron to the groom in the dickey. "We're not made of sugar, any of us." It was raining fast by the time they reached the house. The Baron got out, and stumbled on the steps. He would have fallen, had not Joost supported him. "It's nothing," he said, "nonsense. Only a little giddiness. Hang the doctor. He'd make a man think he was dying, ten years before his time."

He looked at his watch under the hall-lamp. "Ten minutes to six," he said. "Near dinner time. Hurry up. I feel quite hungry."

.   .   .   .

Joost scowled at his own white face in the glass, as he stood washing his hands. The excitement of the visit to the madhouse had kept him up. He was now asking himself what it meant, without being able to find a solution. Did his uncle mean to get him locked up there, unless he obeyed him? Impossible. And yet—with influence! Absurd. Did he intend to warn him, while there yet was time, thinking—as no doubt he thought—that Joost was on the high road to madness already. Yes, that must be it. Joost smiled bitterly at himself, and the glass smiled back. He was nearer crime, he thought, than insanity.

Now he was home again, the whole misery rushed back upon him. Was it possible that he could sit so calmly next to his uncle in the carriage, sit opposite him at table, with this hate burning down into his heart? Could such a state of things continue? Could he live with the man whose one object seemed to be to destroy his life and cause him suffering. No, said Joost to himself, as he blew out his candle and went downstairs. He resolved very decidedly, though as yet without any further particularization, that this present condition of affairs must end. With or without Agatha, he must go out into the world and earn his own bread.

The large dining-room was lighted up. There were candles in the sconces, and a bright oil lamp hung over the square table with its massive silver centerpiece. The Baron was already seated at the head of the table. Behind him stood the butler. Joost sat down opposite.

"Is it raining still, Jakob?" said the Baron.

"Raining fast, sir."

Joost refused the soup. The Baron cast a sharp glance at him and poured himself out another glass of wine. He was, as his nephew noticed, still dressed in that Sunday suit he had put on for his visit to the madhouse. He tucked his white napkin under his chin, probably to save his clothes. It made his red face stand out the more.

Joost refused the second course. The Baron cast another look at him and poured himself out more wine. Neither had spoken. Joost sat looking straight before him, white, dark, glum. He also repeatedly filled the glass beside his empty plate.

The Baron took of everything, and ate noisily, gobbling and choking, and casting more and more frequent glances at his nephew. The butler moved noiselessly to and fro.

The dessert was put on the table. Joost had eaten nothing.

"Get out," said the Baron, abruptly breaking half-an-hour's silence. The patient Jakob passed softly out of the room. He closed the heavy dining-room door on the two gentlemen and left them to their own cogitations. He was not sorry to be outside.

"Joost," said the Baron when they were alone. He poured himself out another glass of wine from the replenished decanter. His hand trembled somewhat—"Joost, I am an ill-used old man. I have been ill-used all my life, and my experience has not been a happy one. Be sure of that. Far from it. But we need not speak of the subject. You don't believe me, do you?"

"What about?" said Joost. "That you were ill-used? I don't know."

" And don't care, I suppose that means. It is true, all the same. And now, see how you behave toward me. Just because, for your own good, I ask you to forget this foolish love story—after all, it is a child's fancy, nothing more—ask you to forget it on your own behalf. It is on your own behalf. Don't you believe me ? "

Joost did not answer.

" Don't you believe me ? " The old man bent across the table.

" No," said Joost with a laugh.

His uncle swore a great oath. He stretched out his hand to his glass, but the hand trembled and struck against the slender stem, upsetting its balance and sending a crimson stream over the white table-cloth. The Baron flung the offending wine-glass into a corner of the room and, stumbling to the sideboard, came back with a tumbler which he filled and drained.

" And so," he began again, " you would marry Agatha van Hessel after all. If I were to die to-night, you would marry her to-morrow ? "

" Certainly," said Joost.

" And van Hessel, damn him, would give his consent too," muttered the old man. There was a long silence.

" Look here, Joost Avelingh," said van Trotsem, bending forward again, his red hands spread out before him. " You shall *not* marry this girl. I have told you myself, kindly, that I am acting for your own welfare. You laugh, and simply answer that I lie. Had you consented, with a good grace, to obey my wishes, there would have been an end of the matter. Now, on the contrary, you force me to take action. You yourself have indicated the road. You tell me van Hessel will never take you without my money. Well, damn you both, he shall never get you with it. Rather than that, I will leave it to Arthur van Asveld."

"Leave it where you like," said Joost. "I have told you once for all, sir, I don't want your money."

"Yes, you do," said the old man, quickly, "for it is your *only chance* of Agatha."

A terrible expression came over Joost's face, a look so dark and threatening that his uncle, half-fuddled as he was with wine, was startled by it. There was murder in that passionate glance. The mouth, dogged and square, set itself firmly, full of dreadful resolve.

"Do not exasperate me," said Joost Avelingh.

"It is you who exasperate me," said the Baron, surlily. "Have I ever injured you? What right have you to speak to me thus? I tell you again, you shall not marry the girl!"

"When have you ever injured me? How dare I speak to you thus? Say rather: When have you not injured me? Say rather: How should one speak to his greatest enemy on earth?" Joost started up and came half-way round the table toward his uncle. "When have you had another object in life but to make me miserable? When have you had another amusement? Nay, I will speak. I have been silent long enough. You shall hear me to-night, if it be the last night we spend together under the same roof. Would to Heaven it were so! It shall be so, so help me God. You, who have persecuted your sister till her death, you, who have insulted and injured my father till he also passed beyond your vengeance, if not beyond your hate; you rejoice to know that you have me still left. You delight in the thought how you have tortured me through all these years, how you still have the power to make me suffer! You have succeeded. I admit it. Rejoice in it while you can. But I defy you. I am no longer a child. Why should I respect your gray hairs? They but witness how long I have undergone your persecutions. Why should I honor our relationship? It but tells me how you treated my mother. I leave this house to-night! I defy you! I shall marry the girl I love in spite of you, in spite of her father, in spite of a legion of devils encamped against us! I shall marry her yet, I warn you! And I shall rejoice the more in our union to know it is against your will!"

He had poured out these mad words in a ceaseless, breathless stream. The old gentleman lay back in his chair staring at him, breathless too. When his nephew ceased, he snatched up a water-bottle and aimed it at the offender's head. It crashed against a looking-glass and sent a glittering shower of glass-splinters and water-drops all over that part of the room. Some of the splinters struck Joost and the water splashed over his back. "You hell-hound!" began the Baron, when at last he found voice—but no, his language need not be written down here. For several minutes he stormed on, swearing and raving in a fury of passion, while Joost stood silent, his arms crossed on his breast, great beads of perspiration coming out on his white forehead. After all, his uncle had him in his power, and he knew it. "For the next two years at any rate," shouted the old man, "we shall see who is master. I will make a mill hand of you, you dog; and you can inherit my millions afterward. You or van Asveld. Ha! Ha! You or van Asveld." He was frantic with rage. His face was livid one moment, and violet the next. He foamed and spat, while with trembling hand he reached out for more wine. And yet, strangely enough, the ungovernable old man in the bottommost depth of his heart respected his nephew more and liked him better for thus standing up and facing him in his wrath.

He tore the napkin from his throat. "I will end it this very night!" he cried, as he staggered to his feet. "No, sir, you shall stay with me this night and many another. You shall stay with me, because I wish it and the law enforces my will. If you disobey me, I will call in my servants and disgrace you before them. And this night, this very night you yourself shall drive me over to the village. It is you yourself, mind, who force me to do it. You have defied me. I could not rest a night with the thought of what my death would bring you! The realization of all your wishes, forsooth! You shall *not* realize them. This night, I promise you, sir nephew, shall make them unattainable forever."

He fell toward the bell-rope and rang violently. A servant hurried into the room. And the Baron, still foaming with passion, could find no other words than " The Chaise!"

PART II.

AFTER.

CHAPTER XII.

CHARITY.

"BUT if you add the garden," said the architect, "you will almost double the expense, Mr. Avelingh."

"And the comfort of the old people," said Joost.

They were sitting in the big library at the Castle; Joost Avelingh before his writing table, the architect a little on one side, in a deferential attitude. A shaded lamp at Joost's elbow threw a glare of light over a large white roll spread out before him, a drawing-plan. By the fire sat Agatha, near a little table and lamp of her own, busy over some woman's trifle of dainty useless fancy-work.

"Oh, the poor people," said Timmers, the architect, "yes, certainly, the comfort of the poor people! Only, really, it appears to me that, with the arrangements you have made already, Mr. Avelingh, the comfort of the poor people will be very adequately—not to say super-abundantly—provided for."

"What is worth doing at all," said Joost reflectively, his eyes fixed on the plan before him, "is usually, though not always, worth doing well. I should say: Yes. Decidedly. Add the garden."

"Very well, Mynheer," replied the architect, who always contradicted his clients just sufficiently to allow himself a door of escape if matters went wrong. "And as you so justly remarked, 'what is worth doing at all is always worth doing well!' And therefore I should advise the garden, as there is to be one in any case, to go right round the building with a good-sized bit in front; it always looks so much better. And what should you say to a fountain in the center, before the grand entrance, just here—he pointed with his pencil—a fountain with a symbolical figure of Charity! Mevrouw—a bow in the direction of the fireplace—might kindly consent to sit for the figure; a most charming—ahem—representation we could obtain. I know a friend of mine—"

"No, no," said Joost hastily. "None of that."

"No fountain at all?" asked the architect.

"The fountain, if you like, but no figure."

Timmers looked disappointed. "Well," he said, brightening up the next moment, "you could have merely a bronze spout, if you wish it, or a dragon. It might play on Sundays and on the birthday of the Founder."

Joost allowed this last suggestion to fall to the ground unnoticed. He sat staring straight in front of him, looking at nothing. The architect, finding it impossible to rouse him, rambled on and, in his dislike of awkward silences, tried to attract Mevrouw's attention.

"And the gardens," he said, "could be laid out by Heesters and Sons, the Amsterdam people. That, of course, is not in my line. I should recommend them, unconditionally. Their taste is excellent. And no doubt, in this matter, Mevrouw will give them the benefit of hers." He drew the drawing a little toward him and got up, addressing Agatha, "What would you say, Mevrouw, to digging a pond along in this direction—it is just the merest suggestion—but, if you would give your opinion—"

Agatha half rose.

"No," said Joost Avelingh, suddenly waking from his reverie, "Mevrouw does not care for these matters. Sit down, Timmers. Leave it to—what's their name? Heesters and Sons."

The architect sat down abashed. Agatha sank back in her chair without a word.

"Yes," said Joost Avelingh, "that is all very well, very well indeed. And I quite agree with what you have been saying, Timmers, and I am sure it will be quite right. And now, I think, we have discussed everything fully and, really, there is nothing more to arrange. So, if you will take these papers—"

The architect held up his hands with such a pitiful, deprecatory expression, that Joost stopped. "Well," he said, impatiently.

"My dear Heer, my honored Heer, there are numbers of things I must still ask about. A great institution is not put together in an hour like a hen-coop. Good Heavens, I shall not get through to-night. You will have to let me come again once more at the very least, before we can even begin taking the tenders."

Joost settled himself in his armchair with a sigh of resignation. The architect began hurriedly—and yet with evident enjoyment—describing his plans and their various advantages. His enjoyment was only marred by the too evident fact that his employer was not listening. Nevertheless, he wandered on through figures, and measures, and technical terms innumerable, till the flow of his eloquence was suddenly stopped by a knock at the door.

Kees Hessel came in; a man deep in the twenties now, stouter than formerly, with honest blue eyes, a bright complexion and a great yellow mustache.

"Busy about the hospital," he said in a brisk, cheery voice, casting his eyes over the great plan after the first greetings had been interchanged. "Well, Mr. Timmers, are you going to immortalize yourself, as well as the founder?"

"I do my best, Mynheer van Hessel," began the architect.

"If there's anybody you're bound to immortalize, it's the old creatures themselves," said Kees. "Once get people into an institution of that kind and they're sure to live forever. But it's a good work all the same, and that's my opinion."

"We shall give them a hard egg for breakfast every morning all round," said Joost laughing, a little boisterously. "We shall put it down in the rules. That will kill them off, if nothing else will. Won't it, Agatha?"

"Yes, Joost," said Agatha gently.

"Some doctors are beginning to teach that hard eggs are the only wholesome ones," interposed Kees.

"Doctors will teach anything," answered Joost, "merely because they know by experience that every new fallacy brings in a dozen new patients. Don't tell me! You forget you are speaking to a medical man."

"A medical baby!" cried Kees, "a medical embryo! Surely you don't mean to tell us that three years loafing through the first half of a University career turns out a medical man! You aren't a medical man, Joost, no, not even in the least degree."

Joost smiled. "You might have laughed at the pun, Agatha," said Kees.

"Yes," said Agatha, "I beg pardon, Kees. I was thinking of something else. I shall, I promise you, next time I come across it. But we were speaking of the building plans, and Mr. Timmers was saying—" she pitied the architect, suddenly interrupted in his explanations, and left out of the conversation.

"Oh yes," said Joost, "Mr. Timmers! I am much obliged to you for all the trouble you are taking, Timmers. We'll talk it over at our ease some other day."

" Would to-morrow suit you, Mynheer ? " asked the architect, gathering up his materials.

" No, not to-morrow. Let me see. To-morrow evening we dine at your father's, Kees, on Wednesday I have the Blind Council meeting, Thursday there's the Town Concert, Board Meeting on Friday. Look here, I'll send you a message. Good-night."

" Good-night, Mynheer. Good-night, Mevrouw. Good-night, Mynheer van Hessel." The architect bowed himself out, his hat in his hand, his papers in a neat roll under his arm. " A rich man," he said to himself in the hall, " and an influential man, but a crotchety."

" What a busy fellow, you are, Joost," said Kees.

" Saturday was free, I think," put in Agatha.

" Yes," replied Joost quickly, " but I like to have a night to ourselves once in a way. Don't you ? "

Agatha did not answer. He might well know she did.

" I have brought you the draft of your scheme," said Kees, producing his pocket-book. He was clerk to the District Court; his uncle in the Hague had got him the place recently in exchange for a vote. " Shall I read it you ? "

Joost nodded assent.

" Avelingh Institute and Establishment," began Kees, " for the Reception and Retention, the Maintenance, Support and Entertainment, and furthermore the General Advantagement and Protection of the Aged Industrious and Deserving Poor, Married, Single or otherwise under the motto ' Virtue Vanquisheth Vicissitudes.' "

No one smiled at this majestic procession of words. Such titles are more or less the custom in Holland, where no infant organization is ever ushered into the world without a name as long as a baptismal robe. The motto also is a national institution, and—common sense coming to the rescue—an Establishment like the above-mentioned would soon be known as the " V. V. V."

" You might leave out ' otherwise ' " remarked Joost.

" That shows you are not a lawyer," answered Kees, gravely.   " No lawyer would ever have said that."

" I bow to the authority of the Court," replied Joost. "We can reserve a certain number of rooms for the ' otherwise.' "

" Article First," continued Kees.   " The Avelingh Institute and Establishment— "

" You people are all the same," cut in Joost.   " You are in a conspiracy to vex me.   Scratch out ' Avelingh.'   I won't have any connection with the affair."

" What ? " cried Kees, opening his blue eyes.   " Not even your name in it?   Oh come now, that is good.   Well, you might have told a fellow !   All very noble and high-minded and that !   But you'll be sorry afterward.   That's my opinion, and I don't consider myself a fool ! "

" I did tell you," said Joost.   " At least, I seem to have been telling everybody the last two days.   I build the whole concern and, when it is ready, I make a present of it to the Commune with a draft of rules, which they can alter or not, as they think fit.   The grant is unconditional.   And I refuse to be connected in any way with the Board of Directors."

" Build a thing like that at the cost of half a million of money * and then put it altogether into other people's hands !   But, my dear Joost, supposing they mismanage it ? "

" I don't care," said Joost.

" Oh very well !   Only I was going to suggest—"

" Don't bother.   Read on," said Joost, peevishly.

" If he prefers it, Kees, you know," put in Agatha from her corner.

Kees returned to his regulations, not without a shrug of his shoulders.   He did not pretend to understand his brother-

* £40,000.

in-law. A good man, certainly, but a peculiar. Changed, in many ways, since he came into all that money. Irritable and boisterous alternately. Not, certainly, as jovial and good-natured as the outside world might think. Kees preferred equable tempers. But what did anything else matter, as long as Agatha was content?

"It is very interesting," said Joost, when they had got about half way, "at the discretion of the Secretary and in the absence of the Treasurer? Yes; is there any more of it, Kees?"

"Only seventy-nine more articles. These things must be done accurately, you know, or you get into any amount of trouble afterward with all the revisions."

"Oh yes, of course. I'm awfully obliged to you for taking so much trouble. It's really very good of you; I couldn't have done it myself."

"You have plenty of other things to do, Joost," said Agatha affectionately. "Your hands are already too full." She could not bear any one to think there was anything Joost could not do.

"They will be fuller soon, for all that," remarked Kees. "Don't forget, you complete your thirtieth year in a month or two. That makes you eligible for the States General, and we shall have them putting you up as a candidate at the next election."

"Yes," said Joost laughing. "Of course we shall. What next?"

"Nonsense, you think it's a joke, but it's sober truth and earnest. Do you think all these good deeds go for nothing?"

"Good deeds—as you are pleased to call them so—are never rewarded in Holland unless there is some political intrigue connected with them," said Joost, earnestly. "We were talking about it at the Club only the other day. Lady Burdett Coutts would have been Miss Coutts with us till the day of her death. That makes it so much easier to do them," he added, more earnestly still.

"Very true, as far as official recognition goes," said Kees. "I grant it. But you can't keep the people from finding out an honest man. All the embroidered coats in the Hague can't do that, however hard they may want to."

"N—o—o," said Joost, hesitatingly, "but—"

"Why, man, you're the most popular man in the province!" the other went on, enthusiastically.

"I never noticed it," Joost interrupted, quickly. "Not among the higher classes, certainly. The very reverse! I should say, sooner, the very reverse!"

"That may be as it may be," his brother-in-law replied, evasively. "Supposing your impression to be correct, it still remains a fact that although we, like all nations that are not governed by one man, are governed by a small clique instead, there are one or two prizes that clique is not able to bestow. Those are the seats in Parliament for large towns or manufacturing centers. And it's my opinion that they'll bring you in for the town in a few months, and really, Joost, I'm not such a fool as you sometimes think. Besides, I've heard more about it than I can repeat just at present."

Agatha had risen and come forward. There was a bright sparkle in her eyes and a flush on her fair cheeks.

"Of course he is popular!" she said. "And of course he is liked and esteemed. He is always saying he isn't, and that everybody hates him, but I tell him it can't be true."

Joost had risen too. He was walking up and down the room with gigantic strides, his tall figure swaying to and fro, his arms crossed across the broad chest. Suddenly he stopped before his brother-in-law and threw back the waving black hair off his forehead with the old movement which had brought on that early quarrel when his uncle struck him. His dark eyes burned like coals from under the broad white brows.

"It isn't true, Kees," he said. "Say you're joking. It's all nonsense; no one ever thought of such a thing."

"It's all nonsense," replied Kees. "At least, I mean your way of taking it is. What's there to be in a temper about? Most men would give half their life to get into the States, if they could get there in this manner. Why, it's the glorious ideal! The free voice of the free people! Occurs once in twenty years, perhaps! You haven't achieved it as yet; but when you do, as you will, I shall congratulate you as heartily as I did when you told me your uncle was dead and you were going to marry Agatha. No offense to the old gentleman."

Joost stood before his desk again, his back turned to his brother-in-law. "You are right," he said in a quiet voice. "Of course it takes one aback. And you think this foundation is responsible for it?"

"This, and all your other efforts. Here you have been for the last ten years taking an interest in all the charities of the province, scattering your money among the halt, the lame and the blind, till you're on half the philanthropic councils of the country, looking up public matters at the same time, working for the new canal to Amsterdam and the steam-tram up to Arnhem, here you are in one word, the man to whom the province owes most, and you don't expect to be popular. I tell you again—you're the most popular man we have."

"It may be true," said Joost. "I didn't notice it, because, you see, I knew my own class hated me, and one comes in contact most with them, of course. It can't be helped. I mean, I dare say it's all for the best. Are you going? Well, good-night. We shall see you to-morrow. Good-night."

Joost remained standing by his writing-table, looking down at the general plan of his almshouses, which the architect had left for his inspection. Agatha bent over her work, stealing glances every now and then at her husband's stalwart form, shaded against his lamp.

"If I thought it was this," suddenly said Joost impetuously, "I should tear the whole thing in pieces."

He was speaking to himself, not to her. Agatha knew, by experience, that he did not wish to be disturbed.

He stood silent for some minutes longer. "I hate it!" he cried out suddenly. "I hate the whole wretched thing!" he turned round to his wife: "I tell you I hate it, Agatha!"

She came to him and put one arm round his neck. "Why do it, if you do not wish to, dearest?" she said. "I never thought you really quite liked it, but you seemed to think you did. Can it not be undone still, perhaps?"

"Can it not be undone?" repeated Joost passionately.

"No, no, I should not have said that. You will enjoy the thought of it afterward, as long as you live. It is a grand work, a splendid work! They are right to admire you for it! And you will feel, when this first impression passes off, what a good deed it is. It is all the nobler to feel like this about the honor it must bring you. It is like you, Joost, my own pure, noble Joost. I honor you for it, and so does Kees; I saw it in his eyes. But you will take courage and see what a blessing it is to be a blessing to others. You are a benefactor of the whole province, Joost. I like to think it! It is a benefaction."

"A benefaction!" said Joost sullenly. "It is an expiation!"

"An expiation! My dearest!"—she clung to him with a frightened expression in her innocent blue eyes. "What do you mean? What makes you say that? I never heard you speak so before, Joost!"

"Did you not?" he answered, turning on her almost fiercely. "Every man has sins and follies enough to expiate, I suppose. Never mind, dearest. There goes the bell for prayers! Go, dearest. I will join you immediately."

He disengaged her arms gently from his neck, and watched her as she unwillingly left the room. " Prayers ! " he said to himself with a bitter laugh, as soon as he was alone. He stood in front of a little leaflet calendar his wife had embroidered for him last year. It hung by his writing-table. His eyes were fixed upon the date.

" The 14th of December," he said. " It is destiny."

CHAPTER XIII.

LOOKS BACK.

JOOST AVELINGH had spoken truly when he said that he was not much liked among the men of his own rank. Since his uncle's sudden death had made him possessor of one of the largest fortunes in the country, many things had happened to influence his development; still, his character had remained on the whole, as characters are wont to do, essentially the same. And Joost Avelingh's character was not one of those which obtain favor in the circle in which he found himself placed. It was not one either to attract particular dislike. His was one of those natures people let alone, because they have nothing in common with the crowd —for no worse reason, if that be not the worst and most unpardonable of all. He was not by any means a genius, claiming and obtaining adoration; he was just an ordinary mortal; a trifle more reflective, and with a trifle more " Seelenleben " as the Germans say, than the common-place people around him. Clever enough to appreciate cleverness in others; in many ways a most unhappy fate.

It has already been said that he neither swore nor drank nor gambled. It may be added that he led a strictly moral

life; in short, he had no aristocratic tastes. Let it be stated
still further that he lived in the country, was a very rich
man, and yet cared neither for shooting nor horse-flesh, and
every one who knows anything about the matter will admit
that the catalogue of his deficiencies is complete. He had
a peculiar theory of his own that whosoever consciously occasions unnecessary suffering to any living creature stands
lower in the rank of creation than any other brute beast
whatsoever, with the exception, perhaps, of that monster,
the cat; and, concientiously sticking to this theory, he had
once asserted at the Club, to the general amusement, that
he had never despised any human being till he met with a
foreign nobleman who kept hunters and harriers. That
nobleman was at the time the Club's honored guest, and
there ensued a great shrugging of shoulders and tapping of
foreheads all round. Many of the young men present regretted only too sincerely that fox-hunting was impossible
in Holland, and hare-hunting forbidden, and that even an
innocent little attempt to get up pigeon shooting had recently been put down by public opinion. "They manage
these things better abroad," said Arthur van Asveld.

On the other hand Joost Avelingh, while he did not
sympathize with the tastes most generally cultivated, had
disagreeable little likings of his own which nobody appreciated. The early habit of reading, contracted in the dull
days of his childhood, still held him in bondage, and that
among a society which never read anything at all but the
newspapers, the magazines, and the latest French novels.
Full of some interesting book he had lately come across, he
had once or twice innocently told others about it. Fool
that he was, he had immediately contracted the fatal reputation of "pedantry," a reputation which the utter fatuity
of months of ordinary conversation would not suffice to
efface. "You are the clever man who reads Taine," old
Beau Liederlen had said to him once, some time after he

had last offended in this manner, "I will tell you what, sir: "*les origines de la France contemporaine, ce sont les co-cottes.*" Every one enjoyed that joke immensely; it was the best that had been heard in the Club for years. And Joost went by the name of "le petit Taine" for some few months accordingly; nobody could exactly have told you why.

Joost, then, was neither liked nor exactly disliked by his associates. They endured him; he was "so peculiar, you know." He could not be ignored; he was too rich for that. And perhaps a little envy crept in with regard to such a very wealthy personage, for £12,000 a year is an enormous fortune in Holland, where many have enough and but few too much. Then there was the unwilling tribute of respect which ignorance always pays to knowledge, however loudly it may affect contempt, and, as has been already said, in Joost's circle the man who read other books than novels and pamphlets on public affairs was at once written down as "zeer knap."* It was no use talking to Avelingh; "he had such ideas, you know." Nobody else had ideas.

On the other hand Joost had been unconsciously building up for himself a great reputation among the lower classes of his neighborhood. When the old Notary first told him that by the terms of his uncle's will, "my nephew, Joost Avelingh, the only near relation I have, and the child of my dearly loved sister, Adelheid" was appointed sole heir of every rood of ground and every brass half-penny the old Baron possessed, the young man formed three rapid resolves in the twinkle of an eye:—to stop studying medicine; to marry Agatha immediately; to live on a fourth of his income and do what good he could with the rest. His uncle had not left a single legacy, but he had recommended his servants to the heir's sense of justice. Joost could not endure to keep about him the witnesses of his daily degrada-

---

* "Knap" is clever, with a dash of actual knowledge through it.

tion. He disbanded the whole staff, indoor and outdoor, pensioning off, where he could, with what his uncle would have called, not justice, but prodigality, and paying the younger servants their full wages till new places were got for them. All went, even the occasional helps, and the man who milked the cows. The lease of the home-farm was bought off at an exorbitant price and a new tenant found. Perhaps the whole measure was not a wise one; Joost had reason to repent it afterward, with regard to one man, at any rate. Despite its generosity, it caused a good deal of ill-feeling at the time in the neighborhood, ill-feeling as inexplicable as it was distressing to the new lord of the Castle. However, he lived that down. Perhaps that outburst of feeling kept him from a project of entirely refitting and refurnishing the house. Such a plan had certainly flashed across his mind for a moment. Agatha, the thrifty, common-sense Dutchwoman would not hear of it. " Why do it ? " she asked. " Everything seems in very good repair. There's only a looking-glass broken in the dining-room, I saw." Yes, Joost knew there was a looking-glass broken in the dining-room.

So he contented himself with fitting up a boudoir for her, and a bedroom.

" The large South room," said Agatha.

" No, not that one, dearest ; my uncle slept there."

" And what of that, Joost ? There's not a room in the house which hasn't been slept in by half-a-dozen people, dead and gone long ago."

Agatha was not sentimental. And Joost felt ashamed to seem so. Sentiment is the one great disease which Dutch society both fears and despises. In its less virulent form of " feeling," the complaint is mostly successfully stamped out in youth. Fortunately, cases are rare. The Dutch put up, in obedience to the law of the land, placards with the name of the infectious disease on the doors of all infected houses:

society sticks its warning on the front of unsound hearts, and the weakness dies off, or kills. And so no cases occur after twenty-five. And that is a satisfactory conclusion.

The South bedroom it was. And Joost installed himself in his uncle's former sitting-room, in the same round armchair at the same old desk.

"Why not," said Agatha.

He moved in one or two bookcases for his favorites, and turned out the old man's pipes and hunting trophies. He turned out also Rietstap's Noble Families of the Netherlands, but he retained the account books of the estate, and conscientiously, painfully, laboriously, he set himself to mastering the mysteries of the management of that large property.

And so nearly ten years had passed. "Slipping away," said Agatha. "Creeping," said Joost. And yet she, the childless mistress of many servants, might have had time enough upon her hands, while he could scarcely have found a moment to call his own, had he so wished it. But he did not wish it. He flung himself into a vortex of various occupations, looking after his estate, not as well as his uncle, certainly, but still quite well enough, considering how irksome the duty was to him, and pushing with unexpected energy every plan that was started for the welfare of the community. "He is aiming at a political career," said the men at the Club, over their whist. He came down there too, of afternoons. In spite of all incompatibility, he, formerly so reserved and gauche, now sought the society of other men. Gauche he was still, but no longer reserved. "Aveling is getting a positive bore with his boisterousness," said Beau Liederlen marking honors. "He never used to be witty, and I can't think what makes him fancy himself so now. His jokes are very stupid, really; and I wish to goodness he would send his laugh to a tuner's. He might have waited for his father-in-law's shoes, in any case; one buffoon in a Club is quite enough." He looked across to where the subject of his remarks now sat silent; alone and haughty, with a dark cloud on his face and a great sadness in his eyes. His lips were moving nervously; they often did, as if in prayer. " He is like a hyæna," said Liederlen, scornfully, " always laughing one moment and preying the next."

Joost, certainly, was fully occupied, and the people were beginning to acknowledge it. He found plenty of leisure for reading, he said ; that meant that he read in the train, in the carriage, while dressing. " No wonder he does not sleep well at night," poor Agatha complained to her mother. " His brain is overwrought."

CHAPTER XIV.

MONEY-MAKING MADE EASY.

" Is the Burgomaster up already ? " asked Joost.

It was a bright, bitterly cold winter's morning. The many windows of the van Hessel's substantial, brown-brick mansion were coated over with fairy traceries of frost-work, the only beautiful thing, by-the-by, about the dull, comfortable house. There were frost and snow on the hard ground and on the trees of the semi-circular carriage sweep. There was snow on Joost's great boots as he stamped up and down on the steps. There was snow, gray and clotted, about the shafts of his sledge. But the glittering sun shone down from the blue sky on the red plumes and gay trappings, on the horse, tossing his bedizened head to the tinkle of a dozen bells, and sending forth great shafts of breath into the clear, cold air.

" Brisk weather, Mynheer," said the red-nosed servant who opened the front door, after having fumbled over the bolts and chain. He rubbed his purple fingers.

" Is the Burgomaster up, already?" asked Joost stamping and puffing.

" I shall have to go and see," said Piet.

Joost waited in the Burgomaster's study. The stove, newly-lighted, was roaring and fussing, without, however, emitting any heat as yet. A portfolio, from the so-called " Reading Society," lay on the table; Joost opened it and looked through the engravings of one or two Dutch and French papers without seeing one of them. He shut the portfolio again, and stared at the stove.

The Burgomaster entered, in a gray dressing-gown and slippers, unshaven as yet, his eyes very sleepy, his hands very cold. Mynheer van Hessel had not changed much during the last ten years. He looked a little stouter, a little balder, a little less red in the face; that was all.

" My dear Joost!" he said. " Oh, of course you are most welcome. But if you had let me know in time of your intentions, I should have told them to keep up the fire all night."

" It *is* cold," said Joost apologetically.

" Cold!" cried the Burgomaster; " the wonder is to think it can ever get warm again. The earth's crust must heat faster than the physicists tell us it cools, I should say. One degree in a million years, isn't it? or something of the kind! Modest kind of person, the earth, eh? Contented so long as she can dip her crust in cold water. I must remember that for this evening, capable of improvement perhaps. And what brings you here?" The Burgomaster settled himself in an armchair, drew his dressing-gown tightly round him, and tucked up his feet against the stove. " Agatha all right, I suppose?" he added, as an afterthought.

" Oh yes," said Joost.

" Ever after that last affair, of course, one feels anxious," pursued Mynheer van Hessel. " Nothing of the kind in sight at this moment ? "

" Oh no," said Joost.

" So much the better."

" I'm so sorry to trouble you at so early an hour," continued the son-in-law. " But I was afraid that to-day especially it was my only chance of catching you, to come almost before you were up. I was afraid the Governor would take up all your time."

" Yes," interrupted the Burgomaster. " And as it is, I haven't got much to spare. The Governor is to arrive at eleven, and the inspection is to begin immediately. I shall have to look over my address presently. ' Highly Honorable Austerity !' Would you like to hear it, Joost? You might give me your opinion."

" No, no," said Joost, with that wretched straightforwardness of his. " I shall hear it presently. We shall have a cold time of it. Whatever makes him choose this season ? I thought they always came in spring."

" This suited him better," said the Burgomaster, looking away in sudden confusion. " And—oh—ah—ahem, you remember what the poet says :

> " ' By " antechambering "—let the truth be told—
> The only thing I ever got—was cold !' "

" I have come," said Joost impatiently, " about important business. I sha'n't take up more of your time than I can help ! "

" No, don't," said the Burgomaster. " That's right. Important business, really ? The Charity-foundation, I suppose. Kees told me last night he had found Timmers with you. Don't you think you had better tell your man to walk the mare up and down? She will catch her death of cold standing there."

"No," said Joost imperiously. "It *is* the Charity."

"Well?"

"I am going to give it up."

"Give it up," cried the Burgomaster in dismay, his feet falling from the stove. "Joost! What do you mean?"

"I have changed my mind. I won't give the money."

"Impossible. Really, Joost, you might have thought of that sooner. I always said the sum was exaggerated, frantic, as you will remember, a tenth would have suited your object just as well. You will remember my telling you that I considered it a positive spoliation of your future children, and you may very well have children still, in spite of these earlier mishaps. I told you all that, over and over again. But the thing's done now. It's too late. No use crying over spilt milk, though I don't wonder you're sorry you spilt such pailfuls."

"Quite true," said Joost; "but I have changed my mind, and I withdraw my offer."

"You can't do it, Joost. You would make an unutterable fool of yourself forever. Good Heavens, how the whole world would despise you! The very thought makes me shudder. Better to let the money go—*now*—than to keep it at such a price."

"The money!" cried Joost vehemently. "*You* can keep the money, if you like. But I am going to withdraw my proposal to use it in charity. I wrote out my letter this morning. Here it is!" He drew out an envelope and threw it on the table.

"I won't touch it," cried the Burgomaster.

"Then shall I take it to your office? It's the official one, you see."

"No," cried the Burgomaster still more loudly, "you shall not. You shall not disgrace yourself for some absurd

n

whim or other! I tell you, you will make yourself generally despicable!"

"Yes," said Joost.

"Is that what you want to do?"

"Never mind what I want to do, sir. I do not want to give my money; let that suffice."

"The man is mad," said the Burgomaster, casting up his eyes in despair. "But you are my son-in-law, sir, and Agatha's husband, and you owe her something. I can not allow Agatha's husband to cover his name with contumely."

"Agatha," said Joost calmly, "will bear her share of my burdens. She is quite willing to do so."

"Reason the more," replied the Burgomaster quickly, "for you to desire to spare her."

Joost winced. He took up his letter again and marched to the door.

"Do you mean to say," cried Mynheer van Hessel, in despair, "that you are going to send in that letter to me as Burgomaster?"

"Yes," said Joost, laying his hand on the door-knob. The Burgomaster sprang up and came running forward with wonderful agility, considering his stoutness. His face was very much discomposed. "Look here, Joost," he said in an agitated voice, "it can't be done. For Agatha's sake; for all our sakes; well for—for mine. Listen. Sit down. There that's better. What was I saying? It's gone too far now. I—I—of course I couldn't know you would draw back like this, and really it isn't gentlemanly of you, Joost, not decent. I mean, I promised Timmers something you see. I—of course, as Burgomaster, as it was to be in my parish, I could use my influence. And I used it, Joost."

"I do not see what that matters," began his son-in-law. "If you are unable to keep your promises—"

"Not exactly promises, Joost. Guarantees; call them guarantees. In fact, I—naturally enough—undertook to sell him the parish ground you fixed on—and—well—I've sold it. And I thought I might promise him the contract, from what you had said, Joost."

Joost sat silent, a slight flush coming and going on his dark cheek. At last he spoke.

"What was to be your share of the plunder?" he said.

"Sir!" cried his father-in-law. "How dare you use such language? What am I to under—"

Joost cut him short with an imperious gesture. "Let us be as brief as possible," he said. "What sum is to be paid over by me to you, without any questions on either side, to do away with this difficulty forever?"

"I refuse to be hectored in this manner," began the Burgomaster anew.

"Will thirty thousand florins do it?"

"Oh Joost, Joost," wailed the Burgomaster, suddenly collapsing. "Are you so much in earnest? Money won't do it, Joost. I'm sorry to say there's another difficulty. You—you are to be trusted, I suppose?" He leered across at his son-in-law, "And you are absolutely resolved?"

"Absolutely," said Joost.

"Well there's been a little unpleasantness about the administration. It's a great shame of the Governor, and he my wife's cousin too; and, really if I were to sum up all his deficiencies: But it's always like that; we minor grandees pay the reckoning. You understand?"

"Partly," said Joost.

"I can assure you—need I assure you?—that I am perfectly innocent. Accidents will happen, and no one can be always accurate. He behaved shockingly; all personal spite! But he might have made things very disagreeable for me. And—and—"

"Well?" said Joost.

"I was obliged to propose this plan of yours, Joost—put it a little, you know, as if it was my idea. You don't object to that, eh? I must say I have often thought a similar institution would be very beneficial. And—and it put the Governor in a good temper, you see."

"I see," said Joost. "And what was the Governor's share of the plunder?"

"Ha, ha," laughed his father-in-law. "Very good, you always were very satirical, Joost."

"And this," said Joost, "this little unpleasantness is what the Governor is coming about, I suppose. And I am to pay off the score?"

The words had scarcely left his lips, when the door opened and Mevrouw van Hessel came in.

"I fancy I must have left my key-basket here, Henrik," she said, "I think it is under the—" She stopped suddenly as she caught sight of the two faces before her. "What is wrong?" she asked with a woman's intuition. She went back to the door and shut it carefully. "What is wrong?" she repeated.

Neither answered.

"Some money question of course," she went on, "I can see that. So much the better, when it is only money, and not a fright like Agatha's illness the other day, Joost. But what is it?"

Still neither man spoke.

"I *will* know," she went on vehemently. "I have seen for a long time, Henrik, that something was amiss. I have waited for you to tell me, because I knew you never kept a secret from me long. If you keep this, it must be a very bad one. But, what Joost knows, surely, I may know; and so you will tell me."

"Yes, yes," said the Burgomaster, "presently. Really, my dear, it is nothing."

"Has he been borrowing money of you, Joost?" asked Mevrouw. "I am afraid there is not so much money as there used to be. But we must not borrow from you."

"No, no, mamma," muttered Joost. "You don't owe me a stiver." He addressed his mother-in-law as mamma according to the invariable Dutch rule. He called the Burgomaster papa too, as in duty bound when he called him anything at all.

"If there is less money, Henrik," Mevrouw went on, "we must live differently. There is nothing to worry about in that. What does the loss of money matter as long as there is no disgrace?"

"True," said Joost, as if to himself. "What does the loss of money matter as long as there is no disgrace?"

"No, no. There is money enough," said Mynheer, peevishly. "I will tell you all about it presently. Only Joost was advising me to give up my place as Burgomaster, and there would not be money enough then. No, certainly, Joost, there would not be money enough then; and what would become of us all?"

"Give up your place as Burgomaster!" repeated Mevrouw, looking in amazement from one to the other. "Why?"

"It was all a misunderstanding," continued the Burgomaster. "But it is settled now. Is it not?"

"Yes," said Joost. "Yes, yes, there really need be nothing to trouble you, mamma."

"Of course," said the Burgomaster brightening up, "I will tell you all about it presently, Marian. Joost, throw that envelope into the fire; I hate to have loose papers lying about. That's right. And now, really, you good people must leave me to my speech. *Hisque feliciter peractis.* What says the poet?

> "'And all agreed it would be best
> To let the little matter rest.'

Good-by, Joost."

"Good-by, mamma," said Joost. "I assure you there

need be nothing to trouble you. Papa owes me nothing.
And I am sure there will be money enough."

"A swindler for a father," he said to himself as he got
into his sledge. "And for a husband a—ah well, poor
Agatha!"

CHAPTER XV.

"ARE YOU ILL, AVELINGH?"

THAT same evening there was a large dinner-party at
the van Hessel's in honor of the Governor of the Province,
come over on a visit of inspection. The Burgomaster,
beaming over his vast shirt-front, genial, smiling, full of
little quips and quibbles, sat at the foot of a great table covered with plate and crystal, round which some twenty-four
guests were grouped. Opposite him, half-hidden behind
fruit and flowers, sat Mevrouw, with the Governor at her
right hand, a little ferrety man with pepper and salt mus-
taches and keen eyes—a connection, you know; at least, he
had married Mevrouw's second cousin. They remembered
the relationship, now he was Governor.

Joost, gazing across at his mother-in-law, said to himself
that she had recently grown much older in appearance.
There was an anxious, careworn look about her eyes which
did not match at all with her stately bearing. And now,
when she ticked her finger against the back of her hand,
there was quite as much nervousness as impatience in the
movement.

"Yes," she was saying to the Governor, "I remember
Leenebet* perfectly well as a child. We used to go picking

---

* Helena Elizabeth.

apples in my father's orchard, and Leenebet always brought me the biggest. She was such a dear, unselfish child."

"I dare say the small ones were riper," said the Governor. "Not such a fool after all, that wife of mine." He was tasting the wine on the tip of his tongue and telling himself that the Burgomaster, whatever else he might mismanage, must certainly be a careful judge of wine.

"Bad for children," he continued after a pause, reflectively. "Raw apples! Give them pain in their insides."

Mevrouw smiled acquiescence without hearing what he said. Her eyes were wandering anxiously over the servants. She could trust her butler, and she could trust the waiter from the village who had come up on these occasions for the last fifteen years. But she could not be certain that the young footman would not drop some dish or other—for had he not spilt the soup last year? and, on the other hand, she *could* be certain—for her olfactory nerves had supplied her with proof positive—that the coachman had again tried the quality of his master's claret. She smiled, therefore, sweetly to the Governor and wondered whether Toon had already had too much and, if not, whether he would last out the bill of fare. There was a buzz of conversation, and a mingled odor of flowers, perfumes, and hot gravy. The guests were thinking of themselves or of the Governor. The Governor was thinking of the wine.

"Yes," Dr. Kern was saying. Dr. Kern was the village doctor, present in his quality as influential member of the Board—"Yes, I very nearly missed the beginning of your speech, Burgomaster, and I should have been very sorry for that. But we doctors are never masters of our time, you know."

"Practically slavery," said a lazy-looking gentleman, opposite.

"It would be slavery, sir," replied the doctor severely,

"if it were not work for so divine a mistress. Now, it is honorable service."

" Oh yes, of course," said the lazy gentleman, who really did not care what kind of work it was as long as he had not to do it.

" Now only this morning," continued the doctor, " just as my wife was fastening the bow of my white tie, Jan Smee's son came running in to say his father had had another of those attacks. So I had to rush down to the smithy with him. I couldn't very well let the old smith die, even for your speech, could I, Burgomaster ? "

" Would it have mattered very much," drawled van As- veld to his neighbor, " if there had been one Smith less in the world ? They are surely a sufficiently numerous family." His neighbor was a kind-hearted girl, and did not see the joke.

Van Asveld was there in virtue of his position as clerk in the Burgomaster's office. Having painfully toiled through the University curriculum and taken his degree, he had re- cently obtained this post, through the influence of friends. The duties were extremely light; the post was a genteel one ; the salary—ten pounds a year—almost paid the Jon- ker's cigar bill in that land of cheap cigars. Our friend had grown still fatter, redder, already a little bald. He looked like one who has lived, not wisely, but too well. He was still unmarried, the fair sugar-planter's daughter having re- fused the honors of the van Asveld coronet. He subsisted, as he himself said, " on the interest of his debts," and no one could see that he was obliged to deny himself anything. There was a suspicion—just a suspicion—that he drank now and then.

" You see one has to be careful with these cases," the doctor went on, prosing a little about his patients as he was apt to do. " It is impossible to foresee what turn they will take. I have told Smee's people a dozen times : he may live till eighty, and he may die to-night. Apoplectic, you know; complications about the heart. Rush of blood to the head. Fit. Off the man goes. Or he gets better, you know."

"And which is most liable to happen when the doctor comes?" asked the lazy gentleman. He asked it in all good faith, thinking he must say something, and not knowing what it was all about. His thoughts were merely talking in their sleep.

His question was answered in all seriousness none the less. "It is most important that a physician should be there," said the doctor, "but it is not absolutely necessary. Any one with a grain of common sense knows what to do. Of course, you unloosen everything, give the patient repose and breathing-room and all that sort of thing, and bring him too in the regular way. I needn't enter into particulars. Every student of medicine can tell you more than is necessary. As I say, common sense helps us a good deal in these matters."

"I thought," said the Burgomaster, "that the man who followed the promptings of his unaided intellect always did just the wrong thing in medicine."

"Oh well," replied the doctor, "I don't belong to the younger school. And as for that, the right kind of apoplexy kills you, doctor or no doctor. Then comes the fit, and then the *coup de sang*, as we call it. It's in cases of the latter sort, that so much depends on common sense. I believe many and many a man has died of strangulation, so to speak, just because of want of some helping finger to loosen his cravat."

"Oh come, doctor," said the lazy gentleman, suddenly waking up, "loosen his cravat! Come, come; you're joking."

"Nothing is farther from my thoughts, my dear sir," cried Doctor Kern. "Now, only this morning I found Baas Smee, gurgling and choking, with purple face, although I've told his wife half-a-dozen times before exactly what she was to do. If I had come half an hour later the man would probably have been dead. Now, he may, as I said, live another twenty years or more. He'll die of a regular fit some day, if he doesn't die sooner of one of these rushes of blood to the head. Of course, if the man were to live reasonably —but there, there! Your uncle, by-the-by, had just such a constitution, Avelingh—" he looked across at Joost, sitting opposite, a little higher up, and playing moodily with his knife.

"Oh—ah—what did you say, doctor?" asked Joost without looking up.

"Your uncle van Trotsem was just such a kind of patient as this good Baas. He might have lived another twenty years for aught I knew to the contrary. Not that I thought he would. But I should certainly have given him one or two more. And I thought it strange—But, there; it's an old story, and no one can care much about it."

"On the contrary," said van Asveld, bending forward, for Joost did not speak, "we are very much interested. You know old van Trotsem was a connection of mine too, doctor."

"Well, I was only going to say, I thought it strange at the time that with his constitution he didn't pull through that attack, whatever it may have been. As for living reasonably, of course—forgive me, Avelingh—but he lived like a madman. Talk of an unsound heart! as I said to my wife at the time, 'An unsound brain into the bargain!' Well, he's dead, poor man, but when they sent for me, and I found him lying there, I said to myself: 'This oughtn't to have been, van Trotsem. Himself to blame, of course. None the less sad on that account.'"

"Are you ill, Avelingh?" asked van Asveld suddenly. The question was prompted by sincere surprise and involuntary sympathy. His eyes had wandered to Avelingh's face, as the doctor ceased speaking.

Joost and Arthur sat opposite each other. Their eyes met. "No, thank you," said Joost controlling himself with a mighty effort and forcing the blood back into his cheeks. He drew himself up and threw forward his chest. "Why do you ask?"

"Because you looked it," answered van Asveld angrily. "Looked as if you'd seen a ghost. Hang it, I don't care." He turned to his fair neighbor : "Are you afraid of ghosts, freule?" he said.

"Yes," replied that lady unconditionally.

"They move in the best families," Arthur went on. "And really almost the only occupation left for a gentleman nowadays is to starve and turn ghost. I wish I knew of a vacancy. It might be worth while to apply. The people in authority seem to forget—" he raised his voice and turned in the direction of the Governor—"that the greatness of Holland, from the time of Brederode upward, has always depended on the young men of its old houses."

The Governor heard him. He smiled a complacent little smile. "I fear we must admit, my dear van Asveld," he said, beaming at the Jonker with a benevolent wave of the hand, "that the young men of the old families so often fail us, that we have to make a shift for it, as best we can, with the old men of the young families nowadays."

"Every one seems singing their own praises," said Bettekoo to her neighbor, frankly and ungrammatically. The Governor was a *parvenu*, raised to his exalted position—it was whispered—because he had surprised an ugly secret about a government tender. Such things happen in all countries. Perhaps the whisper was not true.

"I will sing yours all day, if you will allow me," was the immediate answer, for Bettekoo's neighbor was in love with her and he, she and Mevrouw van Hessel were looking out for a good opportunity for him to tell her so.

But at this moment the Burgomaster struck his dessert-knife against his wine-glass and rose up in all his portly importance. He looked round on the assembled guests; conversations died away with a sudden hush or a nervous little laugh, and a deep silence fell upon all.

"Highly Noble Austerity," said the Burgomaster's sonorous voice, "Ladies and Gentlemen, you will forgive me, if, seeing you all thus gathered together here this evening, I take the opportunity of saying a few words in connection with an auspicious event which has recently surprised and —and delighted—this whole parish. Need I say that I allude to the magnificent offer of an institution for the aged and deserving poor, recently made by my dear son-in-law, Joost Avelingh. That offer has been submitted this morning to you, Highly Noble Austerity, as the representative of our most gracious sovereign; it has met with your full approval, and I do not doubt that it will be gratefully accepted by the Parochial Board at their next meeting. The plans have been already drawn up; the rules made out; and, without going too far, I can safely say that the donation is a regal one, the proposed building a palace, the man who conceived such charity as this a king among benefactors." The Burgomaster warmed to his task. "Ladies and Gentlemen," he continued, "it is a proud moment for me when I can look the king's representative in the face and say, 'The commune in which these things are done is that of which I have the honor to be mayor, and the man who does them is my son-in-law!' And therefore, when the question first came to me : 'Father, shall I do this thing?' my heart leaped up in answer, and with all the strength of my influence as a parent, all the energy of my will and my desire, I answered and continued to answer : 'Do it!' till lo, the thing is done. Far be it from me to assume any undeserved merit—*non mihi tantus honos*, eh, doctor?—but we all know what the poet says : 'A wise word wisely spoken in the wisest hour.'" Ah well, no more of that. Joost Avelingh, it is a wonder-

ful, a beautiful thing to be possessed of influence. The lordship of great wealth bestows the lordship of this world; the
use of it for the benefit of our brethren achieves a title-deed
to the next! I am proud, sir, that, for my dearly loved
daughter's sake, you call me by the name of father. Ladies
and Gentlemen, I invite you to drink to the success of the
Avelingh Institute for the Aged Poor, and I couple with that
invitation the name of the Institute's illustrious founder, my
son-in-law, Joost Avelingh."

The Burgomaster waved his wine-glass gracefully in the
direction of the man whose eulogy he had pronounced. All
other glasses were lifted round the table; there was a murmur of benevolence and admiration, a general flow of interest and sympathy toward the hero of the moment. " Excellent," said the Governor, tapping one finger against his plate,
" excellent, excellent; oh yes, very well indeed." He was
not a little hurt to find that the Burgomaster had passed
him over, and that the toast of the evening, if there was to
be any toasting at all, should not be addressed to him, the
king's representative. Mynheer van Hessel had purposely
acted thus; it was his little revenge for the uncomfortable
quarter of an hour he had spent, before all was smoothed
over, with the husband of his wife's cousin. The importance of the charitable grant seemed to provide sufficient excuse.

Conversation resumed its flow; the endless dessert which
Dutch dinner-givers still affect slowly crept on through its
successive stages; yet the fruits preserved in brandy which
invariably conclude the proceedings were already going round
before Joost rose to reply. He tossed back his black hair in
rising; his face showed pale beneath the dark skin; he
looked stalwart and strong and resolved.

" Highly Noble Austerity, he began, in a clear, calm
voice, with just the faintest, incipient possibility of a sneer
over the ludicrous titles, " Right Nobly Respectable Sir Bur-

gomaster, Ladies and Gentlemen, if I rise to thank you for
your good wishes, as in duty bound, it must be clearly understood that I do not, by such recognition of them, in any way
take unto myself as my rightful property the praises which
the Burgomaster has lavished upon me. What I have done,
I have done from no especially noble motive. I have done
it for reasons of my own. If it conduce in however small a
degree to the happiness of any human being—" his eyes involuntarily strayed to Mevrouw van Hessel—" I shall be
grateful to God. I do not say—as is customary—I shall feel
amply rewarded. I do not look for reward. And none of
us, surely, neither you nor I, nor any fellow-sinner, overlooking our past life, with its bad actions and its so-called good
ones, making up the sum total of our existence, would dare
to bring the balance sheet before the throne of God and
standing there—"

Suddenly the goblet which he held up in one hand broke
right across the slender stem. The upper half slipped down
with a crash of breaking glass and splashing wine. In
another second dark drops of blood fell heavily on the shining tablecloth. The speaker stopped, irresolute, evidently
annoyed. He opened his palm, full of blood and broken
crystal. The speech was at an end. The whole company
sat staring at him in amazement. Once again during that
memorable dinner he found himself the meeting-point of all
looks and all thoughts. Agatha came running round to her
husband with her wretched little bit of embroidered cam-
bric to wash out the wound. The party broke up, leaving
them alone together. " It is nothing, really nothing," faltered Joost.

" He must have held that glass in a vice like the devil's,"
said van Asveld to Kees, as they filed out after the ladies,
" why the stem was actually crushed into pieces."

" Yes; very extraordinary," said Kees.

Dutch gentlemen—after coffee has been served—do not

linger over their wine in the old-fashioned English manner, but they go into the room of the master of the house
and sit for half-an-hour or so over cigars and liquors. When
Joost joined the others presently with his hand tied up, he
was full of jokes at his own great clumsiness, good-humor-
edly patient under floods of chaff, and ready to laugh his
loudest at any pleasantry whatsoever. The doctor cast
searching glances at him once or twice from his kindly gray
eyes. He had known Joost from earliest childhood.

"If the man were not sincerity itself," he thought, " as
any one can see he is, one would feel inclined to think he
was acting a part. But it is nothing of the kind ; I am
sure of it. He is spontaneously boisterous and reserved—
melancholy and gay, but all the moods have some common
source of overstrained excitement. I can't imagine what he
has to excite him. But he was always a nervous, impressionable child. I shall recommend him a cold-water-cure
next summer."

The object of these considerations came up at this very
moment and sat down beside the doctor. " You were talking about my uncle at dinner," said Joost. " Now what,
honestly and truly, as between man and man, do you, with
all your professional experience and natural acuteness, say
that he died of, Doctor Kern ? "

" There you put a very difficult question, my good man,"
replied the doctor, thoughtfully eying his cigar. " When a
medical authority is asked what has actually caused death,
his safest answer is always ' want of breath.' Unless it be a
tile or a chimneypot."

" Yes, yes," said Joost impatiently ; " but supposing you
to be content with approximate accuracy."

" Well," said the doctor. " Of course we have to fill up
our certificates, and I fear we often put in what comes
handy—in all good faith, of course. Mind you, I never
laugh at my profession. It's the grandest one on the face

of the earth. I believe fully in my own powers. Only I believe in my own limitations too."

" Yes," said Joost. And what did my uncle die of?"

" I should say," replied the doctor cautiously, "that the cause of death was a rush of blood to the brain, probably under the impulse of some strong excitement ; and, of course the heart gave way. It had been unsound for a long time, you know. Failure of the heart's action, in fact. But really, as far as some of the symptoms went, he might have choked himself—or—been choked. Strangulation, in fact. Yes—um, um—one hardly likes to say it—but, really, strangulation. However, of course, that is evidently and entirely out of the question. You were with him, at the time, were you not? And really, Avelingh, you ought to know more about it than I can, considering you studied medicine. He had—ahem—been—drinking a good deal, I believe?"

" Yes," said Joost gravely, " he had."

" Just so, in fact, I should say—between you and me— he was more than half drunk. Excuse plain speaking. It is a most exceptional case. Really, without a post-mortem, it would be impossible to say what your uncle died of."

" You filled in ' heart-disease,' " said Joost.

" Undoubtedly ; yes, and truthfully. If his heart had been all right, he would have been alive this day, unless, of course, he was choked—which he was not. And, as I was saying at dinner, he might have been alive in spite of his heart. A strange business ; a very strange business." The doctor smoked reflectively. Joost did not speak. " By-the-by, Avelingh," Dr. Kern went on presently, " I never give professional advice unasked, but, if you were to consult me about a pleasant place to spend a month or so next summer, I should say : try Godesberg. Pleasant place ; a little warm in the full season ; excellent hydropathic establishment. Plenty of compatriots."

" You say so because I broke that glass at dinner," cried

Joost. "You think me nervous! Nonsense, doctor. Look here!" He held out his uninjured hand, to show how steady it was.

"That goes for nothing," replied the doctor. "Mind, our bodies are brittle enough at the best. No use breaking them and spilling the wine. With some of us they're like ginger-beer bottles, and the ginger-beer works from inside till they burst. The human frame divine, you know, and all the rest of it. And—no advice, of course; I never give advice unasked—but if I were you, I should some day (no hurry) go to Godesberg."

"They are getting up to join the ladies," said Joost.

CHAPTER XVI.

THE JONKER'S LEGACY.

The carriages were called at ten; and Joost and Agatha went off together. The various guests began to disperse along their several roads, and van Asveld, having walked up the village-street with a friend, turned down a quiet lane, which led to his own abode. He stepped out briskly, smoking as he went, and reviewing the events of the evening. The great Charity interested him little, or rather he looked upon it with feelings of mingled irritation and disgust. He considered it, naturally enough, as a gigantic bid for popularity, and the only stupidity about it, when viewed in that light, seemed to be that exactly the same object might have been attained with one fifth of the money; four-fifths therefore appeared absolutely wasted even from the donor's standpoint. Why should all the wretched old paupers in the province, after having been happy and contented in

hovels all their lives, want to die in a palace? Surely an
old beggar must feel as uncomfortable in such a mansion, as
he, van Asveld, would be in a miserable hut! Pigs in the
pigsty; horses in the stable. That was the law of nature
and of—ahem—God.

Uppermost in the Jonker's mind was the thought of his
dead cousin's great wealth. "Avelingh must be rolling in
gold," he reasoned, and the recollection of his own conversation with the Baron van Trotsem on the very morning of
the old man's last day on earth, came back to him with re-
vived bitterness. Often and often, since that fatal day, he
had recalled the farewell scene, the old Baron's promise of a
considerable legacy, the cruel disappointment when the will
was proved to speak of no provision at all. Even now, after
ten years, Arthur stamped his foot at the recollection, upon
the frozen snow. "Life had gone hardly with him," he
thought, and not untruly. The failure of that one hope, at
any rate, was as vivid, as irritating to-day, as when first it
became unpleasantly patent to him and to all his creditors.
Somehow he had convinced himself that both Joost and the
Baron had done him a personal injury by allowing death to
supervene before the necessary testamentary arrangements
had been definitely made. He did not reason much about
it; but he liked Avelingh none the better because of that
gentleman's good luck.

From these reflections upon what might have been, the
Jonker naturally dropped into a review of his present financial
position. There could be nothing very attractive in that, and
he was not displeased to find his attention diverted by the
discovery that he was rapidly gaining on some one, who
seemed to be strolling leisurely on, a few paces ahead.
Walking briskly, as he was doing, he had almost come up
to the figure in front before he noticed it at all. "Who could
be out in this lonely spot at such an hour?" he asked himself, "a tramp perhaps? The Burgomaster's clerk must

see to that." Whatever van Asveld might be, he was anything but a coward. He increased his speed and came
alongside of the man. "Good evening," he said. There
was no necessity for courage of any kind. It was only
Joost Avelingh.

"Avelingh," cried Asveld, in great disgust. He had
expected to be able to make a show of his authority.
"What the devil are you doing here, if one may ask?"

"Walking home," replied Joost, quietly. "And unless
you object, I shall continue my road."

"It is no business of mine, of course!" replied the other.
"Only it seems a deuced strange way of getting back."

"I often walk after such an evening," said Joost. It
cools one down wonderfully. Gives one a better chance of
sleep."

It was true. The man who could never be alone or idle
by day, rushing from one occupation to another, reading
even while he thus rushed, the same man would wander out
at night for long lonely walks. Was it because he knew
that, whether in the house or out of it, he *must* be alone at
night? He had put Agatha into the carriage and started
down the dark road by himself. It would take him more
than an hour to reach home, and the night was bitterly cold,
but he had a fur coat on and a cigar between his lips.

"Cools one down! I should think so!" said Arthur.
"No danger of that. Freezes one. How is your hand?"

"Quite comfortable, I thank you," said Joost stiffly.

"I thought you weren't looking well all the evening. I
told you so at the time. You looked as ill as a living man
can look, while the doctor was speaking during dinner about
Cousin Dirk's death."

"It is a painful subject," said Joost.

"Undoubtedly. Though scarcely so for you, I should
say. Oh yes, of course, and all that. No doubt. And I
quite believe you, but if *I* were to say it was a painful subject

for me, a very peculiarly painful one, I am afraid the cynical world would sooner believe me."

"I suppose you mean," said Joost, " that you would have liked my uncle to leave you some money. I have often heard that you were disappointed about some such matter. And I wanted to speak to you about it. But I do not see why the memory of my uncle's death should therefore be peculiarly painful to you. You would not be any the richer, I feel sure, if he were alive to-day."

"No," said van Asveld, brusquely, " but I should have been richer if he had lived a little longer, or he was a damned old liar."

They walked on for several minutes in silence. At last, when Joost spoke, there was an unmistakable tremor in his voice and yet it only gave utterance to the two simple words : " How so ? "

" How so ? " repeated the other, " I can't tell how much you know, Avelingh, and for all I could prove, you may be as ignorant and innocent as a new-born babe. Mind you, I don't for one moment insinuate you are not. Only, I can scarcely understand, that living with you all day, as the old man did, and bursting out into voluble rages as he was apt to do also, he should never have let out anything to you of his plan for me."

" My uncle's volubility," replied Joost, "restricted itself to a very limited circle of—" he was going to say " epithets " but he substituted " interests. " " There is no reason, as you say, why you should believe me, but, if it is any satisfaction to you, I have no hesitation about declaring on my word as a gentleman—perhaps you do not consider me entitled to give that ? "

" Every man is a gentleman," said Arthur haughtily, " in that sense."

" Thank you. On my word as a gentleman, or if you will, my Bible oath that, as far as I had, or have, any cognizance, my uncle, at any rate till the day of his death, had made no plans whatever on your behalf."

"Just so," said van Asveld, "I don't doubt your word. I dare say the old close-fist wouldn't blab. But you yourself make a restriction. Might I ask you to explain it?"

"Why not?" replied Joost. "On the last day of his life my uncle mentioned your name in connection with his will. He told me—why should I not repeat it?—that he would rather leave his money to you than suffer me to disobey him. It was said in a passion, as a threat. That was the only time I heard of any intentions on your behalf. And as I tell you, the words seemed but a passing allusion. I have no more to say on the subject."

"But I have!" cried Arthur hotly: "A great deal more! That remark was not a passing allusion, as you choose to call it. I know better! Perhaps I know more than you do. On the very morning of his death I was closeted with Cousin Dirk, as you will scarcely have forgotten, and when I left him, I took with me the solemn assurance, the all but written guarantee, that I should be handsomely remembered in his will. He passed me his word on it. He told me I might trade on it with the Jews or my future father-in-law. And I tried to that very afternoon with old Moses; only he wouldn't see it, damn him. And he was right in the end, as he told me afterward; the hoary scoundrel! But—for all that—if the old beast had only lived a little longer, I am sure he would have kept his word, for he was a gentleman, hang him, with all his faults, and that's more than many of us can say."

"Do I understand," asked Joost, "that my uncle gave you his solemn assurance on the day of his death that he would leave you money?"

"Yes," replied Arthur, "didn't I say so?"

"And he told you you might trade on—reckon on—his promise?"

"Yes," repeated Arthur, "do you want the whole story again?"

"He did not, I presume, mention any particular sum?"

Arthur hesitated a moment—barely a moment. He recalled the whole conversation of that eventful morning, its minutest details stood engraved in his memory forever: he remembered the terms he had proposed and his cousin's answer to them, and he considered that he was hardly prevaricating when he answered, "There had been a question between us from the first of some forty or fifty thousand florins."

They walked on, after that, side by side, through the dark night. Presently said Arthur: "So you see I have full right to complain that Cousin Dirk's death is a peculiarly painful subject to me."

Joost did not answer.

They reached the house where Arthur had rooms, and stopped.

"Good night, Avelingh," said Arthur, not too ungraciously, holding out his hand.

"I believe what you have told me," said Joost abruptly, standing with his hands in the pockets of his fur coat. "I see no reason to disbelieve it. In a day or two, as soon as I can conveniently make the necessary arrangements, I shall instruct Leening & Co., who are my bankers, to pay over to you the sum of forty thousand florins with compound interest from the day of my uncle's demise."

He turned upon his heel without another word.

"Avelingh," the other called after him, "Good Heavens! Avelingh! Damn it. What do you mean?"

Joost walked on. "What's the use of long deliberations?" he said to himself. "And what does it matter whether he gets the money or some other poor beggar? These things when done at all, are best done quickly.

And if what he says be true, I owe him the money more surely than I owe my butcher's bill."

Arthur van Asveld remained standing by the little wooden garden-gate that waited to admit him. He felt dazed, as a man might feel on being suddenly struck to the ground by a gold nugget, with a rough "That's for you!" His first impulse was not to believe the whole statement, to look upon it as a vulgar joke. But "No," he said to himself the next moment, "we are not on such terms as those with each other. And, besides, he was unmistakably in earnest. Good heavens, what can he mean?" Then came a momentary flush of admiration and gratitude for Joost's generosity. And then again, almost immediately, while he yet stood out there in the cold, the doubt broke in upon Arthur's mind: "Can all be right and square and above hand with regard to Avelingh's succession? Men do not give away forty thousand florins like a pair of old boots. But they will pay out that and more than that, with a reason. Some men's consciences require sedatives—Arthur smiled to himself in the dark—some men's secrets are best buried in gold. Forty thousand florins! What could it mean? He regretted not having asked for fifty or sixty. He was right, for Joost had immediately passed over that "or fifty" as an attempt at mere extortion.

"What could it mean?" He asked himself the question again and again, as he went up to his room. Despite the pleasure of thus finding temporary relief from his most pressing liabilities, the question continued to worry him. Why? Why? "Das geht nicht mit rechten Dingen zu," he said.

CHAPTER XVII.

"UNDER THE SURFACE."

AGATHA drove home by herself in the carriage, listening
vaguely to the regular tramp of the horses' feet on the frozen
snow, and dreamily thinking of many things. There had
been a time when Joost would have proposed to sleigh back
with her through the calm winter's night, and when she
would not have minded the cold, as long as they were together. Did he love her less than formerly? She thought
not. Differently? No; he had never loved her quite as
she loved him. Had she a right to expect it?

Joost Avelingh had sought in his wife what most men
seek: an ornament, a delight, a continual pleasure, but not,
in the full sense of the word, a companion—a pet, dearly
cherished, but not an intellectual equal, to be honored, consulted, esteemed. The force of circumstances, undoubtedly,
would have made it difficult for him to admit her to his full
confidence, but he had never sought or desired to do so.
He loved Agatha with all the early tenderness, " too much
tenderness " might well be said, if there were no danger of
being misunderstood. He admired her pure, fair beauty,
and he wished it to be admired by others. He was proud
of her as she entered a room with all her mother's majestic
bearing, her delicate complexion changing with every impulse of feeling, her eyes shining calm and good under the
coronet of yellow hair. Her beauty had developed into
fuller matronhood as the years went on. He had never
loved her for that beauty only. He had loved her for her
goodness, her sweetness, her purity, all that goes to make a
good woman lovable, and he loved her for them still. He
would do anything—that struck him—to give her pleasure;
any sorrow of hers was a deep grief to him also. He had
espoused her, fully, loyally, with his heart forever; but his

mind's life, the deep, strong current of his thinking soul, flowed up to her, babbled round her, and flowed past.

She gave him more—who can doubt it? She gave him what a woman can—her all. And she was happy, though with a lurking suspicion that she might be much happier still. It was at particular moments especially, when the shadow fell broad across her sunlight, that she sorrowed over it; at other times she would strive to convince herself that what she condemned as shadows were but specks upon the sun. It was not in Agatha Avelingh's nature to bemoan herself, and the wrongs that others did her had to be very large indeed before her eye perceived them. She was always the last to see any injury unless kind friends could point it out.

On this occasion, however, her heart was troubled. She had not liked Joost's mood all through the evening. She had seen—far more clearly than van Asveld—how the doctor's talk at dinner had unnerved him; she had felt all the pins and needles of the Burgomaster's speech in her own breast almost before they reached Joost's; she had been much distressed and puzzled by the incident of the broken glass. She had often felt instinctively that her husband kept his troubles from her. Could there be money difficulties? Hardly. Agatha smiled at the thought. There seemed to be too much money. True, he never spoke to her on the subject, it being one of his theories that women could know nothing about matters of finance, and that it was foolish to instruct them; but she knew, none the less, that Joost was not the kind of man to be much troubled by pecuniary considerations. Something wrong, probably, in one of his many committees or councils. It vexed her more than she would confess that he never spoke to her about all this business, philanthropic, political, or personal, in which he was involved. When she asked: "And how were they in your meeting this afternoon?" he would answer: "Oh,

very good, love, but not as good as you," and stop her mouth
with a kiss. And when she ventured to trot out her wise
observations on the state of modern politics at home or
abroad, he would say, "They ought to make you Prime
Minister, dearest. How nice you would look opening Parliament in your new red velvet dress." What was the use,
then, of asking him what little matter worried him? It
only meant provoking the stereotype answer: "Nothing."
She resolved, as she went up-stairs to her room, to do it all
the same. She looked at the clock. Past eleven. She sat
down in her dressing-gown by the fire.

Twice during these years of her married life the joy of
motherhood had seemed very near to her; twice her hope
had been frustrated, the bright dream had faded into air
like a mirage. She regretted the disappointment certainly,
but when she rose from her weary bed of sickness, her heart,
rebounding to her husband, found no room for loneliness
or repining. For Joost, the regret was a much stronger
one. His had been—and still was—the masculine desire
for a child, a child, namely, not merely for love, but for
honor, ambition, enjoyment, for all its capabilities of greatness and success. It was the only thing he would gladly
have changed in Agatha, the one misfortune he could almost
have reproached her for.

It was nearly twelve, when the husband, softly pushing
open the door, a candle in his hand, suddenly came into the
unexpected brightness.

"Up still!" he said. "I thought you would have been
in bed long ago. I wish you would not sit up for me, dearest. You know how often I have told you I do not like it."

"But I like it so much," she answered, "I can not bear
going to bed and to sleep quite comfortably and unconcern-
edly, while you are still out in the cold, as if we were not
married at all. And it is such a real pleasure to see you
come home."

She spoiled him, this handsome, melancholy husband of
hers. Could she wonder if afterward she had cause to complain of his behavior? Very few husbands can stand being
systematically spoiled.

They began to talk of the evening's experiences, she
making the greater part of the observations upon them, he
answering in monosyllables, mostly. Dutch gentlemen
rarely have dressing-rooms: Joost had one and but seldom
used it. He left the door open and the gas turned up, and
wandered in and out to his wife. He listened to what was
chiefly innocent gossip with a certain appearance of interest. He had almost forgotten the scene with van Asveld,
barely half-an-hour ago. It had made but little impression
upon him. The gift of the money had left him supremely
indifferent. Perhaps, if had weighed the matter in the
silence of his own room, leisurely considering the pros and
cons, he would have concluded not to give Arthur the
money. Who shall say? But now he had acted, as he so
often did, upon a sudden impulse, and he was not sorry it
should have been so. It was an impulse altogether in accordance with his nature and with his present mode of
thought. What did money matter to him? He was only
too anxious to get rid of it in a manner pleasing to his conscience. And to the peculiar promptings of that conscience
the Jonker van Asveld's claims seemed especially plausible.
He did not like van Asveld certainly. Reason the more to
do him the strictest justice. The whole matter seemed
scarcely worth a thought, unless it were to extract a momentary pleasure from the idea of having done what might
perhaps be best. Perhaps it was not really the best? Well,
of such stuff are we mortals made that the second best must
do as well.

And Agatha prattled on of many things while her heart
still dwelt on one. She was yearning to speak to Joost of
his trouble, of his sudden sickness, of the broken glass. An

accident? No, it was more than that. A loving woman
reads her husband's countenance like an open book after ten
years of married life, even when that countenance is as
habitually dark and overcast as Joost Avelingh's. And she
had seen, from her distant place across the table, had seen,
as no other had, the nervous grip tightening slowly around
the brittle stem. What thought tormented him? Had she,
his lawful, loyal wife, not the fullest right to know?

"Joost," she said, with her back turned to him—standing before her looking-glass. "How is your hand?"

"You asked me that just before you started, Agatha,"
replied Joost, a little crossly. "That is not two hours ago.
Are you going to ask me every two hours?"

"I am so afraid, dearest, that some glass may have remained in the wound. It was quite a deep cut."

"A mere scratch. Nonsense, if one had nothing to bear
but that! The hand is all right, I tell you."

"And the heart?" she said, suddenly facing him.

"The heart," he echoed, laughing uneasily, "why,
Agatha, the heart—as they say in the bulletins—is as well as
can be expected under the circumstances."

"I should so like it to be quite happy," she said softly.

"Quite happy!" he repeated bitterly. "Who is happy?"

"They who are at rest."

Again he caught up the word. "Rest!" he said. "You
know what the Bible tells us, Agatha. 'There is no rest,
saith my God, for the wicked.' We are all wicked, I suppose?"

There was an unpleasant lightness in his tone that jarred
upon the words.

"Yes," she answered more softly still. "We are all
wicked, and that perhaps is why the peace of God, when
once it comes, is said by that same Bible to pass all under-
standing."

"Then it's no use trying to understand it," remarked Joost.

"No, dearest, but I believe each individual soul can *feel* the answer to the question whether it is at peace with God or not."

He did not seem to listen much to what she was saying. "Rest!" he cried. "Peace! Beautiful words, in sooth. We mortals have not learned to be so ambitious. We do not ask for cooling breezes, only for a little tempering of the flame. 'Reach down thy finger and touch but the tip of my tongue!' Our hearts are burning."

Agatha drew near to him. He almost pushed her from him.

"You religious people," he said, "talk about all the pains and penalties in the beyond. Penalties for what? The pleasures of the present? Great God! if Hell be yonder, then what is this? And do thy creatures pass from suffering to suffering? From hell of earth to hell of hell?"

"Joost! Joost!" cried Agatha, "Oh dearest, sin alone is suffering! And they who pass from sin to sin forever, must pass forever from woe to woe."

"Sin," said Joost gloomily, "the wrong choice between good and bad, it is a mistake, an ignorance, a fatality—call it what you will. Call it all things but a conscious self-injury. We men are not such fools as that. Never mind, Agatha. Keep your happiness. You need not understand."

"One thing I understand," said Agatha. "You are wretched."

"Wretched!" said Joost. "No. Who is wretched? Who is happy? Wretchedness is an immeasurable capability. I have not reached its limits yet. Perhaps only touched the surface. No, I can't say I am fully and sufficiently wretched. Oh, Agatha, Agatha, life is an awful thing."

"And death more awful yet," murmured Agatha.

" Is it?" said her husband. "That question remains un-answered still."

He lay far through the night staring into the darkness with wide-opened eyes. His wife dropped asleep at his side. He listened to her breathing, and he, who had always re-fused to let her share his sorrows, yet felt unconsciously ir-ritated that she could sleep thus tranquilly after their con-versation. It was very rarely that he gave such utterance to his thoughts. And he could not have told himself this even-ing why he had so suddenly opened a window, as it were, into his heart that even this woman he loved best on earth might look so deeply into it. He had done so, impelled to break through his reserve by all the emotions of the day. And she slept. Why should she not? What could women with their easier, lighter, smoother natures know of a man's life-struggle against fate? He turned restlessly on his pillow. " Life is an awful, a horrible thing," he said to himself " But to bear is to conquer," he said.

CHAPTER XVIII.

MURDER WILL OUT.

Two months had elapsed since the events narrated in the last few chapters. The new year had come to life, creep-ing slowly out of its infant torpor and waking up, bit by bit, beneath his coverlet of snow. He had not yet passed into the stage of blustering boyhood; that would come in time, when the winds of March arose. At present there was si-lence still; frost and snow, the strange silence of winter, when the waters lie bound, and the earth lies muffled, the silence as round a dying bed or by a baby's cradle. And the new year stirred in his sleep; and men said: "Hush! he is waking!"

A lonely traveler was coming along the straight, desolate highway. The morning hung low: dull, and gray, and cloudy. There was no one in sight but this solitary pedestrian. A country cart had met him some time ago, and jogged away into the misty distance, right on, down the narrow line of road. He had eyed it, in passing, with exaggerated interest and then stumbled on awkwardly, swaying to and fro as he went. He was a common man, of some thirty years or thereabouts, poorly and untidily dressed; and although his shambling gait may have been habitual to him, there was something in his swinging progress, as well as in the foolish scrutiny of the cart, which at once proclaimed to any but the most superficial observer, that the man was the worse for drink at this moment—more so—that he was probably not unfrequently in a similar condition.

He staggered on till he reached a little knot of cottages. Here he stopped, gazing stupidly from side to side, with that same look of senseless interest. Gradually his sunken eyes seemed to brighten, as if with a smile of recognition: he stumbled forward, pushed open a low door, and disappeared into the interior of a tiny public-house.

"And what may you want, my good friend?" queried the master of the house in no very friendly tone, as the newcomer slouched up to the bar.

"A borrel," was the surly answer.

"Well, you can get that, though I should say, by the look of you, that you had had quite as much as was good for you already."

The other did not answer immediately. The publican carefully measured out a small glass of the commonest gin and placed it on the counter.

His customer took it up and, holding it by the foot, began slowly, thoughtfully, luxuriously, to suck in its con-

tents.   His little blood-shot eyes twinkled.   Half-way
through, he rested with a deep-drawn sigh of enjoyment.

"I reckon I've never had enough, from your point of
view," he said.   "As long as I've got half a dozen cents left
to pay for more."

"The police would tell you a different story," replied
the publican.

"The police!" cried the wayfarer, with a snort of contempt.   "There's all the difference in the world between
the police and a—public—house—keeper."   He evidently
enjoyed this sentence and the tone of contempt he threw
into the last words extremely.   He repeated them slowly.
"It's just the employers and the employed," he went on.   "If
there were no public-house keepers—damn it—there need
be no police.   You're just the beaters, you are, when the
police go hunting."   He spoke in a slow provincial drawl,
and—having said his say—sucked again at his little spirit-
glass.

"Yes," remarked the publican spitefully, "and fellows
like you are the quarry."

"Right you are," said the other, "and the quarry was
the most respectable party in every hunt that ever I
saw."

The publican did not reply.   He limped away—he was
a lame man—to another part of the bar.   The fellow was
only repeating—he felt sure of it—some of the foolish temperance talk that has recently come into fashion, and it was
a matter of principle with the publican never to pay any
attention to temperance people.   "It unsettled your ideas
of right and wrong," he was wont to say.

The stranger finished his glass with a smack of the
lips, and pushed it across the counter.   "Give me another,"
he said.

"Cents first," said the publican, tersely.

His customer winked and slowly produced from a ragged pocket ten copper cent-pieces, which he spread out in a straggling row before him.

The publican leisurely refilled the little glass.

"Always the same, eh?" said the other, winking again. "Smart as ever. Not a day older than ten years ago. I know you."

"Do you?" asked the publican with a keen glance. "I haven't that advantage with regard to your Honor."

"No fooling!" said the fellow fiercely. "I know you, I tell you, Wurmers, you old thief. Knew you ever since I was a child. You must be pretty near eighty, you old Methusaleh!"

"No calling names!" cried the publican more fiercely still. "What do you mean, you scoundrel?"

The other instantly collapsed. "Methusaleh was a damned respectable party," he murmured in a cowed tone.

"Yes," said the publican, "but thieves aren't, whatever *you* may think. And as for Bible history, a drunkard might remember there were no publicans before Noah."

"Well, I know you at any rate, Wurmers, I tell you. It's not the first borrel I've had in your house, and the gin's as watery as ever."

"You're drunk," said Baas Wurmers. "You're drunk enough to taste water in hell-fire."

"Drunk, am I?" screamed the other. "You wouldn't have spoken like that to me the last time I stopped at your house. I was in a handsome chaise then, and sitting behind as good a horse as ever stepped, I was."

"You're drunk," repeated the publican. "You look like the kind of party that drives a handsome chaise, you do."

"I didn't say I was driving," replied the man. "And I didn't say it was my chaise. I'm an honest man I am, as honest as adverse circumstances will permit. As good as a publican any day!"

J

He struck his fist violently on the edge of the bar. The wood was old, like the publican, and rotten. It cracked across under the blow, or rather, a little crack the master of the house had noticed for many a year, spread suddenly into one of larger size.

The man stopped, looking at his handiwork in some alarm.

"That's damage," said the publican quietly, "to be paid for."

The delinquent moved awkwardly to the door.

"No you don't," cried the little old rogue, limping round the bar with wonderful agility. "No you don't. Pay first, and make yourself scarce afterward. Show your cents!"

The other with a rueful countenance, turned out two empty pockets.

"So you spend your last copper on gin, do you?" cried the little publican, hopping from one leg to the other, as well as his lameness would allow. "And a wife and children at home crying for food, very likely! Ugh—to think of it! But you don't get away, my fine fellow, till you've paid me for what you've broke!"

"I haven't got the money, as you see," said the other threateningly. "And your rotten old planks would have come to pieces, any way. So you'll just let me pass."

He made for the door, but the old Baas flung himself straight at his whilom customer, and fastened his skinny arms round the man's unsteady legs, holding him there in a tight embrace, and screeching for help at the top of a shrill discordant voice.

Another little old man came running in—the grocer from over the way. Various women and children from the neighboring half-dozen cottages grouped themselves around the now open door.

"Police! police!" screamed the publican. "They're robbing me! Thieves! Help! Police!"

Police there were none. But the half-tipsy and altogether broken-down personage thus attacked was the last
criminal to offer a determined resistance. He allowed himself to be secured by the two old fellows who had seized
hold of him, and he was led away up the road in the direction of Heist, staggering on between them, with a lessening
procession of children bringing up the rear. During the
first part of the journey old Wurmers was very eloquent
about his fancied wrongs, but his indignant expostulations
gradually dropped into an occasional murmur, and the little
party reached the Burgomaster's office in melancholy silence.

But here all the Baas's indignation overflowed afresh.
The criminal stood by with an agitated expression on his
face. In spite of his ragged appearance, he was evidently
not accustomed to such humiliating contact with the police.

A grave functionary in a dark blue coat—the *garde cham-
pêtre*—took down the old publican's deposition with an indifferent air. It did not seem a very important case, he
thought. The hour was still too early; there was no one in
the office yet. He advised Baas Wurmers to go back to his
gin-shop for the present. The man was a vagabond. That
was all.

The little group dispersed. The constable sat down to a
table covered with papers. The tramp stood at the window
and looked out. Presently the door was thrown open, and
Arthur van Asveld walked in. The constable rose; the
tramp turned from the window and made an attempt at a
military salute.

"Who is this, Stronk?" said Arthur in his official voice.

"A vagabond, Jonker. Brought in just now. Drunk
and disorderly in a public-house on the Hoester Road."

"I will examine him till the Burgomaster comes, and
make out the report." He passed into an inner room. He
had no particular right to examine anybody, being only a

clerk, but he liked to make a show of his authority, fancied or real, and, after all, that may be excused as an innocent enjoyment. The constable followed him with the culprit.

"Your name?" said Arthur, authoritatively, installing himself behind a green table.

"Jan Lorentz."

"Occupation?"

"Gentleman's servant out of place."

Van Asveld surveyed the figure before him. "Out of place for some time, I should think?" he said.

"I have been unfortunate, Nobly Respectable Sir. I come from this neighborhood. I have never been in such a position before. I was born and bred on the finest estate in the country—"

"Silence," said Arthur with great dignity. "Place of birth?"

"The Castle at Hoest, Nobly Respectable Sir."

"Indeed?" remarked Arthur. "Last place of abode?"

"Yes, I was born on the estate, where my father was servant before me. My father was Mynheer the Baron's coachman, Nobly Respectable Sir, and I was for many years one of Mynheer the Baron's grooms."

"Silence!" said Arthur. "You say you were in the Baron van Trotsem's service. You will have to prove that. How long were you employed at the Castle?"

"I have my papers, Nobly Respectable," began Lorentz eagerly, fumbling in a breast-pocket. "I was four years with the Baron after I came back from military service. I should be there still, only the nephew turned us off. And I was present with the Baron in his last moments too! It was a shame to do it, a shameful shame! and no offense to your Honor."

"I can not allow you to speak in that manner of a man in Mynheer Avelingh's position," interposed Arthur sternly.

"Do I understand you to say you were with the Baron van Trotsem at his death?"

"Indeed I was, Nobly Respectable. And I helped to bring him to; only it was no use, because he was dead."

"Silence! Last place of abode? I must once more insist on your answering questions only."

The interrogation continued; the culprit telling the common tale of a character lost never to be recovered: drink, misery, destitution, then more drink on that account, but no crime. Arthur looked at the testimonial Avelingh had given the man on dismissing him with the other servants, it was fairly favorable; undoubtedly it was genuine; Arthur recognized the large, somewhat reckless and restless handwriting of the present Lord of Trotsem Castle.

"That will do," said Arthur presently. "You can go back to your work, Stronk. Let the man remain here. I have one or two things still which I may as well settle before the Burgomaster comes. And you can go on with your reports in the mean time. Sit down there, you, what's your name. The Burgomaster will be in presently. And shut the door as you go out, Stronk; it is really quite cold still."

The constable passed into the anteroom. When the door had closed behind his retreating figure, Arthur got up and came round to the corner in which the tramp had sat down.

"Remain where you are," said van Asveld condescendingly. "And what is this story that you tell, my good man, about your having been present when the Baron van Trotsem died?"

"I was groom, sir, in the Baron's stables, as I told you," said the fellow, civilly. "And I was with him at the time. You may have heard that he died in a chaise on the high road. I was in the dickey when it happened, and I saw the whole thing done."

"Done!" cried van Asveld, thrown completely off his

guard by this unexpected expression. " Do you mean to
say that you saw any deed done that night, which can be
said to have any connection with the Baron van Trotsem's
death ? "

Jan Lorentz hesitated. His one desire was to get away.
He was frightened at the idea of any dealings with the
police, and anxious not to commit himself further. He
felt just tipsy enough to know he must be careful about his
words ; the walk up to the Office had sobered him, and no
one now who spoke to him, as Arthur was doing, would receive the impression that he was much under the influence
of drink ; but for all that his brain—never clear at the best
—felt fuddled and confused.

" Oh, no, nothing," he said awkwardly. " I was in the
dickey, and through the glass in the hood—they had forgotten that little glass—I heard and saw it all, you see."

Arthur bent forward and put one hand on the back of
the man's chair. " I have my reasons," he said, " for sus-
pecting that you know more about the Baron van Trotsem's
death than you care to show. Now look here ; you've got
into a mess with the police this morning. You say it's the
first time ! "

" It is. Indeed it is, Nobly Respectable Sir," cried Lorentz.

" Very well. I am willing to believe you. Mind you
get out of their clutches, that's all. It's always a good deal
easier to get in."

" What am I to do, Nobly Respectable ? I will do anything ! "

" I am sorry for you," continued Arthur, " and willing
to help you out of this scrape. What's more, if you make
it worth my while, I may do a good deal more for you,
mind you, a good deal more. Do you understand that ? "

The tramp shook his head with an assumption of
shrewdness. " I'll do anything," he said ; " you try me, sir."

" So much is not required of you," said Arthur. " The Baron van Trotsem was a near and dear relation of mine. His death took place under the most mysterious circumstances. I have recently been led to suspect that there was foul play somewhere in that business. Now, you tell me you were present from first to last?"

" Yes," said Lorentz. " Yes, that true. I sat in the dickey and saw it all."

" Very well. Now mind you, I shall ask you some questions. Your own future, for a good deal, will depend upon how you answer them. And first; What part did Mynheer Avelingh play in the whole matter? What did he do?"

" N—nothing," said the tramp, hesitatingly.

" Nothing!" repeated Arthur, sarcastically. " Really? Nothing? With his uncle dying at his side? That is very extraordinary! We shall hardly get you out of prison, or into a comfortable means of earning an honest livelihood, by such statements as that. Nothing! Indeed? No fooling," he continued, suddenly changing his tone to one of bitter earnest. " Look here, Lorentz, I can well understand, that if anything evil happened, you were paid to keep silence. And you seemed to have earned your pay. But the other side don't seemed to have looked after you very satisfactorily, and now I'll pay you to talk. I think I shall probably pay you better. There; you can grasp that!"

" Yes," replied the man quietly, " and a good deal more than your Noble Respectability perhaps thinks. And what am I to say?"

" Answer my questions; that is all. And, to begin with the beginning, what did you hear the Baron say in the chaise? Did you hear him say anything at all?"

" Only now and then, Nobly Respectable. But at times he shouted loud enough to be heard half-a-mile down the road. And he abused his young nephew most terribly for wanting to marry the Freule van Hessel, and I heard him cry out a dozen times, quite plain, that rather than let him do that, he'd leave all his money to a certain Mynheer van Asveld."

"Indeed!" said Arthur, looking out of the window. "You heard him say that?"

"A dozen times, so help me God. And it was you he meant, Jonker."

"What?" cried van Asveld. "You know me?"

"As soon as I came in," replied the man, "only I couldn't think clear at first. I can't always think clear. Haven't I seen you up at the Castle in the old Baron's time?"

"And so," said Arthur, speaking more to himself than to his companion, "the old man was driving across to the Notary—we knew that—shouting out all the way that he intended to alter his will in my favor—I don't think any of us were aware of that little item; it was not a detail Avelingh would care to communicate. Why you scoundrel!" he cried, suddenly turning on the frightened tramp. "Talk of getting you out of this scrape. Damn the old gin-seller and his rotten tables! It's worth half-a-dozen gin-sellers to me to know what your keeping boxed up in that drink-muddled head of yours! Tell me what you saw through that God-send of a little glass window, and I'll pay you twice whatever Avelingh gave you to hold your peace!"

"There's nothing I want so much as to get out of this trouble," said Lorentz, cautiously. "And I'm most anxious to oblige you, Jonker. I saw it all through the glass, as I said!"

"Did you see him killed?" cried Arthur excitedly, "Tell me for the love of Heaven, did you see him killed?"

"I saw the old Baron fall back, and then I saw Mynheer Joost throw back his arms and clench—"

"Yes! Yes!" shouted Arthur. "Clench him by the throat, eh? Oh, my God! What are you staring at me like that for, you villain? You fool to take ten years to come and tell me that you saw Avelingh strangle his uncle, when I would have made you rich the day after the deed, had I but known!"

The tramp stood silent, a troubled expression in his eyes. Presently it cleared off, and he cast an unexpectedly acute glance at the excited nobleman opposite him. He was a strange creature, in whose brain original shrewdness and drunken confusion had been fighting for the mastery during several years. There could be little doubt which would ultimately conquer.

"Never mind why you did not speak sooner," Arthur continued more calmly, "the great point is that you have spoken now. So much the better for you in every way. You heard, therefore, as you now declare, the Baron van Trotsem repeatedly express his resolve to alter the will on that fatal night. And you know—none better—how it came that he never lived to do it. It is not chance, my good man, but Providence, that has brought you here this morning."

Arthur walked to the window and stood gazing out into the gray sky. That hour had brought him a revelation so terrible in its reality that he trembled to think of its import in spite of all the hopes and fears of the last months. He had received the so-called legacy in full from Avelingh, and from that moment the conviction had deepened upon him, that the man who paid away so much money, unasked, must have his very good reasons for doing it. The doctor's talk about van Trotsem's death had also rankled in his mind, and, what with one thing and another, Arthur had felt more and more convinced that, somewhere and somehow, a mystery remained unsolved in connection with Joost Avelingh. And yet in spite of this conviction, he told himself that the actual discovery, as it now presented itself to his mind, found him unprepared. It was too awful to think of. Ten years ago, then, the old man had been murdered by his own nephew, and that nephew had enjoyed his ill-gotten gains ever since. To do Arthur justice, the horror of the thing was uppermost in his thoughts at first. But soon the other consideration came working its way to the top. It was not only to enrich himself but to rob another that Joost Avelingh had committed this crime. And that other was he, Arthur van Asveld. But for this murder he might now have been—instead of a beggar as he was—one of the richest and most influential men in the province! he might have been, in fact, in Joost Avelingh's place. The conception was torture to him. He turned away from it, and found himself relentlessly recalled to it, till his heart hated Joost as it had never hated before.

As he stood there, staring moodily at the clouds, the choice between two modes of action presented itself to his mind. He could take this secret to the guilty man and trade upon it. It would be worth a fortune to him. How much, it was impossible to say; enough undoubtedly, to make Arthur rich forever after. That was one course to pursue, the easier, and by far the more profitable. Or he could put the whole matter in the hands of the authorities. There was no profit to be got out of that; only endless worry and exposure and—yes, undoubtedly—and revenge.

"Here is money," he said, turning round, and throwing a goldpiece across to Jan Lorentz. "Go and settle with Baas Wurmers—give him a florin or two—and then get a room in the village. We shall want you, of course, to bear out your statement that your saw Mynheer Avelingh clench his uncle by the throat and kill him. But, mind you: keep a quiet tongue in your head. Not a word, not one word, till I bid you speak. Unless you obey me exactly, you may whistle for another penny of mine."

Jan Lorentz eyed the goldpiece and its giver dubiously for a moment. Then he took up the money, bit it, as if in doubt of its corporeal existence, slipped it into his pocket and slapped his side. It was many months since he had possessed such a sum. His eyes twinkled with delight— possibly with visions of unlimited gin.

He shambled to the door. Arthur followed him and called to the official, still busy at his writing in the outer room: "The man can go, Stronk," he said. "He is a respectable fellow, evidently. I have given him a florin or two to settle with the old publican. Not worth sending up to the District Court, surely."

CHAPTER XIX.

" WANTED."

" I wish I had never begun the whole thing," said Joost dejectedly. "It has brought me nothing but trouble and disappointment from the first."

"It is a good work all the same, and a great one," answered Kees, "and that's my opinion."

Agatha nodded gratefully to her brother. They were sitting together in Joost's room again, and once more the subject of their conversation was the Charity.

It had not gone well with the Charity. In appearance, undoubtedly, things were prospering as they should. The Burgomaster, having once taken up the matter, had carefully nursed his son-in-law's project through all the perils of a Board Meeting, and Joost had in due time been honored with a vote of thanks and an address.

The work of building had not yet begun, on account of the season, but active preparations were already in progress, and the necessary arrangements had been made with various contractors. So far, so good. But Joost, having once been partially enlightened by his father-in-law, perceived but too plainly, how all these concerned in the business were combining to get as far as possible, a maximum of profit out of the concern by reducing the proposed benefit to the poor to a minimum. When everybody—from the highest to the lowest—had received the share he claimed as the price for not betraying his neighbor, it would remain to be seen what was left for the old people. The rules had been adopted "in accordance with the wishes of the beneficent founder," and with some insignificant alterations only, which latter however,—as such alterations will—sufficed to entirely subvert Joost's intentions on several important points.

No wonder, therefore, that Joost considered he had a right to feel aggrieved. He had attempted an impossible thing, and was surprised to find out his mistake. Men constantly strive to keep hold with one hand of what they esteem it their duty to let go with the other. He had been resolved from the first to withdraw entirely from the management of the charity-fund; he refused all honor or influence in connection with it; he sincerely desired that posterity might forget the very name of its founder, and the measures he had taken rendered such a contingency more than probable. And yet he could not bear with equanimity to witness how the money, once out of his control, was used in ways of which he must strongly disapprove. He would have liked to see the whole Charity acting in entire independence of his influence, and yet in exact accordance with his wishes. And now—far from that being the case—the whole thing was being used as a convenient means of putting money into pockets already too full of ill-gotten gains. He might well complain.

"It is a good work all the same," said Kees. "You can't help the misdoings of other men. Charity begins at home in this sense also, that it blesses the giver first, as Agatha said just now. It's quite true, and you'll get your blessing in time."

"My blessing is the last thing I expect to come home to roost," said Joost, a little bitterly. "Nor do I consider I have deserved it. As long as the poor old paupers only get their due. What do you say, Agatha?"

"I can not help thinking," replied Agatha, "that it was rather a pity you ever gave the whole thing so entirely out of your own hands. But that's done now, and past crying for. I am sure you would have managed it admirably, Joost."

"I am sure you would have done all things admirably, Joost," said her husband laughing. "Anything of interest on at the court, Kees?"

"Nothing but endless drunkards and dog-keepers," said Kees. "It's awfully slow work, a little district show like that. What I should like would be a real criminal case to work through from beginning to end, with a regular villain in it. That must brace one up, I should think."

"Unfortunately, regular villains are scarce," said Joost.

Agatha shook her finger at him and laughed.

"You people are about the happiest in the world, I should say," remarked Kees suddenly. "Far too much money; plenty of love; a beautiful place like this; all these good things, and nothing to do but to enjoy them! And now, into the bargain, Joost must go and spend his time in earning golden opinions all over the country, making himself the most popular man in it! Here is the June election coming on, with all the glory it is to bring you in prospective! What more can you desire? I could almost find it in my heart to envy you, Joost, if it were not that Agatha is my sister!"

"Yes," said Agatha quietly, "we have much to be thankful for. I hope, I trust, we remember it."

"The only thing I shouldn't like would be the having

nothing more to be discontented about or to desire," cried Kees laughing. "Oh yes, of course, I forgot," he said suddenly. His florid face crimsoned over. The good-natured fellow looked quite distressed. "There is something wanting, certainly. Oh well, cheer up; that may still come in time."

Joost's eyes met his wife's. A look of love shot into them in answer to hers. He felt very tenderly toward her that night; he could not have told himself why. He got up and kissed her in her brother's presence.

"There is room in house and heart," he said, "and when the angel knocks at the window we shall open *à deux battants.* Till then, what avails it to gaze forth into the night? Enough to know that the issues of life, as of death, are in the hand of God. Come in!"

The last words were elicited by a knock at the door. A servant entered with a note. "From whom?"

"The messenger could not say, Mynheer."

Joost broke the seal; it was wax, flattened with a piece of current money. His eyes ran over the brief contents, and his face expressed blank amazement. Then another look began to creep across it, and he allowed the paper to fall to the ground. He bent down to look for it; felt for it a minute or two, though it was lying just in front of him, and then raised himself again with the missive in one hand. His face was set and calm.

"You need not wait," he said to the servant. "I will let the messenger have the answer immediately. He turned to his bureau, hurriedly wrote a few words on a scrap of paper, ran to the door, then stopped as if a sudden thought had struck him. "Oh, Kees," he said, "would you mind giving the man this for me? They are sometimes so importunate, if one speaks to them one's self. Awfully good of you, if you would go down to him a minute."

"Certainly," said Kees starting up. His brother-in-law pushed him into the hall. "Just see the address is all

right!" he called after him. Kees glanced at the address,
stopped abruptly under the hall-lamp, tore open the paper,
and stood irresolute.

Joost had shut the room-door and come back to his wife.
Once more he kissed her on the forehead. But before he
resumed his seat a fresh thought seemed to strike him.
"Oh, I ought to have told Kees," he cried, once more turning to the door, "that he should"—he closed the door behind him.

He found his brother-in-law still standing under the
hall-lamp, the open paper in his hand. "Come into the
dining-room," he cried hurriedly, "as I told you to do."
He threw open the door as he spoke. A servant was clearing away the dinner-things. "Tell the man down-stairs
there is no answer," he said. "Stop. Give him that." He
threw a small coin across the table.

"What does all this mystery mean?" queried Kees.
He still held his scrap of paper in one hand. It was addressed to him, and inside were written the words: "Wait
for me in the dining-room, Kees."

"Read this," said Joost, holding out the letter the messenger had brought him. On half a sheet of paper these
sentences were traced without heading, signature, date or
any other mark of identity:

"An accusation of the very gravest nature has been
lodged against you this morning. If your conscience condemns you, cross the frontier immediately. You have an
hour's start and will not be pursued too fast. There is no
extradition-treaty with Uruguay."

Kees stared blankly at Joost; then he read the contents
of the note over again; and then he once more lifted
amazed eyes to his brother-in-law's face.

"A hoax," he said at last. "Who can have done it?"

At this moment there came another knock at the door.
Joost started as if the blood-hounds of the law were already

on his track. It was only the servant, returning to continue his work.

"Wait till you are called," cried his master in a passion. He flung to the door and locked it.

"A hoax," repeated Kees.

"I do not think so," said Joost. He took up a dessert knife from the table and began playing nervously with it.

"Not?" cried Kees. "Why, surely you don't mean to say it's earnest? Joost! And what would the accusation be about, pray? You'll tell me you know that, next."

"No," replied Joost. "I don't say that."

"You think it's meant seriously, and yet haven't an inkling what it's all about."

"I did not say that either."

"Let's be practical, Joost; the time they allow you is short enough. Have you any idea what this paper means?"

"No," said Joost—"Unless—" he paused.

"Unless what?"

"If your conscience condemns you," repeated Joost. "A vague term. Whose conscience condemns him not?"

"Not every man's conscience condemns him of grave crimes against the law of the land," said Kees with ready good sense. "Nor does yours, of course. So there's a mistake or slander, or something. Except it be a hoax. Let me look at the paper again."

He took it to a shaded lamp on the sideboard, and studied it carefully. As it happened, he was a bit of an expert in handwriting, having amused himself with graphology at college. His ruddy face grew suddenly white.

"As I live," he cried, "the hand is—yes, though it's evidently feigned—I would swear to it being Doverel's himself."

"Doverel's!" cried Joost. "The public prosecutor's! Surely, he has no reason to shield me."

"It is Doverel," said Kees in an agitated voice. "I see

his handwriting daily at the court. He has changed it for this note. It is he, all the same. Joost—Good Heavens— Joost. If you can understand anything of this, Joost, you've not fifty minutes to get out of the house!"

"And why should Doverel warn me?" said Joost.

Van Hessel, more accustomed to such matters, could have given several reasons, had he been calm enough to do so. His hand trembled. "Joost," he stammered. "My dear fellow, forgive me. Of course you are innocent, whatever the charge may be. I didn't know what I was saying. Of course you will stay quietly here. It is absurd."

"I shall stay," said Joost.

There was a moment's silence after that. Joost continued to play with the knife he held in his hand. He threw it up several times and caught it by the handle. His brother-in-law stood staring at the terrible missive, too amazed and stupefied to give advice.

Presently Joost spoke. "No extradition treaty with Uruguay," he said. "Could I get away yet, I wonder, if I wished to?"

"You could," replied Kees, waking up, as it were, from a dream. "If you leave the house immediately, the police will not pursue you just yet. That is what the letter means. Doverel has his own reasons for doing a man like you a service. But in an hour or so—half-an-hour now—they may be here. Sooner, if the letter has been delayed."

Avelingh walked up and down the great room with rapid strides. There were drops of cold sweat on his forehead. He stopped opposite his brother-in-law.

"I shall stay," he said again.

"Of course," said Kees. "It will all be cleared up in a day or two. It's so extraordinary; I don't know what to say or think. You can't imagine what they may be aiming at? You really can't now?"

Joost threw back his hair from his brow. "No," he

K

said. " What crossed my brain just now was too absurd,
too unlikely. No, Kees, in the sight of Heaven, I have
no idea what the charge can be."

" I thought so," said Kees, heartily. " I mean, I knew
it. Only, of course, one is so utterly amazed and confounded. I can only say again: you must forgive me, Joost."
The two men shook hands.

Another knock came at the door. They shook hands
again, and then Kees went to open it. The servants stammered excuses. Two gentlemen were asking for his master.
He had asked Mevrouw, and Mevrouw had said he must
knock.

" I will go to them," said Kees.

" No," cried Joost, standing at the far end of the room.
" Show them in here."

He had been playing with the silver knife. A moment
ago, however, he had laid it down and taken up a large steel
one in its stead. Playing thus, half carelessly, he had once
or twice made a rapid pass with the shining blade near his
throat. Only a feint or two at the best. Who shall say
what was passing in his mind?

A moment later two strangers entered, grave-looking
men in dark clothes. " Mynheer Avelingh?" said the
elder interrogatively.

" Yes," replied Joost.

The first speaker hesitated, and cast a glance at Kees.

" My brother-in-law, Mynheer van Hessel, Clerk of the
District Court," said Joost.

The stranger looked relieved, but he hesitated still.

" This gentleman may hear anything you wish to say,"
continued Joost.

" Anything?" queried the other with a marked accentua-
tion of the word.

" Anything and everything," said Joost.

" It is an unpleasant task that brings us here, Mynhee"

Avelingh," continued the officer, "but we are only carrying out orders. I very much regret that those orders should have been necessary."

"Do your duty," said Joost briefly.

The police officer seemed to be unfavorably impressed by the fact that his arrival did not occasion more surprise. It was as if he had been expected. And yet such visits as this in a gentleman's mansion were surely unusual, to say the least. He looked from one gentleman to the other and hastily concluded that Joost must be guilty. Policemen are almost always dominated by one hasty impression, and allow themselves to be actuated by that impression alone. Fortunately, their experience insures a fair chance of its being a correct one on the whole.

"My duty," said the man, roughly, "is to arrest you, in the King's name." He showed his badge of office as he spoke.

"And what," asked Joost, "is the charge against me?"

"That," replied the officer, "you will hear later on. Put down that knife, if you please, Mynheer." Joost flung the knife he was holding to the table, with a laugh so fierce that his three companions involuntarily started back.

"What is the charge?" said Kees. "You heard this gentleman mention my quality. I am Clerk of the District Court. What is the charge?"

"If you wish it," answered the officer, in a sulky manner, "I suppose there is no especial reason for my not telling you. The charge is an exceptionally grave one—it's just murder. That's all. There's an accusation lodged against Joost Avelingh for the murder of his Uncle, Dirk van Trotsem—Dirk, Baron van Trotsem, it is, I believe."

Joost began to tremble violently over his whole frame. He felt that all three men were watching him intently, but he strove in vain to steady himself. There was a moment's terrible silence; then, controlling himself as best he could, the accused man hissed out: "Are you flesh and blood, or devils?"

And a few seconds later he added, in a still lower gasp: "Or angels?"

In spite of the sick terror at his heart, Kees wondered at the words. He involuntarily recalled his father's frequent assertion that "Joost was so melodramatic," and he would have smiled, if there had been room in his thoughts for anything approaching a smile, as his eyes turned to the commonplace-looking men before him.

Neither of the officers took any notice of Joost's exclamation.

"I must request you to follow me," said the elder one, "we have a carriage in waiting down-stairs."

"Yes," said Joost. "I understand. I presume I may take leave of my wife?"

"Certainly. But we must be back in town to-night."

"I shall not require long," replied Joost. He turned to his brother-in-law. "Good-by, Kees," he said. "I do not know what you may think, but I can assure you by all that I hold sacred that such an accusation as this never came into my head. When I hesitated just now, it was because a wild suspicion crossed my brain that some dealings in connection with that wretched Charity—but there; I knew the idea to be absurd at once. Such things are not punished. Good-by, Kees. Tell your people at home, and—and"—his voice faltered—"take care of Agatha. I swear to you I never dreamed of the possibility of this; I am as utterly amazed and bewildered as you can be."

Kees Hessel wrung his brother-in-law's hand. The tears stood in the honest fellow's eyes. "I don't doubt it," he said. "It will all be set right in a day or two. Some one's gone mad somewhere, evidently. That's the solution. And till we find it out, I'll fight for your innocence against the world." He ran after Joost as the latter was passing out of the room. "Take plenty of money with you," he whispered. "The more the better. Money buys pretty well everything, nowadays."

Joost crossed over to the study where Agatha was sitting quietly at her work, the tea-things waiting at her side, the kettle singing on its little peat-stove. He was about to shut the door behind him, but one of the officers interposed. He turned fiercely on the intruder. "Excuse me, no," said the man, "the charge is too serious a one. We can not let you out of our sight."

Agatha looked up in mild surprise. "Dearest," said Joost, leading her to the other side of the room, "something very extraordinary, very sad, has happened. Can you bear trouble?"

"Yes," said Agatha, "with you. What is it Joost?"

"And disgrace?"

She hesitated. "Yes," she said again. "Because it would be unmerited. But, oh, darling, what is it?"

"Those two men there are policemen. They have come here with a charge against me. Some one has accused me—of an awful thing—of—of—the murder of my old uncle, Agatha."

"Murder!" she repeated, vaguely. For a moment or two the word seemed to make no impression on her. She clung to him with an anxious, questioning look upon her face.

"Yes, dearest. How the charge is made, by whom—how such a thing is possible, I am striving in vain to understand. It is so. I must go with them to the town to-night, Agatha. Now!"

"Go with them? Oh, Joost!" She burst into tears.

He pressed her to him in silence. "God will take care of you, my own darling," he murmured, at last. "God help me. You must pray for me all the time. Oh, my dearest, that I should bring such grief upon you!"

She lifted up her head from his breast and dashed back the tears angrily. "You will come back to-morrow," she said. "It is ridiculous. They will see you are innocent to-morrow."

The officer took a step forward, and coughed softly. They had forgotten him.

"I am ready," said Joost, turning haughtily. He disengaged himself from his wife's embrace and came forward.

"He is innocent!" cried Agatha, almost defiantly. "He is innocent! He is innocent!"

Joost paused for a moment in the door-way.

"God only knows," he said to himself. In that moment his heart, in its forlornness, went out to his wife in love and admiration as it had never done before.

CHAPTER XX.

"GIVE A DOG A BAD NAME."

THE country was ringing with the news. A man of Joost Avelingh's wealth and position arrested for murder! The thing was unheard of. And although his name only appeared in initials in the papers, according to the queer continental custom, yet everybody knew—on the day after the arrest—who was meant by "an influential inhabitant of Heist, J. A." The provincial paper, indeed, suppressed the news altogether during the first few days, from a laudable, if foolish, desire to maintain the dignity of the higher classes in the presence of the common people, and one or two disreputable society-journals sent interviewers to Agatha to ask her how much she would pay to have the item kept out of their budget (the interviewers were not received, be it said by the way); but the independent radical dailies published leaders — which gave much offense in all Government circles, as they were intended to do—urging the authorities to do their duty, and darkly hinting at precedents which led them to infer that the criminal would get off scott free.

Certainly no one could complain that the prisoner, once arrested, was treated with exceptional lenity. No distinction at all was made between him and a common criminal, even there where it might be argued that similar treatment resulted in actual inequality. At least, such small favors as he could succeed in obtaining were acquired in the strictest secret from the prison warders at perfectly incredible prices, and their existence was vigorously denied in the semi-official newspapers.

He was locked up in a prison-cell and left to himself. When there, he received an intimation that he might select an advocate to act for him, but he was only allowed to see that personage at rare intervals, and meanwhile the secret inquiry into the case—the "instruction" as they call it—proceeded. Dutch criminal procedure is very different from English; it may be generally described—in spite of numerous deviations—as having been modeled very closely after the French. This book has nothing to do with the question which system is preferable, but it must be stated in explanation of what follows, that the foreign investigation starts from the diametrically opposite point of view, as compared with British ideas, that a prisoner, if there once be sufficient ground to arrest him, may safely be presumed to be guilty till you have proved he is innocent, and that, therefore, the one great object always to be kept in view is the criminal's confession, to obtain which all efforts of the preliminary examiners co-operate. On the other hand, the Dutch have abolished all juries. A Court of several judges —varying in number, according to the gravity of the case—

decide on all questions whatsoever. So much it seemed necessary to explain.

The examining judge, then, was using all his efforts to extract a confession from Joost Avelingh. This was the more desirable because of the great scarcity of evidence against the accused. But all threats and stratagems proved equally vain. The prisoner, confronted with the chief witness against him, heard the charge with evident surprise. He was accused of having seized his uncle by the throat and having strangled the old man by tightening the comforter he wore. The evidence of the doctor and the notary corroborated this view, as appeared still more fully at the trial. But the prisoner absolutely and consistently denied it. They had to bring him back to his cell in despair.

In the mean time, Kees Hessel worked for him with unflagging energy. Some little privileges were obtained, as has been said; " it need not be inquired too particularly by what means," cried the radical press. He was allowed to see his wife once or twice; but the interviews—agonizingly painful as they were—could bring neither of them much satisfaction. During the month or two of the weary preliminary inquiry his health broke down visibly. The wretched food, the want of exercise, the anxiety, the harrowing examinations; all these combined to do him injury.

" The prisoner," said the papers, " insolently persists in refusing to confess his guilt."

The opinion of the country went dead against Joost. For much of that opinion, of course, the newspapers were responsible, and these—in so far as they were written for men of the lower classes—attacked, in the offender, the gentleman of position. There was a nervous dread everywhere that he must escape, as so many other men had done before him, or that, even if he were condemned, he would be immediately pardoned. Herein, however, public opinion went wrong. It forgot, or ignored, the fact that Joost, though a gentleman and a man of great wealth, had no patrons or protectors among the influential members of his own class. And he had not. On the contrary, he was generally disliked by the very men who could best have helped him. Many of them had hated him for his hard-working, honest efforts to "curry favor" with the poor, for his great wealth and so-called good luck, for the talents and ambitions and noble desires, which made him so unlike one of them. They rejoiced at his fall, and now kicked him when down.

"That's what comes of being cleverer than your neighbors," said Beau Liederlen. "I always foretold he would come to grief. When a man in our circle has too much brains, he makes a bad use of them, say I."

Kees Hessel, therefore, had a bad time of it. He went from house to house, and from man to man. He was voted an insufferable bore in the Club smoking-room, but a right good fellow all the same.

"Talk of something else, Kees," people said to him. "We'll believe the man is innocent, if you'll talk of something else." In the female drawing-rooms matters were made still more difficult for this special pleader. When he started the subject, he was met by an icy stare, and pause, and then that most cruel crusher of all, a sudden change in the conversation. They thought it bad taste in him to allude to the matter at all, the man being his sister's husband. There was not a woman of her own class, except her mother, who could unbend sufficiently to show Agatha any sympathy.

Only the little dressmakers and milliners, the little servant-girls, and the "unfortunates" spoke and thought pityingly of the woman left deserted and despised in her great mansion. They stopped before the shop-windows where the "portrait of the murderer" hung, and they pitied him too a little, "because he looked so melancholy, and had such lovely dark eyes."

The van Hessel family had enough need of comfort and

sympathy, though they did not get it. The Burgomaster seemed hopelessly crushed by this misfortune, the greatest imaginable in his eyes : disgrace. He grew visibly thinner, his large limbs lessened under his garments till the latter flapped loosely about his frame. His carriage lost all its ancient strut, and a look of unmistakable worry settled on his face. He would have avoided the Club, had not his son insisted on his appearing there.

"We are innocent," said Kees, "and we intend to show it in a few weeks."

It was Mevrouw who at this moment showed strength of mind for the whole family. She calmly accepted the position in which she found herself, neither flaunting her pride in the face of a righteously indignant world, nor abating one jot of it to please those who were eager for her humiliation. No allusion to the matter crossed her lips, except when she once or twice—just at the right moment—feelingly mentioned, " our great sorrow " in passing, or on one special occasion haughtily vindicated the innocence of " one whom all his relations love and admire." She had never cared much for Joost, there was too little sympathy between their characters; nor had she ever advocated his marriage with her daughter, in spite of his wealth, but she stuck to him now in her own cold imperious manner. And to Agatha her heart went out in love and tenderness indescribable. She had hurried up to the Castle immediately, and all through those two terrible months of anxious waiting she stayed with its sorrowful mistress.

Bettekoo's lover broke off the match on account of the undesirable connection. So Bettekoo was sent for to the Castle also, and the three women wept together. And yet, despite their common misery and humiliation, there was not one person in the whole family, after the first frightened amazement was over, who believed in Joost's innocence except Agatha and Kees. Verrooy made himself agreeable to his wife about "the murderer" on every possible occasion, and by asking his children how they liked having a convict for an uncle.

And Agatha? Her servants liked her; they had every reason to do so. They were bound to her by many ties of kindness in the past. They tried to show her their awkward sympathy as best they could. The laborers on the estate, the poor in the neighboring cottages; there were tender hearts enough, eager to weep with her and for her, and many a little token of affection found its way to her heart. But none ever spoke of Joost. "Murder!" It was such an awful thing, and all believed him guilty. She felt instinctively that it was so. And what then did sympathy, however well-meaning, avail her? It was not recognition of her sorrow she wanted, but assertion of his innocence. His innocence against the world! She did not leave the grounds, except to go to church, during all those weary weeks. It was shameless of her to appear there, said the ladies and gentlemen. But what cared she, though her most intimate friends looked away as she passed down the aisle, and though not one hand was stretched out to her in the entry?

The little girl at the turnpike came running to her with her accustomed smile and courtesy, and the child's mother burst out crying as she threw open the bar. And Agatha returned to the Castle, with her mother at her side, and spent a quiet afternoon alone in the beautiful gardens of her desolate home.

And God was very merciful to her. For He tempers the wind.

CHAPTER XXI.

JAN LORENTZ.

THREE gentlemen were leisurely walking down the village-street on their way home from the Club late one evening in April. They were Liederlen, Verrooy, and Doctor Kern.

The village of Heist, though still called a village, is larger than many a country-town. It is surrounded by a number of villas and small gentlemen's seats, and the inhabitants of these villas have built themselves a very comfortable edifice at one end of the principal street, where they can play whist in the afternoon, and *vingt et un* in the evening. Sometimes, when the gambling runs high at night, as it is very apt to do, the Club-lamp will twinkle far down the deserted street till the sun mingles his fresh rays with its sickly light.

It might burn on into the small hours on this occasion for all the three gentlemen knew or cared. They had left the smoking-room at 10 o'clock, as was their habit. Verrooy did not gamble; his wife would soon have stopped that. Liederlen played cards all day, but for the sake of the game. He would have played all night, only he could find nobody to sit down with him, except for high stakes after ten. As for the doctor he did not know the difference between diamonds and clubs.

"I have always contended he was guilty," remarked Liederlen, as they strolled down the quiet street. Of course they were talking of the great case; who ever talked of anything else in Holland that April? "I have always contended he was guilty, and I shall say so in spite of Kees Hessel's bluster. They ought to lock that fellow up too, till the whole thing is over. Here he has been boring us again to-night. And, after all, the whole flood of his eloquence proves nothing, actually nothing, except that he means well; and that did not require proving of Kees Hessel."

"Of course he is guilty," said Verrooy. "And really, that wretched groom might have spoken up ten years sooner and saved us all the disgrace. It will cost me my chance for the Burgomastership of Zielen, and I really thought I had succeeded this time."

"His poor wife," put in the doctor, pulling away at his short pipe with a thoughtful air.

"Nonsense, doctor," cried Liederlen. "Wives must take their chances, and, I dare say she knew all about it. She's had her share of the spoil, at any rate. Why, they won't be able to touch the money, as it is. I never pity a woman with good health and fifty thousand * a-year. Such a woman was never unhappy yet; she couldn't be."

"I am not sure about the guilt," began the doctor timidly. He was a nervous, thinking man, who did not like to enunciate combative opinions.

"Oh, come! come!" cried both his companions.

"I was present at the preliminary proceedings, you see," the doctor went on quickly. "Of course that's all a secret, and I am a principal witness, unfortunately enough; I would have given my best skeleton to keep out of the matter, still I may say this much that if I were a judge and a medical man in one, I should not attach too much importance to the testimony of the witness who's supposed to prove the whole thing."

"Jan Lorentz!" cried the others.

"Yes, Jan Lorentz."

"Why, van Asveld says it's convicting," remarked Liederlen. "He says that when he first heard the fellow describe what he'd seen, he felt as if he were actually pres-

---

* About £4,000.

ent. The story is most exact, it appears, and the Notary bears it out."

"Van Asveld is free to have his impressions as I am to have mine," said the doctor. "And my impression is, though I cannot prove it to be the correct one, that man Lorentz is both a feeble-minded and a foul-minded personage. He is very shrewd in one way, as such persons often are, and the juge d'instruction evidently believes thorougly in him. It remains to be seen whether the judges will, when the actual trial comes on. I should say he drinks, though this is between you and me, for I've never seen him in any way the worse for liquor during the examinations. But, still I should say that he drinks. I should even say that he has probably had delirium tremens once or twice. I wish I could examine him closer."

"Even if he drinks," said Verrooy, "that proves nothing as to his veracity. He wasn't drunk when he sat in that dickey ten years ago."

The doctor shook his head. "Whatever his faculties may have been," he said, "they're not to be trusted now. He had a good brain once, and that makes the struggle all the more intricate. I wish the judges would order an inquiry into his mental condition and put in some man thoroughly capable of judging. I wish they'd let *me* have a look at him. But there he stands, quite calm and collected, and gives his evidence, and it all goes down like melted butter."

"Well?" said Verrooy. "What more can you want?"

"I should like to see him an hour or two after he's given his evidence," said the doctor quietly. "I should like to know what his brain was like when the tension was past."

"As for drinking a glass too much now and then," remarked Liederlen. "Why, the charge might be brought against many veracious people—van Asveld himself, for instance."

The doctor looked over his shoulder with a quick, half-frightened movement. "Take care," he said, "van Asveld was to come after us. He only stopped to finish his quarrel with van Hessel."

"He does drink too much at times; I am sure of it," said Liederlen.

"He may," said Doctor Kern. "I have no opportunities of judging."

"Joost Avelingh did not drink, not he," sneered Verrooy. "All proper and respectable, and too good to play whist, and so on. Only a little murder now and then, just to show you he had foibles like other men."

A quick step was heard behind them. "*Quand on parle du diable on en voit la queue,*" said Liederlen. "Here van Asveld comes."

"I can't imagine how he can walk so quickly, with the weight he has to carry," remarked the doctor.

"Weight! I should think so," quoth Liederlen. "Nigh on a hundred kilogrammes, and the house of van Asveld and all its fortunes into the bargain! Well, Asveld, who had the last word? Ten to one you can't guess what *we're* talking about!"

"*Rira bien qui rira le dernier,*" said Arthur, as he came up. "Van Hessel will sing a different tune next week. I hear the trial comes on next Tuesday."

"So much the better," grumbled Verrooy. "We shall have it over."

"So much the better, undoubtedly. We shall hear the truth at last," said Liederlen. "I have been thirsting for authentic news all these weeks. They ought to make the preliminary inquiries public. Why, the whole country is clamoring to know particulars, and nothing has transpired. I envy you, doctor; you ungrateful man for complaining!"

The doctor only replied with an emphatic "Humph."

"I hear seats are at a premium," remarked Arthur. "As you say, the whole country is in a ferment for news. That comes of all the preliminary secrecy."

"It is said one or two ladies applied for cards," put in Verrooy, "but we don't quite see the desirability of admitting them, just yet, over here."

"It's a pity, I think," cried Arthur. "I should have had his wife and mother up to see the show. To see the scoundrel standing there with his smooth dark face and lying away his soul. It will be a sight worth gazing on. They have not got him to confess as yet. It's my opinion they never will. The pious, silky villain."

"You are very certain of his guilt," remarked the doctor.

"Certain! I would stake my name on it! Who can doubt it! I could find it in what is left in me of a heart to weep for the poor old gentleman."

"Your soft-heartedness does you credit, sir," said the doctor gravely.

"Yes, damn it; your soft-heartedness does you credit," sneered Verrooy. "And your uncle—cousin—what was it? —ought to have taken it into account in his will, van Asveld."

The all-absorbing interest of their conversation had led these gentlemen when they reached the bottom of the street, to turn and once more saunter up it. As they passed under the light of one of the few widely scattered lamps, a man, who had been fumbling at a street door, shrank back into the shade.

"Who's out at this hour?" laughed Liederlen. "Go to bed! Go to bed! Can't be respectable."

The doctor was nearest to the individual in question. "As I live, it's Jan Lorentz," he said, stopping short. "Good night, Lorentz."

"Goo'—nigh'," said a thick, unsteady voice in answer.

"I thought so," said the doctor quietly. "Drunk!"

"Drunk!" cried van Asveld, with an oath. "I don't believe it! Not a bit of it!"

"You need not," said the doctor.

They stood in a half circle round the wretched creature cowering against the door-post. He had visibly started at the sound of van Asveld's voice, and seemed very much terrified. He stammered something about "Come again next—hic—morning. Too late now. Goo' nigh'."

"Here, I must talk to this fellow" said Arthur, in an agitated voice. "Don't wait for me! *Au revoir!* See you to-morrow."

"I should like to have examined this subject," began the doctor.

"Oh, examine him some other day," interrupted Arthur. "Do, please, leave me alone with him. Do, my good Doctor, go home before it gets so very late."

"Yes, yes," cried Verrooy. "Don't let's loaf about here. It's quite time we were back. Come along, Doctor; you go my way."

The doctor, always unwilling to oppose, allowed himself to be led away, and Arthur found himself alone with the tipsy man, face to face in the dark, desolate street.

"You *are* drunk, you scoundrel," he said fiercely.

Jan Lorentz could not summon up impudence enough to deny the charge, but he seemed inclined to resent the form in which it was made. He scowled at his accuser in a very ugly manner.

"You swore to me," said van Asveld, violently, "that you would keep steady till this business was over. After that you may drink up the whole devil dissolved for aught I care. But you swore you would not touch a drop during these few weeks. You know you did."

"Yes," murmured the drunkard, "so I did. And so I will. I haven't had a drop till this evening. And I won't

L

again. It was only just once, so help me—; and my throat was just simply burned up."

"Damn you," said Arthur, angrily, as he turned on his heel.

"Damn me!" muttered the drunken man to himself with another tipsy "hic." "It looks very like it at present, but it won't be your doing, my fine master; no, nor your preventing, but just my own choosing; worse luck."

He began fumbling at the door again, making vain efforts to open it with what was evidently too small a key. He might have continued this labor indefinitely, but suddenly the door was thrown open from the inside, and a flood of light, and a flood of shrill feminine eloquence, poured out upon the bewildered being. His landlady stood before him, in undress and a furious temper.

"And this is how you come scraping and scratching at the door in the middle of the night, is it?" cried the lady, "as if you hadn't a key to let yourself in by, every bit like a dog rather than a rational being, and talking and quarreling outside in the dead hours of silence, waking up honest people that were in bed and asleep, as you ought to be. You ought to be ashamed of yourself, Mynheer Lorentz, though I say it, who never was." The good lady having wound up her oration with this rather enigmatical finale, opened the door wide, and stood on one side, candle in hand, to let her lodger pass.

He stammered a few words of excuse, and lurched up against her in his anxiety to keep on the further side. She saw how matters stood at a glance, and immediately, contrary to his expectation, the springs of her eloquence dried up.

"Aha," she merely snapped, in a tone pregnant of vague terrors in the future. "Drunk! we shall see! So *that's* the kind of lodger the Jonker van Asveld recommends to people as thoroughly respectable. We shall see."

"It's no use talking to a drunken man," this wise woman used to tell her cronies. "For it only hardens them. And so you go and spill all your powder before you had need to use it at all, you see. Now, take my advice and wait till next morning, when all the drink has gone out of them, and then, the lower they happen to be, the hotter you give it them. Once you get them under your thumb that way, and you can keep them there a month—with management. With good management, of course. Don't I know. Didn't I have seventeen years of it with my good husband; God rest him? And wasn't he as sorry the last time he got drunk—and he so weak, he spilled half of it, but he managed to get drunk all the same—as the first? Almost, at any rate; and that's saying a good deal, I can tell you, neighbor. You look at other families, and find out if it isn't. But you bully them when they're in liquor, and the liquor gives them impudence to fight it out."

"It was a pity of that good stuff your husband spilt," said the neighbor. "Was it gin now, Juffrouw Kaas?"

Jan Lorentz stumbled up the stairs in the dark, with one or two muttered imprecations. He was furious with van Asveld, whose overbearing manner was beginning to gall him excessively. He was still more furious with himself for having sinned again after several weeks of abstention.

"You don't get a candle from me," his landlady called after him, "and you may just go to bed as best you can."

He closed his door with a grin and a scowl, and sat down heavily on a chair by the curtainless window. Jan Lorentz was not a bad man, but he was a culpably weak one. He knew that, and the thought, while it caused him real sorrow, broke by its very existence such strength as he had.

He had been respectable enough once, when he was a groom in the Baron van Trotsem's stables. The son of that gentleman's coachman, bright, brisk, and good-looking, he had even been reckoned among the élite of the young men of the neighborhood. He had flirted, more or less harmlessly, in various quarters, and had so early acquired the reputation, easily acquired among that simple peasantry, of being a little wild. Then had come, a year or so before the Baron's death, the great ruling influence of his life, as it proved, when he fell in love, heart and soul, with pretty blue-eyed Dientje, a maid in the van Hessel family. But Dientje, who was thoroughly respectable, and a bit of a prude, with her pink print dress and stiff, frilled cap, refused to have anything to say to a young man with "antecedents." A year of hopeless courting followed, and then the death of the Baron intervened, and Jan, turned off with the other servants, drifted away to Amsterdam in search of work. He got a fresh place there, and, Dientje proving inexorable, he fell into bad company and, unable to resist a coachman's constant temptations, began at intervals to take a glass too much. The rest was sufficiently easy—the devil takes care to keep his roads in excellent order ; the best surveyor in all creation is this old gentleman who limps himself—and Dientje, now maid to Mevrouw Avelingh, when she sometimes heard sad stories of " that drunken fellow, Lorentz," would plume herself upon her own discrimination and receive with a smooth little smile the congratulations of her circle of middle-aged spinsters, all as respectable, as primly dressed, and as stiffly capped as herself.

Jan Lorentz had a grudge against Avelingh, an exaggerated grudge, which increased the more he was dissatisfied with himself, for we all like to have our scapegoats. He was angry with the young master for having turned off his uncle's servants, in spite of the generous manner in which it had been done, and he attributed to this measure his removal to Amsterdam, his separation from Dientje, and all his subsequent misfortunes. The more he felt those misfortunes, and the more he regretted them, the more eagerly he turned from awkward self-reproach to abuse of Joost Avelingh.

He had almost begun to believe, that, but for Joost Ave-lingh, Jan Lorentz would have been a happy and an honourable man.

He sat himself down, half tipsy, half sobered, and stared out of the window. He did not like the midnight sky, it gave him vague impressions of heaven, and darkness, and the life beyond. The room in which he sat was a poor one, but neat and clean. On a deal chest of drawers, among two or three untidy articles he had thrown down there, stood a small portrait in a common faded plush frame, the portrait of the woman he had loved, the woman he loved still. It was a coarse photograph, done at some country fair, all pale now and brown and stained. It had never been like her; it was least of all like her now. It was altogether an ugly, vulgar object, and no one who looked at it would have said that it represented a pretty woman. But it was the one thing in all the wide world toward which this poor creature's soul still felt tenderly. The woman up yonder at the castle, living on and changing slowly with the impressions of ten long years, had passed out of his life; he had never seen her; he could not tell what she was like, by this time, in mind or body; but the photograph, individualized into a separate existence, remained with him still. It was the photograph he loved and cherished : the symbol of that pure, pretty, eighteen year old maiden, who had said " No " to him so demurely under her father's apple tree in the time when life was young. And it was from that love that perhaps some day, if ever, in the far future, the regeneration of this man's whole being might go forth. He sighed heavily.

"Is it worth while?" he asked himself. The question had kept coming up in his mind again and again during the last few weeks, and each time he had answered " Yes," though with varying emphasis. " It means money," he said, " plenty of money. And plenty of money means respectability. And if I'm once again respectable, I shall turn over a new leaf, for I'm an honest fellow still in spite of adverse circumstances, and, perhaps, some day I may go up to the Castle, and if I find Dientje still to my taste, well, she might have changed her mind, and who knows? But I must have money first, to come with. No use going to the girls without that. And I sha'n't drink any more."

It was the great dream of his life, intermittent, but constantly recurring, " to be respectable once again." And no poor wretch in whom that aspiration lives can be utterly lost.

CHAPTER XXII.

THE TRIAL.

The Court was crowded. Any one could have foreseen that this would have been the case ; and accordingly ticket-holders had begun to form up in line almost an hour before the doors were opened. As for the ticketless, their chance seemed of the smallest. Yet there was a great, gaping, chattering crowd all down the wide road and on the opposite side of the canal. Policemen in glittering helmets were keeping a path clear for the carriages that drove rapidly up. The crowd chaffed the occupants, and, if it could be done while a constable's back was turned, some wretched little street-boy would even try to raise a laugh by pitching a paper pellet or a handful of dirt into an open landau. For the street boys, tiresome everywhere, are—it must be admitted with regret—almost ungovernable in the larger cities of Holland. Drunken with the national wine of freedom which has always been poured out so generously in this favored little corner of Europe, and unable as yet to moderate their transports, school children and hobble-de-hoys are often a lamentable trouble to the quiet, respectable people who love to go their way in peace. And there is no doubt that at some not very remote period the question of the liberty and license of the streets will have to occupy the attention of the wise men who seek to govern Holland without ruling it; or better still, perhaps, of those home legislators who, by the fiats of public opinion, could do so much to settle the question, and perhaps might even now willingly do so, if nineteenth century philanthropy had not decreed so remorselessly that the boxing even of the wickedest, thievingest street boy's ears by any but the constituted authority is such a severely punishable offense. The human ear—even of the humblest of God's creatures—is a far more sacred thing than any rich man's apples, or white pants, or silk carriage cushions. And it must be protected accordingly—while the apples and carriage-cushions are not. For it is difficult for the constituted authority to catch a street boy. Philanthropy is the same all the world over. And it is a very beautiful thing. But the street boy is pretty much the same also. And he is a nuisance.

This, however, is a digression hardly warranted by the fact that the ragamuffins of a certain large Dutch town were amusing themselves in their peculiar manner on the morning of the great murder trial. After all, pellets are harmless things—happy the man who got nothing worse! But there were other things to occupy the thoughts of the crowd. The trial itself was naturally on all lips, and in all ears. The opinion of great and small, rich and poor, was unanimously against the accused. The mere fact of his being a gentleman proved his guilt to the crowd. No gentleman was ever accused of crimes unless he had really committed them, and the pity which one might naturally mete out to a poor man and brother, victim of plutocratic legislation, was changed to execration and righteous vindictiveness now the criminal was himself a plutocrat. It had got known, besides—and the fact had been widely disseminated by all the papers from an early stage—that the murdered man had been the murderer's protector and benefactor from his infancy upward; that he had fed, clothed, nurtured, and educated him, and had made him his heir. As a return for this life-long benevolence the nephew had killed his uncle so as the sooner to possess himself of his inheritance, and he had in reality enjoyed that inheritance during ten long, guilty years! When the melancholy prison-van made its appearance, yells of hate and fury rent the air. Agatha heard them, waiting with a sick yet prayerful heart in a hired room close by the " Palais de Justice ; " the prisoner heard them as he sat in his little, carefully locked box. They drove him under a covered archway and shut the gates. There were hundreds of men in that surging, ragged crowd eager to strike him to the ground, hundreds of women who, if once he lay there, would not have hesitated to trample on his heart. The case had somehow got hold of the popular imagination, and public feeling ran high.

Inside the building the sentiment against the accused, though more refined in its expression, was not a whit less strong. The great hall was filled to overflowing with men belonging to the upper classes; all the seats reserved for persons of distinction were occupied by those who had a full right to be so designated ; the lawyers were passing into their particular quarters; the representatives of the press were quarreling for a seat. There was not standing-room by the time the judges filed in, trying to look as important as possible in their long black robes. The case, being one of so grave a nature, had come on before the Chief Court of the Province. The hall was wide and lofty, full of light, and even cheerful. The judges sat in armchairs behind a green table on a dais at one end of it, with a great statue of Themis above them holding her scales awry. To their right was the public prosecutor, also in his robes, and opposite him the clerk of the Court. Immediately below the dais stood the bench for the prisoner, who had his counsel near him, though out of reach of his hand or voice. Behind the prisoner, again, sat the witnesses.

The judges being seated, the preliminary rustle died away in a few nervous coughs, a laugh here and there, the fall of an umbrella, and then a gradually deepening silence. In the hush the voice of the President was heard, low at first, declaring the sitting opened. The inevitable formalities were gone through amid evident impatience, and a whisper arose every now and then above the monotonous voice of the clerk. Then the case was called. Two thousand pairs of eyes were directed to a little door near the dais; and several policemen brought in Joost Avelingh.

He stopped for one instant in the doorway, and cast a swift glance over the sea of faces turned toward him. And in that brief moment it seemed to him as if he had taken in the expression of each individual countenance. He had seen his father-in-law looking utterly dejected; he had met Kees van Hessel's anxious, wistful gaze; and braved Arthur van Asveld's arrogant, confident, and contemptuous one. He had faced hundreds of wrathful, scornful eyes on every side, and felt as if torrents of hatred were pouring down on him from all directions. The feeling had left him calm, almost indifferent. He was accustomed to the dislike of his own class. One thing indeed had moved him strongly, it was that yell of hatred outside the walls. For a man with Joost Avelingh's love of admiration and need of affection that experience was one of more than endurable bitterness.

The prisoner passed to his bench, bowed to the President, who took no notice of the salutation, and sat down. All through the proceeding his demeanor was, of course, most closely watched. It did not give satisfaction. Once or twice he shrank back, as if in pain, and people said he was cowardly; once or twice he looked calmly round, and they complained he was impudent. For the most part he sat immovable, with his arms crossed over his breast, and his dark eyes fixed on the presiding judge.

The act of accusation, as they call it, was read, a lengthy document, quite a small book in itself, setting forth the whole story of the crime as it presented itself to the mind of the public prosecutor—the Advocate-General, to give him his proper title. This document—really nothing more than a written brief against the prisoner—attacked him with violence from the very first, and ascribed to him, besides the crime now actually under consideration, as many more as it could conveniently insinuate. The man thus accused appeared to listen with great composure. The audience, however, at least the non-legal part of it, got impatient, and began to whisper in friendly ears that the same thing might have been said with half the words in a quarter of the time. But the slow, monotonous drone went on as if it would never come to a conclusion. It did so, nevertheless, unexpectedly; the President nodded; somebody coughed; and soon after the examination of the prisoner began.

In Holland, as in France, there is no examining or cross-examining of witnesses by the bar, the general impression being that the lawyers' object on such occasions is too often not to guide a witness into telling the truth, but to confuse him into telling a lie. The presiding judge examines, and he alone. It is true that the public prosecutor and the prisoner's counsel may suggest the putting of some particular question, but young barristers are loth to avail themselves of that privilege, for the President is very apt to take such suggestions amiss, as implying a lack of ability in him with regard to the conducting of the case. Both systems appear to have their advantages, and their disadvantages.

The prisoner stood up to be examined. As he did so, even his enemies—and who but Kees Hessel was his friend in that large concourse?—even his enemies acknowledged the dignity of his bearing. He might be nervous afterward under the statements of some of those called to give evidence against him, but in his own answers he was firm and collected. The attitude he assumed was insolent, said the lawyers, for he admitted everything but the crime itself. Only the evening before a last desperate attempt had been made to force a confession from him. It had failed, and the failure was resented accordingly.

"Your name?" said the President.

"Joost Avelingh."

"Your profession?"

"I have none."

"You have no title of any kind? No university degree?"

"None."

"No occupation?" The President, a red-faced little man, leered at the prisoner over his round spectacles. Joost smiled—a bitter little smile.

"I am a member of the Council of Management of some ten or twelve charitable societies," he said, "and on the Board of some half-dozen Industrial Companies; that is all."

"Yes," said the President, "I know. You have found charity a convenient cloak to hide a multitude of sins."

Joost's soul flinched, if that expression be permissible. The outer frame stood calm, erect and stately; the eyes were gazing at the statue of Justice above the little President's head.

The usual questions followed, and then a closer inquiry began into the circumstances of the crime itself.

"You admit," said the President, "that the Baron van Trotsem, your uncle, took you into his house when you were a destitute orphan of five, and that from that moment until the day of his death, he fed, clothed, and educated you, and that finally he appointed you his heir?"

"Yes," said Joost.

"Did you know during the Baron's lifetime that his will had been drawn up in your favor?"

"I had reasons to suspect it from frequent allusions which he made."

"Had you, in spite of all you owed him, any cause—in your own opinion—to dislike the Baron van Trotsem, or to feel a grudge against him?"

"Yes," said Joost in a distinct voice. "We did not get on well together, and he made me very unhappy." He refused to see the anxious signs his advocate was covertly making him. The poor man desisted in despair.

"That is vague," said the President, "and unsatisfactory. Were there any special grievances which you could bring forward?"

"My uncle," replied the accused, "had resisted my wishes whenever he could do so. He had refused to allow me to take up a legal career, and had insisted on my studying medicine without any adequate reason. He had forbidden me to marry the lady who is at present my wife, also without in any way explaining his action in that matter."

"Ah!" said the President. People looked at each other. It seemed as if the President's portentous exclamation was echoed from every lip.

"Many a man," continued Joost's examiner, "has been compelled—by his very affection—to resist youthful desires, to choose another profession for a son or ward, to deny his consent to an early marriage. In such cases the 'reasons' usually appear 'inadequate' to the sufferer. Are these all the offenses you charge your uncle with?"

"I charge him with nothing," replied the prisoner, "I answer your questions as best I can."

"And you admit that you hated him?"

"Yes," replied Joost softly.

Once more quick glances were interchanged. The counsel for the defense cast up his eyes to heaven and folded his lean hands over his black robe.

"On the evening of your uncle's death you had had words with him?"

"I had."

"And you knew, when he ordered his carriage, that he was about to drive to the Notary to alter his will?"

"I did."

"You knew you were bringing him there, and that it was his intention to disinherit you in case you married the Freule van Hessel?"

"Yes."

"He had told you so expressly?"

"He had."

"And you killed him before he could reach his destination?"

"No." Joost's voice rang out clear and full.

"That will do: Prisoner, you may sit down."

After that the witnesses were called, the witnesses for the prosecution; there were none for the defense.

Jan Lorentz gave his evidence brightly and decidedly enough. He deposed to having heard the Baron's threats and insults, and he declared that he had wondered how flesh and blood could stand them. His evidence exculpated the prisoner to a certain extent, but at the same time it made his action seem all the more probable. His account of the events of the evening flowed on smoothly till it reached the description of the moment when the crime was committed. Here the witness faltered, contradicted himself, stopped.

"Take care," said the President sternly. "You repeatedly stated in the preliminary inquiry that you saw the accused seize his uncle by the red neckerchief he wore. That statement is fully corroborated by the evidence of the Jonker van Asveld, who says that you first made it to him when you were arrested on a charge of vagabondage, thereby causing him to communicate with the necessary authorities. Do you maintain it now?"

The witness looked round nervously at Joost Avelingh, then at van Asveld. His eyes wandered rapidly over the glass ceiling of the hall back to the President's face.

" Yes," he said.

The impression, at the conclusion of this witness's evidence was unfavorable to him, but still more so to the prisoner. From the clumsy attempts he had made to " say a good word for the accused," and from his hesitation over facts he had stated plainly on earlier occasions, it was evident to every one who could put two and two together that the man had been tampered with by the murderer's friends. Money, you know, will do a good deal in the world, and this Lorentz is but a poor devil, they say.

The Notary described the arrival of the chaise with the dead man at his house. He created a great sensation by solemnly affirming that the red comforter was drawn into a tight knot round the neck of the corpse, a knot so tight indeed that it must, in his opinion, have been purposely tightened. The prisoner was once more called forward.

" Can you explain the tightness of the knot round your uncle's neck ? "

" No," said Joost.

" While he was lying in the chaise in that condition—dying—that, at any rate is *in confesso*—what did you do to relieve him ? "

" Nothing," said Joost.

He felt the absurdity of the answer, even while he made it. There was not a man in the hall who believed him on this point—not even Kees Hessel.

" You may sit down," said the President.

The Notary continued his account. It ended with the recital of the prisoner's last words that fatal evening. " When I told him the Baron was dead," said the Notary, " Mynheer Avelingh broke out into a wild cry. ' I knew

it!' he shrieked. 'I would give the world it were not so.'
That was all he said at the time."

"Can you explain that exclamation!" asked the President of the prisoner.

"I do not wish to do so."

"You will scarcely pretend, I suppose, that it was caused by grief for the loss of the man whom you regarded—as you have just admitted—with feelings of such strong aversion?"

"It was not," said Joost.

After that came the doctor, who was vague and undecided, as it is the nature of many conscientious medical men to be—of none more so than Doctor Kern. There were signs, he admitted, which pointed to strangulation, but as it was certain that the dead man had previously had a fit of some kind, it was almost impossible to say whether the tightening of the comforter, which accounted for the symptoms alluded to, had occasioned death, or had perhaps merely accompanied, or even immediately succeeded it.

"You mean to imply," said the President, "that the Baron might, judging from the condition of the brain and heart, have died before the neckerchief was drawn tight?"

"That may have been so," said the doctor. "Immediately before."

"On the other hand, the tightening of the neckerchief may have been in itself sufficient to cause death?"

"I can not say," replied the doctor. "It depends first on how tight it was drawn, secondly on how long it had been tightened before the Notary loosened it; thirdly on the appearance the corpse presented immediately before, and immediately after the unfastening of the knot. I did not see the corpse till half-an-hour later, and there was no post-mortem examination. I can not say."

"But you must say, sir!" cried the little President pettishly, "the whole case turns on it."

" Then God help the prisoner, Mynheer the President. If my evidence and Jan Lorentz's be all the proof against him, God grant him a good escape."

" Silence ! " cried the President, " you were not asked for any such expression of opinion. Step down, sir."

The Jonker van Asveld was next called. He described his first interview with Lorentz. He also bore witness to the bad feeling existing between Joost and the Baron. He spoke affectionately of the latter. People pitied van Asveld and sympathized with him. He had behaved very well they said.

It transpired in the course of the examination that Arthur had received money from Joost. The whole story of the legacy came out, to the amazement of the audience.

" Prisoner," said the President, " can you explain how you came to give such an enormous sum as forty thousand florins to the witness, merely because he asked for it ? "

" I considered it my duty to do so," said Joost.

" Ah, conscience is a wonderful power," said a clergyman to his neighbor, " no rest, you see, no rest."

The Court adjourned at this stage of the proceedings. There were three men in it, at that moment, and three only, who did not believe the prisoner guilty; they were Kees Hessel, Joost Avelingh, and Jan Lorentz.

Criminal cases do not take long in Holland, when once the stage of publicity is reached. The hardest work has been got through in the long and careful inquiry, which may be looked upon as a full rehearsal for the grand representation. And there was no insurmountable mass of evidence on this occasion. The witnesses had been heard before the luncheon recess; the pleading would take place immediately after. The case might be concluded before nightfall. All but the verdict, be it understood; that would not be pronounced till a week later.

They locked the prisoner in a cell, while waiting for the Court to reassemble. Joost Avelingh felt relieved to find himself again alone. He had spent several weeks in almost continued solitude, broken only by the rare visits he received, chiefly from officials, and the inquiries held from time to time by the Juge d'Instruction. After the long stillness of that narrow prison the blinding light of the great judgment-hall, the continual movement of such a mass of human faces, had strangely disconcerted him at first. He was almost glad to be back again in the shade and the silence. He sat down on a coarse wooden bench and reviewed the morning's proceedings as best he might. He could not shut his eyes to the fact that matters had gone very much against him. And no doubt it was true, as his counsel had told him in passing out, that his own evidence had done most to damage his cause. "If you are condemned, Mr. Avelingh," the lawyer had said, not without a shade of bitterness in his tone, "and there is every reason to fear you will be, you will have yourself to blame. It would have been better to confess altogether, than to confess as much as you have done, and then deny the rest."

"I have confessed the exact truth," replied Joost Avelingh.

The other shrugged his shoulders. "That is often the unwisest thing of all," he said.

And now in the quiet of this little cell the accused again told himself that he had done right. Self-deception there may have been in his conclusions, but they were undoubtedly sincere. No man need incriminate himself, he reasoned, but no man may tell a lie. I have answered each question put to me according to my inmost conviction; I need not answer questions they do not put. The charge against me is utterly and irremediably false, and I plead "Not guilty" with all my heart and soul.

Strange to say, these last weeks since his arrest had been in many ways the happiest of all his life. There had, of

M

course, been the cruel sorrow of the sorrow his wife was enduring for his sake, but when he put the thought of that
away from him, his heart gained strength and happiness
from the struggle he was passing through.   This story
trumped up against him, was a lie, and the battle with the
lie, by throwing the reality temporarily into the shade, and
crushing it down out of sight, brought him a sense of relief
and of rest which he had not known for many years.   He
accused himself now of morbidness, of hypersensitive con-
scientiousness; he laughed at the thought of his own former
doubts and fears.   This was what men punished; this, what
the world called sin.   And he a fool, a dreamer, he worried
his brain about little things!   He turned on one side on his
hard prison pallet and slept till the warder awoke him.

Such had been his thoughts.   But now, while waiting
there in the interval of his trial, he first began to realize
what condemnation might mean!   He shuddered at the
idea, and once more his mind reverted to Agatha.   He knelt
down on the stone floor and prayed God to have pity upon
her.   And then the blue-coated officials came with their
bunches of keys and led him forth again.

As soon as the Advocate-General had got through the
opening sentences of his address to the judges, it became
apparent to all present that it was exceptionally hostile to
the prisoner.   Joost Avelingh himself felt that, with growing
conviction, and bent forward in an attitude of anxious inquiry.   It was terrible to think what opinion this man must
have formed of him.   Was it but the expression of the
thoughts of all around?

The Advocate-General painted in glowing colors the
benefactions which Joost had received from his uncle in a
long course of years.   He represented the boy as taciturn
and undutiful from the first—there was evidence enough
to prove it—and the old man as violent and headstrong
undoubtedly, for so old men often will be, but kindly and

well-intentioned on the whole. He described the crime which had been committed—of the crime itself there could be no doubt—as entirely attributable to cupidity, resentment, and youthful passion. For the latter, he said, some excuse might certainly have been found—the accused had most probably truly loved the woman he afterward married—but that excuse disappeared before the fact that there was evidently as much cupidity as love in the motive which actuated the murderer. And if love was a noble passion, and even lust perhaps a palliable one, cupidity, the sordid desire of an old man's gold, was the lowest, the most demoralizing of all. The crime was an exceptional one. The guilty man belonged to a class in which criminals were rare—not because the men of that class were better than others, but because they had less temptation to transgress. The victim was an old noble, a person of great wealth, rank and consequence; he had been foully and secretly murdered by the viper he had taken to his bosom. During ten long years the malefactor had enjoyed all the fruits of his horrible deed, and in that period he had sought to procure for himself a reputation for charity—and perhaps, who knows?—to lull his guilty conscience to sleep by lavishly dispensing his ill-gotten treasures. But at length the slow step of Justice had tracked him, for her advance is sure, if slow. The crime, truly, had been as was said, exceptional. The punishment of this generous, gentlemanly, God-fearing parricide must be exemplary and exceptional too! A slight burst of applause, suppressed immediately, greeted the conclusion of this eloquent harangue.

What could the counsel for the defense—himself convinced of his client's guilt—bring forward in reply? He tried, as best he could, to disarm the evidence of Jan Lorentz; he pointed out the discrepancies in the doctor's professional statement; he reproached the Notary bitterly for not having given information earlier to the police if he con-

sidered the circumstances of the death at all suspicious.
He attacked that Notary with a vigor which showed that
he was seeking a safety-valve for his pent-up feelings. He
would not be so angry, said the old lawyers, shaking their
heads, if he did not feel that his was a losing cause.

As for his client, the advocate did not say much in his
favor. He felt that he could not. Something got up into
his throat and choked the words down. But he could
truthfully and conscientiously assert that in his opinion the
so-called legal evidence which the Dutch law demands had
not been sufficiently produced and that therefore, whatever
men might think for themselves, the judges, as judges,
must acquit a man whom they could not legally convict.

"My client has declared his innocence," said the Counsel," and the law has not succeeded in establishing his
guilt. If he sinned, he sinned alone in the darkness, and
in the darkness his deed has remained. And sin, ere the
law can touch it, must lie red and glaring, an offense to
all who tread the highway, in the resistless light of day!"

A voice from the gallery called out "Jan Lorentz!" in
allusion to the words "alone in the darkness." There was
another burst of approval. Joost Avelingh, for the first
time during the long trial, hid his face in his hands.

It was growing dark when the Court rose. They were
lighting the street-lamps. Outside, a turbulent crowd still
waited, eager to get a glimpse of the prisoner, hoping to
hear something of what was going on inside, if it were only
the latest news of the proceedings. A broad stream of
black-coated gentlemen flowed out and mingled with the
populace. Everbody was discussing the events of the day,
the attitude of the prisoner, the statements of the witnesses,
the address of the Advocate-General. The black van again
rumbled under an archway, amid the disappointed hootings
of the roughs. The prisoner got into it. He was less
calm and firm now, it was said, than at the beginning of

the trial. His courage seemed to be giving way. He had asked, immediately on coming out, to be allowed to see his wife. The verdict would be given, as usual, after an interval of a week.

<hr>

CHAPTER XXIII.

THE TURNING-POINT.

" YES, I've done it," said Jan Lorentz, " I've done it, and now I want to know what I'm to get for my pains."

" You had your regular indemnification as witness, hadn't you?" said van Asveld with an awkward laugh. " If not, you can still apply for it."

" Don't humbug me," cried Lorentz fiercely, " you'll be so good as to give me a definite answer to-day, Jonker."

" Don't shout in that way," said Arthur. " I'm not deaf, and, if I were, it would be better to carry on our negotiations in writing than to yell at each other in this manner. I do not as yet know what negotiations need take place. What do you want of me?"

" What do I want of you?" repeated Lorentz in wrathful amazement. " Why the money, of course, which I was to have for giving my evidence."

" Let us understand each other," said Arthur, sitting down at his table and measuring imaginary lines with a ruler which lay there. " You were in possession of certain facts which it is in itself a legal offense not to communicate to the authorities; you alluded to them in the course of an interview with me, an official interview, mind you, and I, of course, having received your information, in my official capacity, passed it on, as I was bound to do, to the Public Prosecutor. That functionary examined you; he could not well act otherwise. In due time the case came on for trial, and you appeared in it as witness. So far, all seems plain, and there is nothing unusual. For which of these successive developments—all growing out of each other, it appears to me, as the leaves of a plant—if you understand so poetic a simile—do you expect to be exceptionally rewarded?"

Jan Lorentz looked mystified. "I want my money," he said doggedly, after a moment's pause. It seemed the safest thing to say.

"Would you," began Arthur again, smiling sweetly, "oblige me by answering my first question before we proceed any farther?"

"Jonker, I don't care. You promised me my money, and I must have it. You promised that you would pay me for giving my evidence. You very well know you did."

"As you will not answer my question," said Arthur in a tone of gentle complaint, "I suppose I must continue without knowing your opinion. Now, here the personal consideration comes in—" the stout Jonker rubbed his hands. He was not as has been said, a particularly bright personage himself, and he therefore intensely enjoyed intellectually mastering this ignorant creature—"the personal question comes in. For reasons of no further import to any one but myself I have special cause to regard Mynheer Avelingh with disfavor and I cherish the memory of my—venerable, let us say—venerable, uncle. I therefore take a peculiar, and perhaps abnormal, interest in this confession of yours, and to express the satisfaction I feel at your having done your duty, simply your duty, mind you, the duty of every honest citizen, I obtain your release from custody by myself paying off your damages, and—"

"And?" said Lorentz, his eyes growing bright and cunning again.

"And you reward me, you scoundrel, by asking for more!"

Lorentz was thoroughly taken aback by this unexpected conclusion. "You promised," he stammered again, "you know you promised to give me more than Mynheer Avelingh ever did. Not that Avelingh ever gave me anything!"

"By your own confession, then," said Asveld coolly, "if those last words be true, I have already redeemed my promise. But, look here, you needn't think that a man of my rank will deny his word to a poor beggar like you. I told you I would give you money, as you say. I was a fool to do it, and really I can scarcely account for my behavior now. I was very excited—but that is neither here nor there. Money you shall have."

"How much?" said Lorentz.

"One can see you are not accustomed to do business with gentlemen. On the day of the verdict, if it goes against Avelingh, as it certainly will, I shall give, although as I say, you have done nothing to earn them, but because I have passed my word in a moment of excitement, I shall give you a hundred florins."

"A hundred florins," repeated Lorentz slowly. "Pooh," he suddenly said.

"Do you mean to say, damn you," cried Arthur in a sudden fury, "that you consider the sum too small?"

"Pooh," said Lorentz again. Yet at the same time he began to tremble violently from suppressed excitement, which his enfeebled frame was unable to support.

'Damn you twice over," cried Arthur, in a still louder voice. "Get out of the room this instant before I knock you down-stairs! Get out, I tell you!" He ran round to the door and threw it wide open. Lorentz shrank back. He was frightened. He was not a man to threaten, but there was a look in his eyes which well might have made Arthur pause and parley. But the Jonker—all his pride up in arms at the insult his generous offer had received—and, really, in making it he had been moved by a magnanimous impulse to redeem a promise thoughtlessly made—the Jonker pointed haughtily to the door. Jan Lorentz crept cautiously past him, and slunk slowly down the stairs.

"Disgusting," said Arthur to himself, as he shut the door. "What are these insolent beggars coming to, I wonder? Here do I, hard-up as I am, offer this man a present of a hundred florins, merely out of a conscientious desire to keep my word to him, and look what I get in reply. And surely, I owe him nothing. I may have said that morning: 'I would have given anything,' or 'half the world,' or something of the kind; I really don't remember. People use such expressions every day. And the idea of taking one at one's word. Half the world indeed! It's as much as I can do to keep my tailor in a fairly good temper and persuade him to let me have a new coat."

So reasoned Arthur van Asveld, not altogether unfairly, and threw himself down on a sofa with a yellow-covered novel in his hand.

The man he had so ignominiously dismissed, walked slowly down the village street toward his own home. There was an angry look in his eye and there was fury, red and raging, in his heart. He was not accustomed to feel strongly—his soul had lived in a thickening haze for many years—and the very violence of his emotion alarmed him. One thought was beating at his brain: this van Asveld had cruelly wronged him, and he was unable to retaliate. And before the wrong so suddenly made apparent, his bright daydream of future respectability seemed to vanish into space. Worse than that, he had sold his soul for gold, and found himself defrauded of the price. For Arthur, looking at the question from his point of view and entirely unconscious of any foul play, it was perhaps not unnatural to conclude, that he owed the man nothing but a reward which his excited promises had rendered inevitable. But to Lorentz who regarded the matter in quite a different light and believed himself to have been inveigled by van Asveld into statements he would never otherwise have made, it seemed that nothing but wealth almost unmeasured could make good such a sacrifice of peace.

He stumbled on then with a fierce, ungovernable fury at his heart, largely made up, though he knew it not, of remorse and despair. He hated Arthur. But he was powerless to hurt him in any way. He was equally powerless to undo the wrong he had done. And so, to the end, he must continue to serve the Jonker's purposes, and be laughed at, after all, for his pains. He was angry; he was glad he was angry. He thought with a dim foreboding fear, how miserable he would be when the anger passed away. At van Asveld's bidding, or persuasion, call it what you will, he had abstained from drink almost entirely of late. The more fool he! He resolved to do so no longer. He would have a drink that night—" a regular good one "—and that would put a little strength in his veins. It would warm up his hatred of his enemy, too. Yes, that would be the best thing for the moment, a " regular good, thundering drinking-bout ! "

The mere idea seemed to invigorate him. He turned down toward the shop over which he had his room. He was in a mood which would either drive him to the devil forever, or rescue him on the very brink of the precipice.

As he entered the shop, he saw that a woman was standing at the counter, talking to the mistress of the place. Both were crying. At least, the one whose back was turned to him had her handkerchief before her face, and Juffrouw Kaas, his landlady, was also allowing the great tears to course slowly down her fat, red cheeks. With Juffrouw Kaas weeping was a cheap luxury, to be enjoyed as often as a rational occasion presented itself, sorrow and joy being alike available, although sorrow was decidedly preferred.

The sorrow of others, of course. That goes without saying. It was so much more thrilling and emotional than joy.

Lorentz was about to find his way up-stairs, as was his wont, with a surly "good evening" to the shop-woman, when she stopped him with a little cry of delight. She often stopped him—or tried to do so—because he was the best authority upon the great trial and could give the latest news. She was proud of him on that account and had made peace with him in spite of various little deficiencies she would never have borne in any other lodger. She often told herself he should go as soon as the trial was over. But till then he was well worth keeping. He gave her quite an important position among the numerous gossips of the neighborhood. She was "Jan Lorentz's landlady" nowadays, almost more than Juffrouw Kaas.

"Why, here is Jan Lorentz himself," cried the good Juffrouw. "Oh dear! Oh dear! Mynheer Lorentz, this is Mejuffrouw from the castle. And oh dear, dear, to think of the sorrow up there! It's terrible to think of!" And Juffrouw Kaas fell to crying again.

The woman by the counter took her handkerchief from her eyes and turned round quickly. Jan Lorentz found himself gazing upon the same countenance which had lived on in his dreams all those years. It was but little changed; a trifle rounder, perhaps, and fuller; that was all. The same prim, innocent expression; the same pink cheeks and clear blue eyes. These latter were dimmed with tears at the present moment, but their owner looked all the sweeter in her sorrow. It was Dientje.

"And oh the agony up at the Castle," cried Juffrouw Kaas. "Oh my dear Dientje! My dear Mr. Lorentz it is heartrending to think of it!" She burst out crying afresh, and Dientje, who had kept her eyes till then fixed immovably on her former lover's face, also suddenly buried them afresh in her handkerchief.

Jan Lorentz gazed at her for one moment, and then, turning, fled up-stairs, as fast as his shaky legs could carry him. He reached his garret in safety and there, throwing himself down on the bed, he sobbed like a little child.

CHAPTER XXIV.

DAS EWIG WEIBLICHE ZIEHT UNS HINAN.

It was true, as Juffrouw Kaas had said, that the grief at the castle was heartrending. But if that worthy woman had seen it, she would probably not have emitted any such opinion. It is far more likely that she would have remarked on the coldness and indifference of these rich people who sit silent and sleepy while their husbands and sons are being dragged away to prison. And she would have tried to picture to you some conception of her own sorrow, if any similar misfortune had been possible in her case. But, thank Heaven, no; hers was a respectable family. "Though, really, no offense to you, Dientje, for Mr. Avelingh was always as pleasant-spoken a gentleman as ever I came across."

The agony through which Agatha Avelingh passed during that final week of suspense was too awful for utterance. She bore it, then, almost silently, and, but for an occasional pressure of the hand or look of affection, even her own mother scarcely dared to express sympathy. In such a terrible crisis as this what could words, however tender, avail? They spoke sometimes for a few moments, in a half-frightened whisper, of the incidents of the trial, or of some circumstance which concerned the case. But both women seemed to be afraid of stirring the depths of their sorrow. It was a relief to Agatha to weep with Bettekoo over her minor troubles, and they talked freely together, and frequently, of the faithless lover.

On this particular evening they were sitting in Joost's room around a lingering fire, for it was the end of April and the days were still chilly. Agatha, somehow, liked to spend most of her time in that room, in spite of the pain which each familiar object caused her. She preferred passing the hours there in silence, working at some trifle that occupied her fingers and let her thoughts go free. It would have been better, perhaps, had she thrown herself into a full stream of continued effort, as Joost had done when his troubles overmastered him. She admitted it to herself, but she could not find strength to begin. She had striven, and with partial success, to occupy her thoughts in the previous weeks, but during this last period of suspense between the trial and the verdict, anxiety—breathless, heartbreaking anxiety—conquered every other impression. And this evening—the evening before the decisive day—she sat by the fireside with Joost's belongings all around her, and, as she bent over her crochet, her whole soul was with her husband in his prison-cell.

Kees Hessel had come up to see his mother and sisters. He joined them frequently of evenings after his day's work was over. And they would sit and talk of many things, while thinking of one. And if Kees could bring a whisper from the outer world, however insignificant, which seemed to turn the faintest current in Joost's favor, he would spread it out before them, and they would reason over it together, till it looked like a mighty wind that was bringing them hope and good news. They talked of the trial openly every now and then, when the tension became unbearable, and strong feeling broke through the dyke.

Kees was telling a long story now as he bent toward the fire with outstretched hands, of the comical courting of a young man of their own circle, who, having heard that the girl he was enamored of, had a weakness for gingerbread, had sent her the whole of her name in great gingerbread letters: Sophia Dorothea van Duivenvoorden, a cartful of honey-cake. They were laughing at the story with what small courage for laughter they had. Even Agatha smiled a wan little smile.

"And they say," concluded Kees, "that she ate it all up in a month, a letter a day from the first to the thirtieth, and then, having no more gingerbread on the thirty-first, accepted him in the course of that morning."

"Kees," said Agatha, with her eyes on her work, "will they condemn him?"

"I don't know," replied Kees, staring at the fire. "I daren't say, Agatha. I daren't hold out any false hopes to you. Things are very much against him."

"Have you then heard anything new?"

What could he say to her? They had been telling at the Club that afternoon that the judges were unanimous. So much had leaked out, as such things will. It was hardly likely that they would be unanimous in a resolve to acquit him.

"There are always rumors of various kinds afloat on such occasions," he replied uneasily. "It's no use worrying you with all that people conjecture. But I can not deny that we must prepare for the worst."

"Oh, Kees, he will be condemned!" she said, and she dropped her face on her hands.

There was silence in the room for some minutes. Mevrouw van Hessel made a movement as if to go to her daughter, but sank back in her chair again undecided.

Agatha looked up, "And when he is condemned," she said, "it will be on the evidence of Jan Lorentz."

"Not on that alone, Agatha. That would not suffice."

"No I know," she said, a little impatiently. She was going over the ground in her mind again for the hundredth

14

time. "Of course they must have the other witnesses to complete it. But you yourself think, Kees, do you not?—" She turned to him with a sudden appeal in her eyes—"that the legal proof of the deed has not been furnished?"

"I do," he answered. "I have said so dozens of times to whomsoever will hear me. And it's my opinion, but people think me a fool."

"But the judges may share that opinion? He may get off on that score, even if the world still thinks him guilty."

Kees shook his head doubtingly. "He may," he said.

"But he will not!" cried Agatha. "And yet, if Lorentz's evidence were not there, he could never be condemned! There would be no talk of legal proof at all!"

"If it were not for Lorentz's evidence," said her brother, "there would never have been any case at all. There would have been really no proof, legal or otherwise. The others merely complete his story and give it an air of probability. They furnish the judges with the necessary pretext to condemn the accused on what is practically the testimony of one witness. Hundreds of men are judged in that way. It's all fair and square as a rule. You can't let every murderer go free who hasn't invited two friends to come and see him do the murder."

"When he is condemned," said Agatha, "it will be on the evidence of Jan Lorentz."

"Well, yes. Have it so, if you will, though that's not the way we lawyers put it."

"And this man says," Agatha went on after a short, thoughtful pause, "that he saw Joost clench his uncle by the throat and strangle him with a neckerchief."

"So he says," replied Kees.

"He lies, Kees."

"I have no doubt of it, dearest. If I did not think he lied, I could not believe Joost to be innocent, as I do from the bottom of my heart."

"Yes, he is innocent," said Agatha, aloud, to herself. "Let us never forget that that is the great consolation. Oh, mother, if he were guilty, it would be unbearable."

"Doctor Kern and I were talking about it only this afternoon," remarked Kees. "The Doctor has veered round a good deal lately. Not about his evidence; he sticks to that, as indeed he easily can, for it may mean everything or nothing. But about Lorentz. He believed in Lorentz quite at first. Now, however, for the last week or so, he has altered his opinion. He has been watching him closely, and he tells me he thinks the man is playing a part, or telling a got-up story. Money may be at the bottom of it. Nothing else well could be, one would say. I have sometimes wondered whether Arthur van Asveld, with whom the whole thing began, can possibly—but no, the idea is too absurd. Besides, van Asveld couldn't pay the price usually charged for a villainy, even if he wanted to. No, no; it's a mysterious business altogether."

Agatha started up. "I must go and see this man," she said. "Mother will you go with me?"

"My dear girl," cried Kees in alarm, "what are you thinking of? It would be no manner of use! Only bring you fresh trouble."

"This man," said Agatha, "swears he saw my husband do a thing I know he did not do. I must find out why he swears it. I have often thought I should wish to see him and ask him. I have put it off till now, but, somehow, the thought of—of to-morrow gives me courage. Let us go at once."

"I think it is unwise," said Kees. "It is only exposing yourself to unnecessary insult. Let me go, if the thing is to be done, though I do not see what you expect to gain by it."

"No, no," cried Agatha. "I must go. I have resolved now to see him. And mamma will accompany me. Ring the bell, Kees, and tell them to get a carriage ready."

Kees obeyed her. No one could contradict her well at this moment, or cause her the most trivial unnecessary displeasure. Her maid was sent for, but the answer came back that Dientje had gone up to the village, it being her evening out. Mevrouw van Hessel quietly got her own and her daughter's wraps, and in another twenty minutes they were bowling swiftly along the road to Heist.

Kees Hessel had been able to tell them where to find the man they were in search of. The carriage took them to the Burgomaster's, and from thence the two women walked a distance of some fifteen minutes along a still country road. It was barely half-past eight when they turned into the village-street.

They reached Juffrouw Kaas's little tobacco shop, and Agatha entered first. A thick gray veil she wore completely hid her face. She stood for a moment irresolute by the counter. The little shop-bell tinkled on.

It brought out Juffrouw Kaas in a great hurry. Lady-customers were naturally an unusual thing with her. The good woman's face was redder than ever, but she had dried her tears.

" Does a person of the name of Jan Lorentz live here ? " Agatha was beginning. She stopped in dismay. Through the open glass door she saw her maid sitting near a cosy tea-tray in the snug little room at the back of the shop. Fortunately her mother caught sight of the girl at the same moment and rapidly signed to her not to betray them. Good Juffrouw Kaas looked from one to the other with evident curiosity.

" Jan Lorentz is my lodger," she began. " Do the ladies wish to speak to him ? If so, I will run up and tell him ? "

" No," said Agatha. " I could not think of causing you that trouble. We will go to him. He is in his room, you say ? It is at the top of the house ? "

"Oh, Mevrouw, it is not a place for ladies like you! And who knows but he may have been having a drop too much again. He offends in that way just a little occasionally. I must admit that he does. I was not aware of any such thing, you may be sure, Mevrouw, when I let him have my room."

Agatha could not repress a slight shudder. But at the same time, she passed to the steep staircase at the back of the shop and began to mount it without further parley. Her mother followed her. They could trust Dientje.

"I must request you," said Agatha, stopping on the stairs and raising her voice purposely so that the maid might hear, "not to follow us. It is unnecessary. The door on the second story to the right, you say? Thank you. I wish to speak to this man alone."

Dientje was naturally tingling all over with curiosity. But she would keep Juffrouw Kaas downstairs now, all the same.

The two ladies groped their way up and found the door. They knocked; a gruff voice bade them enter. There was a little fumbling to find the door-handle at the dark stairhead—you could not call it a passage—and then Agatha opened the door and walked in. Her mother followed her.

The garret was dark but for such light as came in through the curtainless window from a clouded moon. A man sat on a chair, cowered up somehow, with his arms on the back, and his head in his arms. He did not look up. He thought it was Juffrouw Kaas, come to prattle about to-morrow.

"You are Jan Lorentz?" said Agatha, pausing near the door.

He started at the strange voice. "Yes," he said, getting off his chair and standing awkwardly beside it. "Yes, I am Jan Lorentz."

N

Agatha took a step forward into the dim room. "And I am Mevrouw Avelingh," she said.

He staggered back and reeled backward, clinging to his chair. "What do you want with me, Mevrouw?" he stammered forth.

"I am Mevrouw Avelingh," she continued, speaking hurriedly as if she were afraid to trust her own voice, "the wife of the man who is to be condemned to-morrow. He will be condemned on evidence which you have given. And I am come to ask you why you gave it, knowing it to be a lie?"

He stood staring at her. Even in the semi-darkness she could see his wild eyes. She faced him, throwing back her veil so as to see the better and speak the clearer. Her fair face seemed to gather toward it all the scattered rays of light in the little room.

"For you knew it to be a lie," she went on more hurriedly still. "And you know this very evening, sitting here alone in the darkness, that it is a lie you have spoken before man and before God. I ask myself how it is possible that you can abide thus with your own thoughts in the stillness of the coming night, that you can go to sleep, to rest, with the thought upon your heart of what you have done, of what you are doing still. Tell me, do you sleep?"

"What do you know?" murmured the wretched man, sinking back on his chair. "What do you say? What do you mean?" She came yet more forward into the vague light of the window. Her face, with its aureole of golden hair, standing out from the dark indistinctness of her clothing, seemed to him like an angel's, without corporeal frame. Mevrouw van Hessel stood back in the shade by the door.

"How do you sleep?" repeated Agatha, vehemently. "Can you sleep? I do not speak to you of the misery, the utter, unfathomable ruin you are bringing upon the innocent man, upon me, his wife, upon us all who love and cherish him. I do not wish to dwell upon them. They must be present with you night and day, in your dreams, in your waking thoughts for, after all, you are a human being and have a human heart, even although—but no, I am not come to reproach you. You must be too miserable to need any reproach from me. And as for *my* cause, for my husband's —oh, however I long to obtain his deliverance, I would leave it in the hands of the God who has said : ' Vengeance is mine ; I will repay ! ' "

She stopped a moment, but it was only to gasp for breath. The bowed and broken man before her gave a faint groan but never moved.

" It is of yourself I would speak," said Agatha, softly. " Of your own hopes, your fears, the conscience that lives within you. Why do you do this thing ? All the misery it is bringing upon others ; all the misery it has brought and still will bring upon yourself—is it worth it ? You are young still, like the man you injure. You suffer already. I can see it ; I thank God for it. He is more merciful to you even now than you know. But the twinges of conscience you feel at this moment are as nothing to the remorse which later years will bring. As the years pass on, carrying this brief life away with them, as you grow older and wearier and see pleasures fade away in air which now still attract you, as you watch death and its awful certainty of judgment draw-ing nearer, miserable man, what an agony will be yours ! " Her voice faltered. She steadied it. " I tremble," she went on, " when I think of the future you are preparing for me. It is almost too horrible to think of. But I tremble yet more, when I turn to the future you are preparing for yourself, even on this earth, and in the eternal retribution be-yond. I dare not let my thoughts dwell upon it. Oh God, have mercy upon this most wretched man ! " She burst into tears.

" I plead for myself," she said more calmly, as soon as

she could speak. "So be it. I have a right to claim my due. And I tell you that you have lied, and still lie, in the sight of Heaven, that you are lying away a good man's, an innocent man's whole life. I *can not* ask what are your motives. Whatever they are, they shrink away too miserably into nothing before the horror of your deed. Men tell me you want money. Poor fool, had you come to us, we could have given it you! Poor fool, had the world's wealth been offered you, it would not have been worth the agony which God Himself has already set gnawing at your heart. What are you seeking? Happiness? Pleasure? Enjoyment? They will go from you forever with the setting of to-morrow's sun!"

Jan Lorentz raised his head. "Go!" he said, huskily. "Go! Whoever you are, have mercy upon me! Go! I can't change anything now. It's too late."

"Oh let me plead with you," cried Agatha—so near that her clasped hands almost touched his shoulder. "For myself, if you will, and for you! For you, most of all. You are delivering over my husband to an earthly tribunal. You will see him stand there to-morrow and, knowing him to be innocent, will see him condemned. And for me that means many years of suffering: thirty, forty, perhaps, if it be God's will, but they will end, and God will approve us innocent. But you—you are delivering up yourself; yourself, your own heart and soul that you love, the eternal within you; you are delivering up yourself—perhaps in thirty years, perhaps in forty, perhaps in an hour from this moment to the judgment-seat of Almighty God!"

There was a ring of real grief in her voice and even of compassion that thrilled through the poor villain whom she addressed. She believed what she was saying with all the strength of her being. She pitied him. In the midst of her own terrible anxiety and sorrow, she pitied him, even him, the man who had wronged her so cruelly. He felt it with a pang

of inexpressible shame. He believed what she was saying to
him; his own heart's experience already bore it out. His
anger had died down from the moment he first saw his old
love once more looking at him. The tears, long strangers
to his eyes, had left his heart strangely tender. And now
there came surging in upon it all his fear and disappointment, all his misery and remorse. His past life lay open
before him, like a desert devoid of fruit, and the future
seemed to rise beyond it, black and vast with eternal doom.
It was more than heart of man could endure. He started
up with a despairing shriek. Its echo rang for many days
in the ears of his two hearers. And as he uttered it, he fell
heavily forward on the floor.

The shriek, piercing, as it did, through that quiet little
house, brought up the two women who had sat wondering
till then in the little back-parlor. Juffrouw Kaas had ceded,
much against her will, to Dientje's entreaties that she should
remain below and not trouble the unknown ladies, but those
entreaties had required renewal, as it was, almost every five
minutes, and now, when that cry broke the stillness, the
landlady was half-way upstairs before Dientje properly realized that she had left the room. So the maid rose and followed her.

The man lying evidently unconscious, Mevrouw van Hessel's practical energy asserted itself. She knelt down by
him and raised his head immediately; she would have got
him on to the bed with her daughter's help, had not
Juffrouw Kaas come running in before she could do so.
Juffrouw Kaas had certainly made a pretense of knocking
at the door on her way, but she had not paused one instant
for an answer. " I thought murder was going on here,"
she gasped, with her fat hand on her ample bosom. " Oh
dear ladies. I thought he was murdering you!" Juffrouw
Kaas had never run upstairs so fast in her life.

As she choked over the words a moonbeam, emerging

from a cloud, fell full into the little room. The sky was clearing. In the bright light the fat little tobacconist immediately recognized the Burgomaster's wife. She dropped a courtesy. "Mevrouw, the Burgomaster," she said in a low voice. "Dear, dear, to think of it! Mevrouw, the Burgomaster!"

Madame van Hessel rose from her knees. She took hold of the amazed Juffrouw by her fat shoulders and walked her incontinently out of the room. Dientje stood on the landing, uncertain what might be desired of her. Mevrouw called her in, and then shut the door and turned the key upon Juffrouw Kaas.

"We can't have any extra, unnecessary trouble," she said. "Heaven knows we have quite enough already without that."

Together the three women moved Jan Lorentz on to his bed, and Mevrouw van Hessel, producing a small scent-bottle, rubbed his forehead and hands with eau-de-cologne and water. After a few moments he moved, heaved a deep sigh, and opened his eyes. They rested immediately on one of the three faces anxiously bending over him. "Dientje," he said in an awe-struck whisper. She shrank back. An expression of such anguish came into the sick man's face that Agatha, putting her arm round her maid's waist, once more gently drew her forward. Jan Lorentz lay still, gazing at her for several minutes. To her they seemed hours. At last he said, still in a very feeble voice: "I forget how it was. I think I must have fainted. I think it was an angel told me not to sin against God, and I was frightened."

It sounded almost childlike in its simplicity, coming from that guilty man. No one disturbed his thoughts, and gradually the truth came back upon him. "I have been dizzy like that once or twice before," he said, "and my brain goes round. It's the wretched drink. Oh, God, if I could escape from the drink! It has made a devil of me."

"No, no," said Agatha. "Do not speak like that! Oh, let me tell you! There is pardon for you! There is mercy! Oh mother, how gladly I would speak to him, if it did not seem as if I were goading him on to destroy his own earthly happiness, that my husband's and mine might be saved."

Jan Lorentz did not seem to hear her. He was lying with his old love's hand clasped tight in both his own.

"The angel was right, Dientje," he murmured. "I believe that God sent her to me. I must not be my own accuser before the judgment seat of God."

CHAPTER XXV.

THE VERDICT.

"Silence!" cried the usher, settling his broad orange scarf as he spoke. The presiding judge took up one of the documents lying before him. A nervous thrill of expectation ran through the vast concourse. The prisoner knitted his eyebrows slightly. It was noted with some surprise that Kees van Hessel was not present, as he had been all through the day of the trial.

The judge began to read the verdict in a shrill voice, full of abortive attempts at impressiveness. It was a long document, comprising several folio pages and giving, first an accurate summary of the facts of the case, and then a full exposition of the legal consequences the deed must involve. Seven minutes were spent over the descriptions in the first part; the President cleared his throat and coughed solemnly as he turned over page after page. At last, however, long after every one was tired of hearing facts enumerated which most men by this time had unwillingly learnt by heart—at last the legal part of the document was reached. The Presi-

dent laid down the paper and blew his nose. Then he
glared round at the expectant crowd before him, took off his
spectacles, wiped them, resettled them carefully over his
eyes, glared round again at the public and resumed his reading. The prisoner uncrossed his legs, and then crossed them
again. Much of what the President read was a repetition
of the address of the Advocate-General on the day of the
trial. The same charges of ingratitude and avarice were
brought against Joost. Full attention was accorded to the
testimony of Jan Lorentz, the principal witness. It was
supplemented by that of the Notary and the Doctor. And
taking all things into consideration, and reckoning that the
motives for the deed and the circumstances immediately
connected with it, everything, in fact, but the actual com-
mission of the crime—had been confessed by the prisoner,
the judges came to the conclusion that they were justified
in declaring that the necessary legal evidence had been supplied, and on the ground of that evidence, and all that had
come to their knowledge in connection with it, they found
the prisoner " Guilty of Murder."

CHAPTER XXVI.

AFTER THE VERDICT.

As the concluding sentences rolled forth sonorously
from the President's lips, a commotion, which had been
increasing for the last few minutes at the entrance to the
judgment hall, assumed such proportions that it attracted
attention from those who sat higher up. People began to
look round and to cry " Hush ! " One or two of the judges
themselves looked across, and the youngest of them, bending sideways over his armchair, spoke to the colleague who

sat next to him. The President looked nervously to the right and left, out of the corners of his eyes, but read on, his rubicund face growing purple. He had reached the last words of the verdict; the declaration of the prisoner's guilt had already passed his lips; nothing now remained but the sentence: "Find the accused to be guilty of murder," read the President, "and accordingly—"

"Stop!" cried a shrill voice from the back of the hall. "Stop! Stop! Don't sentence an innocent man!"

The President involuntarily checked himself and glared over his paper. All eyes, even the prisoner's, were turned in the direction of the principal entrance. Men started up from their seats; those at the back jumped on to the benches and looked over their neighbors' shoulders. In the confusion one or two chairs were upset with a crash; exclamations of sudden irritation or curiosity broke forth on all sides. A wave of hushed sound and checked movement passed over the vast assembly. Men were restraining themselves still under the influence of the place and the occasion, but the decorum of the court of law was broken for the moment. The prisoner—his view obstructed by those who had risen behind him—sank back on his wooden bench and shielded his eyes with one hand.

"Silence!" said the little President, in high indignation.

But no one heeded him. For all were gazing at the lanky figure of Jan Lorentz, struggling with two policemen, just within the entry.

"No, no!" cried Jan Lorentz, in the same shrill, excited voice. "Let me speak while I dare. He is innocent! I have lied against him! Let me speak!"

"Let him speak!" cried a chorus of voices from various parts of the building. The President's renewed call for silence was overborne in the protest. Even the judges who sat next to him were agitated by a human curiosity, which induced them to half rise from their chairs. A knot of gentlemen round the combatants by the entrance forcibly rescued the man, who was struggling and shouting with what weak strength he had, from the hands of his assailants, and bade him go on to the front in God's name! And others in the body of the hall, alternately making way for him and pushing him forward, bore him up on a wave of excitement to the very feet of the President. He arrived, gasping for breath, his shabby clothes torn, his face white and haggard, his eyes staring in front of the dais, by the side of Joost Avelingh.

The President was an old man. He had grown gray in the law-courts. But he had never seen such a sitting as this. And he was at a loss how to act. In his anxiety to preserve his own dignity and that of the Court, and yet at the same time to do no injustice nor offend public opinion, he hesitated altogether, and looked from one colleague to the other.

" Let him speak ! " cried one or two voices again. It was simply curiosity that actuated all present.

Jan Lorentz, standing there, with his gaunt frame thrown forward, his lean hands clasped convulsively round the railing, to the left of the prisoner, the whole man trembling with emotion and struggling to find utterance— Jan Lorentz availed himself of the President's momentary indecision, and in the sudden silence he began to speak. He poured his words forth in short, rapid sentences, hurrying on, as a man hurries who does not trust himself to finish what he has begun.

"It is false!" he panted, "my evidence! He is innocent! I did not see it! I did not say it! I did not wish to! The Jonker asked me! And he said I had said it! And it was all a mistake! And no one let me go back! And I hated Mynheer Avelingh! But he is innocent!"

The young judge at the further end, forgetful of all

propriety, started up and ran around to the President. The one between them also turned his head, and a hurried confabulation took place. The President made a rapid sign of assent, and addressed the man standing before him.

"As you have said so much," he squeaked, frowning severely, "you may as well say more, and explain, though you can not excuse, your most unseemly interruption. What have you to tell?"

"I never saw Mynheer Avelingh draw the handkerchief round his uncle's throat," replied Lorentz more collectedly. "No, so help me God; all the time I was looking through the glass in the hood I never saw him touch his uncle at all."

"Man!" said the President impatiently, "take care what you are doing. Justice does not allow herself to be played with. If you have received money to come and tell this story, you are not only a scoundrel but a fool."

The President was not a shrewd judge of men, despite his position. For it did not require much insight to perceive that this one was undoubtedly sincere.

"I am telling the truth," cried Jan Lorentz anxiously. "I am, at last! I can't help it! Oh gentlemen, for the love of God in Heaven, don't make it harder for me than it is."

A murmur of sympathetic approval ran through the hall.

"Do you mean to say," asked the President, "that you, fully realizing the consequences of what you are doing, persist in your declaration that you have borne false witness in this court in the case of the Crown against Joost Avelingh?"

Lorentz began trembling violently. He supported himself against the balustrade by an effort, and slowly gasped out—

"It is true. Yes."

Low as the words were, there was scarcely a man in the hall but heard them, amid that breathless silence.

"And Avelingh is innocent?" cried a voice from the gallery.

Jan Lorentz bowed his head in acquiescence. It dropped forward on his hands.

The Counsel for the accused started up. "I give notice of Appeal to the Supreme Court," he said. He scarcely knew what he was saying. How could he remember he had no right to say it then?

A shout rang through the hall. Then another! And another! Men started up on the benches and chairs again, and waved their pocket-handkerchiefs, and cheered. These phlegmatic Dutchmen, roused out of their habitual apathy, broke forth in an enthusiasm they would have been ashamed to confess. It was too wonderful, the awful certainty, the sudden hesitation, the rapid light and shade! And now the deliverance! The hearts of the spectators boiled over. They cheered. They scarcely knew whom they were cheering; Jan Lorentz or Joost Avelingh?

The President rose, purple with passion. "This must end," he cried, "immediately! Arrest that man! I suspend the sitting! Clear the Court!"

After all, nothing was proved as yet; nothing was even changed. The judges, to a man, disbelieved this improbable story. The witness had been tampered with; or he was mad, or drunk. He would retract to-morrow, and get off with a comparatively mild punishment for contempt of court.

But the public thought differently. One of those inexplicable, unreasonable waves of feeling which perplex those who govern nations swept suddenly over the vast crowd that had been present at the scene just enacted. The reaction was the greater because of the opprobrium which had been heaped on the prisoner. Without pausing to ask whether Jan Lorentz's statement really did away with the charge against the man already condemned as a murderer, the mul-

titude, full of the unexpected words: "He is innocent!" acquitted him in its own mind, and would have released him
where he stood. Some confused account of what was going
on inside the building spread rapidly to the thousands outside, and the foolish cry, "Long live Joost Avelingh!" once
started, no one knew how, was taken up and repeated again
and again by the populace. Gentlemen of high position
pressed forward round the prisoner, as he was being led away
in custody, and shook hands with him. Kees Hessel, who
had come down with Jan Lorentz, struggled toward his
brother-in-law and threw his arm around his neck.

"I knew you were innocent, Joost," he sobbed, "but I
did not expect to hear others repeating it! You are innocent! Hear them! You are innocent!"

"God alone knows," said Joost Avelingh.

CHAPTER XXVII.

AVELINGH v. AVELINGH.

SEVERAL weeks elapsed after Jan Lorentz's confession,
none of the principal actors in the tragedy could ever exactly tell how. Joost Avelingh had been taken back to his
cell, there to await the result of the action brought by the
Crown against the perjurer. For the value of the latter's
retraction must be carefully tested before the appeal in the
earlier case could come on. The Magistrates—the legal
world generally—were of opinion at first, that the witness's
original story was the true one, and that the explanation he
now gave had been put into his mouth by the friends of the
murderer. And to the objection that he would then be lying away his own liberty, they merely replied that even that
sacrifice might easily have been made worth his while by

people who were as rich as the Avelinghs. To obtain such
a result, a man or woman possessed of millions would willingly spend hundreds of thousands in any case, and many
a man, especially a young one, would gladly undergo several
years of confinement with the hope of a fortune at the close.
It was a difficult matter. If the man stuck to his statement, it would be impossible to convict Avelingh, even
though the judges might feel confident the statement was a
false one. But the proceedings for the charge of perjury
must, in any case, come on first.

This was the opinion of the authorities and the legal
luminaries. But the world at large did not take their view
of the matter. It had got into its head that it had ill-used
Avelingh, and so it veered round to the other extreme and
made much of him. It may be confidently affirmed that it
would have acted exactly in the same manner, whether the
accused man was actually guilty or not, for the world, as we
all know, lives by impressions, and public opinion seldom
does a thing by halves. The men who had been present
during Lorentz's confession had very generally accepted its
sincerity, and it was they who spread the story far and wide.
And that same evening, in spite of one or two warning
voices here and there, the country had declared for Joost.
A large number of newspapers hung back at first, undoubtedly, but that was because their earlier opinions, unlike
those of the changeable crowd, had the disadvantage of still
being there to bear witness against them, and they shrank
from disproving all the subtle arguments of the day before
yesterday. But, the press being, after all, quite as much the
slave as the master of that spoilt overgrown child " The
Public," it was not long before " our more judicious readers "
began to find out " that we have always drawn attention to the
weak points in the prosecution." And, having once got so
far, it was easy for the radical " Cry of the People " to attack the legal institutions of the country, which made it so

simple a matter to condemn an innocent man. It was not only that insignificant organ, however, that fell foul of the magistrature. The "Cry of the People," when it goes forth, must always be raised against some scapegoat or other, and, Jan Lorentz being more or less interesting on account of his "martyrdom of virtue," it was evident that only the authorities remained to be blamed. Everybody who was angry with himself for having originally taken a wrong view of the case—that is to say, almost every inhabitant of the country above the age of fifteen—abused the examining judge and the Advocate-General for having led his judgment astray. Somehow, everybody forgot to call the newspapers to account, probably because those papers themselves were now engaged in the campaign with such laudable vigor. And so public discontent, after having wandered from one to another—like a ball on a bagatelle board—finally settled down in its favorite little hole: the "Police."

Joost Avelingh sat in his prison-cell. The authorities were angry with him for having "through his perversity," as they put it, brought discredit upon them, and the severities of prison discipline were but little relaxed. They allowed him to see his wife once or twice, in the presence of a warder, and he learned from her lips how she had been the means of saving him. He learned also that his innocence had already obtained credence with all but the magistrates. And, in the revulsion of feeling he perhaps realized more fully what an agony there had lain for his sensitive, love-loving nature in the hatred and wrath of a nation risen up against him. Few men pass through the ordeal, few men would be morally so unfit for it as Joost Avelingh. It has been said of him that his nature in his youth "wanted to be put out in the sunshine." At least, so it ever seemed to him and his friends. But the Supreme Wisdom that ruled his life decided otherwise, and he passed through the very blackness of night.

Coming out, then, as from a tunnel, blinded with the sudden radiance, his heart leaped up and staggered within him. During all those weeks of prolonged suffering, the physical side, so to call it, had scarcely troubled his repose. The imprisonment, the restraint, the deprivations, he had hardly counted these at all. His ordeal had been altogether a moral one, and, besides the inevitable separation from his wife, it was in the judgment which the world had passed upon him that his torture had asserted itself, as his punishment would have lain there, had the law finally condemned him. It seemed, then, when once, in the silence of his cell at evening, he heard a passing street-boy call out: "Long live Joost Avelingh!" that the windows of Heaven fell open and filled the dark earth with light. It was not that he cared for the silly cry and the ephemeral popularity it brought him, but that in the thought that once more his fellow-men esteemed and honored him he drank as it were the new wine of life.

Had he a right to such esteem and honor? He could, perhaps, scarcely have told himself. In the novel delight of living which came over him during these wonderful days he would certainly have answered yes, but he would not have accounted to himself for the answer. The circumstances of the trial had worked a great change in his nature, subverting to a certain extent his ideas of right and wrong. A man does not pass through such an experience and come out unharmed. He had learned—he would have been surprised, had he known how unexpectedly and how thoroughly—what a difference there is between calling one's self a sinner and being called a sinner by the law. He knew well enough that he was not a good man. Above all, he had had weighing upon him for many years the half-admitted consciousness of a great transgression. He had played with it, and mourned over it, and repented and done penance for it. He had been miserable over it just with that amount of misery which makes a man interesting to himself, and contented with the working of his own conscience. He was not, he told himself, as the mass of men around him who sinned carelessly and smilingly on without pausing to deplore their weakness. And his own "soul-suffering," his "expiation," his "inmost weariness,"—perfectly sincere as they ever remained—were not unpleasing to him, for they seemed to him like a patent of his soul's nobility, credentials which assigned him a superior rank among God's creatures, that something divine within the best and bravest which brings them comfort in the triumphant knowledge that they who most aspire most often go astray.

It will readily be believed that Joost Avelingh himself had not realized these considerations which were actuating him. It would have been absurd to expect him to do so. He realized the result. He was unhappy, so sincerely and earnestly unhappy that in spite of all his efforts to avoid reflection, he had once or twice in inevitably quieter moments been brought face to face with the idea of suicide, and had not recoiled from it. His love for Agatha—and perhaps still more, her love for him—had struck down the thought to the ground.

He had confessed his sin to God, he told himself, and obtained no pardon for it. He had striven to expiate it in the sight of Heaven, and the expiation, returning as a ball thrown upward, had brought him honor, gratitude, praise; and, as if a curse had rested on it, the good he had striven to do had changed to evil. He had held out his gold to the sick and the necessitous, and it had turned to ashes in his hand. The fault was not his, but God's.

Then came—as a thunderbolt from a clear sky, in spite of all his self-deception—the accusation of murder. What he thought, what he believed, what he felt in the first moment of that discovery, he never could explain in after years. Not God, not his own tender conscience, not the

o

lifelong grief that gnawed at his heart—others, rough, rude voices, the police, the law, the press, the whole world, accused him of a crime, accused him of the worst crime of all, murder. Was the accusation rational?

They did not come upon him, mind you, and tell him without further preface, that he had deliberately strangled his uncle with a neckerchief. Had they done so, his experiences might have been different. It is hard to say. But when he first learned in the repose and fancied security of his own home, sitting there quietly in his study-chair between wife and friend that a " serious charge had been brought against him," his first impression naturally was that there must be some mistake. For—in spite of the long schooling of his heart to one idea, or perhaps just on account of the fixed form in which that idea had thus been cast—he could see no connection between his own accusations of himself and such as the law might bring against him. Or it may be presumed that he just saw enough connection—for one moment—to explain a passing confusion and then clearly separate the ideas forever. In an instant's flash of thought—quicker than any visible spark—the fancy crossed his brain that God might have taken up arms against him ; but the next moment he remembered that God does not grant such revelations of His justice. Knowing, therefore, that such accusations as he might whisper against himself could not be the same as those the world would bring forward, his mind turned to other possibilities and, after wildly grasping at the recollection of all the peculations in connection with his charitable grant (not that he was to blame in that matter), desisted in despair and truthfully declared itself utterly at sea.

Then came—a few minutes later ; but a few minutes are often a long period in the story of a soul—the express charge of murder. It was that word which flashed across his brain the thought of a divine revelation and brought to his lips the hesitating words or " angels"? with which he had greeted the police-officers to Kees Hessel's amazement. " Or angels," remarked the younger policeman to his comrade when they found themselves alone. " What foolish things some of these criminals say, to be sure!"

Joost Avelingh now found himself thrown into utter confusion. He knew perfectly well that the law could not accuse him of murder. At least, he had always taught himself to believe that it could not, whatever doubts may sometimes have crossed his mind on the subject. He had often, undoubtedly, brought terrible accusations against himself, and, sitting there as judge, jury, prosecutor, witness, and defendant, had never come to a satisfactory verdict. He had grown accustomed to the case of " Avelingh against Avelingh "; it had become quite a part of his existence. It dragged on forever, and he could not well have got on without it, though he paid the costs with the peace of his soul. " The Crown against Avelingh " was a very different matter. " The world against Avelingh " was agony indeed.

He was rescued from the confusion into which he had fallen by the specification of the charge of murder which had been brought against him. He found himself confronted with Jan Lorentz; he heard the man's story; he was asked whether he pleaded guilty or not guilty. He could give but one answer, and he gave it immediately, and persevered in it all through the trial. He was not guilty. Whatever accusations a too sensitive conscience might sometimes suggest, this charge of willful murder was absurd, scandalous; an infamy. His heart gathered strength at the thought. Fool that he had been to dream of God's retribution, here was he brought face to face with an outrageous, libelous attack upon his good name and fame. He owed it to himself, to his wife, to society itself to defend himself with all the means in his power. Summoned to confess, he refused with righteous scorn. He turned upon the witness and told him that he lied, as he did. He repeated haughtily and consistently, that the charge was a slander, that he was innocent of the deed it attributed to him, He could not do otherwise ; he was perfectly justified in doing what he did.

And so complicated are these hearts of ours in their perceptions, that it remains true—as has already been said—that Joost Avelingh, in spite of the grief of separation, in spite of the agony of general opprobrium he was enduring, found cause for comfort and rejoicing in these days of distress. Can a man be happy and wretched at the same time ? The rational answer is No. And yet Joost Avelingh, when he came out of prison with a sprinkling of gray over his jet-black hair, could only tell that for some thoughts and at some moments the happiest experience of his life had come to him in a cell. As the certainty of his condemnation grew more manifest, the undercurrent of elation, indignation, protestation, self-glorification—call it what you will; it was something of all four—broadened through his soul. It was a new feeling to be accused unjustly, to know that there was nothing in his heart deserving such persecution, to endure to a certain extent the martyrdom of injured innocence. It was a new thing to be a far better man than the world acknowledged, and it brought its peculiar compensations. Before the trial was over, Joost Avelingh felt better satisfied with himself than he had ever felt before in his life. It was the one great result which his ordeal produced, at first, at any rate. The slow evolution of feeling had been too continuous to be suddenly annihilated by the unexpected conclusion. Rather, it found itself confirmed by the voice of public opinion. He came out of prison at peace with himself and the world. All his little self-accusations had faded into the glaring light of the prosecution for willful murder. He stood out in that white light, and men cried: "He is innocent!" Joost Avelingh did not echo the cry, but he accepted it. And the voice of the people, recognizing again his claim to esteem, was inexpressibly sweet in his ears.

He went back to his wife, when at last the prison doors were opened, with a love for her in his heart such as he had never felt before. It is not necessary to ask whether it was greater, whether there was more of it; it was different. If he had contented himself till then, in his intellectual pride, with thinking that a man's love to his wife must be all tenderness and petting, he could no longer deny Agatha that element of respect and admiration which he had till now unconsciously withheld. She had achieved a claim to his lasting gratitude which his heart must bend to admit. It did so most willingly, most gladly, but it bent none the less. He need not—he did not—love her for what she had done; he had always loved her; but now in his love was irresistibly intermingled the memory of the debt he owed her, and that love was beautified and elevated by the thought. "Not such a great thing after all," may be said, but it was great enough, if deeds are estimated by their consequences. And it was great in its devotion, in its courage, and most of all in its mastery of a human soul. Joost Avelingh had nothing to do with the various influences which had effected the alteration of Lorentz—and, in truth, Agatha's coming had been but as the fall of a stone in a brimming cup—to the husband it was his wife who had saved him, and there was heaven in the thought. It was she who, by the words she had spoken, by the thoughts to which those words gave utterance, had vanquished as vile a heart as ever lied on earth. It was she who, when all others stood back careless or powerless, she the woman, who had stepped forward and achieved what neither her brother nor the lawyer would even attempt. When she came to him in the governor's sitting-room, upon his liberation, he could only fold her to his bosom and clasp her there in silence. But it was some days later, as he walked slowly up and down his study in his old accustomed manner, revolving many things, that he suddenly stopped before Agatha, and bent over her hand and kissed it. And she, looking up into his face and smiling, was astonished at the look of tender reverence she read there. But she never guessed the meaning of that kiss.

Supposing that formerly he had loved her for her beauty only—though that would be but a very one-sided way of explaining his affection—it would have been all the more desirable that his feelings should undergo a change. For her beauty, in spite of her youth, had not remained uninjured by the sufferings she had gone through. She had never been as lovely as Joost thought her, but the pure, sweet, somewhat haughty expression of her fair face had a great charm in it; and that it would always retain. "She is very much aged, nevertheless," said her acquaintances. "It is wonderful what a few weeks will do. She must have felt terribly cut up about the whole matter. Poor thing!" Her eyes had acquired a troubled expression. There were hard lines here and there about the mouth and forehead, and there was gray—as with Joost—in the masses of golden hair her husband and mother were so proud of. Everybody called upon her again now, and everybody told her that they had wanted to come and comfort her all along, but had dreaded being thought indiscreet. "I assure you, my dear, I had ordered the carriage the very instant I first heard the terrible news," said one lady, "but my husband came and told me he was sure you would rather be left alone. 'If my wife were being tried for—were arrested like that,' he said, 'I am sure I should not like you to come bothering me.' Wasn't it unkind of him, my dear? So I just changed my mind and drove to the pastrycook's. And I was so sorry for you; I could not sleep all night for thinking of you, though Everard said it was the tarts. Men are so unfeeling; are they not, Mynheer Avelingh?"

Joost had become an object of the greatest interest.

People asked him impertinent questions, which he did not answer. He turned on his heel once or twice, very abruptly, and left some fair catechizer all perplexed in the middle of the room. Decidedly, Joost was not destined to shine in polite society. "I can't understand," the parish clergyman's wife complained to Mevrouw Verrooy. "I only asked him what his favorite text had been in prison, and he stared at me with those great eyes of his and said it was very warm. He is not an agreeable man. I do so hope, for his poor wife's sake, that confinement has not affected his head."

Agatha sat and received her visitors and was amiable to them. She was grateful, too, that they should make much of Joost, and she tried hard to convince herself that they had acted with superfine delicacy—a delicacy not properly appreciated at first sight, you know, but easily intelligible, if you give your whole mind to it—in not coming to see her in the days of her distress. She found herself uncharitably hard to convince.

CHAPTER XXVIII.

"LIBERTY LOST AND REGAINED."

BUT before Joost Avelingh could be liberated Jan Lorentz had to be condemned. The thought—although he admitted its seriousness—did not much trouble Joost, for in the long solitude of his confinement he had learned to consider the false witness with feelings of overwhelming hatred and contempt. Can it be wondered at? When they fetched him from his cell, it was to confront him with this creature, who coolly stood there lying away all that made life endurable. So thought Joost; and the wrong thus done him was so unfathomable that he could not but hate the man, even while he despised him. It is not true, by the way, surely it is not true, though it has been often repeated, that hatred and scorn can not mingle together in our thoughts of one and the same person? However that may be, Joost Avelingh felt too intense an aversion suddenly to pity the perjurer when the confession of his crime had been wrung from him. He considered that he but received what he merited; and the more he recalled his past wickedness the more he appreciated Agatha's victory in bringing the scoundrel to book.

For Agatha the circumstances were different. She also had good reason to shrink from all sympathy with Lorentz, but she could not forget her last sad impression of him, received on the night before the verdict. It still seemed to her as if she saw the wretched garret with the moonbeams shifting across it and playing over the bed on which he lay. She could not forget the misery on his pale face and in his broken voice. She had watched him there through the whole anxious night, first with her mother, then with Kees, who had been sent for to join them and take down the guilty man's deposition, and from first to last with Dientje. Jan Lorentz had lain through the greater part of the time with his fingers tightly clasped round his old love's hand, gazing at her as if he would drink his fill of her face, and murmuring occasionally some words of self-disparagement. Not of endearment; he would never have allowed himself to give utterance to these. The woman had passed beyond him, irretrievably; none the less could he cherish and honor the thought of her. He was not ill; that is to say, his weakened frame did not feel weaker than yesterday, but the storm which had been sweeping over his spirit during the last few days and had now culminated in this renunciation, had left him prostrate in mind and in body. He was inexpressibly weary, as a man after the crisis of a fever. But he was also out of danger. In the fight in his soul the right side had won.

Beggared, broken in health, utterly forlorn and miserable, and now tormented by the stings of conscience, what could he do but give up the struggle? He had always retained his fierce grudge against Joost, but it had never been his intention to bear false witness against him, and, in spite of his dislike, the possible injury to the accused soon outgrew any vengeance he might have reckoned on. It was true, as he said, that he had been unconsciously led into making his original statement, and that he had never intended to do so. He was not a sufficiently bad man to wish to deliberately ruin the happiness of several innocent lives, if he came to think out the subject. The hope of gain, and the desire to free himself from a disagreeable dilemma, had probably actuated him in the beginning, and also, quite as much as both these, the fear of going back on the statement he was once reported to have made. How he had first made it he did not clearly remember. His impression was that van Asveld had tricked him into it, knowing it to be untrue, but therein he wronged the Jonker, who had merely read his own thoughts too readily from the lips of another, and who firmly believed, even after the condemnation of Lorentz, that the man had been bought over for a small fortune by Agatha Avelingh.

Brought face to face with his lie in all its nakedness and barrenness, Jan Lorentz could not continue to play a part he had from the first been but loath to undertake. He betrayed himself, and, once discovered, was a lost man, as far as keeping up false appearances went. Not that he immediately desired to sacrifice his liberty. His surrender was, perhaps, at first more the result of moral and physical weakness than of any higher resolve. It is always more or less difficult to tell a lie consistently, and this liar's staying power gave out. But also, it must be admitted, his heart was not in it. He was not a sufficiently bad man not to desire to be a better. And when the wave of conviction rolled in upon him, it

struck against no granite rock. He went down before it
from debility as much as from deliberate choice. But he
was almost glad when he was down.

That did not mean, however, that he bore gladly the
consequences of his deed. Nor were they such as men accept lightly, whatever may be their consciousness of guilt.
In that never-ending night when he poured forth his broken
confessions, exculpations, entreaties to the sympathetic, silent women by his bedside, his hand clasping that of his old
sweetheart, he had often faltered and shrunk away with
sudden indecision. And even then when, having spoken,
he fell back and lay still, but for an occasional murmur, he
had realized with terror what his self-surrender meant. But
the sequence of his action swept down upon him, irresist-
less from the first. He bowed his head, and did not try to
resist it.

But gradually, with the rest his avowal brought him and
the knowledge of doing right, now inseparable from his
misfortunes, courage and a certain contentment came back
to the man. He went through the trial for perjury victo-
riously, even though it ended, as it inevitably must, in his
condemnation to a long term of imprisonment. One bright
point, which Agatha timidly pointed out to him, he seized
with avidity, fixing his eyes upon it till it illuminated the
darkness. This imprisonment would give him an opportunity, such as he could nowhere else have found, of escaping
from the power of the drink. "Yes," he said, "with God's
help, there is that to live for. And when I come out of
prison, Dientje? When I come out of prison?" He lingered wistfully over the words. She drooped her eyes to
the ground and did not answer. There was no need to un-
deceive him now, should she so wish it. And many years
would pass before he saw the sun again.

In the course of his examination Jan Lorentz admitted
that he had told a lie at first, had adhered to it through the

inquiry, and sworn it during the trial. He had not seen Joost touch his uncle on the night of the old man's death. But he pleaded, truthfully, that he had never intended to say so in the beginning, and that the story had been forced upon him, somehow, by van Asveld. The Jonker, called to explain this, pooh-poohed—also truthfully—the idea, and swore that his first doubt of Jan Lorentz's sincerity had arisen on the day when the verdict was given. The judges believed him, and absolutely disbelieved Lorentz, for van Asveld was a gentleman and the prisoner a self-avowed liar. It went very much against the accused that he thus tried to explain away his guilt and lay the blame on another man's shoulders.

Had he seen nothing, then, he was asked, from his place in the dickey? And it came out that he had. Had it not been so, he would probably never have told even his trumped-up story at the trial. He had seen Joost clench the reins tightly, and drive on as if hell and death were pursuing him —as they were. It was this he had been about to tell Arthur when the latter's impetuous conviction led his thoughts astray.

And he had seen more. For he had seen that the old Baron himself, when he fell back in the chaise, clutched at the neckerchief round his throat and fumbled at it for a moment. Then the dying man's hands fell to his knees, and the cloth remained unloosed. Had he tightened it in his hurried efforts to unfasten the knot? Probably that was what had occurred. The doctor repeated his original statement. When called to see the corpse, he found evidences of strangulation. They were not sufficient to prove death from that cause. As a rule, the symptoms of strangulation were unmistakable. That was not the case with the deceased. The deceased had been dead "about half an hour." There had been no post-mortem examination. There ought to have been. He could not say deceased had died from strangulation. He thought it highly improbable he had done so. It was impossible to speak positively. As doctors talk, unable, after all, to look before and after, however good their will may be. There was hardly a medical man in the country who did not vehemently impugn Doctor Kern's evidence, and declare that, if *he* had been called to view the body he would have been able to accurately diagnose the state of affairs. Every tyro could see whether a man had died from strangulation or a fit. "Or from both?" asked Doctor Kern sardonically.

And so the prison doors closed upon Jan Lorentz. And the world forgot him. Only two women in it, though they never breathed his name to one another, remembered him in their prayers. And God remembered him; and the Lord Christ came to him in his solitary cell.

CHAPTER XXIX.

A "LETTRE DE FAIRE PART."

JOOST AVELINGH was once more at the Castle. The June election had swept by and was a thing of the past. It was true that Joost's name had been brought forward as a candidate here and there in the past winter, but nothing positive had been decided upon, and his brother-in-law may have given too loose a rein to a naturally sanguine temperament when he spoke with such assurance of his chances. Whatever these may have been originally, by the time the electioneering campaign came on Joost's name was enveloped in a whirlwind of obsecration. It swept by; and before the end of May he was liberated and restored to his rank, but then other candidates had been nominated, and the election was at the very door. Joost never even remembered it. He had other things to think of, assuredly.

Gradually, however, he returned to his occupations, and the first painful impression wore off. He resumed the management of his estate; he took his place again at his numerous committee meetings. The men of his class were much more cordial to him than formerly. It seemed as if every one were anxious to make up to him for wrong thoughts of him in the past. The Supreme Court had—unwillingly and ungraciously—acquitted him; and society, angry with itself for having believed in the guilt—the criminal guilt, be it remarked—of one of its members, did all that it could to atone to him for its injustice. The common people of the neighborhood merely returned to their allegiance; they had cause enough to feel grateful to Joost. Wherever he came, he was received sympathetically. He went out more " *dans le monde*," and people said : " He was really not so bad when you got to know him. And they had certainly treated him ill, poor fellow!" The first time he drove into the chief town of the province he was recognized; and a small crowd —largely composed of street-boys—cheered his carriage.

He also resumed his charities, and now dispensed them more openly than formerly. There was no more of the shamefaced attempt to buy off his conscience; he had come to look upon these matters, as has been said, in a different light. And for that reason he admitted Agatha into his confidence, and they talked his plans over together, to her great delight. Till then he had excluded her, from no motives of unkindness, but because he told himself he had no right—nor she either—to draw any pleasure or profit from such perfunctory benevolence. He was less sensitive now. The trial had hardened him. And he resolved henceforth " to do good and fear naught,"—not even himself.

So he slipped into the position of a wealthy, beneficent, active and prosperous country gentleman. He kept his per-

sonal tastes more in the background in his intercourse with
those who did not share them, and it was noticed that he
had lost in prison the boisterous and unnatural bursts of
gayety which had made Liederlen liken him to a hyena. He
was never outrageously funny now.

Large-handed charity is not of common occurrence. It
is more frequent, perhaps, in Holland than in most countries, for it must be admitted of the Dutch that, with all
their faults, they are, on the whole, a generous people, willing to alleviate suffering where they can, and to dispense
hospitality, as the nations of Europe have good cause to remember. But even in Holland a munificent man stands
out as a harbor-light, to which all the shipwrecked on life's
solemn main immediately direct their course. Joost Avelingh's post-bag brought him a daily batch of begging letters, some of them heart-rending, some of them side-split-
ting, all of them full of faultless misfortune. He attended
to an inordinate number, and Kees Hessel, who would have
shared his last crust with a beggar, said that from a politico-
economical point of view his brother-in-law did far more
harm than good.

One morning a paper with a deep black border lay
among the other letters on the breakfast table. Joost tossed
it to his wife unopened. "Cards for somebody," he said, as
he took up a newspaper. It sounded a little heartless, perhaps, but had the loss been in his own immediate circle of acquaintances, he would have heard of it before receiving the
"lettre de faire part." Agatha unfolded the paper and read
out with some astonishment the demise of an old clergyman
in a village in the North of Holland, a man perfectly unknown to her. "My beloved husband, Hieronymus Hellevaer, at the age of eighty-three," said Agatha. "Poor old
lady! And who is the Right Reverend, Very Learned Heer,
Dominus Hieronymus Hellevaer, Joost?"

"Hellevaer," said Joost thoughtfully, laying down his

paper, " Hellevaer, Hellevaer." I can't remember the name. But I've heard it somewhere, all the same. Let me see "— a sudden expression of displeasure passed over his face— " Oh yes, I know now," he said. " Certainly, that was the name of the clergyman who was present at my father's death and who—who sent me to my uncle. It is the same, I suppose. Did he live till now? He must have been very old, I should think. Where do they write from?"

" Eighty-three," replied Agatha. " From Tjumstjumperadeel."

" What a name?" said Joost. " He must have got another parish. It was at Overveer that my father died."

They went on with their breakfast in silence. Presently Joost said, a little bitterly " Poor man, he did me a bad service. I suppose I ought to forgive him. He meant it for the best."

" It was for the best, after all, surely, Joost," said Agatha.

He looked at her for a long time with a vacant, dreamy look, without answering. Then he said : " Do you know, Agatha, what my father wanted to do with me?"

" No Joost. How should I? You never told me."

" He wanted to send me to the orphan asylum."

" To the orphan asylum? My dearest!"

" My father was a wise man, Agatha. Perhaps it would have been better."

He cast a glance over the lofty room in which they were sitting, with its oak-carvings and frescoed walls, and out at the great windows over the broad meadow in front of the house and the green woods beyond. It was a lovely August morning, glittering with light and balmy with approaching heat. The smell of the roses came in under the striped awning.

" Perhaps it would have been better," he said. He said it dreamingly, questioningly, and, as the words left his lips, his coachman knocked at the door and came in to ask for orders — as Dutch coachmen do toward the end of breakfast.

"You must go over to the dealer's this morning," began Joost in a practical tone. "You can take the bay filly, and warn him that I won't keep the new pair, if the off-horse shies again at the steam-tram as she did yesterday. And if you come across the steward, send him up and tell him to bring the estimate with him for that wall at the back of the lower lane cottages. Is there anything he can get you from the village, Agatha?"

He lounged away to the window and remained standing there till the man was gone. Perhaps he remembered his uncle's warning that it was not a little thing to give up all this.

It seemed as if his return to his old surroundings after the sudden deprivation which he had undergone, had awakened within him a greater taste for luxury, or, at any rate, a greater enjoyment of it than he had felt before. It had never been his weakness to take especial pleasure in such beauty as only money can buy; he had always delighted in the fields, and the woods, the birds and the sunshine, such enjoyments as God gives to all. He appreciated them now with a keener relish after the close confinement he had suffered, but he also began to notice more the comforts and advantages which only wealth can bestow: the great house with its beautiful old furniture, the stables, the gardens, even the well-appointed and well-furnished dinner-table. The difference with his plank bed and a little pannikin of weak pea-soup was too great for human flesh not to linger complacently over it.* He was not a luxurious man, far

---

* It may surely be doubted—in the interests of equality—whether it is just to suppress those arrangements by which criminals of the better class are enabled to procure themselves food a trifle superior to the common prison fare.

from it, but he realized as he had never done before, what a difference there is between affluence and penury, between comfort and privation. He clung also, more than had been his wont, to the old house for its own sake; he wandered through the woods and said, not only: they are beautiful, but also: they are mine!

"It is difficult to forget," he said, when the servant was gone, still staring out of the window, "and, whatever they may say, it is difficult to forgive."

Agatha looked a little puzzled. "Surely you do not feel you have anything to forgive that poor old man, Joost?" she said. She was washing up the tea-things. The Dutch use costly porcelain as a rule—brought from Japan and the Dutch Indies, often a couple of centuries ago, when they still made fine porcelain over there—and Dutch housewives invariably look after it themselves.

"I was not thinking of the Domine,"* said Joost. "I was thinking of my uncle."

Agatha put down her little fringed towel and went up to her husband. She laid her head on his shoulder, and he, looking moodily down on it, askance, from where he stood close against the window, his hands in his pockets, he noticed once again the frequent gray hairs among her thick golden tresses.

"Are you angry with his memory still?" she asked softly.

"Yes," he said grimly. "I hate him even now. I have always hated him. It seems as if I had always hated him. Look at the wrong he has done me, and you."

"Not me," she said in surprise. "He would have, perhaps, if he could. But he was prevented. It is wonderful to think how he was prevented. If it were not that it looks as if one rejoiced at his death, I have often thought that

---

* Minister.

P

God brought you and me together in a very special manner, Joost."

Joost did not answer.

"And so you must forgive your uncle for the sake of that."

"He always wronged me," said Joost, "and therefore I suppose I must always have hated him. It may be un-christian, but it is very natural. I can not remember his doing anything for me, or with me, unless it was to make me wretched." He shuddered. "He must have been a very bad man, Agatha," he said.

"I did not like him, certainly," replied Agatha, frankly. "He was very cross and disagreeable, and I could not for-give him for being unkind to you, Joost."

He caught at the expression, for his mind was full of it. "Could not forgive him," he repeated. "There, you see, you say it yourself!"

She nodded her head at him, laughingly, in spite of his earnest tone. "Nonsense, Joost," she said, "the poor man is dead ten years and more."

"I can't help it," said her husband fiercely. "I hate his memory. He has ruined my life, and I hate him for it. I am glad I do. It makes some things much easier for me."

CHAPTER XXX.

DOCTOR AVELINGH'S THEORY.

BARELY a fortnight after the arrival of the "*lettre de faire part*," Joost Avelingh found a thick packet in the post-bag bearing the same postmark: Tjumstjumperadeel. He opened it, and a closed envelope fell out, with a sheet of notepaper folded round it. The sheet of notepaper proved to be a letter from the widow Hellevaer, and the letter was as follows : "Highly Nobly Born Heer,"

(In a land of titles, like Holland, the begging letters are always extra polite).

"HIGHLY NOBLY BORN HEER,—It is a painful task for me to recall myself to the recollection of your Nobleness. And perhaps it is wrong of me to seek to do so, for it is more than twenty-five years ago since I kissed your Nobleness farewell in the drawing-room of Castle Trotsem. But I can not forget that it was my beloved husband who, having been the friend of your honored father, Doctor Avelingh, and having received you from his hands in the hour of his death, was the means of restoring your Nobleness to your uncle the late lamented Baron van Trotsem. He and I both rejoiced ever since most sincerely at your good fortune, and were glad to think that my dear husband had been instrumental in preparing it for you. He was taken from me, by the inscrutable decree of the Almighty, on the fifth of this month at thirty-three minutes past seven in the morning, and died in peace of an influential attack of the chest—he had been asthmatic of late years, though otherwise in good health, praise God. And while I rejoice that he should have been spared to me so long, I can not deny that his loss is therefore the greater trial to me. But I will not complain, knowing that it is our duty to be resigned under all our afflictions, which endure but for a moment. I am old and shall not live much longer. But at present I am left almost destitute and with but few friends, most of whom are prevented by their own limited means from assisting me, as they would be only too desirous to do. I rejoice to think that my dearly beloved husband's intervention saved Your Nobleness at the time from all the horrors of poverty and public charity. Excuse, Highly Nobly Born Heer, my importunity. I found recently among my husband's papers some documents which will probably have some value for your Nobleness, and which are of no further importance to me. I send them, therefore, to your Nobleness, and it is the anxiety to let you have them which explains this letter and must excuse it.

"Hoping that your Nobleness will favor me with an early reply, for, indeed, I sorely stand in need of it.—I remain, Highly Nobly Born Heer, Your High Nobleness's old friend and humble servant,

"PIETERNELLA KIP,

" Widow of the Right Reverend Very Learned Heer Dominus Hieronymus Hellavaer."

Joost laid the letter down, with a smile over the "influential attack," and an inward resolve to inquire into the woman's condition. And then he turned to the little parcel of papers she had sent, as an excuse for her appeal, it must be feared.

He examined the papers listlessly. There were one or two letters from the Baron van Trotsem, treating, as briefly as possible, of business matters with regard to the death of Joost's father, funeral expenses, sale of furniture and so on. They were yellow and faded with the lapse of years. Then came a fresher looking letter, and, tied up with it, a sheet of tinted paper, covered with writing in a big florid hand. A vague recollection of having seen that document before flashed across Joost's brain, but he could not account for it. He turned to his uncle's letter and read :

"DEAR DOMINE: I am obliged to you for your letter and inclosure, which I return as desired. It shall be as the man wished, but I must effectuate the thing in my own manner. I can not endure to appear in any way as if I carried out his orders. Nor can I bear the thought that the son would probably immediately consent to do for the

sake of his father, whom he has never seen and to whom
he owes literally nothing, what he will refuse to do for my
sake, although he is indebted to me for all he possesses. I
am resolved therefore that he shall do it for my sake, and
for my sake only, and I must request you not to communicate with my nephew on the subject.

" Yours, etc.   VAN TROTSEM."

Joost took up the inclosure alluded to, and glanced over
the first lines. He started, flushed up, turned to the signature at the back of the paper, and began reading again.
The letter was signed : " Joost Avelingh." He was gazing
at his dead father's handwriting for the first time in his
life.

" MY DEAR HELLEVAER "—thus ran the letter—" Let
me remind you once more of our conversation of the other
evening. I repeat that it is my earnest desire, more than
that, it is the one wish of my heart—I can scarcely put the
matter too strongly—that my dear boy should in time take up
my profession. You laugh at my theory on the subject, but
your laughter is accounted for, excuse my saying so, by
your ignorance. Had you studied the question as I have,
you would judge differently. ' Heredity ' has always been
my hobby ; my university-dissertation treated mainly of
that subject, and I have occupied myself with it ever since.
I feel sure that, if the same profession were followed up
through several generations with us, as it is in the East,
and as it used to be in Europe, we, with our modern opportunities of study, would attain to an excellence never
dreamed of before. I flatter myself I am a better doctor
than my father was, and I feel confident that my son will
in time be a better doctor than I. The difficulty lies in the
fact, which I have noticed with care—I may say, that I
have discovered it, in so far as it is the result of scientific

observation—that sons, as a rule, after having in their childhood declared for their father's profession, manifest an aversion to it in later youth. This dislike, natural enough and
easily explainable, for they see all the outer annoyances and
none of the inner compensations, comes to the front at the
very time when they are called upon to make a choice, and
the parent, instead of treating it as an excusable symptom,
allows it to decide the child's future. I have noticed exactly the same phenomenon in numerous families. And
my own little Joost, if you now ask him what he wishes to
become when he is a man, will promptly tell you 'A doctor
like papa.' By the time he is eighteen or nineteen he will
most probably say, 'anything but a doctor,' but, if wisely
guided, he will live to thank his father's penetration. I
hope to superintend his studies myself, but should fate prevent me from doing so, I most earnestly entreat you or
whoever may have the care over his future life to remember
that it was his father's wish, I would almost say his command, that he should study medicine.

" JOOST AVELINGH."

The younger Joost read this letter twice over with eyes
of immeasurable amazement. A flood of memories swept
back upon him ; he must have a moment's time to think
them out. His father—the bright phantom of his infancy,
the "Beauty" of his childhood, forgotten now for many
years, yet vaguely cherished like a moss-hidden grave—his
father stood out before him again under the full light of
this letter. He cast a long glance at the big portrait, en-
larged from a photograph, which he had caused to be made
some years ago, and which now hung over his writing-
table. His eye lingered over the dark face, with its obsti-
nate mouth, and strong, energetic expression. There was
much in these to remind you of the son, but the romantic
part of Joost's nature, inherited from his mother, was al-

together lacking. Joost also had his stock of energy, though it may have been less prominent than his father's. The members of his various committees could testify to its being there.

The doctor had been a headstrong man, and the letter was a headstrong letter. Joost remembered now where he had first seen that sheet of pink tinted paper; in the Baron's hand on the day when the old man made known his wishes to him with regard to his future career. Many of the circumstances of that interview now rose up before him. He took up the two letters again, his father's and his uncle's—and once more read them through.

His father, then, was responsible for that one great injustice which he had always laid at the Baron van Trotsem's door. As for the theory exposed in the document he held in his hand, it was a hobby such as all men have, all medical men especially, and the son was to be sacrificed to it. He did not believe one moment in the correctness of his father's views; he felt convinced that, come what might, he would always have felt the same unchangeable aversion to a profession, the material side of which was so especially distasteful in his eyes. His father was wrong, undoubtedly; but all that was done now, and over. The results remained only as far as his uncle was concerned. Surely the Baron had been to blame, also, in assigning no reason for his behavior. His letter certainly explained the motive that had prompted him, and Joost could not but admit that it was an explainable and almost excusable motive in one with his uncle's character. He knew how the Baron had hated the doctor, also not without cause. He was obliged to admit that he—Joost—had clung to his father's memory and closed his heart to his uncle. It was the Baron's fault, he told himself. The answer came back immediately: " True, but the Baron did not realize that." And he could understand, however much he regretted it, the frame of mind which had made his uncle declare: "He must do it, if his father so willed it, but he shall not do it for that father's sake, but for mine." Joost knew his uncle's character well enough to recognize at once, that it was like the old gentleman's ideas of duty and paternal authority to respect the dead doctor's wish, and that it was as much like his silent, vindictive surliness to pretend that that wish was his own.

But after all, then, his father was primarily to blame! Joost found the discovery influenced his thoughts of that dead parent more than he had imagined it would do at first. However he might withstand the charge, he felt the great onus of cruelty gradually slipping from his uncle's shoulders. He could be angry with the Baron for not telling him more, if he chose to be so; he could no longer be angry with him for not having left him free in the choice of a profession. With an impatient exclamation he gathered up all his papers and went across with them to his wife. It was but too true, as he had said a few days ago, that for him to hate his uncle made many things seem easier. It was a comfort to think he had such good cause to hate him still.

CHAPTER XXXI.

JOOST'S LABORS FOR OTHERS BEAR FRUIT FOR HIMSELF.

"You are to be 'High and Mighty'* after all, Joost," cried Kees Hessel, panting behind his brother-in-law in the village street of Heist. "I have been all the way up to your place to tell you about it, but Agatha said you were down here. I left her a high state of glee, I can assure you."

---

* Title officially given to the Dutch States-General.

"How so?" said Joost. "What has happened? Tell me all about it."

"I'm awfully glad I'm the first man to bring you the news," replied Kees, recovering his breath and puffing away at his cigar. "I made sure some one would have talked about it to you as soon as I heard you had gone to the village. And I like to have the telling of pleasant tidings when I can."

"Then tell them," cried Joost, laughing. "What has happened? Out with it."

"This has happened," said Kees solemnly. "Pernis, who, as you know, was elected in two districts at the last election, takes his seat for the Northern division, and so leaves ours once more vacant."

"Yes, yes, I know that," interrupted Joost impatiently. "And also that William the Third is King of Holland. But I am waiting to hear something new."

"Wait then," said Kees, imperturbably, "and let me tell the story in my own way. Our district being vacant, the electioneering clubs have been talking about What's-his-name, and So-and-so, as they always do at first, but in the mean time some half-a-dozen citizens of the working class put their heads together, call an independent meeting, and nominate—you."

"When did this meeting take place?" asked Joost, the color rising into his dark cheek.

"Yesterday evening, my dear sir. And the crowd took up your name immediately and screamed themselves hoarse with it all over the place."

"But that does not elect me," began Joost. "The electioneering clubs— "

"The electioneering clubs would scarcely have chosen you; you are not partisan enough. But the promoters of yesterday's meeting have forced their hand. They daren't split the vote, you see, now the people have come out so strong on your behalf. I came across the Secretary of the 'Central' this morning, and he tells me that they're going to have a meeting on purpose in two days, and put you up, so as to be beforehand with the other party. And he hopes you'll accept their programme."

"I shall do no such thing," said Joost.

"Came across the Secretary" was a euphemistic way of putting it, for Kees had lingered in the neighborhood of the Secretary's house for more than an hour that morning, in the hope of meeting that gentleman and hearing what he had to say.

"Then will you come out on the other side?"

"No," said Joost. "I shall stick to my own colors at first, in any case."

"By Jupiter, it's magnificent," cried Kees, in high enthusiasm. "A representative of the people, chosen by the people for the people, without any party intrigue. The thing's never been done before, Joost! You're bound to pass, my boy, and I wish you all success. What a happy fellow you'll be, and how heartily one can wish you joy of it, when one remembers all your former troubles. What a splendid career! Or, as Agatha puts it, what a vast sphere of usefulness! Bless her good little heart!"

"Yes," said Joost thoughtfully. "It is a vast sphere of usefulness, and a splendid career. Should I really be the first independent member, using 'independent,' of course, in its technical sense of 'belonging to neither party?' I suppose I should."

"You would," said Kees, "and that's why I call it **magnificent**. It's just the people who've pointed you out, and said, 'We'll have that man and no other.' And it's never happened before."

They had reached the entrance of the Club. It was thither their steps had been tending. The clock had struck four, and the building would be filling by this time.

Joost pushed open a double green-baize door, and walked in. A large room with a comparatively low ceiling, a great round table in the middle, full of newspapers, and a number of little tables in all corners, surrounded by quantities of leathern easy-chairs. All the chairs occupied by men, smoking, with a little glass of orange-colored bitters or white gin in front of them ; a buzz of talking, a rustle of paper, and a thick cloud of blue smoke over it all. Through two doors at the farther end a distant view of men moving round billiard tables, with the constant shock of balls sounding across, and —on the left side, in the card-room—quartettes of white heads, black heads, and bald heads bending over their whist. A general confusion of sounds, and the occasional clear clink of glass, as a waiter moved about between the groups. A small Club such as every provincial town in Holland can produce.

Joost's entrance was the signal for a general commotion and flutter of interest. People laid down their papers and turned half-round in the heavy chairs, or glared furtively at the new comer over the top of the *Town Gazette*.

Joost advanced to the table, his stalwart figure looking all the taller by the side of his shorter, stouter brother-in-law. Several of the men sitting nearest got up to congratulate him and to ask him what his intentions were. Van Hessel's story was certainly true. Within two minutes Joost heard it on all sides. He was to be proclaimed candidate for the States-General in the next meeting of the Central Club, hurriedly called together for that special purpose. It was true, as Kees had said, that the people, by their spontaneous and altogether unprecedented action, had forced the hand of the wire-pullers.

It can not be said that the congratulations Joost received were very hearty or sincere ones. He was certainly not the candidate the politicians by profession would have chosen. A man must obey orders in the game of party politics; and that would be no army whose every recruit aimed at posing as a general. Most of the gentlemen of Heist, therefore, while they were quite willing to forgive Joost for the injustice they had done him, and receive him again into society, told each other that to send him up to represent the district in Parliament was quite another matter altogether! Everybody tried to find out at once what his party politics would be. That he would have none, no one believed, even though he repeatedly affirmed it.

"All very well," said Beau Liederlen, running his fingers through his carefully curled gray hair, "but the man who goes in for wine-drinking must decide whether he'll have red wine or white. *Et ceux qui ne veulent ni l'un ni l'autre ne reçoivent pas de pots-de-vin du tout, mon cher.*" Beau Liederlen was one of those people without occupation, whose utterances no one takes seriously—not even they themselves —or he would hardly have dared to say that. He lounged back to his card-table, where he was playing whist for half-penny points.

Arthur van Asveld sat at the large center table, his hat on his head, his hands in his pockets. He bent lower over a newspaper, with a dark frown on his face. He was fatter and redder than ever of late. It can not be denied that he was beginning to look a little bloated; his big stupid eyes had often a glazed stare in them which by no means improved their expression. It was said pretty plainly now, that the Jonker drank too much. He was clerk in the Burgomaster's office still: there was not much chance that he would ever be anything else. The Burgomaster sighed over him, and would gladly have got him promotion. Mynheer van Hessel had emerged from what he called "that unfortunate little injustice in connection with my son-in-law" in a triumphant, if extenuated, condition. He had soon fattened out to his original size, and he was now as bright, smiling, pompous, and prosperous as ever. He had also unpacked again, and repolished, his little store of quotations and witticisms. He designated the pink Jonker invariably as " my rosy cross " in allusion to the well-known lines of a Dutch poet:

> " A cross with roses
> Is each man's fate."

He was not much liked, somehow, poor man, in the village of which he was Burgomaster. People were always describing him as a worthy creature "after all." The Governor of the Province did not speak of him even in those relatively complimentary terms.

When Joost came out of prison, van Asveld found himself placed in a difficult position. Personally he remained convinced of the liberated man's guilt, and therefore refused all intercourse with the Baron van Trotsem's murderer. The refusal had been made the more awkward for him by Joost's walking up with outstretched hand, as if nothing had happened, the very first time they met at the Club; the Jonker had put his arm down by his side, and there had been an end of it, though many of Joost's warmest partisans had been very violent about it, and Joost himself had suppressed a momentary impulse to knock the fat nobleman down. The magistrature, as has been said, although the necessary evidence had escaped them, were not altogether willing to admit Joost's complete innocence, and van Asveld, who had gone through all three trials, may therefore perhaps be more readily forgiven for sticking to his original impression. He cut Joost dead, although Liederlen told him frankly, it was execrable taste of him to do so, and, constantly as they met, the two had not exchanged a word since the day when Joost had paid over his forty thousand florins to van Asveld.

The men in the front room of the Club, then, crowded round Joost this afternoon and talked of his political prospects. Some of them, even at this early stage, began recommending special, or even individual, interests to his protection.

"When you are Deputy," said one of his colleagues in the direction of the Local Steam Tram company, "you won't forget the concession up to Hoest, Avelingh."

"Oh, as for that," cried a little lawyer from the town. "We can't have you people pushing all your local claims to the front. The interests of the whole district, and of the principal part of it, especially, must be considered in the first place. No, no Avelingh can't take any particular notice of the half-dozen enterprises he happens to be concerned in himself."

In the mean time van Asveld sat by, with sullen face, listening unwillingly to the chorus of acclamation around the man he hated.

"You are a damned lucky fellow, Mynheer Avelingh, to have that whole trial shindy kicked up round your name," remarked a young nobleman, whose ancestors had exhausted the stock of brains in the family. "A damned lucky fellow, as things have turned out. Don't you think so, van Asveld?"

"I?" said Arthur, thus unexpectedly addressed, and thrown off his guard. I think—if any one cares for what I think—that some people "—he disdained the subterfuge—"that Mynheer Avelingh has invested his money very well, and that it is beginning to bear very good interest."

The words were spoken very deliberately and distinctly. An awkward silence fell on the party of gentlemen grouped round the table.

"Do you mean to infer, van Asveld," said Kees Hessel hotly, gnawing at his big blonde moustache, "that my brother-in-law has bribed people into bringing him forward?"

"I am not in the habit of inferring," answered Arthur, lifting his heavy eyes to Joost's face with a look of ineffable

contempt. "Bribery! Nonsense. No. There is no bribery in Holland. But how do the pious people put it?
'Charity suffereth long and is kind.' Charity proves wonderfully kind sometimes—to the charitable."

"If one elector has received his charity, it is you"—began Kees. Joost stopped him.

"Address yourself to me, sir," he said, returning Arthur's contemptuous stare. "If you accuse me of owing a
large amount of such popularity as I may possess to ill-advised
charity, I can only admit that there is much truth in the
accusation. But I believe that the assertion is still more
correct, that I am largely indebted to the unjust scandal
which has been connected with my name, and for which
I, at any rate, can not be held responsible."

Arthur shrugged his shoulders. The truth of the assertion was very unpalatable to him.

"There are various ways of getting money, Mynheer
Avelingh," he said with much meaning. "And there are
various ways of spending it. Each man has his own way.
If I were in possession of your fortune, I should buy kisses;
you buy votes. You are the wiser man, and, I presume, the
happier." He had risen while speaking, and now turned on
his heel and left the room.

"Come away," said Kees, taking his brother-in-law's
arm. "You needn't look so white, Joost, for anything that
cad happens to say. You know we have always called him
a cad ever since our college days."

"Yes," answered Joost, as he allowed himself to be
drawn forth from the stifling atmosphere inside into the
warm evening air. "Yes, but I am not sure it was the
right epithet to apply to him. I don't think he is exactly a
cad."

Joost found his Napoleon waiting at the inn where he
always put up, and soon he was bowling swiftly along the
highroad behind as fine a pair of spanking grays as ever shied

at one of the numerous steam-tram cars, which ruin the narrow Dutch roads for the rich while they make them accessible to the poor. Joost Avelingh had interested himself in these means of locomotion. He could not complain.

He found Agatha, as her brother had foretold, in a high state of glee. She was only anxious to know how Joost would take the news. And when she saw that he uttered no protest, but plainly, if somewhat passively, accepted the situation, she openly declared her satisfaction. It was true that Joost did not now, as on the former occasion, declare his unwillingness to accept the projected honor. He seemed to acquiesce in it, not altogether ill-pleased at the splendid opportunities of usefulness which it opened up to him. It would give him, besides, a much desired distraction, rousing all his energies and bringing them into play.

" I want work," he said, tossing his head like a horse that sniffs the battle, " hard work, and plenty of it. It is wonderful how much a man can do in a day, if he gives his whole mind to it. And I like giving my whole mind to business. I like being thoroughly and consumedly busy. It does me good."

Agatha could not help agreeing with him. He had fallen once or twice of late into his old moody fits. Ever since the widow Hellevaer had sent those musty old letters, he seemed to be less cheerful. He had shown his wife the letters, and discussed them with her, but it was as if a small cloud had again come between them, untraceable and inexplicable, but no less a cloud on that account.

It was a great joy, then, to Agatha to let her mind dwell upon this public recognition of Joost's merit, and all the honor and advantage it would bring him. For herself she cared little, and yet she delighted to think that she also would henceforth be associated with his plans and projects, and that he would allow her to work them out with him. It compensated her, to a certain extent, for the loneliness of that great childless house. Agatha had never been able quite to forgive her friends and relations for their desertion of Joost in the hour of trouble. They had believed the charge against him. There lay the sting. Actually believed it! Incredible as it seemed to her, she was obliged to recognize the fact. And it vexed her, and imbittered her intercourse with those whom she had always loved best.

CHAPTER XXXII.

INTERVIEWING THE CANDIDATE.

"Yes, gentlemen," said the Burgomaster with his old wave of the hand, "yes, I think I can promise you that."

He was standing in the middle of the vestibule of Trotsem Castle. Opposite him were drawn up in straggling line some half dozen old farmers in their tight-fitting black clothes, black caps and stiff black stocks. The only bit of color about these old gentlemen was the dark red of their clean-shaven faces, or an occasional glow of fading yellow among the grizzly stubble that showed under their caps. All wore earrings; all held their hands twisted round by their sides, and all hung their heads on their breasts, while their little eyes twinkled up at Mynheer van Hessel. The Burgomaster beamed down upon them.

"Sit down," he said, "sit down. My son-in-law will be with you immediately."

The boers all shuffled a little uneasily, but no one availed himself of the invitation to drop down on the oaken bench which stood just behind them.

"I quite agree with you," continued Mynheer van Hes-

Q

sel, " that it would be an immense advantage to your village
if the canal passed by it. There is a great deal in what you
say that strikes me as singularly accurate and—and well put.
There is no doubt that the—ahem—the new canal would
confer great benefits upon your village if it passed that
way."

" Juistament,* Heer Burgomaster," said the spokesman,
a fine, hale, cunning-looking old boer of some seventy win-
ters. " It is just as your Nobleness says."

" Ja ! " echoed two or three others, shuffling to and fro,
" it is just as the Heer Burgomaster says."

" Not that there is not another side to the question,"
continued Mynheer van Hessel, " it seems more natural, and
it is certainly much more simple, to let it take the short cut
by Zielen. The Government will look at it in that light,
you may be sure."

" Zielen is a place of no importance, not like our village,
as the Heer Burgomaster knows," said the old boer. " It
remains to be seen, with the Heer Burgomaster's permission,
what the Government will do."

" It will cost fully seventy thousand florins more to go
round as you wish it," remarked Mynheer van Hessel.

The boers all looked at each other. " We would never
vote for a candidate who took the canal round by Zielen,"
said one—the youngest, apparently pulling hard at a shining coat button.

" Juistament," muttered all the others.

The Burgomaster knew that. It was what they were
come for. Next spring a canal was to be cut right across
the province, and in the natural course of affairs it would
have nothing to do with the populous village to which these
people belonged. But it might be made to twist past it at
considerable extra expense, and these, the notabilities of the

---

* Pronounce yoistementt, a corruption of the French justement.

neighborhood, had come up to inquire which way the candidate would exert his influence, before they gave their vote.

"The advantages to your part of the province are manifest," said the Burgomaster hastily, "I feel confident you will find no man more willing than my son-in-law to admit that. He will be in immediately, and will tell you so himself. He is a little chary of his words, and rough in his way of putting things, but you mustn't mind his manner. Besides, of course, as candidate, one must be careful what one says. All your words are used against you. And, mind you, let me tell you this before he comes. You don't expect him to be such a fool as to say plainly that he'll do what you want, do you? Eh?"

The boers looked uneasily at one another. No one spoke.

"Because, look here," the Burgomaster came quite close, and tapped the old spokesman on the breast, "if you expect that, you needn't wait for him. I know Mynheer Avelingh; he's no fool, as I say. As deep as some of you boers, whom no one ever tried to cheat yet without cutting his own nose off. He doesn't commit himself, not before the election. He won't have any newspaper reporter finding out and printing that he's promised you the canal. Not he. You know what the poet says :—

"'If speech be silver, silence must be gold.'

You know that, eh?"

Half the boers nodded.

"Well, let me tell you one thing. Mark my words," the Burgomaster impressively shook his finger to and fro in front of the old boer's face. "To say one thing and mean another, that's the money a political candidate has to pay with." He drew himself up in triumph and surveyed his audience. "And therefore," he continued, "I know my son-in-law, and, of course, as his—his fatherly counselor—I largely advise him and give him the benefit of my experience. And I am acquainted with his views of this subject. You understand me?"

"*Ja, ja,* Heer Burgomaster," said the boers.

"Of course you do. I wish I always had such fellows as you to do business with, instead of my burgher people. We should get on better. Very well; I may tell you that if the candidate says; 'I won't do it,' he won't, and there's an end of it. But if he says: 'I shall do what's right. I shall examine the matter and arrange for the best,' or anything of that kind, then he will. And don't expect him to break his own window-panes by a promise in so many words, for he won't do it. Nobody would. And if you want that, you may as well go home at once."

"We should have liked a definite promise," said one boer.

"Then go to the other side," cried the Burgomaster impatiently. "I dare say they'll promise anything. It's the definite promises that nobody keeps. And here you'll get what's far better, an indirect one. At least from the candidate. *I'm* a free man, and I don't mind going farther and saying: 'We'll do what we can.'"

"Will the Heer Burgomaster give us that in writing?" interposed the youngest boer again.

"I should not mind, but what's the use?" replied van Hessel. "It's not like a promise to pay. We'll use our influence. Whether I say that or write it, it comes to the same thing. You don't expect us to shout out our views on the house-tops — although house-tops are the best things for *views,* eh?" (Nobody saw this. Besides, a Dutch boer never laughs.) "It's backstairs influence you and I want, I suppose. It's backstairs influence does it. And backstairs influence you shall have. Half-a-word's enough to a good listener. Mind that, when you speak to my son-in-law. Half-a-word's enough to a good listener. Fine weather for the crops, eh?" And the Burgomaster talked about the agricultural outlook till Joost Avelingh walked into the hall.

The preparations for the election were in full swing now, and the candidate had a busy time of it. He looked bright and energetic; it was true, as he said, that the bustle and hard work did him good. He stopped, when he saw the little group round his father-in-law, and looked inquiringly from one to the other. The worthy Burgomaster rapidly introduced the deputation, and explained the object of their visit.

"I am much obliged to you," said Joost, "for the trouble you have taken in coming to see me"; he had learned already, to a certain extent, the little ways and tricks of a successful politician. "I shall of course do what I can to further your interests, but I can not promise anything with regard to the canal."

The Burgomaster winked at the deputation. Nobody winked back, but there was the slightest twinkle of sympathy in one or two of those cunning little eyes.

"I have not studied the subject at all, as yet," said Joost. "I should say, superficially speaking, that the canal would naturally go by Zielen. But I must examine the matter first."

"Of course, of course," interposed the Burgomaster. "Naturally by Zielen, but there may be other reasons— other reasons which we shall easily discover, why it should not."

"There may," said Joost, "but I must wait till I have discovered them."

"Zielen is not in your district," said one boer, with a sharp look.

The Burgomaster trembled for the effect of this speech. "You may be sure," he said, hastily, "that we shall act as seems best."

"Yes," said Joost. "I shall do what I think is right, as far as possible. Be sure, gentlemen, that I shall further the interests of my district, and of your part of it, with all the means in my power. I shall do what I can for you. But I must do what is right. You will take a glass of beer?" He passed on to the dining-room. The Burgomaster winked once more to the deputation, and put his finger to his lips.

CHAPTER XXXIII.

MORE ABOUT THE MAD COUNTESS.

"It was quite right of you not to commit yourself," he said to Joost as soon as they were alone. "And, really, the idea of the canal going round in an unnecessary curve like that is too absurd, and could only come up in the heads of clownish peasants like those creatures. But you can always talk about it to the minister afterward and tell him you don't expect him to listen to you but that you do it "*pour acquit de conscience.*"

Joost did not answer. He was wondering how long he would keep his hands clean in the struggle of political life.

"But now to talk of something else," said the Burgomaster, walking to another part of the room and earnestly scrutinizing a picture which hung there. "I am sorry to say that I also must have a little conversation on business with you, Joost."

"Indeed!" said his son-in-law. A cloud came over his face. He did not like talking about business with Mynheer van Hessel.

"Yes," replied the Burgomaster, still deep in contemplation of the work of art before him. "Yes. It is always

more or less unpleasant, but it is unavoidable. You know
I hate beating about the bush. Let us be brief, and frank.
I will be frank above all things. Even my enemies admit
that I am the soul of frankness. Very well. I must make
a clear statement. Some people would call it a confession.
Let me rather describe it as an elucidation of such action as
I may have considered myself obliged to take under peculiar
circumstances. Confession is such a misleading word. You
are with me so far?"

"Farther," said Joost with a lowering smile. "If you
want money again, please tell me at once how much. I
can't promise I shall be able to give a large sum this time."

The Burgomaster turned from the picture and came forward, holding up both hands deprecatingly. "Money!"
he said, "money, dear boy; I do not want money.

> "'I ask not silver, ask not gold,
>   I claim the love which you withhold.'

Not that you withhold your love from me—far from it—
but the poet says so, and I am not responsible for his sentiments. No, I am not going to ask you for money, but your
generous offer makes what I was going to say so much easier.
I have got to speak of some money I owe you and unhappily—at present—can hardly refund."

"I know all about that," said Joost hastily, "why speak
of it?"

"Ahem," replied the Burgomaster. "It is not that.
Hardly that. I am not alluding to the small sum which—
well, well; we will drop that subject as you wish it. This
is a different matter; no connection with any arrangements
of yours. Altogether unknown to you in fact."

"Indeed?" said Joost. "Then can't it remain so?"

"It might, perhaps," answered the Burgomaster, a little
ruefully. "But no,"—he struck his manly breast—"I consider it my duty to make you acquainted with the facts.

And I hope you will appreciate my uprightness in so doing. It is painful as you can imagine, for a parent—"

"Yes," interrupted Joost, hastily. "And now, briefly, if you would be so kind,—as you promised—and frankly, what is it?"

"I had a sister once, Joost. I do not suppose you were aware of that fact?"

"No," said Joost, with genuine astonishment.

"She was older than I was. She never appeared in these parts."

"She died young, I suppose?" said Joost.

"Hardly. No; I should not say she died young. She disappeared young; let us put it like that. When she was about twenty years old, she unfortunately went off her head; turned crazy, you know; very regrettable. And so—eh—they locked her up. Very sad—eh—very sad. Same thing had happened to her aunt before; made it all the worse."

"I had no idea of this," said Joost. It was very sad, as you say, for the lady. Does Agatha know of it?"

"Not she. In fact nobody knows of it. At least, nobody who would speak of the subject. She was—mercifully—abroad at the time, and my father gave out that she died there. He did not want it to damage my prospects, and he knew, poor man, that *his* eldest sister's madness had kept his other two sisters—who weren't crazier than most old maids—from marrying all their lives. So we brought poor Agatha home and locked her up in the provincial asylum, and kept it dark."

"Agatha," cried Joost, with an involuntary shudder.

"Yes, that was her name. One of the daughters in our family has been called Agatha for at least six generations," said the Burgomaster with evident pride.

Joost shuddered again. "How could you call your daughter Agatha?" he asked.

"Why not?" said the Burgomaster in astonishment.

"I don't know," said Joost. "The name—" he shuddered again. He had always had an inexplicable horror of madness in all its forms. At that moment he remembered his visit to the asylum with his uncle on the day of van Trotsem's death.

"Nonsense, Joost. I have always said you were so melodramatic. You must have it from your poor mother who made that runaway match. It *was* a foolish match; old Trotsem was right there. And I dare say she repented of it."

"And what about your sister? What connection had she with the money you owe me?"

"I am coming to that. Of course, my poor sister being mad, hopelessly mad, as all the doctors said—and in spite of their unanimity she never got better, but she was always of a contrary nature from her birth—I might naturally be considered her heir. In fact, I could really be looked upon as the *de facto* owner of her property already. Does the law admit that mad people can have property? Evidently not. And that's why we appoint a trustee or curator."

"The opposite conclusion seems as reasonable," said Joost. "Were you curator?" He threw a good deal of unconscious meaning into the last three words.

"I was. And I may say that the deceased had no cause to regret it. She never wanted for anything, and a first-class lunatic, as you may be aware, is a very expensive thing."

"But if the money was her own?" said Joost.

"Just so. She never wanted for anything. But the money was not her own, exactly. And in fact—look here, Joost, this was how the whole thing came about. My sister had no money, and I had none either—you know that; for you found it out when you took my poor Agatha without a penny; my money is my wife's—and really, I do not know what would have become of her, if your uncle van Trotsem, who was the soul of generosity, had not stepped in and provided for her for life."

"My uncle van Trotsem!" cried Joost in amazement,

"my uncle van Trotsem was not the soul of generosity, nor anything like it. What made him do that?"

But the Burgomaster hurried on with his back turned to his son-in-law: "And I must tell you briefly and frankly, Joost; briefly and frankly: that he settled during his lifetime, in fact, shortly after my father's death, a sum of eighty thousand florins * on the poor creature for life, the money to be administered by me and the yearly interest to go to her support. And I can assure you most solemnly—I can swear to you—that she received every penny that was due to her until the day of her death, which occurred a month or two ago, I regret to say."

" But what induced my uncle to make such an arrangement?" queried Joost.

" I always said it was a bad arrangement, not square and above-hand, you know. And I am glad to see you agree with me. But your venerable relation, who, perhaps, was stingy, as you say, thought differently, and he made the extraordinary stipulation that the capital should revert to him or his heirs at her death. Only, as we were all anxious that no one should know anything about the sad circumstances, it was to be refunded to the heirs as repayment of money the Baron had lent me."

" And the money is gone?" said Joost.

" I regret to say, my dear boy, that there is not as much money left as I had hoped there would be. Through no fault of mine, I can assure you. Unfortunate investments : Misplaced confidence. You know what the Scripture saith : ' Riches make unto themselves wings and flee away.' No one, I can assure you, is to blame, but the money is unhappily not forthcoming."

" Then why tell me of the whole matter?" said Joost. " I did not know about it."

---

* Some £6,500.

" For that, my dear boy, nothing is to blame but another man's fussy interference. It was a great mistake of your uncle to mix up a Notary in so private a matter, and appoint him co-trustee. And now, though I have told the Notary a hundred times to leave near relations like you and me to settle such matters between them, he insists upon seeing your receipt for the money. He has worried my life out of me these last three weeks." The Burgomaster heaved a deep sigh.

" I see," said Joost. " And how much of the money is left ? "

" Well, if you wish it, I believe it might be possible to say that five thousand florins were left—but really—"

" I see," said Joost. " So you want me to sign a little paper stating that I have received eighty thousand from Mynheer van Hessel in payment of a debt contracted in my uncle's lifetime."

" Really, Joost, there is no hurry. At least, there would not be, if that unconscionable Notary had any sense of decency. Of course, I have told him how busy you are with your election just now. But he won't listen; and if you *could* oblige me—*Bis dat qui cito dat*, you know."

" I must think of it," said Joost, shortly. " I believe I shall have some conditions to propose. The whole story has taken me utterly by surprise. I can not understand my uncle's action in the matter."

" Well, to tell you the truth, there had been some flirtations, all in secret though, between him and my sister. Your uncle was a young fellow of twenty or so. His father wouldn't hear of it. Stupid old man, I suppose. And Agatha went mad, and your uncle remained unmarried and loved his sister instead, who wasn't born, I should say, at the time. She would have gone mad in any case, I suppose, like her aunt. But I don't know what your uncle thought, or didn't think. All I know is he looked after her, and I believe he used to go and see her even. Rum story. Sounds quite romantic. Queer old chap, your uncle. I have sometimes thought his refusal to let you marry my girl had something to do with a romantic fear he had she might go mad in time, like the other two women."

The whole connection rushed in upon Joost with terrible certainty. He was amazed at himself for not having perceived it before.

"Do you mean to tell me," he cried, starting up, "that my uncle was bound to secrecy about this horrible family-secret of yours, and that you now come and tell me my wife is going mad, and you both knew it?" He seized the old man by the breast and actually shook him.

"Joost, my dear Joost!" cried the Burgomaster, retreating rapidly, "you are outrageous. Really, I can not allow this. I must beg of you—There is no question of mental derangement in Agatha! She is perfectly well and sensible. Really, my dear Joost!"

Joost recovered himself with an effort. "I beg your pardon," he said, "the news upset me. I think you had better leave me for a little."

"I assure you Agatha is not at all like her aunt. The poor old lady was as silly as silly can be. She called herself Countess de Montélimart, an absurdity; and even at her death she left me a parrot and a canary she called her children, and she sent me word that two others had died. I had their necks wrung immediately; the parrot might have told unpleasant tales."

"Leave me now," said Joost in a dull voice, "I will let you know about the money. I shall make a condition about it; that is all. Good-by, Burgomaster." He leaned his elbows on the desk, and hid his face in his hands till the Burgomaster had softly left the room.

Even then he retained the same position. He was slowly recapitulating the events of that fatal fourteenth of Decem-

ber, his uncle's last day on earth. He knew now the reason
why that uncle had opposed his marriage, a reason prompted, after all, whatever might have been its real value, by the
interest the old man felt in his nephew. And a solemn
promise, given to the father of four marriageable daughters,
had bound over the Baron to a silence he could not even
break when his ward's happiness came to be concerned in
the matter. The old man's words came back to Joost now,
across the years, with frightful clearness, no longer as cruel
threats and meaningless taunts. The kindness, misplaced
as it had been, and awkward and unintelligible, had been
truly kindness of its sort. No one, overlooking the past,
could say that Joost's had been a happy boyhood, or that
his uncle had done aught to brighten it, but the great
charges of cruelty, which Joost's heart had always preferred
against his guardian, had vanished into air, and, in the sudden alteration, it seemed to Joost himself that he had lost
tangible hold of all unkindness whatsoever, and that nothing remained to him but the great sense of the life-long injury he had done, in thought and word, to a man who had
suffered years of continual misrepresentation on behalf of
his sister, and of his sister's child.

"What does it matter?" he said, raising a hot face from
his hands and throwing back his hair. "What does it matter after all? The result is that he made me miserable."

It was true, if you will. Yet he sank his face on his
hands again with something like a groan.

CHAPTER XXXIV.

BLINDFOLD NOT LOVE, IF LOVE BE BLIND.

"I was coming to you, mamma," said Joost, reining in his horses.

"And I to you," replied Mevrouw van Hessel, from her victoria. "I got your note this morning."

"And I yours an hour ago. Shall I join you?"

"Let us get out," said Mevrouw, in French. "We can walk up the road a little, and talk without the servants hearing."

Joost jumped down and held out his hand to assist his mother-in-law in alighting. They strolled up the dusty highway side by side. It was a beautiful September afternoon, warm, and fresh, and exhilarating, with a clear white-flecked sky and soft tints on the trees. Neither spoke. It seemed as if both had some difficulty about beginning. Joost stole one or two side-glances at Mevrouw van Hessel, still portly and stately of bearing, but with a careworn expression on her features and intricate lines on the lofty forehead, only partly hidden under braids of snow-white hair.

"Your letter said you had something you wished to speak to me about," he remarked at last.

"Yes, Joost, I have, but I do not know how to begin," she answered. "I am so afraid of offending you. It's a difficult matter for old people like me to interfere with you young ones, and it's especially unwise of parents to meddle in any way in the married life of their children. If I had not been so convinced of that, I should have spoken about it long ago."

"Fie, mamma; that was not right of you," said Joost kindly. "Surely you have a claim to be heard, if you deem it advisable. You must speak now, at any rate."

"I must," said Mevrouw, "or I should not have broached the subject at all. But, Joost,'—she turned round and looked full in his face—"I warn you, I am going to interfere and give advice. Can you bear it from me? If not, better tell me at once, and we'll say no more about it."

"I can bear a good deal from Agatha's mother," said Joost. "For I know that her one thought is Agatha's happiness."

"Yours too," said Mevrouw quickly. "Yours too, most certainly, for you are my son also now. But it's just the happiness of you both I want to speak about. Only I am so afraid of implying that I fancy you don't try to make Agatha happy, which is just the last thing I am wanting to say: I know you are indeed very happy together, and that ought to make it easier to tell you that you might be happier still. There. It is out, and you must forgive me. I am sure you might be happier if you gave her your full confidence, Joost."

"You have reason to believe Agatha is not as happy as she might be with me!" said Joost a little bitterly.

"There you rush off into extravagances at once. My dear Joost, I used to think myself a wonderfully sensible woman; I have begun to have my doubts on the subject of late years, but surely I must be exceptionally stupid, if I can not make myself plainer to you than that. If I thought you made Agatha unhappy, or if she had spoken to me on the subject, as you seem to infer that she has, should I have begun this conversation with you at all?" She laid her hand on his arm. "You need not answer me, Joost. Least of all need you furnish me any explanation. Only it appears to me that Agatha is unusually depressed, especially of late.—Is there, perhaps, some trouble about this election which is coming on next week?—and I should say—you must forgive a mother? Nothing but a mother's love for her child would make any one speak on so unpleasant a

subject, but, although she has never said a word to me about
it, my impression is that you are keeping something back
from her and that she knows it is so. It is probably the
merest trifle, Joost, and therefore it seems such a pity. She
has not been well these last weeks. She will not tell you,
perhaps, but she is decidedly ailing. Try and find out what
is troubling her. And now you will forgive me, will you
not?—and we shall never speak about it again. Tell me
what it is that made you ask me to come up to the Castle."

"You may be right, mamma," said Joost gravely. "At
any rate, I am much obliged to you for speaking so kindly
about it. Believe me, I am in a very difficult position. I
must first get quite clear in my own heart about it all! It
seems to me as if I should find no time to think till this
election is over. Fortunately it is close at hand now. The
last weeks have been very hard weeks for me. But I shall
still try to act for the best.

"And now let us talk about something else," he continued, changing his tone. "All that you have said about in-
terfering between married people, mamma, is most true and
most applicable to me. I, also, have been hesitating for
some time. And you will forgive me—will you not?—if I
speak now?"

Mevrouw van Hessel stopped in the middle of the road
and stared Joost in the face. The two carriages, following
slowly some fifty paces behind them, immediately stopped
too.

"It is only this," Joost went on hurriedly, "I should
like to be quite sure that papa has not been unfortunate in
money matters. I have feared for some time that it may
have been so from what he has said."

"Oh, is it only that?" said Mevrouw van Hessel. She
had been asking herself if Joost fancied he had discovered
secrets more nearly touching her matrimonial happiness.
She would have laughed at him, and rightly, in that case,

for the Burgomaster had quite faults enough of his own, without any need of inventing others for him. She drew herself up. " Really, Joost," she said, " I should think we had better leave papa to manage these things for himself. He is the best judge of his own financial position, surely."

" I do not think so," said Joost coloring. " You must bear with me now in your turn, mamma. You can imagine it is far from agreeable for me to broach this subject. And I also have awaited, not weeks but months. It is of no direct importance to me, as you will admit, but I must tell you plainly that unless somebody stops the Burgomaster, you will be—ruined."

It was best to call things by their names in dealing with Mevrouw van Hessel. Joost knew it. She bit her lips, and walked on rapidly for some moments.

" Let us see exactly how we stand," she then said. " It is true that you would not speak without good reason. You have cause to believe we are ruined already.".

" I do not say that. I do not know. But, if possible, I want to prevent it. I want your permission—I would do nothing without that—to go with Kees—"

" Does Kees know ? " interrupted Mevrouw anxiously.

" Not yet, I think. To go with Kees and ask the Burgomaster to let us see exactly how matters stand."

" He will not do so," said Mevrouw.

" I think he will. I believe I can persuade him. Then, if things are as bad as I fear, we must insist that the administration of what is left of your money pass into other hands. And if he refuses or makes new debts, we can always threaten him with—it can't be helped—a curatorship."

" Never," said Mevrouw.

" Remember," said Joost gently. " There are your daughters to think of. Agatha is provided for. Verrooy, I suppose has also a sufficiency. But the younger girls—"

R

She signed to him to desist. They walked on again by each other's side.

Presently Mevrouw van Hessel stopped. "So be it," she said firmly. She beckoned to her coachman.

"Poor Papa," she added, as if speaking to herself.

"Poor Mamma," said Joost. He took her hand and would have bent over it, but she drew it quickly back. "No sympathy," she said in a hard voice.

The victoria drew up at her feet. She got into it and then, bending over the side as Joost lifted his hat, she burst out in rapid French: "Oh you men, you men! We believe in you, love you, trust you, serve you; we live for you; we would die for you—and you repay us! I thought I knew all his secrets, and no doubt I knew all—but this one. He so careful to smile it away; I so fond to ignore it! Go back to your wife and tell her whatever you are hiding. Better the worst of confessions than a life of deceit! Home, Jacob."

The victoria drove rapidly off. Joost, crying to his coachman to begone, struck moodily into a bypath across the fields.

It was no wonder that Agatha should have noticed the alteration which had slowly come over him in the last fortnight. The rest which had followed on his acquittal of the charge of murder had not been of many months' duration. And the successive discoveries he had made with regard to his uncle's treatment of him had shocked and unsettled his soul to its very foundation. In the suddenness of the change, he now exaggerated the old man's goodness, as much as he had formerly undervalued it, and all the anger and hatred he had long cherished in his heart turned rapidly and irresistibly against himself. The whole atmosphere of unkindness and injustice which had lain so thick around his youth, seemed to fade away and dissolve. He caught at it in vain, and—foolish man—would have striven to retain it, but he only found himself face to face with the sunshine pouring down into his own black, ungrateful heart. And his generous nature—for it was thoroughly and affectionately generous—accordingly broke loose in unmerited self-reproach. At first, of course, the discovery he had made, largely as it affected his uncle's memory, did not influence his own remorse for the sin he had committed, for he was perfectly conscious that it is not a rule of ethics that you may injure a man who has behaved badly to you but may not injure the man who did well, yet, nevertheless, gradually his impressions shifted like a dissolving view, and, to say the least of it, his altered thoughts of the Baron materially inclined the plane of self-recognition down which his heart was already running. And Joost's was a very human heart. It did not work out its problem according to the rules of the psychologists, and two and two did not always make four in it, but very often five.

He hated himself now, not with the pretty half-pleased consciousness that he was properly self-reproachful, and distinguished shades of gray where most people talked of white, but with the fierce dissatisfaction and restless self-contempt of one who knows that, despite the scorn within him, no human being can ever really deserve contempt alone. He hated himself as a man of purer, nobler aspirations who had lived a lie and loved it while he lived it. God! that these hearts of ours should take so long to learn that wrong is hateful, not only because we have been taught to think it so, but because of the misery it brings us!

Joost found himself a prisoner—as we all are more or less—in the environment he had built around himself. The next step was not only difficult, but uncertain. The love he owed his wife came into consideration; the happiness he owed her — to her who had suffered so much for his sake—no less. The new sphere of usefulness opening up before him—and close at hand now—with its special attrac-

tions for a man already occupied as he was, could not be
lightly overlooked. He had told himself, when first the
news was brought him, that this time the summons came
from a higher Power than human intrigue, and that he
must obey it. It was this idea which had chiefly helped to
overcome his scruples. He may be pardoned for the
thought. For he had been nominated in an entirely new and
striking manner—directly by the people—and the trials he
had gone through had served as a preparation for that
nomination; with his income of twelve thousand a year he
was one of the wealthiest, and therefore one of the most
powerful men in the country; he was yearning to benefit
those who would elect him, his head full of schemes both
practical and unpractical. Should he give up all prospects
of future utility, should he destroy his wife's felicity for an
idea? Would he, in doing so, not rather disobey the Providence which had led him thus far? He paused under the
trees of his own beautiful home-park, and struck his hand
against his forehead. The next step must be the one now
before him. The election was coming on in a few days. It
must come. Till then he could do nothing. He resolved
to let much depend on that. And would not his success
on that occasion be a divine answer to his doubts, a message
bidding him go forward in God's name and do well? For
his heart recoiled from the other extreme.

CHAPTER XXXV.

THE ELECTION.

A DUTCH election is a very different thing from an English one. There is quite as much excitement and acri-

mony; there is perhaps less bribery, but more intimidation; there is an equal amount of false representation of the candidates on the other side. All that is unavoidable, and will remain so, as long as men are men, and gold is gold. We call it " political life among the masses " in Holland : in England it is accounted for—is it not?—by the fact that " party feeling runs high in the borough " ? After all these nineteenth-century communities, big and little, Celtic and Saxon, are very similar in their tastes and distastes. In the autocratic East the ignorant multitude still venerate the Czar, and the great Padishah; the West has grown more cosmopolitan, and its nations blend their adoration in common worship of the same Golden Calf. The new religion is called Democracy, and the polling-days are its high festivals.

But whatever happens in Holland on such occasions, happens behind the scenes. There are no placards, no ribbons, no banners, no musicians, no processions, no polling-booths, " no nothing," in fact of all that goes to make an English election amusing.

Carriages, without any visible emblem, are employed to convey lazy, or sick, or decrepit electors to the public building in which the usual urn has been set up for the votes. Unwilling or half-hearted individuals are hunted up in their homes and reminded of the duty they owe Church and State. For the political struggle in Holland unavoidably turns almost entirely on the question " Orthodox or liberal in matters of religion ? " Circumstances have so shaped the destinies of the country that for the present no other battle-ground seems possible. We can not, unfortunately, agree beforehand on the stakes of our political tournaments, or the English would never have chosen " home rule."

The contest is intense with all the vindictiveness and intolerant enthusiasm of religious dissensions, but the Dutch are a quiet people, and their animosities lie low. The foreigner who arrived in one of their cities would certainly not

know that an election was going on there and a certain
number of the inhabitants of the place itself—the quiet old
maids and the happy people who never read the papers, and
do not know whether the Clericals or the Liberals are in
power—remain in blissful ignorance of the fact from first to
last. The whole city retains its wonted aspect ; only in the
immediate neighborhood of the " bureaus " a line of silent,
determined looking individuals may be perceived slowly
filing past the solemn officials, with their voting-papers
clenched tightly in their hands. And drunkenness there is
none.

On the evening of the day set apart for the voting in the
chief town which had nominated Joost—his was a by-elec-
tion, you remember, caused by an unexpected vacancy—the
candidate had come down to Heist, so as to be more within
reach of the telegrams which came pouring in as the votes
were counted. There was more opposition, after all, than
people had thought possible at first. The side which had
not proclaimed Joost as their candidate—merely because the
others were beforehand—had tried in vain to get him to
formally accept their political programme in all its particulars, none the less ; and, when this failed them—he had taken
no definite engagements upon him, even with regard to the
Club which was pushing him—they quickly put forward a
man of their own. The people had nominated Joost ; the
choice of his antagonists, accordingly immediately fell on a
large employer of labor—and that divided the votes. Many
of the gentry, too, hesitated about giving their support to
Joost Avenlingh—he was too popular a man to their taste—
and they carried their unwilling servants and tenants with
them. The new idea of independent selection met with a
good deal of quiet disapproval. There was cause enough
then to scrutinize anxiously the telegrams which succeeded
each other in intervals of a few minutes only.

Joost, Kees and the Burgomaster sat in the latter gen-

tleman's private room around a table strewn with papers.
Kees had a great sheet before him on which he was jotting
down the figures as they altered; Joost sat with his arms
crossed and his lips compressed; the Burgomaster lay back
in his chair and blew rings of smoke from his cigar. Only
four or five days ago—immediately after Mevrouw had given
her permission—Joost had brought his father-in-law to book
in Kees's presence. Mynheer van Hessel had protested innocence at first and righteous indignation. He had talked—
with his hand on his heart—about " *integer vitae scelerisque
purus* " and " teaching your grandmother to suck eggs,"
but when Joost took him aside and plainly told him that the
settlement of that little bill of the curatorship and the contentment of the troublesome Notary depended upon this
primary arrangement, he acquiesced, though it took two
hours and a half of pleading and protestation to get the
truth out of his good-natured, untruthful old head. At last
it became plain that, if Joost's claim were sunk altogether,
enough might be saved from the wreck of Mevrouw van
Hessel's fortune to allow the family to live on quietly with
considerable retrenchment. The money must henceforth be
managed by the two younger men, Mevrouw van Hessel to
receive the interest in monthly installments. The Burgomaster cried, called himself a bitterly ill-used old creature,
and then—after having likened himself to King Lear—gave
his son a long description of a parody of the tragedy he had
seen in his youth, and roared with laughter over the comical
character of " *la trop cordiale Cordélie.*" In the mean time
Joost sat ciphering at a side-table. When he brought back
his terms, the Burgomaster assented under protest; he only
stipulated that the post of his own private expenses should
remain untouched. " I can't smoke another brand of cigars," he said, " I'm too old; and I must give your mother
her silk dress on her birthday, Kees. She's had it for the
last thirty years, and she couldn't live without it."

So Joost bought the repose of his mother-in-law and her daughters for eighty thousand florins.

"Why, things aren't half as bad yet as they might have been," said Kees, who, like the rest of the world, knew nothing about the terms of this compromise. "I only hope we haven't been too hard on the poor old governor." Joost went and told Mevrouw van Hessel, who sat anxiously awaiting the result of the conference, what decision they had come to. The carriage must be suppressed; a servant must go, if possible, and one or two laborers also. The dinner parties must be made less frequent and more simple; the girls must give up a large part of their allowance.

"Is that all?" asked Mevrouw. It seemed to her that the sacrifice was too little, for she had prepared herself for the worst. Joost, looking at the tall reposeful woman wondered whether she had schooled her heart to the workhouse. Compared to what she had been accustomed to from her birth, this new life would be penury, misery, drudgery, and she seemed resolved not to let him see she disliked the idea. The Burgomaster crept in with a rueful look, and kissed his wife cautiously on the back of her neck.

"Ichabod. Ichabod," he said. "The glory is departed from Israel. And as for the carriage, it is but half an economy, for we shall be spending two thirds of the money on boots and cabs." "Half" and "two thirds"; the confusion, by a comical chance, happily illustrated the worthy man's ideas of finance.

And now the three gentlemen sat together in the Burgomaster's room. That unpleasant little discussion about money-matters was never more alluded to between them. And for the moment, at any rate, each one's thoughts were occupied with the election. Joost himself, carried away by the excitement and that craving to "come in first" which overmasters man and beast in every contest, was "in it" heart and soul. He snatched the telegrams and tore them open. "We *must* win, Kees," he said.

"Of course we shall win," replied Kees.

"I only wish Agatha had been able to come with me."

"Is Agatha less well again? I thought she was looking poorly," said Kees, "she has got quite gloomy of late. You must cheer her up."

"Woman is the weaker vessel," interposed the Burgomaster sententiously; "this excitement is doubtless telling upon her. They are not able to bear worry as we are. Look how your mother fidgets, Kees, when she has to go to the station. Agatha will be all right when this election is over." •

A telegram was brought in as he spoke. They were counting rapidly over yonder. Joost—so far—was but two or three hundred votes ahead of the other man. There could only be a few more hundreds to count altogether.

"Why, almost every elector in the place must have voted," said Kees.

"There are too many electors now by far," grumbled his father. "Things were better in my day when only those could express their opinion who had something to lose if the voting went wrong."

"I don't know, papa," said Kees. "The people with something to lose are too apt to think themselves the only people who should have something to gain. And that's my opinion."

Another telegram. Only three hundred more voters in the district, and Joost still ahead!

"How many votes have the outsiders?"

"There will be a second ballot," cried Joost, fretfully. "What a calamity! Another fortnight of suspense! I can't stand it."

"To think of its being so contested," said Kees. "I should never have thought it possible at first. The other

side have fought bravely. Do you know, the most ridiculous thing of all is the part that van Asveld has sought to
play against you. They tell me he has made himself quite
useful to the others, if only by going about everywhere and
calling you a murderer and telling every one that the magistrates do not believe in your innocence. And to-day, I
hear, he has been driving a break all over the town at a
frantic pace, bringing up voters from the other ends of the
earth. How that fellow hates you! And all on account of that
money. I don't believe he would have got it in any case."

Another telegram. A considerable accession of votes to
Joost. He had passed the absolute majority. More than
that, he had already, although the other candidate was but
a couple of hundred behind him, exceeded one half of the
number of votes which could possibly be registered, even
though all the electors of the district should avail themselves of their right. He was elected.

"Elected! hurrah!" cried Kees, throwing up a pen-
wiper—the first thing he could lay hold of—and catching
it as it fell. The Burgomaster blew out his most perfect
little smoke-ring, and lovingly watched it, as it floated up
toward the ceiling.

> "The world, which fools so foolish call,
>   Is not so foolish after all,"

he said; "it can give wonderful proofs of sagacity sometimes. I congratulate you, my dear Deputy, from the
depths of a father's heart. This is a proud moment in the
annals of the family."

Joost stood motionless, with the telegram in his hand.
"It is God's answer," he said to himself.

Kees drew the slip of paper out of his hand. "Avelingh,
3,010," he read hurriedly. "Possen, 2,770. Others, 30.
It's all right, Joost. There are only six thousand electors,
altogether. Never mind further telegrams."

"I must be off home," cried Joost; "I want to tell Agatha. Send my man round, please. He was not to unharness."

"Let me go with you," said Kees. "Don't be afraid. I sha'n't intrude."

"All right," Joost called out. He was already in the hall. "I'll just run in to the others, and then we can start."

They had heard his voice as he opened the door, and they all came streaming out of the drawing-room. There were acclamations and congratulations and hand-shakings innumerable. The servants crept up to the top of the stairs and looked across curiously. The butler ventured further into the hall, and congratulated the family. A new light flickered in Mevrouw van Hessel's pale eyes. A flood of brightness seemed to be poured out on the whole household after the depression and gloom of the last few days. For the excitement of the approaching election had not been able to dispel the heaviness which the family misfortunes had brought in their train. The van Hessels were glad to have something to rejoice at. So they laughed, and shouted: "Long live the Deputy!" and escorted Joost in triumph to his carriage, which had come round to the front door.

"Mynheer is elected," cried Kees to the coachman.

"Yes," said Joost, as he stepped in. "Drive as fast as you can!" The brougham, with the two brothers-in-law inside it, dashed away into the darkness of the soft autumn night.

Kees rattled on all the time about the incidents of the struggle, but his companion answered him in inconsequent monosyllables only. His heart was overflowing in a very triumph of rejoicing, and sparkling with the intoxicating glitter of victory—like a goblet of champagne newly filled—all a-tremble with its own golden froth. Victory, victory for this bright delicious moment! Oh that he could seize at that fleeting experience, and, shivering the wine glass, could grasp one fair fragment in his hand forever. But the golden bubbles fly upward and burst on the surface. Pooh, it was not the broken glass he desired, but the wine that tingled in it, and the wine is best for drinking when its effervescence is stilled. In the future, the calm, hardworking future now opening up in the distance, the true triumph would lie. God had answered him and had bidden him put his hand to the plow and not falter. There was work to be done, plenty of it, for those with heads—and above all with hearts—to do it. All that he had achieved for the toilers of his own province till now was as nothing to what he could do for the nation! Work for the poor and the oppressed, the wretched factory girls and the little children, the paupers in the workhouse, the unfortunates in the streets. God had answered him and had said to him: " Go forward and do it." Till now there had been sorrow enough in his life, and temptation, and trial. They were preparations for the sphere of usefulness to which he was to be called. And now let him use his little day, while he could, nothing wavering. The night cometh in which no man can work! He leaned back in his corner, his whole frame in such a tremble of exultation he dreaded lest Kees should see it and laugh at him. The carriage passed swiftly up the avenue to the Castle, its lamps flashing on the great, century-old trees. It drew up before the house.

Joost sprang out. The great door was thrown open. In another moment he was in the hall. He ran to the drawing-room, and, finding it empty, passed hurriedly into Agatha's boudoir. A lamp was burning ; a small fire was lighted ; her books lay about and a piece of unfinished needlework. She was not there. He ran back to the hall. Kees had just reached the mat. " Mynheer is elected," said Kees to the manservant.

" Where is Mevrouw?" cried Joost exultingly, as he hurried across to his own room and threw open the door.

The servant came after him. Joost, turning suddenly, saw that the man's face was white and scared.

" Mevrouw is not well, Mynheer," said the servant. " Mevrouw is upstairs. The doctor is with her."

" The doctor!" Joost had dashed across the vestibule again, and was half-way up the staircase when he met Doctor Kern. That gentleman put his arm through his and drew him down again into his own room. He had heard the sound of wheels, and had left the sickroom to meet the master of the house.

" What is it, doctor?" cried Joost. " Nothing much, surely? Let me go to her!"

" My dear sir," said the doctor gravely, " not in this condition. Calm yourself. Mevrouw has been taken unwell; somewhat suddenly. I am glad the servants had the good sense to send for me immediately. I have done what I can. We must wait and see."

" But what is it?" cried Joost impatiently. " She was all right this morning. Only a little tired, she said."

" Hardly all right," replied the doctor. " The worst of these abominable women is: they *will* not complain. If they would only cry out before they were hurt, as we men do, they would never get into any such scrapes."

" She is very ill?" said Joost. " She is dying? She is dead?"

" Tut, tut, tut, my good Heer. No, she is not dead yet. One would think you believed I had buried her while you were away. She is not dying either, but I tell you the whole truth. She is certainly ill."

" Let me go to her," said Joost, making for the door.

" You shall, if you choose, though it is not much use, for she is unconscious. That is the worst; I can not get her back to consciousness."

"What is wrong?" said Joost. "For God's sake, what is wrong?"

"Sir," said the doctor gravely, "I can not tell you definitely. I am afraid there is some mischief with the brain. Mevrouw has evidently had much to worry her lately. She has, of course, undergone quite exceptional sufferings at the time of the trial, but it seems as if the results would have manifested themselves sooner and not so many months afterward. Still, there is no saying, and probably this fresh excitement about the election has completed the work. 'Inflammation, Congestion,' are ugly words, but, really, we need not be surprised if Mevrouw were to have a serious cerebral illness. I could find causes enough to explain it, unless indeed—" the doctor paused and cast a sharp look at Joost. Was it accident or design?—"unless you perhaps can account for this special attack by some special circumstance, Mynheer Avelingh?"

"She came through the trial wonderfully well," interposed Kees. "I was with her constantly all the time. It is only these last weeks she has been so changed. But while Joost was in prison she did not seem to suffer physically at all."

"The strain may have been all the greater," said the doctor.

"I don't think so. She was so convinced of his innocence, you see. Showed her sense by never doubting for a moment. And that's sure to carry you through, at least in my humble opinion. It's the idea of guilt that kills."

"Doubtless," said the doctor, dryly. "Well, well, we must hope for the best. I have to go back for something, but I shall return as soon as I possibly can. You may go upstairs, if you like, Avelingh, but—as I tell you—Mevrouw is unconscious and will probably remain so. If she should begin to talk, it will in all likelihood be nonsense. You mustn't mind that. I have told her maid what to do.

Seems a sensible woman, that maid. Some connection with Jan Lorentz, hadn't she? By the by, do you know anything of Jan Lorentz?"

"No," said Joost, huskily. "I will go upstairs. Come back as soon as you can." He passed into the hall. "Avelingh is elected, doctor," he heard Kees saying. "It's a pity things should just come out like this. Very unfortunate."

"Elected, is he?" said the doctor. "I suppose I should congratulate him. I ought to have asked after it. I really quite forgot. He is a very lucky man! I only hope his wife will some day appreciate his good luck. My great fear is, van Hessel—knowing what I know—that, if she has such an illness as this and recovers, she will never talk sense again in her life."

CHAPTER XXXVI.

JOOST SURRENDERS.

JOOST AVELINGH went up to his wife's room.

The doctor's last words had been spoken low, but Joost, stopping for a moment in the hall to pass a hand over his eyes and collect his bewildered thoughts, just caught them. He stumbled upstairs, opened the bed-room door, and walked in.

God had answered him. There lay his wife, white and motionless, with staring, meaningless eyes, under the white coverlet—unconscious, insensible. A shaded lamp burned on a side-table; Dientje, the maid, rose softly from her chair near it, and came forward. He motioned her away—toward the adjoining dressing-room—and then sat down alone by the bed.

God had answered him. In the pride of his heart he

had sought himself an answer, and had triumphed at the
thought that it should be a pleasing one. But the very fact
of his yearning for a sign in the heavens was the surest
proof that the oracle in his own heart had spoken already.
It had been speaking through all these months, as each successive experience led him nearer to the truth ; all the shouting and din of the election had not been able to silence its
voice completely; and now, over the tumult of this wild
hour of false exultation, it shrieked aloud ! The intoxica-
tion of the moment died away from him, leaving him the
more dejected. And the hatred and contempt of himself
which the last weeks had fostered once more overflowed his
heart.

God had answered him. He sat staring at the senseless
face before him, and he read the answer there. He did not
believe in such connection as the doctor seemed to snatch at
between Agatha's illness and the trial. Living with her day
by day, he had seen her well and happy, triumphant even,
in the recognition of his innocence. The change had come
suddenly; in the last fortnight, perhaps. He had watched
it; her mother had spoken of it; her brother—but he had
watched it, and seen it for himself. It was God's reply to
all his lying self-exculpation, to his life of deceit. The curse
of her race would fall, surely and swiftly, upon this innocent
wife of his, for so, mysteriously, yet wisely doth God visit
our sins upon our loved-ones. Or, in his mercy, he would
take her to himself and leave her husband comfortless, him
whom no comfort could advantage, and whom misery alone
yet might save. But, whatever the future might fashion, it
would bring them separation—Joost's heart cried out that
it must be so, and the last words the doctor had spoken
were become an irrevocable decree to him. He understood
that it must be thus. He was unworthy to live longer by
the side of this woman whom he cheated, and, whether by
death—to relieve her—or by insanity—to punish him—she

would pass out of his existence. She would never speak to
him again. Never! In that thought he first realized how
unutterably he loved her, with a love which had grown
from a boy's rash fancy for a pretty face, through trials and
mutual enjoyments and deepening sympathies, into the very
essence and existence of the soul. And yet his first yearning was not to retain her, if God bade her pass from him;
it was only that—oh, by all his unworthiness of her, by his
guilt and her gentle innocence, by his passionate love and
her answering affection—by their oneness—of *Thy* giving,
great Father—he might obtain mercy to confess his iniquity
in her sight. For death was not death to him in that moment, nor detachment separation. And ere she—his soul's
diviner part—pass on to fuller purity of knowledge, he
would gather from her lips that she had learned his secret
on this earth, had understood it, and forgiven him. Not,
not to be left here standing with eyes that can not pierce
the darkness, and yet with a hope that told the loved one
loved him still, and now read the soul he had so shrewdly
veiled before her, and now—mayhap—mourned forever for
a unity, high and holy, broken and trodden under foot.
Oh God, have mercy!

He sank down by the bed and buried his face in his
hands. And in the untroubled silence his heart cried aloud.
It was of God that he must obtain forgiveness in the first
place, and he knew it. But his prayers, in that turmoil of
feeling, were of the woman he loved.

Agatha lay silent. She neither spoke nor moved. It
seemed natural to him it should be so. It was as he had
expected. She would never speak to him again. Never.
And his secret would remain his alone.

He still rested his face on his hands and, as he knelt
there, his whole life seemed to rise up before him in its sequence. And, gradually traveling upward, his thoughts
stopped at the days of the trial.

s

The recollection of Jan Lorentz fastened upon him. He could not shake it off. What was the man thinking of at that moment alone, probably, in his prison cell? What was his life? What were his griefs, his pleasures? Did he repent of that night in which his heart had returned to its duty and he had released Avelingh at the cost of his own liberty? Who shall say? He got up and went into the next room. The maid was sitting there.

"Do you know anything of Jan?" he asked abruptly. She started, but she did not ask what Jan he meant.

"I had a letter from him only this week, Mynheer," she said, "he says he is well-cared for and happier than he had thought a man could be in jail. He says he is happier than he has ever been. He says he is at rest."

Joost did not reply. Even while the maid was speaking, a sudden burst of loud music broke the stillness of the calm evening. He tore aside a curtain. There were lights, and moving figures under them, dancing to and fro among the shadows of the trees.

A procession of some kind was coming up the Avenue.

Joost ran downstairs. He met his brother-in-law in the hall.

"Good Heavens, they're coming to serenade you, Joost," cried Kees. "What will do you? What an unfortunate moment! How is Agatha?"

"No better," said Joost. "Tell them, some one, to stop that confounded music."

A servant ran out, and Joost followed on to the terrace, scarcely knowing what he was doing, or what would happen next.

The crowd with their torches and lanterns, their music and banners, were already in front of the house—they had struck up within a few paces of their destination, so as to make their surprise more complete. The appearance of the man they sought was the signal for a burst of cheering.

Cries of " Long live Joost Avelingh ! Long live the Deputy ! " broke forth on all sides, and the music fell in with
the *fanfare* which Dutch custom prescribes on such occasions. The crowd began to sing; " Long shall he live in
glory," the Dutch equivalent to " For he's a jolly good fellow ! " and it was several minutes before silence could be restored. Ultimately, however, the last sounds died away. A
great stillness followed. Everybody expected the Deputy
would now speak.

Joost's voice rose clear and stern on the hushed air.

" Friends," he said, standing on the terrace, with Kees
a few paces behind him. The confused glare from the
torches fell on the stately house and on the tall form and
white face of its master. " Friends, I am grateful for your
kindness. Believe me, I am truly grateful. But do not
expect me to say much to-night. My wife is lying up
there," he pointed with his right hand—" dying—perhaps
already dead. And I "—he faltered; a whirlwind of confusion swept over him.

" Good-night," he said.

The crowd—amazed, frightened, thoroughly disconcerted
—turned to slink away by twos and threes. But even in
that moment of misery he could not bear to do an unkind
action.

" My brother-in-law will receive you in the stables," he
called. " In the stables ! Me you must excuse ! See they
get what they want, Kees," he said, " beer and—something."
And he crept upstairs again.

" Long live Joost Avelingh ! Long live the Deputy ! "
the words went ringing in his ears still. They had always
seemed very sweet to him. Praise, love, admiration—the
very ecstasy of living. He pressed his clammy forehead
against the window-pane and looked out upon his broad
acres lying in the shadows, and his heart within him grew
strangely still.

He turned away, and stood one moment gazing down at the motionless face uplifted toward him. And then he flung himself down by the bed in an agony of tears.

"O God," he cried, "I surrender. I surrender. I have striven in vain to expiate my own faults, to shape my own life wisely, to do well in thy sight. And I have failed. I am guilty! I am guilty! Have mercy upon me a sinner, O God!'

He lay there: how long he never knew. He was recalled to the world around him by a soft voice saying "Joost."

He lifted up his head. Meaning had again returned to those staring eyes. They were looking affectionately at him.

It did not surprise him that it should be so. He understood that his prayer had been answered, and that the spirit, already drawn toward another world, had been checked on its threshold to hold parley with him once more.

And, as one who speaks a last word to the dying, he said solemnly: "Agatha. Listen to me. I am innocent in the sight of man, and guilty in the sight of God."

She made an effort to speak, and failed. She lifted her head slightly, and tried again. And the words came back to him in a trembling whisper.

"I knew it, Joost."

And, wonderful to relate, in spite of all his fears of the last hour, that also—in that moment—now she said it, did not seem strange to him.

She smiled to him, a pitiful little smile, full of hope and comfort, and moved her hand. And he seized it, and clasped it, and held it tight on the coverlet, and, laying his head down upon it, he covered it with his kisses and his tears.

"It is the doctor," whispered Dientje at the door. "The doctor has come back," said Kees.

Joost Avelingh came out into the light.

"She is better, Doctor," he said. "She will never go mad. I have fought with myself for her, and regained her from God."

He went downstairs slowly, with Kees still close beside him.

"I must see van Asveld to-morrow," he said.

"Van Asveld? My dear fellow? What in the world?—"

"Yes, I must see van Asveld. Agatha agrees, for, when I said 'van Asveld?' she nodded assent. It had better be to-morrow. Will you bring him up here to-morrow, Kees? I can't very well leave the house just now."

"But he won't come."

"He will. Tell him it is on most important business. In connection with my uncle. He will come."

The doctor came running down-stairs after them. "My dear Avelingh," he cried, "I congratulate you. I can't understand it. But she's better; there is no danger of congestion now. You will have to keep her very quiet, all the same. Perhaps I was a little too anxious, but she certainly was very ill when I came."

Joost turned round and looked at him.

"Did I not tell you so," he said, "before you had seen her? We are nearer to God than we know, Dr. Kern."

"We are not near to God at all," said Dr. Kern to himself, as he got into his gig. "There is nothing but matter and force, and the two produce such fools as Joost Avelingh."

The doctor himself had once said: "Then God help the prisoner," but perhaps he agreed with Beau Liederlen: "que, 'Dieu' c'est une façon de parler dont on ne pourrait plus bien se dispenser." And to Joost Avelingh, kneeling far into the night by his wife's bedside, came the revelation of the one Reality of which all this life is but a shadow that recedes.

CHAPTER XXXVII.

"COULD WE DO ELSE?"

"And you are willing it should be so, dearest?" said Joost.

"Quite willing."

"And you realized, as far as possible, what it involves?"

"I believe so. I have had time enough to think about it."

"Only since yesterday evening!"

"I have thought about it before, Joost."

Joost walked to the window. "How long is it," he asked without looking at his wife, "since you—since you knew—about this? How did you know it?"

Agatha smiled faintly. She was lying back on a sofa, still looking very white among the cushions. "I learned it in a foolish manner," she said, "in such a simple, old-fashioned, terrible manner, Joost"—she shuddered slightly— "For the last two weeks, or perhaps three, you have been talking about it in your sleep, and you told me the whole story bit by bit. I didn't understand in the beginning, but, after the first night or two, the whole thing became clear to me. And then I understood it all."

"It was dreadful," she continued after a moment. "Most dreadful of all to think you were keeping it from me. We can bear it together, Joost. We could not bear it alone. I could not. You see how it has been. I had strength for the trial—but not for this. And yesterday, somehow—I do not know how—I felt I could bear it no longer. And something in my heart gave way and I fell. And I remember nothing more, but hearing beautiful music, until I awoke and looked into your eyes and knew that there was nothing between us any more."

Had the band and the shouting—more effective than all

the doctor's stillness and soothing—recalled her wandering senses? It were impossible to say for certain.

"And when I understood it all, Joost, I understood you for the first time," said Agatha. "And so, now that there is communion between us again, darling, this avowal has not estranged us, but brought us much nearer to each other, much nearer. And therein lies cause for lasting happiness. It has stood between us, more or less, through all these years. And now nothing shall ever come between us any more."

"And you are willing?" said Joost again.

"I am willing to bear all consequences with you," replied Agatha, "could I do else? Or less?"

"Yet I ask myself: have I a right of my own free will, to condemn you to such a punishment?"

"A punishment! No, Joost, do not call it that. It is but the natural development of our actions, surely. Nothing else—as I say—nothing less, would satisfy us. Let us seek satisfaction first. We have been miserable long enough."

"We!" said Joost. "I! No! I can not say that either; I have been guilty, and we have been miserable. I should be happy to-day, were it not for the thought of the sorrow I have brought upon you."

"The sorrow and the joy, Joost," said Agatha. She was too weak to rise from her cushions, but she held out both her hands to him. "The sorrow and the joy. Do not try to separate what is interwoven for all time. And whatever the future brings us, we will rejoice to bear it together, my husband."

CHAPTER XXXVIII.

WHAT SHOULD IT PROFIT A MAN?

"Yes," said Joost to the servant who knocked at the door. "Show the gentleman into my study."

He came forward once more to his wife's sofa. "It is to be then?" he said.

"No," she replied, looking full into his face. He started involuntarily. "No, it is not to be, if you hesitate over it. Let us not be sentimental. Let us, least of all, make sacrifices for an idea which later reflection might disprove. If there be a choice in our hearts, an alternative, we will not do it, Joost."

"I hesitated for your sake, Agatha," said Joost; and he passed into the next room.

Kees van Hessel stood near the writing-table, with a puzzled look on his face. By the mantelpiece sat van Asveld, looking puffy, and blown, and discontented. The fat Jonker was beginning to bear visibly about him the effects of his intemperate habits. He rose, slowly and awkwardly, as the master of the house entered. Joost Avelingh eyed him with ill-concealed disgust.

No one spoke for a moment. "We have come, you see," said Kees at length, "as you wished." He was glad to break the embarrassing silence.

"Yes," said Asveld, "and I am waiting to hear, Avelingh, what are your reasons for requesting me once more to enter this house which is full of such painful memories to me, as you are aware, and in which I had hoped never to set foot again."

"You must excuse my deferring my explanation a few minutes longer," answered Joost; "I am waiting for a fourth person who was to be here by eleven. It is now five minutes past. I believe I see the gig coming up the avenue."

Kees opened his eyes still wider. Avelingh stood without taking any further notice of his visitors, and the Jonker—after having waited in vain to be offered a seat—sank back into his easy-chair again. Presently the Notary walked into the room.

After the preliminary greetings—while the Notary still stood pulling off his gloves and staring from one to the other, wondering what he had been sent for—Joost began speaking, suddenly, without further preparation.

"Mynheer the Notary," he said, you will admit, I doubt not that the proceedings in the trial in which you also appeared as a witness against me ended with my complete acquittal of the charge that had been trumped up against me and that henceforth the law can not touch me?"

"Of course, Mynheer Avelingh," said the Notary.

"Of course," said Kees.

"And you, Mynheer van Asveld," continued Joost, "you will not, I presume, object to that conclusion?"

"How can I?" murmured Arthur. "You know my private opinion. What foolery is this?"

"And furthermore," said Joost, again addressing the Notary, "you will admit that, whether I had been condemned at the trial or not, I should have always been, as I am now, the lawful possessor of the whole fortune left by my uncle unconditionally. Is it not so?"

"It is, my dear Heer," said the Notary, "but I can not understand—"

"And you," Joost went on, turning to Arthur, "you know it is so—do you not?"

"You have no right to put me meaningless questions," replied the Jonker, "and I shall not answer them. Is this what you wanted me for?"

"The meaning is coming," said Joost. "My property being unconditionally my own, I can do what I like with it; can I not, Notary?"

" Always subject to the restrictions of the law," answered the Notary. " Yes."

" That being clearly understood," Joost went on, " and all the circumstances being fully admitted on both sides, I wish to state that it is my intention to make over to the Jonkheer Arthur van Asveld here present, without any reservation whatever, the whole estate real and personal, which I inherited from my uncle the Baron van Trotsem."

" Joost," cried Kees, " are you mad ? "

" What nonsense is this ? " said Asveld rising in a fury. " I ask once more ; have I been sent for here to be made a fool of ? You mistake me very much, Heer Deputy, if you think you can play off your jokes upon me ! " he made for the door.

" Stay," said Joost. " It is no joke, but terrible earnest. If you wait, I shall prove it to you. The Notary will draw up the necessary deeds, and you shall see me sign them."

" But, my dear Heer "—began the Notary.

" The Notary will do no such thing," cried Kees. " He will understand at once that delay is necessary—" he cast a meaning side-glance at the little gentleman in black, who quietly returned it. " Of course such arrangements may sometimes be desirable, Joost, but they render a number of formalities indispensable. A list of the property will have to be made out. Van Asveld may thank you for your kind intentions on his behalf, and then we had better disperse in expectation of further arrangements. Nothing can be done to-day, can it, Notary ? "

" Certainly not," said the Notary. " I will see about getting the necessary papers ready, and that will take me some weeks ; it is unavoidable."

" Damn me," cried Arthur, " I won't thank anybody for nothing. You may carry off your mad brother-in-law to the Asylum as best you can, van Hessel, but you needn't look for help from me! And now, sir, mad or not, I shall trouble you to get away from that door."

"Yes," said Joost, without moving, "you think me mad, Kees, or unstrung, or excited or something. Think it'll be all right to-morrow. You are quite mistaken. You can go in there, if you like and ask Agatha; she knows what I am doing. I intend to give up this wretched inheritance, and if you'll listen, I will give you my reason. Stay there, you," he cried, addressing Arthur, "I could knock you down with half a hand, and I shall do it, if you move."

The words were true, but Arthur was the last man to pocket such an insult. He dashed at the door; Kees Hessel flung himself between the antagonists. "No quarreling," he said. "We want cool heads here, and that's my opinion."

"Have you all forgotten the trial?" asked Joost, desperately, "and the charges brought against me? My motives for my action are simple enough, when one comes to think of it. I have reasons for being positively certain that my uncle's warnings were not mere empty threats, but that he was fixedly resolved on the day of his death to make a will leaving all his possessions to van Asveld, in case I at any time married the woman who is now my wife. I have in the last few weeks learned particulars, utterly unsuspected till then, which, while explaining my uncle's course of action and showing me that I had been wrong to look upon it as a passing caprice at the time, have convinced me more fully still of the immutable character of his resolve. Had he lived an hour or two longer van Asveld would have been in my place. For I should certainly have married all the same, if ever I could have done so. He did not live an hour or two longer; never mind why not, but for me the moral obligation remains the same."

"You have been slow to discover it then," said Arthur.

"True," replied Joost, humbly. "You must forgive me

for that. And also for the actual pecuniary loss the delay may entail. Remember, you have no legal right to a farthing. And I stipulate that you receive the estate and the personalty as they now stand. You will find them intact, but the interest has been spent, and with regard to that you will ask no further questions. For myself I shall retain nothing but such trifles of personal property as my wife may wish to take away with her. At the time of my uncle's death he had in his keeping my own small private fortune, inherited from my father, amounting to three thousand three hundred florins odd. I consider it my duty to retain that also. I do so, because I am entitled to the money, and because it is incumbent upon me not to leave my wife entirely destitute. You can take the rest."

"What am I to believe?" asked Arthur, turning to the Notary.

"Accept it," cried Kees in despair, "accept it, and believe what you like afterward. Believe what every sensible man would. Very well, Joost, we quite understand you, and it is undoubtedly true. And the notary will arrange it all for you without loss of time."

"I am not a child," said Joost fiercely, "to be humored and played with. I am a man in full possession of my senses and I am acting advisedly and within my legal rights when I fling away this cursed money for another man to pick up. Will you, Sir Notary, draw up this deed or shall I send for another man?"

"Of course," said the Notary, "if you wish it, and if you can rationally explain it—it is very extraordinary—Nothing of the kind has ever occurred to me before during my long practice. And I must be sure—forgive me Mynheer Avelingh"—he edged away a little behind Kees—"I must be sure that I am dealing with a sane man before I proceed."

"You may well make that proviso!" cried Kees. "Good heavens, Joost, what has happened to you? Let us go to Agatha and talk the matter over with her, as you say. Do you forget, man, how you are beggaring her, robbing her in this manner of the very means of subsistence? Heer Notary, you can see he is not himself. He has been overexcited by the election. We will talk of it again tomorrow." The poor fellow was beside himself with anger and distress.

"Yes," said the Notary, "we will talk of it again tomorrow."

"We shall do no such thing," said Joost. "You will tell me now, sir, before you leave the room, whether you intend to draw up this deed of gift or not. It is to be a deed of gift, you understand, free and unconditional, of the estate real and personal, as it stands at present."

"I can't write it out here at this moment, with you waiting," said the Notary peevishly. "I haven't got the stamped paper."

"I do not expect you to do so. I give you a day or two; make it as short as possible. But I must know before you go whether you intend to do the work for me."

"Why, yes, why should I not?" said the Notary hesitatingly. "I as well as any other man; you can always see later on whether you sign it or not," he added, his eyes once more seeking van Hessel's face.

"Rather than have you sign such a document as that I'll call a family council," cried Kees. "I'll have you put under a curator for madness or imbecility, or prodigality, one of the three! The third in any case."

"You will do nothing of the kind, Kees," answered Joost sadly, "not when you know the peculiarities of the case. And you wouldn't succeed if you tried."

"I have stuck to you through everything, but I desert you now," shouted his irate brother-in-law. "Have you considered for a moment what you're doing? Is this money which you are spending wisely for the benefit of thousands to pass into the hands of a fellow like that,"—he pointed to van Asveld—"a drunkard, a profligate! No, you need not make faces at me, sir; it is true enough and you know it. You are all that and more. And if I were to tell you so to your face at the Club, you wouldn't have the heart to deny it."

"I have thought of that," interposed Joost, "but I can't help it. The money's not mine. I'm not so sure it is desirable it should be his, but, once more, I can't help it. I give him the benefit of the doubt whether it would really have been his, if my uncle had lived. I am confident it would not have been mine."

"Then that is settled," said the Notary, who was getting impatient and had another engagement. "I draw up the deed; and, by the time it is ready, I shall see how matters stand."

"And in the mean time?" queried van Asveld.

"In the mean time, sir," said Joost, turning fiercely upon him, "I must bid you hold your peace and wait."

"Bid, bid," answered Arthur, "I do no man's bidding. Not even a madman's."

Joost came close to him. "I have only this to tell you," he said, "you have heard my intentions. If I find that you whisper one word of them to any living soul before I let you do so, I refuse to sign; so keep a quiet tongue in your head. And don't drink."

"And I have this to answer," replied Arthur; "I don't believe you, and when I find out for certain that you sent for me here to insult me and make a fool of me, I'll have my revenge, even if I become a murderer for it, like you."

"And how about the Deputyship, my dear Mynheer Avelingh?" asked the lawyer, pausing in the door-way.

"We shall see," said Joost.

CHAPTER XXXIX.

JOOST MEETS VAN ASVELD FOR THE LAST TIME.

IT was a fortnight later. Agatha and Joost were once more together in the old sitting-room—his room—in which they had spent so many happy evenings during the dozen years of their married life. This was to be the last day of their stay at the Castle. To-morrow they would leave it for-ever. They had succeeded in convincing Kees after long discussions and expostulations—"half convincing him" were perhaps the correcter expression—that they were acting for the best. He had given way unwillingly, when all the circum-stances had been made known to him, and had consented to keep their secret, as they wished, till Joost should think fit to proclaim it. And now, after much hesitation and pro-crastination, the necessary deeds had been duly drawn up, signed and registered; the last formalities had been accom-plished that morning, and, in fact, Arthur van Asveld was actually owner of Trotsem Castle already, with the right to take possession to-morrow. Joost had demanded to be al-lowed to remain till to-morrow. For to-morrow he would be admitted to take his seat as Member of the States-General. He had taken the necessary steps to obtain that admission. He had been flooded with congratulations, letters and cards and addresses, from all parts of the country and he had quiet-ly received them and laid them on one side. " Let me wait ? " he replied to all Kees's inquiries, " Grant me at least this one satisfaction that I may choose my own moment to speak."

" And you are not sorry Agatha ? You don't regret it ? " Joost was saying on that last evening. It was the fiftieth time he had asked her that question. He could not help it. It came to his lips unbid. And she gave him no answer but a kiss or a smile. " Not even now ? Not even since you know —"

"Not even since then, Joost."

"And we shall go away, dearest? We shall try to get work in the Dutch Indies or America. We shall be happy there together. And I have my three thousand florins. They will suffice till I find something to do. It is too late to regret now that I did not stick to my profession."

"No, Joost, we shall stay here," said Agatha, "as you said at first. You were right. I would not tempt you to run away. We shall stay, and that will be our punishment; we will bear it together."

"But you—" began Joost.

"I shall go with you to the Hague to-morrow," said Agatha quickly. "You know you have promised to let me live as close to your heart as possible in future, Joost; and that is to be our great happiness henceforth."

"And so good-by," said Joost, with a long look at the shadows deepening in stately sweeps over the golden autumn chestnuts, "good-by to Trotsem Castle."

Even as he spoke, the door was thrown open, and Kees Hessel came rushing in, with a pale, frightened face.

"Joost" he cried, "van Asveld! you must come to him at once! He is dying! You must come at once, or he may be dead!"

"What has happened?" asked Joost in great agitation. "What has happened, Kees?"

"I hardly know," said Kees hurriedly. "It appears that this afternoon, after having got the documents registered, he went out and had one of his drinking-bouts. In honor of the occasion, I suppose. And, coming home drunk, he seems to have slipped at the top of the stairs and fallen headlong. He's injured internally. The doctor said he couldn't live twelve hours. All the more dangerous, you know, from his being drunk at the time. And you are to come instantly, Joost."

"Why?" said Joost. "Has he asked for me?"

"He can't speak, but they think so. He nodded or something. And so they sent to let me know."

Joost hurried upstairs to get his coat, and Kees, left alone with his sister, came up to her, trembling with excitement. "Who knows what change this may bring," he said, "if he dies? Agatha, it may all pass by like a nightmare!"

"I do not think so," she replied. "The sin remains, and its consequences must remain also. The death of no individual can change that."

"You are resolved to be beggars," said Kees testily. "What will you live on? You know, Agatha, Papa is comparatively a poor man too, nowadays."

"Joost will find work," said Agatha, "and he will support us. And oh, Kees"—she blushed shyly—"I must tell you. If God is merciful to us this time, there will be three of us to support."

"A child! Oh, Agatha! And, with that knowledge, you can defraud the unborn babe of its rights!"

"We did not know at the time, but, had we known, what else could we have done, Kees? We may be mistaken, but, dear boy, we go wrong in good faith. And it seems to us there is no other course."

"You are fools," said Kees with a break in his voice, "or innocents, the whole three of you. And you were much better in some other world, where people reason as you do; and that's my opinion; and I don't know which is the greater fool, Joost or myself. God bless the whole lot of you, Agatha."

Half-an-hour later Joost stood by van Asveld's side. They had not been able to move the Jonker, and he lay as he had fallen, all in a confused heap, at the bottom of a steep, straight staircase, leading up from the shop over which he lived. It was a poor little shop with a sanded floor, the stairs of common unpainted wood;—the staircase, often almost like a ladder, is the weak point in all Dutch houses,

T

be it said. An oil-lamp was burning with unsteady light
in the growing darkness. There was a strong smell of
paraffin, and, mingled with this the fumes of wine made
themselves plainly manifest. Joost noticed this last horrible item with a shudder. He looked at the doctor, standing,
sullen and useless, against the wall, at the landlady, a woman
with a hard face and stony, indifferent stare. What surroundings to die in!

He knelt by van Asveld's side. The Jonker groaned
heavily and opened his eyes. They were fast glazing over,
but they brightened with sudden interest when they fell
upon Joost. The old hate had gone out of them. He
struggled to make himself understood with faint murmurs
and attempts to move somewhat, but in vain, and he was
getting excited over these useless efforts, when Kees suddenly perceived that he was endeavoring to reach the point
of a piece of paper which stuck out of his coat-pocket. Van
Hessel drew it out at haphazard. He recognized it at once;
it was the deed of gift. He held it before the dying man;
and van Asveld's eyes immediately expressed his satisfaction, while he began to make fresh signs, which Kees and
Joost, though this time they seemed plainer, yet hesitated
to understand.

The doctor came forward. "He wants you to tear up
that paper," he said. "It is evident."

Joost held it in his hand. It was, as Kees had said, the
deed of gift. Kees bent forward. "Tear it up!" he whispered in his brother-in-law's ear, "if he dies, the money goes
to his half-sister in India. The Notary will keep our secret."

This paper was, of course, only a copy of the original
deed, for the Notary had the latter in his keeping, but Kees
did not doubt that, now the secret was still theirs, the man
of law, on the doctor's evidence, would consent to annul it.
It may be questioned, however, whether the lawyer would
have dared to do so.

"I can't," said Joost in a low voice. "And if I could, I wouldn't. Once more; let the cursed money go. I've never wanted it, and what I did, I did not do for the money. I might have kept it even now, only people would not have believed me. Let it go."

The dying man, having rid himself of the paper, which had seemed to oppress him, appeared to forget it. He probably believed that his wish with regard to it had been fulfilled. He was sinking fast. With an intense effort he opened his eyes and smiled to Joost. Joost took his hand and retained it in his own. Arthur feebly returned the pressure, and when Joost would have withdrawn his arm, a troubled look came over the Jonker's features. And so Joost knelt there, cramped at the stairfoot, silent and solemn, with his hand clasping that of the man who had hated and persecuted him, the only being on earth toward whom he yet felt ill-will. The flickering oil-lamp played over the Jonker's face. The doctor and Kees stood motionless by the wall in the narrow passage. The landlady had withdrawn, fretful and grumbling. And so, with Joost's face looking down upon him, sad and serious and pitiful, Arthur van Asveld died.

"And it's very sad," said the landlady querulously, as she let the two gentlemen out, "and a great trouble altogether, not to speak of the damage, with the doctor locking the shop-door and preventing my selling a thing all the evening. It's very hard on me, gentlemen; it is a considerable pecuniary loss."

Joost threw a dollar on the counter without speaking, as he passed out. It was the old habit; he forgot that dollars would be precious with him henceforth.

CHAPTER XL.

THE CONFESSION.

THE members of the Second Chamber of the States General were settling down in their places; some eighty gentlemen of various ages, the grizzly predominating, with here and there a shining bald crown or a head of yellow curls, all uncovered according to the inviolable foreign rule. The hall was like any other similar council-chamber, only smaller than most, well fitted for the purpose it was intended to serve, with a number of seats on both sides of a green covered table, retained for the ministers, and the President's chair facing the throne. Everything as simple as possible, perhaps a little too simple, some might think; no robes or or wigs, or maces of any kind, very unlike the British House of Commons, but not different from the parliament chamber of any other small European state. Grave, solemn, orderly, decorous; none of the turmoil Englishmen have grown accustomed to. A certain impressiveness in the very simplicity and repose. There are never recriminations or personalities, or unpleasantnesses of any kind in the Dutch House of Commons. There is no Irish question to produce them. There is never an " Incident." And the Dutch, cool, phlegmatic, fish-blooded, as unlike the French or Irish as it is possible for one human being to be unlike another, live under the unadmitted impression, most certainly an erroneous one, that the man who expresses himself forcibly or enthusiastically must naturally be in the wrong. And so the tide of parliamentary eloquence flows on without a ripple, for a ripple in that quiet country would be marked with a danger-buoy at once.

The galleries were filling—not an event of daily occurrence. A good deal of curiosity was being manifested in the country about the new Deputy, as well on account of his

past history as, more especially, on account of the circumstances under which he had been elected. People in the
Hague were anxious to have a look at him. It was reported
that he was handsome; he was certainly interesting, he was
wealthy; he had passed through a trial for murder and been
acquitted, he had been nominated in a public meeting by the
people—the populace, they said in the Hague—without the
interference of any political club, a dangerous precedent,
but an incident which showed the man's great popularity in
his part of the country. A popularity actually gained, as it
appeared, not by speechifying, but by spending his money
for the benefit of others. Very extraordinary. So society
sent some of its members to criticise Joost Avelingh. It
was quite worth while wasting an hour of the afternoon to
see him take his seat.

The galleries, then, were soon filled to overflowing. The
ministers drew up their arm-chairs to the table, and, bending over to each other, whispered about public business.
The President, an old gentleman of reverend aspect, looked
about him inquiringly, up at the galleries, down at the
Deputies. "Right," and "Left" dropped on to their re-
spective benches. Bits of conversation here and there flickered and went out. A great silence fell upon the assembly.
The President opened the session. The business of the day
began.

Joost had been greeted with a cheer by the small crowd
outside, as he drove up in a cab—from the station—with his
wife by his side. He entered the building alone. The loiter-
ers evidently approved of his bearing and general appearance. They cheered him again. He raised his hat slightly
in reply. It was the last time the world cheered Joost Avelingh.

In the House itself his appearance created no enthusiasm. Both parties considered him more or less as an intruder.
He had been forced upon them. It was not desirable—from

the point of view of party politics—that the electors should
get into the way of sending up independent representatives.
The whole system of parliamentary government on which
modern prosperity hinges would become impossible if such
an exception were to develop into the rule.

The President—specially deputed to do so in this case
by royal authority—called upon the new member to take the
Oath of Allegiance. Joost Avelingh stepped forward, but
before he proceeded to do as was expected of him, he asked
permission to make a personal statement. There was a moment's hesitation. The request was altogether an unexpected one. The President, though he felt it his duty to
rule it out of order, shrank from doing so immediately.
Joost took advantage of the delay and began speaking.

" Mynheer the President," he said, standing out, straight
and stalwart, the black hair thrown back from his brow, " I
claim your permission, as I said, to make what I have called
a personal statement. It may be unusual to do so ; I have
no doubt that in so young and so new a member it will be
considered presumptuous. I must beg of your charity to
allow me to have my own way for a moment. I shall take
up as little as possible of the time this assembly owes to the
country.

" But I also, Mynheer the President, consider that I owe
something to the country ; I owe it this statement. I owe
such explanations as I am desirous of giving, to your august
chamber, to which I have had the honor of being called ; to
the electors who did me that honor—an illustrious one as I
am only too deeply conscious— ; to the country at large,
which is witness of my election. When I first found myself
designated as representative of the people, I accepted the
position which was offered me. If my projects have changed
since then, I owe it to myself and to all men concerned, to explain them. It is therefore I have considered it my duty not
to withdraw in private but publicly to explain my action here."

He stopped to draw breath. A faint murmur ran through the house. Curiosity was visible on all the faces turned toward him, curiosity and astonishment, not too benevolent, a general expectation—and dislike—of some approaching "scene."

"I was accused," Joost went on, "as all will remember, in the course of the spring of this year, of the murder of my uncle, Van Trotsem. I was brought to trial, and first condemned, then acquitted. The case came on ultimately in the Court of Appeal, and that Supreme Court decided that I was innocent of all instrumentality in the death of my uncle. It decided wrongly. I was guilty."

He uttered the last words very softly. His head sank on his breast. But the next moment he lifted it up again with a proud movement, and spoke in the same clear voice he had used at first. When his confession left his lips, a thrill struck through the ranks of his hearers; it was not an expression of kindly sentiment. There was the same curiosity as before, but no sympathy with the speaker. And among his brother-members many a thin lip curled up with a smile of half-skeptical contempt.

"I was guilty," said Joost, "but not as the world counts guilt. Do you care to hear the story? I owe it, as I said at first, to you, and still more to the men who gave me their votes. When I drove by my uncle's side on that terrible evening, there was rage and hate and disappointment uncontrollable in my heart. I hated him—never mind now whether rightly or wrongly; I believed, oh so rightly—I hated him, as few men ever learn to hate a fellow-being; I hated him for all the misery of a lifetime laid at his door. It matters not that now I know I wronged him—at least, in part, the greater part,—that now I perceive how much of what I accused him of was false, and understand that he strove according to his lights—his weak and misleading lights—to do his duty by me. I owe it to his memory to declare that publicy, but none-the-less, as I sat by his side that evening, I hated him, not without full cause.

" At the time of his death my uncle, as was shown during the trial, was driving to the village-notary to alter his will. It was not his intention simply to disinherit me— that would, I may truthfully say, under ordinary circumstances have left me more indifferent than most men, but it was his intention deliberately so to word his dispositions that my marriage with the woman I had chosen for my wife should become forever impossible, unless she married, as I knew she never would, in deliberate defiance of her father. I knew, as I sat there beside him, that I was hurrying on—every ring of the horse's hoofs bringing me nearer—to the ruin of my new-found happiness. And I owed my life-long wretchedness in the past, in the present, and now in all the future, to the meaningless, cowardly cruelty, as I thought, of the man at my side.

" But before we reached our destination, my uncle, who had been ailing all the evening, and of the precarious state of whose health I was well aware, fell back in a fit. What thoughts rushed through my brain in those few terrible moments I could never clearly recall. But one thing I can attest before Heaven, I did not think of the miserable man's gold. I thought of my love, of the will lying uncanceled, of the wrongs of the past, of the great wrong still undone. It seemed to me as if God intervened on my behalf and struck down this persecutor in the way. I drove on. I had studied medicine, I knew that immediate help was often decisive in these circumstances. I believe I realized that at the moment. I looked neither to right nor left, but drove on. I *could not* stretch out my hand to assist this man. I *could not* have stretched it out to hurt him. Yet I heard him gasp out, as he fell back,—once,—twice: ' Stop ! ' I heard him. The words have rung in my ears ever since.

" I drove on as fast as the horse could tear forward. I

felt that the sooner we reached the village the sooner other help would be forthcoming, and the sooner the agony of my struggle would cease. I hoped, I yearned that such help might save him. But I could not, once more, I could not stretch out my own hand to the work.

"I did not see him touch his neckerchief. I saw nothing; I heard nothing after that first despairing cry. I was blinded, maddened by the hope, the fear, the doubt the hate, the terror within me. I desired but one thing, to reach the village, and let it end.

"So much I have to confess, and no more. I am told that even if I had stopped the chaise and given my uncle such assistance as I could, he would probably have died from the attack which struck him down. I willingly believe it. I have told myself so, often and often again. It appears probable. It will never be certain on earth.

"And for me remains that unanswered appeal; it will remain till my death. There remains the knowledge that I desired this man's destruction, and that if Christ's teaching means anything I am a murderer at heart. Many hundreds who hear my story, and to whom Christ's teaching means nothing, will laugh at my sufferings. Those who can measure crime only by the damage it does others, and not by the ruin it brings upon ourselves, will bid me take heart and be merry, or laugh at me for a fool. But I know, and many, I rejoice to think, despite the sadness of the thought, many will know with me that Christ has told men truly, that sin is a thing of the thought, not the deed. And I must bear my burden. I used to think, that if I could obtain an affirmation to the question whether the dead man would have died, even though I had checked my course and helped him, this cloud of accusation would roll from me. I would give my life to obtain such an answer, but I thank God that it would not fully content me now.

"Why I have waited to speak till now, and why I speak

at this moment—I am willing to tell it to whoso cares to hear, but this is not the time nor the place for further confession. The gradual enlightenment of a soul is too long and too strange a story for these walls. Suffice it that I confess the measure of my guilt. I confess no more. The law can not touch me; and, when it sought to do so, I defended myself against false accusation, as each man has a right to do. But such accusation as is my due I now bring against myself. One thing more! I might, perchance, have retained the money I inherited from the Baron van Trotsem; I have resolved not to do so. First, because otherwise my confession—as the judgment of men is wont to go—would have lost more than half its meaning; and secondly, because I wish, as far as possible, to annul all advantages which have accrued to me from my uncle's death. I can not annul my marriage. Besides, it may yet be asked, whether circumstances might not, after all, have made that marriage possible. But it is certain, at least to my mind, knowing my uncle as I did, and knowing also his reasons for acting, that he would not have changed his views of it. I can not, therefore, retain both my wife and my money, for the possession of both together is—may be—the result of my sin. I let the money go without regret. I thank God I can say that, and cling the closer to the great treasure he leaves me. A succession of considerations and discoveries, of no importance here, have taught me to realize lately, more than ever, that the money is not rightly mine.

"And now, Mynheer the President, I must thank you and this honorable assembly for having borne with me so long. You have thereby enabled me to explain, as far as I am able, the motives which actuate me in withdrawing from this Chamber. It is not right that a man with such a confession on his heart should sit in your midst. And I wish to tell those who have contributed to do me this honor, that not the least part of my punishment is the knowledge that

I have closed to myself a sphere of usefulness in which I should have been proud to work with all my strength. Yet it is right that it should be so. God has forgiven me. But I can not forgive myself."

He ceased speaking. All those faces were still turned toward him, still curious, doubtful, smiling. There was a dead, cold silence; and in the silence Joost Avelingh stepped down, with head erect, and face firm-set and sad, and walked across the floor and out at the great doorway of the House.

Outside, at a side entrance, in the deserted street, the cab was waiting with Agatha in it. He got into it, and they drove away to the station, and reached their modest lodgings as the autumn twilight fell, cold and gray, upon the dying leaves.

And that evening Agatha made tea for her husband with the silver tea-things she had brought away with her from the Castle. They were comfortable and cosy by the lodging-house fire. Joost read "Faust" to her, as she sat at work on one of the first articles of what was to be a very modest home-made layette. And, half-way in the great Cathedral-scene, he suddenly broke down and bent forward his face over the book with a burst of happy, though regretful tears.

CHAPTER XLI.

THE WORLD'S FAREWELL TO JOOST AVELINGH.

PEOPLE speak variously of Joost Avelingh, but as a rule he is treated either with anger or with contempt. In his own class especially the feeling is very strong against him.

One half of society abuses him for not having spoken sooner; the other despises him for having spoken at all. The half which takes his confessions seriously is horrified at the thought of the countenance it gave to a murderer. It trembles to think of the wickedness of a man who could do such a deed of villainy and then quietly enjoy its fruits during a dozen long guilty years. It understands—only too well—that he was forced to break the silence at last, un-willingly, no doubt, and half-heartedly, but compelled by con-science to speak at last. It does not believe Joost's descrip-tion of what it invariably alludes to as " the murder." And it says that some day the wretched man will complete his story and confess his whole crime exactly as he committed it. For conscience, when it once seizes upon a criminal, will not let him rest till it has avenged society (and saved the criminal's soul), and this man certainly has a conscience; he may be thankful for that. And the proper, orthodox, respectable people, who are better than their neighbors and know it, hope that Joost will still some day listen to the warning voice within him which has already brought him so far. But in the mean time, while he persists in denying his guilt, they can hold no intercourse with him.

The other half, the people who lived lightly and would let others live lightly too, are not so especially angry with Joost, but they speak of him with good-humored scorn. " He should have let well alone," they think. Many of them, also have a lurking suspicion that Jan Lorentz's first evi-dence unconsciously gave the true account of the story : and that the only mistake was about Lorentz having seen or not seen what occurred. " Well then Avelingh was a lucky man, and had a lucky escape, that is all. He should have known it and kept a quiet tongue in his head. As for associating with a man who owns to such an ugly blot on his history, impossible, not to be thought of, altogether absurd ! " And even those who gave him the full benefit of the doubt agree

in condemning the extravagant " scene " which he " got up "
in the Chamber.   The Legislative Assembly is not a theatre,
they say.

"But Avelingh was always so melodramatic," complains
Burgomaster van Hessel.   The Burgomaster laments over
his own misfortunes and bitterly abuses his son-in-law.   He
was furious with him at first, and refused to have anything
to say to him; he even attacked Kees most vehemently for
having abetted him in the past, and for seeking to stand up
for him now.   Mevrouw van Hessel was obliged to make use
of all her influence to patch matters up as best she was able.
" He has gone mad," said the Burgomaster at last, with a
sigh of acquiescence.   " Yes, send for him, and I can tell
him so.   *Quem perdere vult Deus*, you know—and he certainly talks very piously—*prius dementat.*"

Joost lives with his wife and a little son of some six
months or so in tiny lodgings at Heist.   Some few people
take his view of his duty and his efforts to do it, and among
them is the village Notary, who has taken him into his employ
as a clerk, and at present he earns eighty pounds a year in
this manner.   But better times are coming, for a gentleman
of Amsterdam who took a great interest in the case, and who
appreciates the advantage of having a perfectly trustworthy
man in his office, hopes soon to find work for him there at
a salary of £250 a year.   Joost and Agatha are to go up
to the capital next autumn.   They will not be sorry to leave
Heist, although they have bravely borne the brunt of public condemnation there as long as it seemed unavoidable.
Even in Amsterdam their story will pursue them wherever
they go; but they will not go to many places outside their
quiet little home, and they will soon slip out of sight—as they
hope to do—in the crowd of the great city.

Among the multitude, which once lifted his name to the
skies, the report has got current, somehow or other, that
Joost is a murderer.   This being so, no one can understand

that the police do not arrest him, and a great deal of ill-will is felt against the authorities in consequence. One or two radical newspapers—not over-scrupulous about the means they employ—persistently hold up his case in the eyes of the populace as a proof that justice only strikes down the poor man, and lets the gentleman go unhurt.

And so the world judges the sin of Joost Avelingh. And he, remembering the Apostolic "if we would but judge our-selves," cares neither for its present injustice nor for its past approval; cares not more, at least, than it is in human flesh to care. For a warm affectionate human nature as his, can not see slip away from it love, admiration, honor, so much that makes life sweet, without regretting them. Yet he knows that he did not see them slip away, but willingly gave them up. And he still thinks he did right. He loves his wife and child the more dearly: he trusts God the more closely. And his heart is at rest.

THE END.

D. APPLETON & CO.'S PUBLICATIONS.

www.ingramcontent.com/pod-product-compliance
Lightning Source LLC
Chambersburg PA
CBHW060526030726
47498CB00004B/1091